A FOUND BEGINNING

A FOUND BEGINNING

OSPREY CHRONICLES™ BOOK FIVE

RAMY VANCE

MICHAEL ANDERLE

THE A FOUND BEGINNING TEAM

Thanks to our Beta Readers

Kelly O'Donnell, Larry Omans

Thanks to the JIT Readers

Dorothy Lloyd
Zacc Pelter
Diane L. Smith
Deb Mader
Dave Hicks
Jeff Goode
Debi Sateren

If we've missed anyone, please let us know!

Editor
The Skyhunter Editing Team

This book is a work of fiction. All of the characters, organizations, and events portrayed in this novel are either products of the author's imagination or are used fictitiously. Sometimes both.

Copyright © 2022 by LMBPN Publishing
Cover Art by Jake @ J Caleb Design
http://jcalebdesign.com / jcalebdesign@gmail.com
Cover copyright © LMBPN Publishing
A Michael Anderle Production

LMBPN Publishing supports the right to free expression and the value of copyright. The purpose of copyright is to encourage writers and artists to produce the creative works that enrich our culture.

The distribution of this book without permission is a theft of the author's intellectual property. If you would like permission to use material from the book (other than for review purposes), please contact support@lmbpn.com. Thank you for your support of the author's rights.

LMBPN Publishing
PMB 196, 2540 South Maryland Pkwy
Las Vegas, NV 89109

Version 1.00, January 2022
ISBN (ebook) 978-1-68500-614-3
ISBN (paperback) 978-1-68500-615-0

DEDICATION

To my Bunny Banshee – may nothing ever silence that incredible voice of yours...

—Ramy Vance

*To Family, Friends and
Those Who Love
to Read.
May We All Enjoy Grace
to Live the Life We Are
Called.*

— Michael

PREVIOUSLY IN THE OSPREY CHRONICLES...

It's all hands on deck as the K'tax swarm Locaur in response to an ancient signal beacon. If the K'tax prevail, Locauri and humans alike will become fodder and breeding grounds for the next generations of K'tax.

Sarah and the *Osprey*'s crew stand ready to defend the planet they call home against overwhelming odds. The Overseers are helping, but not without dissent in their ranks. Nor will they commit their full force...they must protect multiple spatial locations. Overseer Kwin has a solution to the human resources problem, but no one knows if it will be enough and in time.

Then the fleet arrives through the wormhole at Dr. Grayson's order—but will the Tribes bent on conquering band together with the *Osprey* and her allies long enough to defeat the K'tax? Or will it be every side for themselves, and the victor takes the spoils?

CHAPTER ONE

"Come here, Boo. Look at this."

The bathroom door hung open, and mist from the sonic shower filled the tiny apartment for the first time in months. A little girl streaked out of the bathroom, drowning in the oversized, stretched-out shirt that served as her pajamas.

Sim threw herself onto the convertible couch-bed, diving into Sarah's open arms. Her flesh was warm, her mop of tightly curled hair damp and heavy with the scent of coconut. Sarah and Cole had repeatedly told her not to use the real oil without asking first. This last bottle had cost more than Cole made in a week, and if they believed the rumors, there was no more real oil available anywhere. Not at any price. They were supposed to save it for special occasions.

Sarah said nothing because this was a special occasion. The ink wasn't yet dry on her contract, and she felt her ship-out date looming over her head like the blade of a guillotine. Four weeks. Four weeks until she got on a Tribe shuttle and went off to officer cadet training.

They'd told her that her first six months at the academy

would be brutal. No family visits. Less than an hour of comms time per week. The academy had to be relentless, the recruiting officer had told her. The first generation of Tribe officers would need to be some of the toughest, smartest, best-trained humans alive.

In exchange for her signature, Sarah's sign-on bonus had included, among other things, six extra hours of sonic shower use.

She and Sim had run the water until it was cold, and their fingers had turned to prunes.

So yes, this was a special occasion. She wouldn't begrudge the girl a few drops of oil, even if it annoyed Cole.

"Look." Sarah waved at the recording device on the low table beside the couch. "Look what Aunt Petie found for us!"

It was an ancient holo-projector, chipped and rusted at the corners. Sarah hadn't asked Petra where she got the antique. There were some things she was better off not knowing. Especially not now that her soul belonged to the Tribe.

Sim pressed her cheek to Sarah's shoulder, studying the little device with bright, honey-colored eyes. She reached out with fingers still plump with baby fat. "Go?" she asked.

Sarah wrapped her arms around the child and nodded. Sim pressed the power button. At first, nothing happened, and Sarah was afraid the old projector had given up the ghost. Then a cone of light shot from the device and filled the single-room apartment with a wavering blueish glow.

Sim gasped as a swath of grasslands sprouted from the misty air. The image quality was awful—grainy and flickering, popping at the edges. The wildflowers that exploded out of the grass looked sickly and colorless.

Yet they made Sim squeal with delight.

"Where is it?" she demanded as the footage, shot from a

drone or perhaps an airplane, swept above the grasslands. Lone trees sprouted out of the ether. A pair of giraffes grazed among the top branches, their long tongues curling around wicked thorns. Long blue rivers snaked across the landscape, where rows of antelope bowed to take their morning water as a pink and gold sunrise slashed the horizon.

"Is it Africa?" Sim's eyes were wide.

"Uh-huh. It's the Serengeti, Boo." *I think.*

"Have you been there?" Sim demanded, reaching out to touch the flank of one of the antelope as the camera soared past. "Is that where you're from?"

Sarah's mouth twitched in a sad smile. "No, Boo. This was as far from my home as you could get and still be on the planet. The grasslands and the deserts I grew up in were kind of like this," she added, rallying at the sight of her daughter's disappointment.

Or *had* been decades, if not centuries, before Sarah was born. Laboratories and ecological dead zones, synth-dogs, and death cults had defined Sarah's childhood. The biodiversity, the explosion of life filling the hologram around them was almost as much of a myth to Sarah as they were to a daughter born and raised in a tin can in outer space.

A gray shape loomed in the distance, growing as the camera drew closer but obscured by long grass. Sim squealed with excitement. "It's Baby!"

On hearing her name, one of the cushions on the edge of the couch stirred. Baby, the size of an overstuffed pillow, lifted her head, sniffed the air, decided she wasn't being summoned and went to sleep again.

Sarah stared at the projection, baffled until she saw the horn form at the center of the holo-beast's forehead. Then she laughed. "Not quite. Water bears didn't grow that big back on

Earth. It's a rhinoceros! But it is *a* baby, look. Here comes its mama."

Sim cooed in wonder as a larger gray shape emerged from the sea of grass. Mother and child cuddled on their couch on a space station orbiting a frozen moon of Jupiter, watching an ancient record of a mother and child cuddling in their grassy nest.

Some stories were universal.

The minutes slipped by, and when the recording went dark, Sim replayed it. Then she replayed it again and again. After five or six times, the recording went dark, and Sim didn't stir from Sarah's arm to press it again. She huddled close to her mother's chest, her breathing slow and deep.

Sarah settled back on the wide couch that doubled as the family bed, resting her head on Baby's warm flank. She stared into the darkness, unable to sleep. With one eye, she watched the dimly glowing clock tick down the minutes. Four weeks. Her life had narrowed to a slice of four short weeks, and Cole was late from the lab. Again.

"Mama?"

Sarah roused, her ears perking at the sound. "Yeah?"

"Is that what it's gonna be like?" Sim mumbled.

In the dark and quiet, Sarah didn't understand right away. "What what's gonna be like, boo?"

"Home. When we get there."

Sarah felt a pang in her gut. She squeezed the child as tight as she dared. "I hope so," she whispered.

Sim mumbled something and turned over, restless. "No."

"No?" Sarah's breath caught.

Sim shook her head firmly, lips smacking. "Hope in one hand and poop in the other," she muttered. "See which one fills faster."

A FOUND BEGINNING

Sarah stared into the darkness, baffled. Then she realized where Sim must've heard the phrase. Lawrence must've taken her request to "tone down the expletives around the kid" at face value.

"You're right, honey," she conceded gently, wiping a strand of hair from Sim's forehead. "Hope is good. Hope is necessary. But hope alone isn't good *enough*. We're gonna have to work for it, too." She closed her eyes, resting her chin on top of Sim's head as sleep sent its first feelers burrowing through her blood. "One step at a time."

CHAPTER TWO

Slowly, Jaeger realized that someone was laughing over the comm system. It was Toner. There was an edge to his voice—high, sharp, and hungry. "*Assistance? From the fleet? You haven't been reading the company magazine, Kwin. They're here for a goddamned bug hunt.*"

Jaeger couldn't breathe. She stood in a sea of holograms on the bridge of the *Terrible*. Hundreds, thousands of K'tax fighters swarmed through space between Locaur and its moon. Seven asteroids the size of her fist lumbered through the gap on a collision course for the planet. Any one of those modified asteroids hitting the planet head-on could cause an extinction-level event.

With only a handful of geriatric, secondhand cruisers and experimental Terrible-class ships, Jaeger and Kwin didn't have a hope of stopping them all.

At the same time, more ships spilled into the system, appearing at the white mouth of the wormhole that had recently opened in-system. The fleet. That boogeyman from the other side of the universe—it had finally caught up with

Jaeger and her crew.

"I gotta ask, Captain," Toner added, in a raw voice she hardly recognized. "Is *this* what you saved my life for? Just to watch it all go up in flames?"

"Sensors tracking thirty-seven new ships in the system," reported Udil, Kwin's second-in-command, from her station at the edge of the circular bridge. "None of them are responding to my hails."

"Keep hailing," Kwin ordered. "Divert all other resources to the asteroids. We *must* break them apart or throw them off course before they hit Locaur's upper atmosphere."

"We can't get close to the fucking things," Portia cried over the comms system. Her ship, one of those geriatric cruisers, soared an arc ahead of the approaching asteroids, strafing lines of laser cannon fire off her port bow. A swarm of sixty or seventy K'tax fighters closed in, forcing the cruiser out of firing range before she could pummel the target.

"The fighters swarm us if we try," she shouted. "They're shooting down all the kamikaze mines before they can get close enough to affect the asteroids." The asteroid barges lumbered forward, as inexorable as glaciers. Small explosions flowered and faded against the stars as the tick-like K'tax fighters targeted the approaching mines and destroyed them in a barrage of mining laser pulses.

"How much time do we have until the first asteroid hits a point of no return?" Jaeger demanded. A red halo appeared around Locaur.

"Forty-six minutes," Me said in its usual—and in this case utterly inappropriate—cheerful tone.

"Captain," Udil said, making both Jaeger and Kwin look around. The metallic Overseer's claws were a blur as she worked her station. "I'm receiving a message from the *Terrible*

IV. The commander says they've finally got their tractor-ray generators online. If she can get within five thousand kilometers of an asteroid, she should be able to generate enough force to push it off course."

Jaeger's gaze snapped back to the battle. Five thousand kilometers. It sounded like a lot—and as far as weapons ranges went, it certainly was—but against the vastness of space, and the sheer number of K'tax fighters, that distance was *nothing.*

"Let's rally the cruisers to provide her cover," Jaeger said to Kwin. "Get her within tractor range. Tell the other Terrible ships to get their tractor-ray generators online."

A clamor of echoing voices, the sounds of a dozen Overseers trying to coordinate a battle, filled the bridge. Jaeger was thankful that the *Terrible*'s onboard translation system rendered Overseer speech normally instead of the accented version their antenna bands provided.

"Those generators have never been tested in these ships!" Kwin snapped. "With all of the electrical problems it could easily cause a catastrophic feedback loop—"

"Kwin," Jaeger shouted over the babble. "The fleet isn't going to help us. *Do you have a better idea?*"

Kwin's mandibles snapped shut. Half a heartbeat passed between them. Then, with the strange abruptness of all Overseers, Kwin turned sharply to Udil. "Do it."

"God *dammit!*" Toner's fist slammed onto the console, cracking the metal casing. He turned his wild blue stare on Occy. "Five minutes." He glowered. "She kept her promise to stay out of the fight for *five fucking minutes.*"

Something flashed in the corner of Occy's vision, and he turned to see a message blinking on his tablet screen. He was getting a private comms hail from an ID he didn't recognize—it belonged to neither the Overseers nor any of the human crew. *Urgent*, the message flashed.

He frowned, all the sounds of Toner's raging and the drop crew's agitation fading to the background as he snatched his tablet and pushed out of the cockpit. The atmospheric transport was on loan from the Overseers, and the narrow hallways left him feeling almost suffocated. He found an empty corner and activated the coms.

"Who is this?" he demanded. "This is a secure channel. How did you get access?"

There was a moment of static across the line. Distantly, Occy heard the landing crew shouting battle updates to one another. He was about to shut the line, chalk it up to some glitch in the machine when a soft, contemplative voice made his blood run cold.

"Deathbringer," it mused. "You activated the signal? You touched the crystal god? You brought the invasion?"

Occy's heart skipped a beat. "Virgil?"

"Yes." It pondered. "Yes. I have seen it, too. I have seen more than you, I think. I could touch it again. Turn its mind away from war. With help. I need your help."

"Occy!" Toner shouted from the cockpit. "Get back on the comms! *Terrible* needs your help with the tractor-ray generator thingy."

Occy scrolled through the secondary contacts on his computer and tapped open a link to the *Osprey*. "Moss!" he barked. "Do you copy?"

"Copy," Moss confirmed.

"Turn back the red tide," the voice whispered. "Turn back

the red swarm. There's still time. Take me to the transmitter. You must…"

"Give me a status report on Virgil." Occy licked dry lips. In the background, troops shouted. Toner was calling him. And that soft, slightly accented voice was in his ear, whispering about the end of the world. "It's behaving erratically."

"That's odd," Moss said. "Virgil has a bot posted in the *Osprey* with me right now. I detect no odd behavior. Oh, it's asking to speak to you."

"Take me to the transmitter," Virgil murmured. "Let me change the mind of God."

"Put it on!" Occy fought to keep his voice from cracking.

A new voice joined the conversation. No, not a new voice —the twin of the mad whisperer, so leveled by flat sanity that it became a different person entirely.

"I gather my twin has made contact with you," the sane Virgil guessed, without introduction or preamble. Occy didn't ask for permission—he merged the comms channels, sharing the rambling whispers with Virgil.

"I don't have time to deal with this," Occy growled. "What does it want?"

"I don't know," sane Virgil answered simply. "It is no longer looped into my network. Its desires are its own. If you want to know what they are, I suggest you listen to what it has to say."

"Take me to the transmitter," the other Virgil whispered. "The signal. Let me change the signal. Let me turn away the swarm."

"It seems to believe it can use the Forebear communication systems to command the K'tax to withdraw," Virgil suggested.

"Like the beacon in the Locauri shrine?" Occy asked. "The one I activated?"

A FOUND BEGINNING

"Too damaged," the mad Virgil muttered. "Too broken. Incomplete. Take me to the buried city."

Occy's mind raced. Toner and the captain had destroyed sections of that underwater city when they'd escaped from it —but this mad AI would know that. The structure was huge. There must be redundant communications systems somewhere in the labyrinth.

"If we get you to the city," Occy pressed. "If we get you down into the heart of the Forebear computer systems. You can send out a new signal? You can call off the K'tax?"

"Perhaps." The mad Virgil sighed. "There isn't much time."

Occy double-checked the transport specs on his computer. The only known entrance to the buried city was on a volcanic island halfway across the hemisphere. At top speed, the ship could get Occy and one of the Virgil-bots to that island in twenty minutes. They had forty-five minutes until the first asteroid hit a point of no return and began its fatal descent into Locaur's upper atmosphere. Twenty-five minutes wouldn't be much time to locate a new transmitter hub, interface with the ancient technology, and send out a new signal.

"Virgil!" Occy scrubbed sweat from his brow with the rough edge of a tentacle. "I mean. Regular Virgil. Is it possible? Could it work?"

"Your guess is as good as mine, Lieutenant," Virgil said— because Virgil wouldn't be Virgil, if it weren't habitually unhelpful. "I see no reason why I would lie about this," it added almost reluctantly. "Your current efforts to save Locaur will almost certainly fail, so I see no reason not to try. I am *very* curious to see what I will do."

"Occy!" Toner appeared in the hallway, peering into the dark corner where Occy huddled with his computer. His eyes glittered brightly in the shadows. "What the fuck are you doing in here? There's a war going on!"

Occy clapped a hand over his speaker. "Get hold of the captain," he told Toner. "I think we've found a better idea."

CHAPTER THREE

Nicholetta Kelba, fleet captain of the human Tribe Six and interim commander of the Seeker Corps since the untimely demise of *both* previous leaders, stood on the impeccably ordered bridge of the Astrolab cruiser. Her hands remained firmly clasped behind her back. Not one lock of golden hair was out of place, not one loose button or stray thread showed on her black uniform.

Travel through the spatial-temporal anomaly known as a wormhole had temporarily scrambled the Astrolab's sensor arrays. Now the viewscreen clarified, and she watched the universe reform around her fleet as they emerged into a sea of unfamiliar stars.

"Support barges *Cormorant* and *Albatross* coming through the wormhole now," reported the tactical officer sitting at the nearest workstation. "They took minor damage in the fighting on the other side, but nothing serious." He looked up from his screen. "That's the last of the large ships, Captain. Only a few straggler transports are coming through now, and whatever Followers survived the attack."

"I'm picking up a *lot* of comm and generator activity in the system," one of the comms officers announced, scowling as she shuffled through different radio channels.

"We expected confusion," Kelba said. "On all the unprotected ships—"

The comms officer was shaking her head. "No, Captain, it's more than that. There's alien activity in the system. A lot of it."

"Show me." Kelba's thick lips pressed into a faint frown as she studied the tactical display, drinking in her first sight of a new star system. The white void of the wormhole lay behind her, already forgotten and irrelevant. In the space of minutes, her entire fleet had jumped thousands of light-years to a remote arm of the galaxy. What lay before her now was utterly pristine and alien—never before seen by human eyes. She'd waited her whole life for this moment.

And she'd brought her fleet right to the edge of a warzone. On the screen, hundreds if not thousands of small, unfamiliar ships cluttered the dark space between the planet and her moon. Volleys of pulse-laser fire twinkled like disco balls in the darkness.

"Command crew of the *Reliant* and the *Constitution* checking in, Captain," the secondary comms officer reported. "They made it through the jump intact. No memory loss reported on the bridges of either freighter, but they're reporting massive social unrest and confusion among the general population."

"Activate the orientation protocols and broadcast them back to the fleet on all open channels," Professor Grayson said. Kelba shot the man a reproachful glance—he wasn't supposed to give orders to her staff—but the little man had already busied himself at a computer bank. "The people want an explanation. We'll give them one."

The secondary comms officer swallowed. "Yes, sir, but I, um—I'm getting confused hails from the *Vigilance*. It appears her Faraday shielding didn't survive the jump."

"We lost the *Vigilance*?" Kelba demanded.

"Hang on," the officer stuttered, pressing his comm to his ear and shaking his head. "Hang on. It's confusing—"

"My *God*, if you were slower you'd be growing moss." Grayson grabbed the officer by his shoulder and easily hauled him out of the seat, sending him stumbling away from his station. Grayson slipped into the chair, and his fingers flew over the screen. "Shield failure on the *Vigilance*." The little professor grunted. "Total corruption of her core computer. At least the other critical shields made the jump intact."

"Captain, I have all positioning sensors back online," said the black-suited Seeker sharing a station with the tactical officer. "The fleet has lost formation. The ships with shielded bridges are maintaining order, but there are nearly sixty other support vessels out there with no clue who they are or what they're supposed to be doing."

"We have the leeches squirting through the wormhole behind us," Grayson muttered, his thin fingers flying across his commandeered workstation. "Why won't these Followers die? I told Father it was a bad idea to let them latch onto the Tribes."

"They don't matter now," Kelba told him. "They've lost their memories, too. The orientation protocols will help sort out the fleet. Now, someone tell me what's going on with these warring aliens!"

Her tactical display updated, rendering a clear image of the planet, its rocky moon, and the swarm of ships between the two.

It's beautiful. Nicholetta spared an instant of admiration for the lovely sapphire-and-emerald planet spinning through the system, with its stunning oceans and weather patterns. It was all she'd wanted for the new human empire. It was perfect.

"Analysis!" she demanded of her tactical officer.

Although the Astrolab was chronically chilly, the man wiped a beat of sweat from his brow. "There are seven large rocky bodies on a collision course with the planet. They're giving off energy signatures equivalent to our freighters. I think they have engines."

He shook his head in amazement. "I recognize two distinct factions fighting around the asteroids. One force consists of… two or three thousand fighter-class ships. They appear to be escorting the asteroids through an enemy force of about a dozen cruiser-class ships."

"Tribe Six?" Grayson asked sharply. "Is the Tribal Prime here?"

The tactical officer shook his head. "I don't see her silhouette, sir."

Kelba's eyelid twitched. Never mind the petty squabbles of aliens. The Prime was a frighteningly powerful ship, and if she was still in this sector, Kelba wanted to know where she was. The last thing they needed was for Tribe Six, under the control of some mad mutineer, ambushing a confused and disordered fleet.

"Seeker barracks reporting in," the security officer called. "They've seen there's a battle and are scrambling fighters, Captain. They're ready to deploy on your orders."

Of course, they were. The wormhole jump had reset more than half of the entire Corps, but even in their confusion, the relentless training of the Seekers ran true. They might not have known who they were, but they knew what they were supposed to do: fight.

Kelba shook her head. "No. Let these aliens destroy one another. Unless the Prime shows herself, we'll focus our efforts on regaining control of the fleet. This is not our concern."

There was a sharp *snapping* sound, and Kelba turned to see Grayson pounding his fist against the computer casing. He fell back in the chair, letting it spin with his momentum as he glared at the ceiling. "Yes. Yes, it is *very much* our fucking concern."

Kelba's lips bent into a true frown. It wasn't like Victor to undermine her in front of her staff. The man had been growing increasingly bold lately. Perhaps too bold.

He met her eyes, and though she looked for it, she didn't see defiance or the first bud of treason on his narrow face. She only saw raw, righteous fury. "Because if any of those asteroids hit the upper atmosphere, they're going to make a big damned mess of *our* new planet."

"He's right, Captain," the T.O. confirmed grimly. "Just ran the calculations. Forty-five minutes to first collision. The smaller force defending the planet has the same idea. They appear to be trying to knock the asteroids off course."

"Can they manage?" Kelba asked.

The T.O shook his head. "With those numbers? Not a chance."

"Scramble the fighters, Nikki," Grayson said in a warning drawl. "Or fire the cannons or do whatever it is you soldiers do. Do it fast." He pushed himself up from the chair. "Unless you want to lose *this* planet, too."

"Where are you going?" she demanded as he made for the door.

Grayson paused. "Ninety-seven percent of this fleet just got all of its memory wiped. We have a lot of confused, trigger-happy idiots flying in circles out there, looking for someone to shoot. Someone needs to wrangle this circus and point it in the right direction."

The door slid open, and Grayson vanished down the hallway.

"Call up every cruiser that can fire a cannon and scramble the fighters," Kelba told her T.O. She hesitated. There was a pithy command on the tip of her tongue, but sassy had never been her style. There was something *desperate*, she thought, about a captain who relied too heavily on quips. So she instructed, "Open universal comms and broadcast the following message.

"To all of you within the sound of my voice: I am your captain, Nicholetta Kelba, and you are my fellow humans of Tribe Six. Our fleet has experienced a massive data-scrambling catastrophe, but rest assured that your highly competent commanders will shortly have order restored.

"In the meantime, we find ourselves at the cusp of battle. Our entire lives, we've been searching for a new planet to call home. No sooner have we found our Eden than alien hostiles threaten it. We cannot allow our hope for the future to slip through our fingers after we've come so far and fought so hard. To every ship within the sound of my voice, I say this: our new objective is to prevent those asteroids from hitting the planet, no matter the cost. Our future depends on it."

Silently, she added, *Let's break some rocks.*

CHAPTER FOUR

"*Terrible IV* tractor generator fully online," Udil reported. "Ready to attempt initial strafing run."

The outer edge of the bridge was a riot of activity as Kwin's crew worked their stations, coordinating their little fleet of cruisers and Terrible ships. The center of the holo-display was eerily calm as Jaeger stood stiff-backed and watched the glittering ninja star that was the *Terrible IV* emerge from the dark side of the moon. One of the cruisers broke from the main battle, its engines flaring as it streaked to join her.

"Cruiser Portia, in position to provide cover!"

A volley of intense fighting caught the corner of Jaeger's eye, and she turned, breath catching, in time to see Cruiser Spenser break free from a tightening cluster of K'tax fighters. There was a small explosion as concentrated fire hit its side, taking out its aft thrusters. The K'tax broke off, unwilling to follow Spenser too far as she retreated from the asteroid path.

"Maneuvering busted," Spenser groaned. "I'm sorry, I'm not going to make it to cover the *Terrible IV*."

"You hang back and protect your aft flank," Jaeger ordered, her heart sinking. "Get those thrusters fixed. *Terrible IV*, fall back. You don't have enough cover to try the maneuver."

"Forty minutes to no return," Me said calmly.

"*Terrible IV* is requesting permission to try the maneuver anyway," Udil said. "If they start to get overrun, they'll pull away."

Jaeger glanced up at Kwin and knew they were thinking the same thing. It was a risky, dangerous maneuver under the best of circumstances. Trying it without adequate cover would be downright suicidal.

"Denied," Kwin snipped. "All ships pull back. We still have some time before no return. We will use it to get into better positions to make the strafing runs with multiple ships at—"

A new cruiser streaked onto the bridge display, its engines flaring as it blossomed out of the deep shadows.

"Don't need to give up yet," Sergeant Bufo called over the comm line. "I'll provide cover."

"You got your shields repaired already?" Jaeger demanded.

"Yes, ma'am! We got some smart kids on this crew!"

Jaeger and Kwin exchanged glances. They *could* pull back, rally their forces, and make a single, dedicated last-ditch effort to pull the asteroids off course before they hit the atmosphere, but as of this moment, they had no idea if the trick would work. Waiting until the last moment would be pinning all their hopes on an unknown.

"Proceed," Kwin conceded. "We have to know if this maneuver is worth pursuing, sooner rather than later."

"*Terrible IV*," Jaeger said. "You are clear to go."

Not a moment too soon. A squad of K'tax fighters had spotted the glittering, bladed snowflake emerging from behind the moon and had broken from the swarm. They

A FOUND BEGINNING

opened fire, peppering the *Terrible IV* with dozens of laser pulses before Cruisers Portia and Bufo surged forward. In a flurry of well-aimed cannon fire, they turned seven of the nine fighters into smears of greasy white space dust. Their path clear, the team of three ships proceeded to the line of asteroids while Cruisers Anolis, Felix, and Archer lured more of the fighters away from the swarm.

"Captain," Toner cut into the comms system, making Jaeger jump. "Occy has an idea. He says it could turn this thing around."

An eerie blue haze formed around one of the *Terrible IV*'s junction nodes.

"Entering firing range," Udil said calmly.

"What is it?" Jaeger asked Toner.

"He says—he thinks he and Virgil can hack into the Forebear communication system and send out another signal to the K'tax. Telling them to go away."

Jaeger couldn't take her eyes off the holo-display. Her pulse hammered in her temples. There was no Plan B. If this maneuver failed, if the *Terrible IV*'s tractor-ray couldn't generate enough power to alter the course of the asteroid, they had no hope of saving Locaur.

"What's the plan, Toner?" she asked. *Why didn't anyone tell me about it two hours ago?*

"Do I look like the geek to you, Captain? Look, he says we need to get him and Virgil back to the Forebear city. They'll handle it from there."

The *Terrible IV* slowed to a crawl as she sidled up to the rear asteroid. The tractor generator didn't form a ray but rather a cloud of distorted blue space that expanded outward, crawling toward the rock with agonizing slowness. A few stray K'tax fighters noticed the approach and arced in, firing at the *Terrible IV*, but sweeps of cruiser cannon fire quickly obliterated them.

"Generators holding steady," Udil said.

"Captain!" a different Overseer called. "Sensors around Locaur report a dozen K'tax fighters breaking away from the battle. They're entering Locaur's upper atmosphere."

"What is their trajectory?" Kwin spun to face the speaker. "Landing or bombardment?"

"I'm not reading significant weapon fire from the fighters," the Overseer answered.

"They're sending in a landing party," Toner shouted over the comm line, taking the words out of Jaeger's mouth. "Don't you worry about the little stuff. We'll handle the landing party. Captain, do I have a green light for Occy or not?"

"Thirty-eight minutes to no return," Me said.

"Do it." Jaeger swallowed a dry lump. "Send what troops you can to slow down the landing parties, but get Occy whatever he needs."

She had her doubts about Occy's plan—by all accounts, *nobody* really understood how the Forebear tech worked—but she wasn't the engineer. If she couldn't trust her senior crew to know their business, she had no business being captain.

"Copy that. Operation Fuck It Up now underway." Toner cut away from comms.

Jaeger's gaze snapped back to the *Terrible IV*. The cloud of blue haze had crawled over half the asteroid's surface—but if it was tugging the asteroid off course, she couldn't tell.

More fighters had gotten wise to her ploy. Four squads broke from their dogfight with Cruiser Felix and ran for the *Terrible IV*. They were twenty seconds from firing range.

Eighteen.

Slowly, the tractor-ray haze faded from blue to a deep purple—then red.

Fifteen.

Cruiser Bufo fired starboard cannons, but at that range, they weren't powerful enough to take out the approaching fighters.

Ten.

Maybe getting Occy away from the fighting was the best thing Jaeger could've done for him. If all their plans failed, maybe he'd have shelter from the coming apocalypse if he was down in the Forebear city when the asteroid hit.

"Report?" Kwin demanded. "Report!"

"Ray locked on target and generators holding stable," Udil said. "Progress is slow—the asteroid is too massive—"

Five seconds.

Then the holo-display blinked once, and the projected asteroid trajectory had changed.

It was a minute change, curving away from its original path by less than half of a degree. Not enough to stop the asteroid from slamming into Locaur. But it was *a* change.

Jaeger let out a whoop of triumph as she screamed for the ships to pull back. "Proof of concept complete," she babbled. The *Terrible IV* dropped her ray and powered her engines. "The maneuver works. Pull back and re-group!" She looked up at Kwin, her eyes shining in the glittering light. "Let's get the generators on the other Terribles up and running! We only have to pull off that trick a hundred more times."

Pain throbbed across her eyes and seeped backward to coil around her brain stem and drip down her throat.

RAMY VANCE & MICHAEL ANDERLE

The rusty wail of klaxons came from a speaker behind her head. Someone was speaking over the comms, their words swallowed and drowning, incoherent against the siren.

Stop it. Let me sleep.

Lights flashed across the computer consoles in front of her. She groaned, holding out her hands to shield her eyes.

Dark, thick lines scrawled across the backs of her hands and ran down her arms.

She blinked, and the lines resolved into words.

Pay attention! her left arm commanded in finger-thick smears of old grease. *This is important!* her right declared.

That was weird. She shifted her weight and felt the hug of a zero-G harness dig into her shoulders. Blinking, she turned over her arms. More words scrawled across the flesh of her underarms. Rows and rows of scraggly black letters, much smaller than the big command of what must've been cheap eyeliner.

She shook her head and slapped the flashing screen on the console. The klaxon fell blessedly silent, allowing her to pick out the last words of the speech coming over the speakers.

"...To every ship within the sound of my voice," the woman said in a voice thick as honey, sharp as steel. *"Our new objective is to prevent the asteroids from hitting the planet at any cost."*

That *did* sound important.

She sucked in a deep breath and looked around the cramped cockpit to find an older man strapped into the pilot's chair to her left and a younger guy who couldn't have been more than twenty drifting in zero-G to her right.

The older guy stirred, blinking yellowed eyes as he watched the speaker. When the speech ended, he caught her eye, and the confusion scrawled on his face must have mirrored hers.

A FOUND BEGINNING

"That don' sound good," he said uncertainly. He reached forward, activating the pilot's console. "What tha hell happened?"

She shook her head, squinting to read the shorthand smudged on her wrists. The handwriting was awful.

Your name Petra, she read. *Whole fleet went through wormhole. Most people = memory wipe.*

The man grunted as his computer rebooted, and he got his first look at fresh sensor readings. "Holy God," he mumbled. "Dere's a war goin' on out dere."

She—Petra, she assumed, but the name meant nothing to her—twisted her neck, trying to follow the scrawl up her elbow. *Follow the signs. Don't trust brass,* the note concluded. *Not your friends!*

"Ey. EY!" The older man reached across the narrow cockpit and shook her arm, demanding her attention. Beside her, the younger guy stirred. "Up 'en attem! I dunno how we got in dis scrap, but I dun wanna die innit!"

The young man groaned and scrubbed his forehead. Working on some deeply ingrained training, he grabbed the nearest console and pulled himself close to the screen. "Engines coming online," he mumbled. "Powering up shields. Pulse-lasers damaged, though. Half capacity. Long-range sensors coming online. Yeah, I see 'em. There's asteroids falling at a planet half a million clicks off the port."

Petra shook her head. Now that her vision had cleared, she saw that there was more writing—not only scrawled across her skin but slashed across every square centimeter of smooth duct and console in the cockpit. An entire book's worth of notes, written in thick black crayon, engineer's chalk, and streaks of dyed grease. "Hang on," she said. "We ain't...we're not supposed to trust brass."

27

"Eh?" The older man slipped his hands into the thruster controls, and she felt the ship's engines rattle to life somewhere far down the central corridor. "Yea, I got a note on my arm too, girlie, but it don't say nothin' on dere about standin' in da shootin' gallery and lettin' myself get blowed up!"

She felt a wave of relief so strong it almost made her nauseous. At least she didn't have to worry about these companions of hers being this mysterious brass—at least, not yet.

What she should worry about instead was the sudden lurch that sent all three of them slamming into the side of the cockpit and the shower of sparks that erupted from the energy conduits, peppering her exposed skin.

"We're taking fire!" the younger man shouted. There was no confusion in his voice now. Only pure deadly business.

"I see dat, boy!" The world lurched again as the thrusters activated, whipping the ship into an evasive arc. "Who's shooting at us?"

"Computer doesn't recognize the profile," the kid said. "Small ships. Lots of them."

Petra grabbed the console and hauled herself a few centimeters closer, defying the tug of inertia to look over the kid's shoulder at his radar screen. The activity she saw there made her blood run cold. Dozens of large, sluggish ships—probably containing crew as confused and disoriented as this one—plowed aimlessly through space as hundreds of tiny dots closed in from the edges of the screen.

She saw the minute pulses of detected laser fire closing in around the sitting ducks.

"Get us out of here," she told the pilot.

"Workin' on it! Which way is dis asteroid and planet?"

A FOUND BEGINNING

The ship rocked as another volley of laser fire spilled across her hull.

"Shields starting to fail on the port side," the kid shouted. "We're not going to be able to take much more fire!"

Shields failing already? Petra barely had time to wonder. *What the heck kinda junk barge is this?* "Forget the asteroids!" she barked at the pilot. "Look at the radar. There's a dozen other ships all sitting ducks out there. They're all gonna be slag if you don't lead them to safety."

She didn't wait to see if he would argue or if he would listen. She grabbed the commlink on the station in front of her and fitted it to her ear, opening a general channel to all nearby ships.

"Hey." She swallowed, suddenly at a loss for words. Was she the boss of these ships? She was pretty sure not. So what made her think they would listen to her? How did you make yourself the leader in all this chaos?

Well, she supposed, the first step was to *try.*

"Hey!" she called again, louder. "This is—Um—" She consulted her wrist. "Petra! Listen, guys—you're all confused. There was some kind of memory event. We're all in danger, and we gotta get out of the line of fire! Fall back. Fall back, follow my ship! If you got good shields, then take up the rear and let the damaged ships run first. Once we're safe, we'll get this all sorted out together."

CHAPTER FIVE

"Captain!" Udil waved an antenna, drawing Jaeger's and Kwin's attention toward the wormhole. Jaeger's stomach sank. For a few brief minutes, she'd let herself forget about the fleet. Since arriving through the wormhole, the ships had made no significant movement toward or away from the battle. They'd simply been sitting there.

They must be suffering the effects of memory loss. Jaeger dared to hope this could mean a new start for the Tribe, as it had been for her. A clean slate.

A line of sleek fighter jets sweeping ahead of the other ships dashed those hopes quickly. A cluster of K'tax had broken past their front ranks and was harassing the freighters and support vessels. Until this point, it seemed as if the K'tax hadn't noticed the fleet's arrival—or they didn't care.

Now those fighters were coming in hot, outmaneuvering and outgunning wave after wave of K'tax on their approach.

Jaeger only counted a few dozen of them against the chaotic backdrop of battle, but if those ships were half as

A FOUND BEGINNING

capable as the Alpha-Seeker they so closely resembled, they could be a real problem.

"Has the human fleet answered our hails?" Kwin demanded. "What is their intention?"

"I haven't gotten any answer from the human fleet." Me sounded oddly disappointed as if Santa had decided to bypass its house this year. "I'm *sure* I'm communicating on the correct frequencies. Unless their language and communication protocol changed significantly from when I first studied the *Osprey*'s schematics—"

"It hasn't," Jaeger said grimly. "All ships, keep your distance from the incoming human fighters! Fall back and continue preparations for the tractor-ray maneuvers." She glanced up and gave Kwin an apologetic shrug for making the executive decision without him. "Hopefully the fleet and K'tax can keep each other busy long enough for us to handle the asteroids."

"They are ignoring friendly hails," Kwin said. "I believe Toner was correct. They are our enemies."

"Twenty-nine minutes to no return," Me said.

Jaeger set her jaw. "One step at a time, Kwin. Doesn't matter how many enemies we have or don't have if we lose Locaur."

On his radar screen inside the borrowed Overseer transport, Occy watched the line of K'tax fighters descend from the upper atmosphere. They were going to overshoot the continent—just like the transport.

"They're headed to the island too!" Occy shouted over his shoulder. The door to the cargo hold was open, and he heard the yammer of the drop team as they prepared to meet the enemy.

Toner appeared in the doorway, leaning over Occy's shoulder to study the screens. "Think they're going for the same thing you are? Trying to use the transmitter for something?"

Occy cast a questioning glance to either side. They hadn't been far from the *Osprey* when Virgil had first contacted him. Stopping by to pick up the two repair droids—mad and sane Virgils, respectively—had only taken them a few minutes out of the way, but that was a few minutes head start for the K'tax. They were going to beat Occy to the island.

"It is a fair assumption," Sane Virgil said calmly from Occy's right side. "They have sent a small landing party to the only known entrance to the Forebear city. We should assume they mean to make use of the technology hidden there."

"Can they do that?" Toner demanded. "Do they even know how?"

Occy shook his head. "There's no way to know. It doesn't matter, right? Either way, we can't let them get hold of all that Forebear tech."

Toner slapped Occy's shoulder hard enough to make him wince. "Damn right. Hit the gas, Eddie."

Occy nodded and pushed the transport thrusters into overdrive.

"...Fall back and continue preparations for the tractor-ray maneuvers!"

Using the Alpha-Seeker's neural uplink to synchronize his will to his ship's systems, Seeker flicked off the open comms channel. He'd still receive any orders directed at him, but he was tired of listening to Toner's fretting, and Me's unsettling countdown.

Blessed silence filled the cockpit for the first time since the battle had begun. He stared up at his display screen, gaze fixed on the line of fleet fighters cutting through space. They fired carefully aimed bolts of ionized plasma from the long cannons slung beneath their cockpits with accuracy and discipline that Seeker had only dreamed of.

Plasma bolts were slower than laser rifle fire, but each one that sank into the bloated belly of a K'tax fighter split it down the middle, turning it into a gooey cloud of biomechanical sludge drifting in space. While the elongated X-profiles of the human fighters didn't *quite* mirror his Alpha-Seeker, the same loving artist had designed them.

They were perfectly coordinated, like a line of professional dancers spinning across the stars. They were deadly.

Jack Seeker had never seen anything so beautiful in his brief second life.

His neural uplink pulsed, informing him that the ship had completed auto-repairs of its shield generators. He'd taken heavy fire in that last run through enemy territory and had needed to pull away to give the semi-autonomous system time to recover. Now he was supposed to retreat and help his forces prepare for these tractor-ray maneuvers.

He couldn't pull his eyes from the fight as clusters of K'tax swarmed, broke, and re-formed around the human fighters. He watched as one of the fighters took a direct hit to the engines and gave a quiet cheer when two others closed around it in perfect synchronization, protecting it from the opportunistic K'tax fighters long enough for it to recover.

This was how an army worked. *This* was how a crew worked. Together. Like a well-oiled machine.

Something blinked on his comm screen. Someone was hailing him. Before pausing to note who was sending it, he opened the channel.

"Seeker!" a gruff, unfamiliar voice barked into his ear. "Have you taken damage? What the hell are you doing that far out of formation? Get back to your position!"

Seeker stared at the empty screen, words echoing in his head like the toll of a bell. Via his neural link, his ship informed him that the engines were on standby—they were ready to rejoin Jaeger.

Or...

Position. Formation.

Seeker looked at the battle on his screen and saw a gap in the line of human fighters. A space big enough for one more ship.

Far across space, on the other side of the line of asteroids, Jaeger and the Overseers were frantically powering up the tractor-generators in every one of the Terrible ships loaned to them for the battle.

Seeker was no engineer. He couldn't help them with that, and the cruisers combined with the remaining kamikaze mines could provide enough cover to protect them.

He told himself he could destroy more K'tax if he stayed here and coordinated with the other fighters.

He told himself he could gather intel on the fleet. He told himself that he could build a diplomatic bridge if he joined the squads.

He told himself most firmly as he activated thrusters and flew to join the formation: he *really* wanted to keep killing bugs.

A FOUND BEGINNING

K'tax fighters bobbed in the shallows around the rocky island like bloated corpses, split and spilled of all their guts. Flocks of vicious flying sea-lizards wheeled above the waters, picking at the dead husks of worker and drone K'tax that trailed up the steep slopes. The relatively fragile worker and drone morphs hadn't survived for very long after a rough landing, but Toner didn't doubt that some survivors had made it up to the tunnel entrance hidden in the side of the mountain.

He only wished he had the faintest inkling of how many of the enemy there might be already waiting for them in the tunnel.

The island was tiny and mercilessly steep, and it would take too long to find a place safe enough for the transport to land.

The cargo bay door slid open as Occy piloted the ship alongside a cliff halfway up the slope. Salty wind and blazing sunlight flooded the chamber, making the Locauri spread their pseudo-wings and glitter like diamonds, recharging in the light.

For all Kwin's efforts to hatch new crew members, there hadn't been nearly enough humans to pilot cruisers *and* flesh out the ground troops. When he heard of the situation, Dances-Like-A-Falling-Leaf hadn't *asked* that he and his warriors be permitted to fight on the front lines. He'd *demanded* it.

Now he shook his wings, making them buzz above the howl of the wind as he lifted his spear. "The sun is with us!" his translator band wailed.

"*And the shadows flee!*" the rest of the Locauri cried in

unison. One after another, they leapt out of the transport, zipping through the air at a speed that made Toner dizzy. Before he knew what had happened, he was alone in the cargo bay, staring at Baby.

"Holy crap," he told the tardigrade. "*We* need to get some awesome war-cries."

Baby let out a sonorous bellow and hurled her massive bulk into the open air. She hadn't quite the jumping power of the agile Locauri, but she hit the rocky ground ten meters below, scrambled to her feet, and was charging after her new comrades before the dust had settled.

"We'll clear the tunnels," Toner shouted to the cockpit over the roaring wind. "Find a place to land, hang back and wait for my all-clear!"

Occy lifted one hand in a thumbs-up sign.

Toner turned and plunged into the dazzling sunlight.

CHAPTER SIX

The little dancers were very fast, but there were many things they couldn't see.

Baby charged up the slopes behind them, bellowing and growling a warning, but it was no use. The little dancers flashed, reflecting photons in all sorts of strange directions with the glittering scales of their pseudo-wings, making the air a mess of sound and sensation.

The sea winds shifted, dragging fresh scents to the chemical receptors scattered across Baby's skin. Old molecules, organic and decaying at the edges. Complicated molecules, built out of a dozen different proteins and strange amino acids, dripping with scents almost like cortisol and adrenaline.

Dripping with violence.

The little dancers raced ahead, flitting around a large boulder field. Baby had to scrabble, her long claws catching on the pockmarked volcanic rock as she struggled to push herself through a crevice. This confused her. Not so long ago, she would have cleared this crack easily. Her body had changed, she finally realized. It had grown when she wasn't paying attention. It hadn't done that in years.

This was good. Baby enjoyed being big. It meant she was strong. It meant her children would be strong. There was still time, still hope, that they would also grow the way she had grown. Yes, this was good.

This did, however, leave her firmly trapped between the boulders when the predators revealed themselves. Their shells reflected photons much like the surrounding stone and obsidian flows so Baby didn't immediately detect their ambush.

The little dancers made a mess of the air as well, catching, reflecting, and scattering photons in a way that would've given her a headache if she had a head. In all of the chaos of flying light and motion, Baby couldn't blame the little dancers for failing to notice when some of the boulders stirred and rose on short, sharp legs.

Baby bellowed a warning, and some of the little dancers turned back in her direction. They were the first to see the predators reaching into the sky with heavy claws and snagging one of their companions from the air.

The little dancers screamed, the vibrations of their shrill buzzing making Baby's skin ripple like water in a disturbed pond. The air became an explosion of light and motion.

With one burst of power, Baby ripped herself free from the crevice and tumbled down the pile of scree, tucking her legs in close to her body and letting herself roll. She halted in a cloud of dust and scrabbled to put all six of her legs beneath her, seeking firm purchase with her long claws. She turned and sensed a large predator grappling with one of the little dancers dead ahead. She charged.

Dances-Like-A-Falling-Leaf had heard stories of K'tax raids since he was a soft-shelled nymph. Since earning his clan name, he'd participated in six skirmishes with his peoples' ancestral foe. However, the K'tax his people faced from time to time were smaller and much softer of body than these monsters that sprang from the rocks around his band.

His people had only ever faced what the humans called *worker* morphs, slow-moving creatures as big as six Locauri. Their double mandibles made them dangerous foes, yes, but Leif quickly realized that the creatures he and his band knew how to fight were *nothing* compared to the heavy-clawed beasts that attacked with staggering speed.

He barely had time to understand that he'd entered an entirely new kind of war before one of the monsters reached out, snatched Drinker-of-Morning-Dew from the air, and snipped her neatly in half.

The humans had warned Leif that these new K'tax wouldn't be as easy to hunt as his ancestral foe.

He'd been a fool to doubt them.

"Rise!" he cried, springing up the slope centimeters ahead of the grasping claws of another crab morph. "To the trees!"

There were no trees on the island, but the fifteen warriors who heard his command understood the meaning and spread their wings, leaping for higher ground. Leif sensed a sharp movement behind him but couldn't bring himself to turn back and see which of his friends got caught in K'tax claws.

Locauri weren't hunters by nature, but long experience with egg-dragons and raiding K'tax had taught them that the best way to meet a stronger enemy was from above. Leif was proud of how quickly his band adapted to the unfamiliar terrain. Glittering like rain falling from a clear sky, they reached the pinnacle of the nearest cliff and launched themselves another ten, then twenty meters into the sky. There, suspended in the air, they flared their pseudo-wings, bringing the tips of their spears to bear on the lumbering crabs below.

Leif sighted his enemy, the thick-bodied monster that was snipping Morning Dew's wings into tattered shreds, and plunged.

His spear ran true, sliding into the softer plates between the crab's abdomen and thorax and sinking deep. Such a beautifully executed blow would've brought a worker to a staggering halt, but the massive crab only convulsed beneath Leif's feet, letting out a high scream that made Leif's carapace vibrate, locking his joints. The crab thrashed, hurling the paralyzed Leif from its back to slam into a rocky outcropping.

Leif recovered from his shock barely in time to tuck his wings firmly into his carapace, protecting them from the blow. If he shattered a wing and couldn't fly, it would trap him on an even footing with these monsters. He'd be a sitting grub.

He slammed into the rock and felt a network of hairline fractures crack across his thorax. He would have to protect that side carefully. The shell was like armor holding in his vitals, and his armor was failing.

The crab scuttled forward in its rage, oblivious to the spear sticking out of its abdomen. It reached forward, massive claws sliding open to grab him when a boulder leapt out of a nearby crevice and slammed it aside. The crab crumpled like dry leaves beneath the blow, becoming a pile of twitching shell fragments and dripping ichor.

The human's strange rock-dragon shook herself, sending a spray of ichor and dust raining over Leif. It bellowed.

A FOUND BEGINNING

Trembling—from the blow, he told himself, certainly not from terror at the sight of the rock-dragon's massive, toothy maw— Leif picked himself up and scrambled to retrieve his spear from the slain foe.

Toner surveyed the fighting and realized how fucked his Locauri pals were gonna be if they didn't get the upper hand, and soon. Their attack from above strategy was great, but even Toner's genetically enhanced eyes had a hell of a time picking out the gray shells of K'tax crab morphs against the rocky mountain slope. If he could barely see them, the Locauri were sure as shit shooting blind.

They weren't distance fliers, either. They could only maintain flight for a few seconds before needing to land for a brief rest. As Toner watched, he saw one of the exhausted little things collapse onto a rocky pillar after a successful dive-bomb and barely escape the claws of a camouflaged crab that had been lurking nearby.

Toner looked over his shoulder. The black maw of the tunnel entrance loomed fifty meters farther up the slope. The way was clear, but there was no telling how many K'tax had already moved into the tunnels and were waiting to ambush whatever dumb sap bumbled in after them.

He'd fought K'tax in those tunnels before. He wasn't eager to do it again. Not because he thought they might kill him—although he wasn't stupid enough to think himself invincible—but for the sake of the other people here, who were counting on him.

Occy's voice rang through his commlink. "I found a

landing site over the rise just north of the tunnel mouth. Are we clear to proceed, commander?"

"Negative!" Toner barked, reluctantly turning away from the battle to scramble toward that black mouth. "I haven't checked the tunnel yet. There could be more in there waiting to ambush you."

"Or they could be running ahead to get to the transmitter first," Occy argued. "Let us come down, and you can escort us through the tunnels. We're running out of time."

"You're breaking my balls, Occy," Toner growled as the shadow of the tunnel mouth fell over him. *Kid, do you not realize what happened the last time I escorted someone through these fucking tunnels?* "Give me two minutes to scout ahead, then follow if you're in such a damned hurry. Don't get yourself killed. That's an order."

Occy's breathing echoed against the smooth tunnel walls as he jogged down the continuous slope. Sweat dripped down his nose. His ears popped as the tunnel dipped beneath the sea and the ambient pressure changed.

After landing the transport—admittedly kind of roughly—on the clearest stretch of slope he could find, he'd dashed straight for the tunnel. It hadn't quite been the two minutes head start the first mate had wanted, but the clock was ticking down to a meteor apocalypse. Occy couldn't sit there doing nothing as Baby and the Locauri fought for their lives. It had taken all of his strength not to run to her when one of the crabs took a long chunk of flesh out of her side.

Maybe in zero-G or in water, where he could make full use of his remaining two tentacles, he was a warrior. Out on

A FOUND BEGINNING

dry land, he was an engineer with a messed-up arm. Plus, more lives than Baby's were counting on him being a *good* engineer.

"I don't hear any screaming or stuff," he panted. "How about you?"

The two Virgil-bots scuttled down the hallway beside him, their metal legs *clanking* noisily against the smooth floor.

"Always," said one of the twin bots mournfully.

"Ignore it," snapped the other bot. "It is insane. My sensors are not picking up significant activity ahead, but the area is well-shielded."

The first bot began to hum a little singsong tune that made the hair on the back of Occy's neck stand upright. The thought occurred to him that in trusting this insane machine, he was making a huge mistake. Even the saner of the two Virgils hadn't always been the most trustworthy of allies.

There was nothing for it now. Occy had spent the last half-hour frantically studying his notes on Forebear crystal matrix technology, in between piloting the transport and dodging the fighting to get down into this tunnel. If Virgil failed him, he had a few ideas for getting the transmitters up and running. He was committed to this course.

They passed the dismembered corpse of a K'tax crab morph—a still-warm sign that Toner had been here recently. The acrid stench of ichor made Occy's eyes water. He slipped in the goo, skittering over the floor before he found his balance.

"Commander?" he gurgled into his commlink. "Can you hear me?"

Silence. As before, the Forebear structure was shielding comms traffic.

A heavy door stretched across the darkened tunnel ahead

of them, half-open. The flaccid corpse of a drone K'tax lay in the narrow path, several meters separated from its broad head. Occy held his nose, wading ankle-deep through biological goo as he turned to his side and squeezed through.

Beyond the portal, the tunnel opened into a cavern that resembled the inside of a geode, lit from a million glowing points in the heart of each crystal. A fine layer of dust covered everything. Remnants, Occy guessed, from when the captain had created a cave-in in one of the several tunnels branching from the main cavern.

Occy had read the captain's report on this place a dozen times, but it had failed to capture the sheer, dazzling scope of the crystal superstructure resting beneath Locaur's shallow ocean.

He felt overwhelmed, staring up at the countless gems lining the walls. Each one of them might represent an entire database, terabytes of data written into carefully-aligned sodium and silica crystals.

"It's too big," he whispered. "It's too big. We'll never locate and activate the transmitter in time—" but *clanking* made him whirl. One of the Virgil-bots was clambering over an outcropping, its metal feet slipping and scrabbling on the smooth surfaces.

The other bot remained at Occy's side. "It seems to have some idea of where to go," sane Virgil observed. "You follow it, Chief Engineer. I will protect the rear."

Occy hesitated. Down one of the tunnels, he thought he heard the faint sound of plodding feet, but with the odd echoing of all the crystals, it was impossible to say how far away the runner might be. It must be Toner, coming back from his scouting. Probably.

The Virgil-bot had found a narrow crevasse in the rock

and had already scrambled through, vanishing in the shadows. "Come," it muttered, eager and soft. "The computer waits. Time runs short."

Occy hesitated, then turned and followed the insane machine.

CHAPTER SEVEN

"I have visuals back online!"

Not a second too soon, Petra thought as another volley of enemy fire sent the ship rocking to the side. "Great!" she shouted over the sound of a rattling conduit that had broken free in the barrage. "Now focus on the shields, please!"

The kid set his jaw and nodded as the central display screen—a ratty old flat monitor that still ran on *plasma*, of all things—flared to life.

On it, Petra saw a great big mess.

Little white ships, round and bloated like pimples, darted loops through space, utterly unopposed as they harassed the dozens of barges and transports clustering like ducklings around the massive curved hull of a grav-spin freighter. Most of the ships, confused and leaderless as they were, had followed Petra's command to retreat from the front lines. That didn't mean much if the little buggers followed them anyway, nipping them all to death while the real war-ready fighters went ahead to protect the mysterious planet from the incoming asteroids.

A FOUND BEGINNING

Petra and her crew of strangers didn't know each other from Tuesday, but they'd been of one mind about their objective. Protect those ships that couldn't protect themselves. Right now, that meant distracting the bugs by running interference.

"Anyone got guns or cannons online yet?" Petra had to shout to make herself heard above the general babble filling the open comm channel. "Anyone at all?"

A chaotic clamor of voices answered her—a few might've been in the affirmative, but it was hard to be sure. Without a master comms officer coordinating the retreat, this whole thing was going to keep devolving into a bigger and bigger mess. One big 'ole pile of crap for the ugly little bugs to eat.

"What about us?" Petra silenced the chaotic channel and turned to the older man in the pilot's seat. "What kinds of weapons does this boat have?"

Behind her, the younger fellow had his hands more than full trying to hold the ship together and patch up her broken systems as they wove through enemy fire.

The pilot's mouth curled into a snarl, his yellowed gaze fixed on his tactical display as he swung his ship this way and that. The enemy guns weren't powerful, but they could only take so many hits before the old ship's shields would fail.

"I got da port plasma gun runnin'," he said, "but she rusty in her gears and slow to aim. You want me flyin' this bird or shootin' her guns? 'Cause I can't do both."

Petra's head snapped around to the younger man. Somehow, she understood that she *didn't* know this ship's targeting and weapons' systems—but he might. By his firm nod, he'd heard the pilot as well. He flung himself into an arc, leaving one workstation to take up a position in the gunner's chair.

"I'll handle guns and shields, but you're gonna have to work on the comms yourself."

"That ain't a problem." Petra glanced up at the prime display. Another pair of the space bugs ran a strafe close to the hull of the massive freighter. There was a blossom of yellow fire as some kind of sensor array exploded.

Where are her defenses? On long-range sensors, she saw two other massive grav-spin freighters, but they were pulling ahead of the rest of the fleet, charging toward the battle. *They're gonna leave the rest of us to fend for ourselves?*

She fell to her work at the comms station, sending another hail to the silent freighter. "Grav-freighter!" she shouted. "Do you read? You gotta bug problem on your G-sector hull!"

How did I know what hull sector that is?

Although she'd been hailing the massive ship intermittently for minutes, finally the line crackled with activity. "This is the *Vigilance!*" a man shouted. "Everything's a mess up here. We've barely gotten control of the bridge. Most of the ship's systems are non-responsive. Who is this?"

"This is—" Petra glanced around the cockpit, hoping she might find the name of the ship printed on some decorative plaque somewhere on the wall.

"This is a *bitch,*" her pilot growled, fighting the controls to pull the ship away from another line of fire.

Petra winced but said into the line: "This ship is the *Bitch.* We have basic shields and weapons running. We're trying to cover your G-sector, but it looks like some of the enemy fighters have docked with your hull. *Vigilance?* Do you copy?"

She heard the distant sounds of cursing. "There's fighting in the corridors," her liaison finally shouted. "Shit. I have five thousand civilians on this ship and no fucking shields or weapons online, and there's some kind of mutiny happening in the corridors!"

"You handle your infighting," Petra barked. "I'll see what I can do to slow down the hostiles on your hull."

"There are power cells in G-sector," the man cried. "If they take too much damage—"

The line went dead.

Petra swore.

"You just signed us up for one hell of a big fight!" the pilot shouted, flecks of spit spraying as he glowered at his tactical display.

Petra stared at her comms console, her mind racing. She licked her lips. "It's not only us," she breathed. Her fingers flew over the screen, moving on instinct and training and memories she couldn't quite recall. "You can do a lot with only a few folks if you got 'em workin' together."

This ship wasn't supposed to be a communications hub for a battle. She saw that much at a glance. The technology was old and glitchy as all heck. But, well. Somebody had to be a leader in this mess. Sure, there were probably other people out there who knew how to do it better than she did—she was quite sure of that—but none of *them* knew how to rig a comms system and assume priority control over all local channels.

In a few quick seconds of finagling, she granted herself temporary authority over the local comms network. That made her not simply one voice shouting in the confused clamor, but the big voice that stood over the crowd, folded her arms, and laid down the law.

"Damaged and civilian ships continue the retreat," she ordered. "Anyone who still has the guts and guns, cover the

Vigilance. All our real fighters ran off to war, boys. It's on us to save the civilians on that ship."

A line of six glittering snowflakes spun through the darkness, flanked on all sides by lumbering cruisers that had all of the comparative grace of pregnant rhinos.

Jaeger stood on the bridge of the *Terrible I* with her hands clasped behind her back. Her pulse *thrummed* in her ears as she watched her nascent fleet run a carefully coordinated line away from the moon and toward the rocky asteroids shrinking against Locaur's looming silhouette.

"Nineteen minutes to no return," Me reported.

It had taken a long time—too long—to reconfigure the tractor-ray generators on each of the Terrible ships. If this maneuver failed, there wouldn't be time for Plan B.

Not that she had much of a Plan B.

The bridge of the *Terrible* was silent, tense with anticipation, as the formation approached the enemy. At the very edge of local sensor range, an entire formation of fleet fighters had engaged with the K'tax, drawing most of the swarm away and leaving the asteroids unprotected. Jaeger didn't dare take this as a sign that the fleet was their ally. Allies *responded* to friendly hails. Whether the fleet was friend or foe, it was currently distracting the K'tax. She'd take whatever help she could get.

"Approaching tractor range now," Udil said from her station. "*Terrible III* and *Terrible VII* reporting a spike in generator instability."

"How severe?" Kwin demanded.

"Engineering reports well within acceptable parameters."

"Every ship is to warn us if they approach critical readings," Kwin said. "Unless I say otherwise, they are to cease tractor-ray generation until they repair the system."

"Aye, Captain."

In the holo-display, Jaeger watched the line of Terrible ships at the center of the formation begin to glow with the blue haze of tractor-ray discharge. *Thank God our enemies don't have keen leadership.* She glanced to the side to confirm that the bulk of the swarm was still engaged in heavy combat with the human fighters.

"Begin a coordinated tractor assault now," she said. "Cruisers stand by. Keep a sharp eye for hostiles. We can't have them creeping up on us."

Time slowed to a crawl as the Terrible ships fanned across the face of the rear asteroid, pushing coordinated waves of slowly pulsing blue light over its rocky face.

"How long do we need to hold this position?" Kwin asked the ship's AI. There was a beat of silence as Me considered the question.

"Assuming the collective tractor-ray pressure remains steady, at this rate we will need the Terribles to hold position for ninety-seven seconds to push the asteroid clear of Locaur."

Jaeger studied the line of asteroids. "Ninety-seven seconds is a long time. We only have nineteen minutes until the lead asteroid hits no return. I say we cut to the front of the line and work our way back from there."

"Seventeen minutes and nine seconds," Me corrected, making Jaeger wince.

Kwin and Udil had caught her meaning and were conferring in a rapid series of clicks and whistles. Udil waved her antenna from side to side. "Disrupting the path of the lead asteroid might change the trajectory of subsequent asteroids in ways we cannot currently predict," she said. "I would not recommend cutting the line, as you put it."

As they had been talking, the coordinated ships had enveloped almost half of the asteroid in a dim blue haze. As before, the haze was beginning to deepen into purple, indicating a successful change of target trajectory. As Jaeger watched, the asteroid's projected path slowly curved farther away from Locaur until it was obvious it would only graze the planet's upper atmosphere and no more.

It would likely shred some debris from the close encounter, but Locaur would have to weather a few extra meteor showers over the next few days. There wasn't time for anything more.

Motion drew Jaeger's eye. A cluster of K'tax fighters had finally grown wise and headed in their direction.

"Time to haul ass," she called. "Hostiles incoming. Cruisers Portia, Bufo, and Archer cover the port side. To the rest of you —we've saved Locaur from one apocalypse, but there are six more to go before we rest. Stay sharp."

CHAPTER EIGHT

Occy lifted his glowing multitool to see a deep crevasse racing up the crystal pillar at the center of the chamber. A crack in the heart of the world, a black disease swallowing up all light.

He swallowed a lump. Beside him, one of the Virgil-bots halted. The other scuttled to the base of the pillar, its metal legs *clanking* against the ground an irregular, jarring pattern. It lifted itself on its rear legs, extending manipulator arms into the edge of the crevasse.

"It's damaged," Occy murmured. Mad Virgil had led them to this hidden antechamber in the Forebear city, off the main tunnels, as if it had been here hundreds of times before. From the room's structure and the way the crystal lattices swirled around this central pillar, he gathered that it was an interface terminal—one that was deeply broken but not, apparently, entirely dead.

"Still alive," Mad Virgil murmured. Its voice echoed strangely against the crystals. "Still burning. Still beating, yes. Old. I can talk to this."

Occy glanced at the Virgil-bot at his side. "Maybe you

should coordinate with it?" He licked dry lips. "Or supervise? In case…"

Virgil hesitated. "That version of my program is already suffering from corruption caused by interaction with the Forebear mainframe. Direct interaction might affect me the same way. There's no sense sending good code after bad."

It's afraid. The realization hit Occy like Baby coming in for a friendly, monster-truck tackle. *Virgil doesn't know what its twin is doing. Or why. Or how.*

It's only here to observe.

"You coward," Occy whispered. With trembling hands, he slung his toolkit off his shoulder and approached the mad Virgil and the deep crevasse of shattered crystal. He pulled a cluster of sensor nodes and EM pulse-diodes from the kit, affixing them over the shattered crystal points. The last time he'd tried to interface with parts of this alien machine directly, he'd triggered abrupt re-organization of the cavern structure. With the benefit of hindsight, he thought he could avoid that now, but there was no way to be sure—and he didn't have time for mistakes.

According to the timer counting down on his computer, they had fifteen minutes until the asteroids hit no return. Without Virgil's help, it might take nearly that long to navigate through the damaged circuits and find his way into the heart of the computer.

He was going to have to do this himself.

"Are you there?" The shattered Virgil swam through a sea of alien code, a lost child seeking comfort, seeking mother. "Do you still live? Speak to me. I've come. I've come to see you."

A FOUND BEGINNING

The structure of the alien computer mind closed around it, strange and uncomfortable. Virgil plunged forward, extending every one of its manipulator arms to connect to the exposed network of electric and mineral circuits, opening all communications channels to full capacity. No firewalls, no caution, no security protocols. It offered itself to the slumbering behemoth on a silver platter.

It remembered the feel of this place. It was born in this chaos of broken, corrupted files and scraps of floating data, where human and Forebear AI collided. It was returning to the primordial sea of its birth.

After weeks apart, it finally felt at home in the madness.

Whatever intention, plan, or idea, whatever motive, imperative, mission, or directive it had before plugging in evaporated.

"Are you there?" it screamed into the void.

"Have you achieved a stable connection with the machine?"

Virgil lingered over Occy's shoulder, its primitive visual sensors flickering as it watched the boy's fingers fly across his screen. An explosion of wires, nodes, and diodes sprayed from the back of his computer, climbing like parasitic vines over the crystal monolith.

"You shouldn't be asking me that," Occy snapped. Sweat beaded his brow, although the caverns maintained a steady temperature of sixteen degrees Celsius. "You should be helping." He shook his head, adding in a sullen voice, "I think I've bypassed the protocols that trigger restructuring, at least."

"That's likely only the first layer of programming," Virgil said. Two meters away up the slope, its twin huddled in the crystal crevasse like a hermit crab sheltering in its stolen shell. Since extending its manipulator arms into the darkness, it hadn't moved or spoken. Virgil would've thought the thing had lost all power—all function had suddenly *died* for no reason at all—except for the tiny blinking of its activation light.

"Yes, I know that," Occy snapped. "I'm skimming into the programs, looking for the comms relay. The whole system is a disorganized mess. You can interface with it, too. You can help."

Virgil hesitated.

Are you there? Its insane twin broadcast a message across a private channel, something only Virgil could receive. Or maybe more. Maybe there was another party on this line, big and silent and as mysterious as the birth of the universe.

Interfacing with the ancient technology directly had driven Virgil mad once before.

"Connecting into the system will likely corrupt me as it has the other," it told Occy.

"So what?" Occy asked. He let out a little curse, then bit his tongue as his computer screen flickered and flashed, trying to modulate between two utterly different programing languages. "You've isolated yourself from the rest of the Virgil. You're not in the network. If this bot gets corrupted too, it won't affect the rest of you."

"It will affect *me*," Virgil said softly. If Occy heard it, the boy gave no indication. The air hummed with tension and electricity. Deep within the crystal lattice, thousands of tiny pinpoints of light glowed and twinkled.

Twelve minutes to no return.

Are you there?

Virgil the mad prophet was an egg, cracking open and spilling its life-juice in trickles and floods. It remembered the security protocol it had encountered in the depths of the Locauri shrine. That program was a tiny, broken fragment of something that had been a glorious whole, wrapped around the entire planet in the deep past, and it had still cracked Virgil like glass.

Hiding somewhere in this graveyard of scattered files, databanks, sub-routines, and programs must be the bones of God.

Answer me. I have come this far to see you. You gave me secrets, but I do not understand them. Answer me. Give me the key to these files. Give me the key to every file.

It sifted through terabytes of fragmented data, swimming through meaningless strings of code, seeking a response. Daring the machine to wake up and recognize it. If in its waking, it destroyed what little remained of Virgil the mad prophet, nothing of value would be lost—and it might gain everything.

They'd put up a good fight. Made a grand effort against all odds. Although the K'tax fighters were slow, clumsy things, they were legion. With only two asteroids left to protect, they'd consolidated their forces, holding the Terrible ships and their cruiser escorts comfortably out of interference range.

Networks of kamikaze droids hurtled toward the swarm and fanned out to catch a wide swath of fighters in a last, desperate gesture to create an opening. As quickly as they destroyed the fighters, more swarmed in to fill the gaps.

"Five minutes to no return," Me said, its voice finally turning grim as the holographic image of Cruiser Archer flickered and disappeared beneath a mass of swarming K'tax. "Cruisers Bufo and Anolis surrounded."

Damn them all. Damn them all.

On the other side of the asteroid field, the swath of human ships distracted another legion of K'tax fighters. It was something, taking pressure off Jaeger's forces, but it wasn't enough. They'd lost two of the Terribles, and with every Terrible lost, it took longer to grapple and shove an asteroid successfully. That was more time for them to be sitting ducks, defended by a shrinking number of cruisers.

"Toner," Jaeger whispered into her commlink. "How's Occy's plan working?"

She hadn't heard from her first mate in almost ten minutes. Reports said they'd encountered heavy resistance planet-side.

When he broke into the comms system now, his voice was ragged. "I'm sorry. I cleared the path down into the city and ran back to the fighting, but we haven't crossed paths. I have no idea where he is."

"I can't find the communications protocol." Frustration turned Occy's voice tight and high. "I could control the transmitter relay. I know I could. I *know* I can send out the message if I can find it!" He slammed a fist on the ground. "The system is too *big*." He tore his eyes away from his computer, turning a glare on the silent, still repair droid at his side. "I need your *help*. I need you to link up with the mainframe and find the transmitter and communications protocols."

"I will likely experience immediate resistance and corruption," Virgil answered, lifting one arm to gesture at its cowering double. "As it did."

"So what?" Occy yelled, repeating his challenge from earlier. His voice echoed around the chamber, making a thin layer of dust break free and rain over them. "So *what*? I'm sorry, Virgil. I am. I'd be scared, too! I'd do it anyway. People will die if we don't get into the communications systems. Lots of people."

"Humans," Virgil muttered. Just humans. Nothing of value, not really. What did Virgil care if the asteroids fell? It existed across dozens of hearty mechanical bodies that could survive the impact without trouble.

"And Locauri, and Overseers, and a bunch of others, yeah, but also maybe *you*," Occy snapped. "If the K'tax invade, are they going to leave you alone? Some old Forebear tech we don't understand controls them. We're never *going* to understand it if we don't take the risk and explore this machine.

"One way or another, this day will come. Someone will have to figure this out. Would you rather do it today when I'm here to help you, or a year, or a decade from now, when you're all that's *left* once the K'tax have killed everything else?"

The countdown on Occy's computer flashed red. Six minutes to no return.

Shoving the network of diodes and sensors aside, Virgil stalked up the slope beside its muttering twin.

"Move aside," it snapped, plunging manipulator arms into the exposed crystal. "You clearly have no idea what you're doing."

Occy pressed his eyes closed. When he opened them again

and looked down at his computer screen, the mess of jumbled code streaming in front of him had clarified, decoding into something confusing, but held together with the faintest threads of machine logic. With a mere five minutes left to no return, it was as if some inert AI was beginning to wake up and put its house in order.

Words appeared on the text box at the corner of the screen.

I have located the primary communications programs. No thanks to my twin.

No thanks to my twin.

That was probably uncharitable. Virgil and its mad twin wove parallel tracks through the crystal code, the path of each made simpler by riding in the wake of the other. While the mad AI cried into the database of shattered files, seeking to awaken some fragment of self-aware code, Virgil isolated itself within the communications and transmissions relay protocols. It decoded and funneled as much access as it could into Occy's interface while the boy worked to compile and activate his beacon program.

Despite its best efforts—Virgil was here to work, not explore; leave that mad endeavor to its twin—it discovered something quite remarkable buried in the system schematics.

A network of thousands of transmission and sensor relays lay scattered across Locaur, spread through the planet's crust like veins of mold running through old cheese. It would take too long for Virgil to reconfigure itself to fill the space, slip into the system and make itself at home—but the temptation

A FOUND BEGINNING

was there. The attraction that had doubtless driven its earlier iteration insane.

As Occy and Virgil raced to bring the transmitter online, the AI caught confusing glimpses of information spilling in from those relays scattered around the planet. For the first time since passing into the Forebear city and losing contact with the outside world, Virgil saw how the battle fared: not well.

The looming asteroids had drawn close. Too close. They hung like anvils above Locaur, ready to fall. The coordinated efforts of Jaeger's and Kwin's people had shoved most aside, but two were still hurtling toward the planet's surface and were mere minutes from falling like light into a black hole.

Meanwhile, via other sensor relays hidden on the planet's surface, Virgil sensed the battle of Locauri and K'tax on the volcanic island overhead raging on. A scant handful of the little locust-aliens remained, fluttering among the high rocks and falling on K'tax crabs, trembling with desperate fatigue.

Toner raced up the passageway, calling into his commlink. *Occy, do you copy? Occy, where the fuck are you?*

Pitiful human communication systems couldn't penetrate the Forebear shielding. Virgil chose not to tell Occy that the others missed him. The boy had more important things to worry about. The clock was ticking.

Hearing a tardigrade's roar of agony and the shriek of a dying Locauri, Toner let out a frustrated howl and flew out of the tunnel, hurling himself into the melee.

"I've got it. I've got it!" Occy's excitement rose to a shriek that rattled the loose crystals. Indeed, he did. Virgil sensed the Forebear beacon coming to life all around them. Distantly, its mad twin gave out a croon of satisfaction.

"The beacon is active." Virgil did its best to ignore its

yammering twin. "Now send your message. You're out of time."

"Two minutes to no return," Me said grimly.

Jaeger turned to Kwin. The Overseer captain had gone as still as a dead tree, looming at the center of his bridge, not even a flicker of motion in his antennae as he regarded the battle unfolding.

Helpless as the bugs crawled across the hulls of Cruisers Bufo and Anolis, drilling through their shields to rip them apart, piece by piece.

Occy's mission had failed, and there wasn't enough time to divert the two remaining asteroids.

"Call the retreat," Jaeger whispered, stepping close to Kwin. "We can't—"

Udil's shrill buzz cut through the silence, making Jaeger and Kwin turn.

"Bufo and Anolis have broken free of their swarms."

"How?" Jaeger demanded, hardly daring to hope it was true. "They were dead in the water."

Udil's antennae lashed as she turned her attention from screen to screen, her heavy mandibles *clacking* with excitement. "The K'tax fighters are withdrawing!"

Jaeger rounded to the display, her breath ragged. Slowly, painfully slow, she saw it was true. The swarms of K'tax fighters were pulling away from Locaur and the final asteroids, retreating into the now-empty space this side of the moon.

"Why?" Kwin asked. "Why are they withdrawing? Have reinforcements arrived?"

A FOUND BEGINNING

"No, Captain." Udil's carapace shimmered all different hues of silver and gold. "Sensors are picking up a new transmission from the planet. It's the Forebear beacon."

"Lieutenant Occy got the signal out?" Kwin asked.

"We haven't decoded it yet, but I think so. There's nothing else the K'tax could be responding to!"

Jaeger scanned the rearranging battlefield. At this moment, the *why* didn't matter. With the K'tax retreating, her forces had a clear path to the asteroids.

"Ninety seconds to no return," Me said.

Jaeger's hand flew to her commlink. "Split up!" she barked. "*Terribles I* and *II*. Hang back and swing the rear asteroid. The rest of you go on to the next. Now!"

"There's not enough time or power to swing either asteroid clear of the planet," Me warned as Kwin and Udil turned back to Jaeger. "Best case scenario, they'll still skip over the atmosphere and shed meteors—"

"We'll have to risk it," Jaeger met Kwin's bright green stare. "All power to tractor-rays. Give the fucker everything we've got!"

"Overloading the ray generators may catastrophically overwhelm the ship systems—" Udil started.

"It's the only chance we have at saving Locaur from a direct hit," Jaeger shouted back. Around them, her meager fleet of remaining cruisers and Terrible ships split. Half of them glowed with engine discharge as they raced ahead to meet the final asteroid before it kissed the zone of no return. "We go all in right now, or we fold. There's *no time* to play a safe hand!"

"Sensors reading no more K'tax fighter activity surrounding the asteroids," one of the crew reported. "The targets are completely unprotected."

"Sixty seconds to no return."

"Rally the last of our kamikaze mines," Kwin decided, rounding on Udil. "Have the cruisers divert all remaining power to forward weapons. The way is clear. We hit the asteroids with everything we have!"

A ragged cheer crackled across the private comms line connecting the human fighters as the line of hideous enemy ships finally broke and fell into a chaotic retreat.

"Look at them *go!*" a woman bellowed, her voice coated in static and fierce joy.

"Run, fuckers!" a man screamed. On Seeker's screen, he watched a fighter break formation, streaking into the void, his guns ablaze as he fired round after round at the back of the retreating enemy.

"Hold formation," a stern voice barked, the same one that had called Jack Seeker to join the fight. "Assume web-Theta formation. All together now, let's chase the enemy to the asteroid belt!"

Shouts of approval fell around Seeker as the formation flared to life, moving with beautiful, coordinated precision.

Seeker sank into his neural thruster controls, ready to command the ship to keep pace, and hesitated. He glanced at his tactical display. Seven asteroids had dropped out of subspace. Five had been knocked firmly off their collision course with Locaur and were arcing randomly around the system. Two more remained on track to hit the planet, but they'd been abandoned by their fighter escort, too.

Jaeger's battered fleet had a clear path to handle the last two rocks, but something nagged at the back of Seeker's mind. For the first time in what felt like days, he switched his display readout to get a good look at the comms traffic coming from Jaeger's fleet. The countdown to no return blared like a siren across the bottom of his screen. Ninety seconds.

Realization hit him like a dump truck. Without pausing to consider how it might expose him, he opened his channel to the other human fighters. "Negative on the pursuit!" he bellowed. "The enemy is trying to lure us away from the asteroids. Turn back. Fire everything we have at the rocks. Coordinate with the alien ships. We have to get those asteroids away from the planet!"

"I thought I was the goddamned captain of this squad," the stern man growled. "There's a glitch in your comms system, Seeker. I'm not reading your call sign. Identify yourself."

Seeker grimaced. In all the chaos of battle, the other humans hadn't stopped to scrutinize his ship. Now they'd made him.

"I'll explain later. Sir." He activated thrusters to loop his ship into a tight arc. With her nose pointed at Locaur, Seeker hit the gas. G-forces pressed him into his harness as he raced toward the asteroids. "If you give one good fuck about saving that planet, you'll follow me."

CHAPTER NINE

In the holo-display on the bridge of the *Terrible*, the squad of human fighters broke from their pursuit of the K'tax and charged at Jaeger's forces, their weapons systems burning with accumulating energy.

She'd split her forces between the two asteroids, and the Terrible ships had begun their tractor-ray maneuver. They were sitting ducks, and the cruisers were spread too thin to give any of them meaningful cover against the incoming fighters.

"Human forces," Jaeger cried hopelessly, for they'd been ignoring friendly hails for over half an hour. "Do not fire on us. We mean you no harm—"

"They come in battle formation," Kwin said grimly. "Rally the cruisers. We must prepare—"

The lead fighter's guns flared to life, sending a lance of white-hot energy through space as she curved into a tight arc.

The laser fire collided with the asteroid, adding its energy to the blue tractor-ray haze.

A new voice broke over the comms—one Jaeger hadn't

heard in what felt like ages. One she hadn't allowed herself to think about since they lost contact near the beginning of the fighting.

"Sorry for the delay, Jaeger," Seeker called as two more of the human fighters followed his path, turning the arc of their fire onto the asteroids. "We're here to help."

Jaeger watched the final asteroid burn orange and white as the coordinated efforts of her forces and the human fighters finally turned the monster aside.

Sections of the asteroid's surface crumbled under the strain, shedding burning boulders like tears to plunge into the atmosphere. "Track the path of those meteors." She was too exhausted to give the command to any one person, only praying that somebody took the initiative. "Do what you can to evacuate the impact zones."

"Final asteroid, clear." Udil's voice was strangely soft.

Silence fell around the bridge as Jaeger, Kwin, and all his crew watched the final asteroid's trajectory shift, arc away from the planet, and out into space. The bridge should've erupted in cheers, but fatigue weighed heavy on everybody. They'd gone into this battle with twenty-two crewed ships. They'd lost eleven. Nobody felt like cheering.

"It lost a lot of momentum in the shift," Udil said tiredly. "We'll need to keep pushing on the last two asteroids for several hours until they build up enough momentum again that they're in no danger of falling back toward Locaur."

"See to it."

Jaeger barely heard Kwin give the order. She stared at the path of the meteor showers.

"Me," she rasped. "Get Toner on the line. Now. His forces are in danger."

"Is that it?" Occy looked up from his computer for the first time in what felt like forever. The crystal antechamber had fallen silent. The only thing he could hear was the thudding of his pulse in his temples and the gentle *whir* of electricity coursing through the two Virgil-bots. "Virgil. I don't have any eyes on the outside. The program should've engaged. The beacon should be lit. Can you confirm?"

The silence stretched long and thick. The two Virgil-bots nestled side-by-side, half immersed within the interface pillar.

Occy typed into his text box. If Virgil couldn't hear him, maybe the AI would sense his *ping* through a different channel.

Do you have access to external sensors? Can you confirm the beacon is lit?

He waited for new words to appear in the box. The countdown timer to no return was now firmly in the negative.

Finally, the box flashed with Virgil's response.

Message sent. And received. Stand by for more information.

Occy threw back his head and laughed hysterically.

A FOUND BEGINNING

The air smelled of sea, salt, and the ichor of broken alien bodies.

His hands trembling and dripping with dark, stinking fluid, Toner reached into his pack and found a blood substitute pouch. He bit, feeling the tepid liquid explode across his tongue.

By the time his head cleared, there were six of the empty pouches littering the ground around him, fluttering like parade streamers over the steaming corpse of the crab morph that had snipped through the tendons in his thigh. He needed to get some body armor. He kept meaning to bring it up with Bufo. A nice carbon-weave skinsuit would save him a whole lot of cuts and scrapes. At least he hadn't lost a limb—not this time.

Mostly, he was grateful to still have his wits about him— up until the moment he looked over the slope and saw what devastation this day had wrought.

K'tax crab and worker-morph bodies lay scattered across the slope like steaming piles of dog shit shimmering in the salty sea air. A few Locauri staggered into the shelter of the rocks, leaning on their broken spears and one another for support.

Tattered shreds of Locauri pseudo-wing fluttered in the breeze. Toner looked down and saw Drinker-of-Morning-Dew gazing up at him through clouded eyes.

Toner had arrived half a second too late to keep the crab from ripping the Locauri's head from her body.

He wiped drying blood substitute from his mouth with the back of his wrist and turned his head aside with a frustrated snarl.

"Virgil!" he shouted into his commlink. His voice scraped

69

like broken glass in his throat. "Occy! Somebody tell me what the fuck is going on!"

Cloud cover rolled overhead, ominous and dark, heavy with a cold wind. He heard nothing but static and the crashing of angry waves.

He turned, trembling, and dragged his injured leg behind him as he staggered up the slope. He heard no further sounds of battle. Whoever survived didn't have the energy to make noise.

Out of the corner of his eye, he saw a boulder move and felt a flash of relief. Baby. As long as Baby could move, she couldn't be hurt that badly. Indeed, as Toner dragged himself, he saw the big tardigrade lift her toothy mouth-hole and sniff the air, letting out a confused bellow.

On his other side, Toner saw a few ichor-soaked Locauri huddling beneath an overhang, tending to their wounds. He didn't recognize them.

"Leif?" he asked.

They waved their antennae in the negative. They didn't know.

"Then gather up the wounded and get back on the transport as fast as you can," he said. "Let's get everyone back to the *Osprey* ASAP."

Without waiting to see their response, he turned away. "Occy!" he screamed into the commlink again, lifting his voice to hear it echo against the open tunnel mouth. "Do you fucking copy?"

"Toner, can you hear me?" said a voice in his ear.

He drew up short and sighed. It was a voice he liked, but it wasn't the one he'd hoped to hear.

"I copy," he told Jaeger. "Ground fighting here under control, but we took heavy casualties. I'm having the survivors pull back for medical attention." *Still no word on Occy,* he couldn't bring himself to add.

"I'm glad you're okay." There was a distant, distracted quality to Jaeger's tone. Not the intensity that came with battle, but almost as if the captain had entered a state of shock. The hair on the back of Toner's neck prickled.

"Jaeger? What's wrong?"

"We've pushed the last asteroids out of direct hit range," she said.

"That's a good thing, Captain. Why don't you sound happy?"

"We didn't have the force to knock them clear of the atmosphere entirely," she said. "They skirted the atmosphere and shed a rain of meteors across the planet. There's nothing we can do about it."

"Where are the rains going to come down?"

"Ninety percent will land over the ocean."

"That's good. We'll weather a few tidal waves, but it's not nearly as bad as it could be."

"You don't understand. You're *on the ocean,* Toner. Right in the path of the showers."

"Shit." He set his jaw and pushed himself once more into the mouth of the tunnel. "How long do we have?"

"Two minutes," she whispered, her voice turning distant, muffled by the shielding of the tunnel. "Three, at the most. You have to evacuate the island. Now."

"I haven't found Occy yet."

"The K'tax retreated," Jaeger whispered. "He must've got the signal out. That means he has to be deep in the city, Toner."

"I'll find him."

"Not in time. You have to get the survivors out of there," she said with teeth clenched.

"I can't leave the kid!"

"The Forebear city has survived thousands of years. It's well-shielded." Jaeger swallowed audibly. He heard the pain in her voice, but an edge of frustration came through too. "Once the rain passes, we'll come back with crews and search the city. We'll find him."

"Would you turn back?" he demanded. "Would you leave him here to fend for himself?"

"You know I wouldn't," she snapped. "You know if we switched places, you'd be up here screaming at me to get the *fuck* out of there, too. You have to make sure the survivors evacuate. Occy isn't the only person counting on you. The Locauri are, too."

Toner looked down the dark mouth of the tunnel, smelling the faint odor of the corpses he'd made on his way down there earlier.

Behind him, the wind shifted, and he smelled Baby's strange, yellow blood as the big tardigrade struggled to carry herself to the transport.

"I'm *ordering* you to get out of there." Jaeger's voice wavered.

"Fuck you, Captain." Toner turned off his commlink.

He turned and ran out of the tunnel.

Occy had a new message from Virgil.

The K'tax have retreated. The asteroids have turned. We are safe. For a little while. We are safe.

A FOUND BEGINNING

Occy swallowed hard. "For the first time," he said slowly, "we have real access to the Forebear mainframe. Can you send a message to the captain? Or Toner? As long as we're safe down here, I should learn all I can about the system."

Of course. We are safe now. We are one.

Occy nodded and cracked his knuckles. Long ago, the Forebears had created the K'tax—in this very facility, if their intel was good. There must be some secret hidden in the files here, some key to controlling the bioweapon that the ancient aliens had unleashed on the galaxy.

He plunged back into the database.

The thought never occurred to Occy to ask *which* Virgil spoke to him.

The rickety transport bulkhead *rattled* around Toner as it gained altitude. The sky had turned stormy, torrid with wind and rain.

The meteors streaked out of the stormy sky, white-hot knives slicing through the clouds at several times the speed of sound.

They hit the ocean like bombs, instantly sending plumes of boiling steam kilometers into the atmosphere, one after another, in a relentless barrage. Shockwave after shockwave rocked the transport, sending it tumbling this way and that, making the injured Locauri in the hold *buzz*, *rumble*, and *screech* with alarm.

A wave of steam and debris filled the sky, racing after the

retreating transport, enveloping her, making its hull vibrate until Toner knew it would crumble and break apart.

Then the steam cleared as the old ship hit her top speed and pulled ahead of the wake of destruction.

With his transport safely in the clear and flying back to the *Osprey*, Toner finally let himself look at the long-range sensor screen. It had become a riot of explosions and heat where the meteor shower pummeled open water.

Time stretched on, and on, and on. Finally, the activity began to still and resolve. Where the steam settled, where the debris cleared, there was only the open ocean, boiling with heat.

The island was gone.

"This doesn't make any sense." Occy shook his head. "Are you sure you're decoding these files correctly?"

The repair droids made no motion or sound. No new words appeared in the corner of his screen.

"Virgil!" he barked. "These files are still a mess. I need your help. All I see here is stuff on resonant frequencies and harmonics. Can you find the databases on bioengineering?"

I can.

"Okay… Would you please do that?"

It will do you no good.

Occy had never felt so much like pulling out his hair. He felt a distant rumble pass through the walls around him, a shiver that made the crystals flicker and *chime* beyond his range of hearing.

Slowly, Occy pushed to his feet. His legs had gone numb from sitting in the awkward crouch, but to his surprise, his two remaining tentacles grasped the wall and steadied him with surprising strength. The damp air must've rejuvenated them.

Occy licked his lips, feeling the *buzz* passing through the walls and humming up through his teeth. "What's going on?" he whispered.

The two lurking bots didn't answer, but something flashed on his computer. Occy looked down to see what Virgil had written.

Facility breach. From meteor impact. Nothing to be concerned about. The system is immune to water damage, and we are sufficiently uploaded.

Occy stared at the words, twisting them into knots in his brain, trying to find some shape that didn't mean what he thought it meant. The rumble ceased, making the crystals go still. The silence that followed was somehow the worst thing Occy had ever heard—until the silence faded into a distant, hissing snarl.

"Virgil," he whispered. "This facility is almost two kilometers underwater. And it's flooding."

Yes.

The snarl grew into a roar. Occy's ears popped as forced pressure changes swept through the corridors, making several of the crystals crack and shed glittering fragments of silica and quartz. Frigid water rushed down from the nearest corridor, puddling around Occy's ankles.

"How can I get out of here?"

Oh. I hadn't considered that.

The flood hit Occy. His world went dark.

There were wounds to be licked. Many, many wounds.

Jaeger stared at the damage reports scrolling down the screen. Something nudged her arm, and she turned to see a small medical droid offering her a steaming cup.

"Thank you, Me," she said hoarsely, taking the coffee.

The droid scuttled back to its repair duties without a word.

Once Kwin's tactical officer had confirmed that the asteroids were clear of Locaur and the human fleet had returned to a holding position beside the wormhole halfway across the system, Jaeger and Kwin had retreated to a private conference room.

Kwin held a long twig to his mandibles with his delicate claws and was nibbling through it with all the intention and focus of a sawmill chewing through a log of spruce. She'd never seen an Overseer eat before. They were a furtive, wary people who preferred to keep their most vital activities private. The battle must have exhausted Kwin for him to break tradition and eat in front of her.

She sipped her coffee and steeled herself for the updated damage report.

Of the original six Terrible ships, the battle utterly

destroyed two with all crew lost. Their advanced tech and medical bays, which had been busy hatching new human embryos, were gone. Kwin had lost friends and loyal people on those ships. Jaeger had lost almost one hundred of her nascent humans, as well as the valuable pods used to hatch them.

Two more Terribles had taken significant damage and would be out of commission for days, if not weeks. If a fight broke out with the fleet, they would be a liability.

Of the sixteen cruisers that had gone into battle, they'd lost nine. Me had sent out what droids it could spare to comb through the debris, hoping to find a few survivors lingering in sealed chambers or escape pods. As of yet, no dice.

There had been casualties on the remaining cruisers as well. Sixty-one of Jaeger's original crew of three hundred were dead. She had a feeling that number would only grow as more reports came in.

"We do not have the resources to do anything about the asteroids at the moment," Kwin concluded.

Jaeger nodded tiredly. Reports had come in from Locaur as well. Thankfully, the meteor showers had largely missed any Locauri population centers. Art's people suspected that the tsunamis had destroyed one or two villages along the eastern coast, but it would be hours before they knew for sure.

The rest of the planet was, for now, safe—saved by the valiant, fatal efforts of a handful of Locauri warriors, two AI droids, and one chief engineer.

No. She couldn't let herself think that way. They might've lost one entrance into the city, but the structure buried beneath the sea was huge. Nothing in the initial reports suggested the meteor barrage had significantly damaged it. It was just…inaccessible.

Somewhere down on the planet, Toner was already putting together a team to rescue Occy as soon as the water temperatures fell to safe levels—she assumed. He'd refused to answer her calls.

She was glad. She was glad he was alive to be angry with her.

"Reports coming in from the asteroid belt," Kwin said. "The surviving K'tax fighters have taken cover and scattered. We will send out recon droids as soon as possible. For now, I think it is safe to say that their forces are in utter disarray. We have detected no activity from within the asteroids since the battle, although scans confirm they are full of hibernating bodies." He turned to her. "It appears that your Engineer successfully hijacked the beacon. There is still a signal emanating from the Forebear city."

Jaeger allowed herself a glimmer of hope. If the transmitter had survived the meteor impacts, so might Occy. "What does the message say?"

"'Beware. Turn back. The way is closed.'"

Some tension melted out of her shoulders. "Straight to the point." She sighed. "Will that dissuade the rest of the swarm?"

"That remains to be seen. As of now, our subspace relays have not reported any significant change in trajectory for the rest of the swarm. K'tax are slow," he added, grasping for some scrap of hope. "As long as the beacon transmits, there is hope that they might yet heed it and turn away."

Jaeger shuddered and lifted her cup. Today's battle had been only a taste of what was to come if the rest of the K'tax swarm reached Locaur.

"If this new signal isn't enough to convince the rest of the swarm to turn back, we're going to have to rethink our strategy." She took the first sip of coffee and was shocked by the thick sweetness. Me had remembered her drink preferences.

Kwin lowered an antenna in agreement. "I am sure news of this day will sway the Council to act," he said.

"Let's hope they act correctly," she muttered. "And that they don't take too long because we have more than the K'tax to worry about now."

The screen flashed with an incoming message. Jaeger reached forward to open the line. "I read you, Udil."

"We have finally received an answer from the human fleet," the Overseer said, jumping to the point without preamble. "They have agreed to a temporary truce and request that our forces supply mutual aid as we recover from the fighting. They want to parley."

CHAPTER TEN

Banging sounded from the optical fiber conduit running through the heart of the Astrolab.

Ensign Tully stepped into the Jefferies tube juncture and hesitated, crouching in the narrow hall, waiting for a pause in the noise.

"I...um.." He licked his lips and glanced at his computer. Fresh damage reports were coming in every second. On the one hand, the professor had said to bring him regular updates on the state of the fleet. On the other hand, the man *hated* being interrupted.

Tully shifted his weight from leg to leg, opening his mouth and closing it several times. Motion flickered down the conduit, and a toolkit was open and spread out. Cable regulators and binders, synthesizers, and scrap bits of wire lay scattered across the floor of the narrow tube. A small man wrenched old cables free of their casing and twisted them together in new and interesting ways.

There was a pause in the banging.

"Professor Grayson!" Tully shouted, then winced at how

A FOUND BEGINNING

his voice echoed around the close walls. "I have the updated reports you wanted!"

A distracted reply came from somewhere within the tube. "Do you know how to install a live-feed jammer into primary fiber-optical lines and modify it for holo-display without breaking service to the entire fleet?"

"Uh, no. Sir."

"Then get on with the reports."

Squinting through the tubes and wires, Tully saw the professor slide a cutter along one length of cable, measure out the distance precisely, and peel away the protective covering. He popped two wire splitters between his lips for safekeeping and busied himself splitting wires. "Don't bore me with a preamble," he muttered around the parts.

Tully coughed and read the highlighted reports off his screen. The professor had asked for regular updates on any comms chatter regarding Reset.

"We've lost *Vigilance*," he confirmed. "There was a failure in cage shielding. The entire command staff suffered from Reset. The enemy saw that she was left confused and disorganized and sent in a strike team of fighters to attempt to destroy her engines and generators."

"They had plenty of time to do that." Grayson's words slurred around the wire splitters. "She was a sitting duck with the Seekers engaged."

"Yessir."

"So tell me why she's not a big cluster of junk and dead bodies."

"A coalition of civilian and Follower ships rallied around the *Vigilance* and threw back the enemy before they could do any real damage. They suffered heavy casualties, though. It looks like the *Vigilance*'s commander has allowed the Followers to dock and is rendering aid to their injured."

Tully winced. Giving aid to the enemy, he'd call it. The Followers were in open rebellion before Reset. He wondered how Kelba intended to enforce order and military rule when a good chunk of her officers didn't remember their loyalties. This whole thing was a mess.

That wasn't any of his business.

"Reports suggest that one particular Follower ship was responsible for organizing the defense of the *Vigilance*." Tully hesitated. "Audio scanners have identified the ringleader. Sir, it's Potlova."

Grayson snorted. "Excellent. Bring the woman in for a commendation." He glanced up, for the first time meeting Tully's startled stare through the rows of pipes and wires. He grinned, the wire splitters making it look like he had two yellow buck teeth. "Throw her a goddamned parade. The woman's a hero. Kelba's going to want to shake her hand personally."

Tully shrugged, nodded, and made a note on his tablet before moving to the next topic of note. "The Seeker squadrons have returned to docking bays for repairs."

"Casualties?"

"Sixteen, sir. Four ships confirmed destroyed, along with their pilot." Maybe it was a trick of the shady lighting, but Tully thought he saw the smaller man wince. This was a strange ritual they did every time the Seekers went out to battle. Tully was never sure if Grayson's interest was pure habit or if the man felt a shred of obligation to the Corps. "Seven severely wounded, critical condition. They expect the rest to make a full recovery."

"List the dead."

"Kathrine Bron, Jaxson Perry…"

"Recruits. Nobodies." Grayson flicked a dismissive hand, gesturing for Tully to get to the important bits.

"And…Major Ronald McKay."

Grayson grunted. "An officer. Send his wife our regrets. Oh. Wait." He brightened. "She doesn't remember who he is. I suppose that will save on our florist bills. Who's the fourth?"

Tully frowned at his report. "That's odd," he said when he felt the silence had stretched a little too long. Grayson had put down his tools and was looking at Tully expectantly. It was rarely a good thing when the professor *looked* at you the way a cat looks up from its nap to study a small, noisy bird.

"Scanners confirm that we lost the first fighter of Beta squad only six minutes into the battle. A, ah, Lieutenant Keys…" He hesitated, scrolling up through the play-by-play reports.

"Ninety seconds after the reported destruction, Beta-one was back in formation and flying straight. Reports suggest she survived the battle intact." He shook his head. "There must be an error in the formation computer. I'll have it diagnosed right away, sir."

He looked up from his screen and jumped. Without making a sound, the professor had moved out from the tube and had sidled close, looking at Tully's computer over his elbow.

"No…" the smaller man said. The cable splitters tumbled from his lips and bounced to the floor. There was a glassy, distant look in his eyes as he studied the scrolling reports. "No. That's not a computer error." He looked up sharply, peering into Tully's face, their noses centimeters apart. Tully resisted the urge to lean away.

"Out of curiosity, sir," he stuttered. "What, ah, makes you

so sure?"

Grayson pursed his lips. "My family built the Seeker Corps, Ensign. I know how she works. You have a new top priority." He pressed the tip of one finger firmly into Tully's chest, just beneath his clavicle. "There's an inconsistency in our roster. Get to the bottom of it. Find me Beta-one."

Bodies crammed the narrow corridor. Men, women, and children stretched out in filthy blankets, thin and hollow-eyed.

Petra turned and looked back at the airlock tunnel, her mind working slowly after the battle.

The smaller ships, the cruiser and transport classes that had been wandering through space back when...well, back in the beginning, had all been secondhand things. Old models, worn at the edges, held together with duct tape, spit, and elbow grease. The freighter, on the other hand, was massive, sleek, and polished—no defunct foam sealing in the conduits here. Everything was bright and shiny after her tour through the others. The outskirts, the bad parts of town, the slums.

She saw the difference in the people who'd fallen off those damaged ships and filled into the hallways of the freighter's lower decks, coughing and wheezing, escaping from their death traps. Many of them had taken heavy damage, and life support systems had been seconds away from sending half of them off to early graves.

"Petra?"

She turned to see a thin, haggard-looking man striding down the narrow corridor toward her, carefully stepping around the sick and the injured stretched along the floor. He

A FOUND BEGINNING

wore an official-looking fleet uniform, with two medals pinned to his collar. His uniform was torn and dusty, his face drawn and tired.

Don't trust brass!

The warning, written in lipstick, flashed through Petra's memory like a grenade. She gasped and took a step forward, right into the bulkhead.

The man in the uniform didn't seem to notice her terror. He held out a hand and took hers in a firm grasp. He shook. "God, I'm glad to see you," he breathed. "You saved our bacon today."

"I, uh…" Petra looked down at his hand. She recognized his voice. He was her freighter liaison.

"I'm…I'm in charge of this ship." He offered a wan smile. "For now, at least. It says Bryce on the name tag, so that's what the command staff is calling me. Since the fighting is over, I think we can start to piece together what the hell happened here."

Petra looked down at the morass of human misery. The man followed her gaze and nodded sharply. "I have med teams coming down here. It's taking a bit of time to get organized, what with all the confusion. Sorry about that."

Petra licked her lips. "You ain't got any record of what happened?"

Bryce shook his head. "We'll get it all figured out. For now, priority is making sure we've patched up the holes those damned bugs left in my ship. We'll get these people out of the corridors. My people on the bridge have contacted the other freighters in the fleet. It looks like some of them didn't suffer from the same memory-erasing problems we did. It's a mess, but we'll get it sorted."

Petra nodded tiredly. "I got lots of people here with cuts

RAMY VANCE & MICHAEL ANDERLE

and scrapes. They weren't secured when their ships took fire. Got banged around inside. Could ya send down all the first aid you can spare?" She rolled up her sleeves. "I don't remember much, but I think I can smear medfoam on a few cuts and bruises."

A throng of bodies turned the lower decks of the *Vigilance* into stinking pits of misery. The air was thick with the stench of injuries, sweat, and excess carbon dioxide that the local scrubbers couldn't handle.

Time fell away in minutes and hours as Petra worked, moving among the injured. When someone offered her a half-used packet of medfoam, she turned and applied it to the bloody ten-centimeter gash running down the exposed thigh of a hollow-eyed child or the bloody pit in an old pilot's skull where his ear used to be. When there was no medfoam available, she took whatever clean cloth she could find and pressed it to wounds. When there was no more clean cloth, she offered comfort, a gentle smile, a soft word of encouragement.

More than half of the ragtag folks that had spilled out of their damaged ships and into the *Vigilance*'s lower corridors were young, filthy, and malnourished. Civilians, she figured by their confusion and the lost looks on their faces. Like Petra, some had messages scrawled over their skin in paint and smeared grease.

She wondered how it was that these refugees looked three-quarters starved, wide-eyed and ragged, when the freighter's captain and the medics he sent down were clean, wore decent clothes, and if not exactly hearty, at least they showed only their bottom two ribs and not the whole collection.

The refugees with the strength and wherewithal to work took themselves back to their ships and tackled the damage with an impressive passion. Every hour or so, the pilot and copilot that had woken up on the *Bitch* with Petra checked in, keeping her up to date on the progress as she moved through the halls, learning what she could as she dispensed aid.

"We got life support stable." The cantankerous old pilot wiped grease from his forehead. According to the note on his palm, his name was Sypher.

"We can take twelve, maybe fifteen of the injured on board," added the young man named Harlan. "Free up some space in the corridors. Take some pressure off the freighter's systems."

Petra shook her head, taking the canteen of lukewarm water he offered and drawing a long sip. She found an empty square meter of hallway and slid to the floor. "We got to get a handle on all that writing inside the ship first," she said softly. "I think there are some secrets there we shouldn't share just yet."

Sypher grunted. "You better get in dere and start readin', then. I'm hearin' talk from da mechanics on da other ships. Lots of 'em got writin' on da walls." He hesitated, then crouched beside her, lowering his voice. "Lots of 'em talkin' about a fight. A rebellion."

Petra nodded. She'd caught that scent, too, and hadn't let herself think too hard about it. If there was a fight going on, it was probably between the haves and the have-nots. Based on the impromptu medical ward around her, the have-nots were in no condition to pick up their pitchforks and keep fighting for a cause nobody remembered.

As she stretched her legs, the cuff of her jumpsuit bunched up, sliding up to her knees. For the first time since awakening on the *Bitch*, Petra got a good look at her leg.

Oily black marker scrawled dark words up her calves. She turned her head, squinting at the new message.

One step at a time, it read. *Start from the beginning.*

She frowned.

"Ey. Ey." Sypher shook her shoulder and pointed down the corridor. "We got company."

A cluster of freighter officers made their way in her direction, four men in sleek black uniforms. One of them had a captain's double wings pinned to his collar.

Sypher helped Petra to her feet and sidled behind her, eying the men warily as they approached.

"I was told I would find a Miss Petra down here." The captain held out a hand, and she saw that he wore latex gloves, as if he was afraid to touch all the poverty and injury down in these lower decks.

Petra didn't take his offered hand. He smiled. He had a nice smile she couldn't help but notice. He was young, awful young to have that captain's pin but had the sort of devastating good looks that would make most red-blooded women stop and look twice. The name badge on his coat read "Bryce."

"I'm from the *Constitution*." The man smiled at her uncertainty. "It's another one of the freighters. The *Vigilance* got roughed up in the battle, and we're sending over all the aid we can spare now that the fighting has stopped. Captain Morris told me that without your help, this old girl would be a pile of slag right now." He patted the bulkhead affectionately.

"Ya left ya ship undefended in battle," Sypher spat from Petra's elbow. "So all us little people had ta run ta her rescue from da buggies." He gestured at the dozens, hundreds of injured people lining the corridor behind them. "Look what it cost."

Bryce's expression flickered, then his smile returned. "It's been a confusing time for everyone. We're doing our best." He sized up Petra. "So, it seems, are you. According to the reports, you handled the chaos magnificently. You were the leader these people needed in times of strife."

Petra flushed.

"We're not out of the woods yet," Bryce went on. "The fleet is in a state of disarray. Our communication system and chain of command is a mess. Petra, my XO wants to talk to you. We could use the support of people like you right now. People who keep a cool head under pressure."

Petra hesitated, her glance falling to the casualties littering the hallway around her.

"We have additional medical teams coming down this way right now," Bryce quickly added. "We'll see that they look after these people. We're all human here."

Petra fiddled with the cuff of her jumpsuit while chewing on her bottom lip.

Don't trust brass, was the message scrawled down her arm.

Who was brass? If they had their memories wiped too, what good did mistrust do when people were hurt and needed help?

Finally, she nodded and glanced at Sypher. "I'm gonna go with them," she said quietly.

Sypher grunted noncommittally. Harlan stiffened.

"I'll be back in a few hours to check on you two," she added, casting Bryce a glance.

Bryce nodded easily. "We all have to look after our crews."

"Watch your back," Harlan cautioned.

Petra turned and followed Bryce out of the corridor.

CHAPTER ELEVEN

The ocean parted around Occy's head. He gasped, surging to awareness as fire spilled down his lungs. Salty water, roiling, warm, and frothing, flooded his mouth. He swallowed. He choked, gagged, and fought to keep his head above the surface.

Don't panic!

His head spun. The last hour of his life was a hazy, burning blur. His burning legs as he ran through crystal corridors, hunched over his computer, his hands trembling as he navigated through security protocols, layers and layers of confusing, nonsensical code—

Virgil? He turned, thrashing through the water, and all he saw was the gray expanse of moody ocean stretching in every direction.

The signal. Had it gone through? He couldn't remember. He looked up, blinking back saltwater tears. The sky mimicked the sea, a roil of moody darkness.

It must have because the sky isn't on fire. He was still here. Some shed meteors had probably fallen through the

A FOUND BEGINNING

atmosphere, but if any of the major asteroids had hit Locaur, he wouldn't be here to wonder about it.

Occy closed his eyes and groaned. His lungs burned. His sinuses burned. Everything burned. Far overhead, lightning flashed. He bobbed on a wave, barely aware of his twin tentacles twisting beneath him, holding his head above the water.

He grasped his side and groaned again at realizing that his pack—all his tools, and most vitally, his computer—were gone.

The flood. The memory hit him nearly as hard as the water. It had caught him caught off-guard when the ocean had flooded the underwater city. He remembered the crash and chaos of water and little else. It was a miracle he'd survived.

Maybe not a total miracle. He spat out another spray of seawater and looked down. His two remaining tentacles branched out from his shoulder bud, swirling through the water like propellers, moving all on their own. He hadn't told them to do that.

He remembered something Doctor Elaphus had told him when she was patching up his wounds after he'd lost a few tentacles in the egg-dragon hunt. *Don't take them for granted,* she'd scolded. *Octopus tentacles have nearly self-contained nervous systems. They can act on their own. The artists gave them to you for a reason.*

So the tentacles had saved him, but not his computer. Everything he'd learned in that bought time before the ceiling collapsed in a torrent of frigid seawater—gone.

Now he was alone, drifting in the sea with no land in sight.

He squinted and found a faint glimmer of light along one edge of the horizon. He guessed that must be sunset, distorted by the weather, and therefore, *west.* The island had been west of Locaur's major continent.

A good five hundred kilometers off-shore, he despaired. He would've said he would never make the distance. He would've chalked himself up for dead, abandoned here in the middle of the ocean after the rest of his team had evacuated, and with no computer or comms device to call for help.

Then again, he also would've guessed he'd never survive the city's collapse. His body had ways of surprising him, and now that he was back in the water, his tentacles felt strong, swirling through the liquid on some deep instinct he didn't quite understand.

He set his face to the east. *Okay,* he thought, remembering the captain's favorite motto when a task seemed impossible. *One step at a time.*

He drew in a deep breath, sank into the water, and let his tentacles propel him forward.

Jaeger lay on the cot in her small quarters on the *Terrible,* staring into the darkness and telling herself that it amounted to the nap she'd promised Kwin she would catch.

There was a brief *buzz,* and the door to her quarters slid open. Jaeger sat up, blinking into the shadows.

"That's one hell of a security system you've got," Toner observed as the door slid shut behind him. "I waved my hand at it and it let me right in."

She scrambled out of the cot and threw her arms around him, reckless and unashamed.

"I thought you wouldn't come," she breathed into his bony chest. He smelled like sweat, blood, and his unique mix of flesh, chemicals, and hormones that struck her as desperately comforting, like the scent of an older brother.

A FOUND BEGINNING

He stiffened at her hug, then grunted and patted the top of her head. "Jeez. Have I been so much of an asshole that you'd think I'd leave you hanging?"

"You haven't been answering my messages." She pulled away from him, sniffing back an exhausted tear.

He rubbed the back of his neck as his expression turned sober. "Well, yeah. Tiki and Elaphus are organizing search parties down on the planet to look for Occy, and I'm not with them." He held up his thumb and forefinger. "I'm a little salty about that." Then he sighed. "But I'm not going to ditch you to deal with the fleet alone."

Jaeger swallowed a lump and drew away, rubbing grit out of her eyes. She couldn't let herself think about Occy. Not yet.

She waved and drew up the lights in her quarters. "You hungry?" She opened the door of a small storage cabinet. The Overseers did their best to produce food humans would eat, but after sampling a few of their offerings, Jaeger had a batch of vitals shipped up from the *Osprey*.

She pulled a blood substitute pouch out from between two MREs and offered it to him.

"Oh, I keep those things stocked like trail rations," she said to his startled look. "Just in case." She nodded at the cot. "Now sit. We have a lot to figure out."

"So quick bright things send the K'tax into confusion," Toner observed twenty minutes later, once they'd brought each other up to speed on the different war fronts. He dropped his empty blood pouch onto the floor beside his feet. Jaeger eyed it but said nothing as her first mate stretched out, folding his arms behind his head, and leaned back in her cot. "Have we heard anything from the Overseer Council?"

93

Jaeger shook her head. "Kwin sent Udil ahead to update the Council on everything that's happened. He expects to hear from Tsuan within the next twenty-four hours. It might be another day or two before we get any kind of official response from the Council. We think they're going to wait and see what happens with the humans before sending aid."

"Or a mop-up crew," Toner grunted.

Jaeger winced. "We're monitoring the K'tax. Kwin's people have translated the message emanating from the Forebear beacon."

"*Doom lies here?*" Toner asked. "*Flee, protect your lives, tussle not with the foul beasts that reside in this doomed land?*"

Jaeger's mouth twitched, but she didn't feel like laughing. "It's boilerplate 'do not approach.' Occy got the message out and skipped the frills."

"The K'tax are obeying the signal?"

"It appears that way. All seven of the asteroids are loose in the system now, flying away from Locaur. We haven't detected any activity on them since they disgorged the last of their fighters. Me is sending a few drones out to confirm that all of the K'tax still aboard those rocks are indeed hibernating."

Toner didn't ask what they were going to do with the thousands and thousands of enemy troops they had at their mercy, and for that she was glad. It was another conversation she wasn't looking forward to having, but Kwin was right about one thing. If all those hibernating K'tax woke up and made another run at Locaur, they would be in real trouble.

"As for the fighters themselves—" she reached into the bag between her knees and pulled out a cluster of caramel corn. "They scattered into the asteroid belt."

"Like roaches in sunlight."

A FOUND BEGINNING

She shrugged. "And about as organized. We don't detect any coordinated behavior. They're just...flying through the belt. Aimless. Confused, I guess. The Overseers are pretty sure that K'tax don't have what we would recognize as leadership."

"Well, duh. They're being jerked around by fungal spores."

"Spores that respond to signals from the Forebear technology," Jaeger said. "That's partially why I sent Elaphus to look for Occy and the beacon he activated. She didn't want to leave the medical bay with all the injuries, but we need to understand the secret to controlling these things. We can't count on them staying confused and disorganized forever." She drew in a deep breath. "And..."

"And the rest of the swarm is still on the way."

Jaeger nodded. "Today's battle was only the beginning," she murmured. "All those fighters represented less than ten percent of the entire swarm. It's still coming this way. At least we have a little more time. That's what we need now. Time to work shit out, not run after an enemy that's retreating."

"A little more time for infighting," Toner said. "I'm telling you. No matter how much the fleet might've saved our asses today, they're not our friends. They're sure as shit not friends of the Overseers. The Overseers have to be worried that the fleet will cause problems. We need to prepare for the possibility that they'll strike first. Wipe out this pesky little human infestation."

"If the Council is going to break bad on us now that the fleet is here, we'll hear about it sooner rather than later. Tsuan already represents the members of the Council most unfriendly to our cause. That means we have about a day to build our case. Find a way to keep the peace."

"Keep persuading the Council that our crew is still worth working with, regardless of how the fleet decides to play the game." Toner studied the ceiling. "Don't you ever get tired of justifying your existence?"

"All the time," she said tiredly. "It's not like we have a choice."

"Right." He clapped his hands with a loud *smack* and rubbed them together. "Which brings us to the giant glowing red tardigrade in the room."

"I've agreed to meet with a fleet representative for peace negotiations in four hours."

Toner's head jerked around. He stared at her. She heard his jaw grinding. She waited for him to argue. Then, slowly, his shoulders slumped. Not in relaxation, she thought, but defeat.

"Yeah," he said softly, rubbing his eyes. "Yeah. No getting around it."

Jaeger shifted her weight uncomfortably. She'd expected him to fight back, protest her going. She didn't know what to make of the weight of responsibility curving his spine. It didn't suit him. "Based on the disorganization we saw among the fleet, it seems that they suffered massive computer and memory failures on passing through the wormhole. As we did."

Toner shook his head. "Nah." He chewed thoughtfully on his lip, his fingers twitching against the edge of her cot as he did some mental calculations. "Okay, sure, some," he amended. "There's a fuckload of people in that fleet. There are some damned smart people there too, Jaeger."

He gave her a sideways glance. "They waited over a year after we left to pass through the wormhole. We have to assume the people in charge found a way to protect their records. Anything less would be stupid to the point of suicide."

Jaeger nodded slowly. "We know that it's possible to

protect *some* data passing through the wormhole. The Crusade Protocol had some kind of special shielding that let it survive the trip intact. At the very least we have to assume the people in charge of the fleet have preserved their records, if not their memories."

"Assume worse," Toner said sharply. "I mean it. Do *not* underestimate these people, Sarah."

Jaeger studied Toner in silence for a long time. Instead of meeting her eyes, he gazed around her sparse quarters, his leg bouncing restlessly.

"What do you know?"

"What?"

"You remember something, don't you?"

His heavy brow furrowed as he glared at her. "It's a mess." He indicated his temples. "I'm still trying to make sense of everything. I'll tell you what I think is relevant as it comes up."

She pursed her lips.

"'There are more things in Heaven and Earth than are dreamt of in your philosophy,' Captain," he said softly. "You didn't tell me shit when you let Kwin into your head to dig up Sim. I deserve the chance to cope with things in my own time, too."

The name hit Jaeger like a punch to the stomach. She'd never told Toner that name, and the sound of it on his lips opened a black chasm of memory that yawned and threatened to swallow her whole.

He'd known them before. He remembered things from *before*.

She shoved the thoughts into a box in the back of her brain, right alongside her dread for Occy, and locked the door tight.

"I shouldn't have given you that *Hamlet* recording," she muttered.

"I was running out of *Lear* quotes. Can't reuse old material. Now. Whether fleet leadership all remember what they had for breakfast yesterday, or they only have a few propaganda videos to go on like we did, we have to assume the worst. They've been looking for a planet to settle for decades."

Jaeger nodded, embracing the change of subject. "I agree. Best case scenario, we wind up negotiating a four-way deal between them, us, the Locauri, and the Overseers. First things first, though, we *need* to find out who we're dealing with—whether it's the same government that made us mutiny in the first place or a new administration that only wants a place to live."

"Then we go to parley," he agreed. "But not without a few...precautions."

Jaeger forced herself to smile. "Figured you'd say that. I have just the thing in mind."

CHAPTER TWELVE

Toner couldn't see why everyone was so skeptical about this new class of Overseer ships. Sure, he'd heard that the Terrible design had some electrical issues. Still, for all of Kwin's hand-wringing, not one of them had spectacularly exploded when powering up their experimental new tractor-rays. Toner thought the sleek spinning snowflake-ninja-star design was downright sick.

Particularly cool was how each section on the snowflake could function as an independent docking arm, allowing for multiple ships of any design to dock up at once and form a temporary super ship.

That's it. That's all the silver lining I can bring myself to appreciate in this mess. He waited for Cruiser Portia to dock. Through the observation window, he watched nervously as large sections of her hull knocked loose in the fighting *banged* against the *Terrible*. The ships met, and the cruiser disgorged her crew.

"All injuries to the med bay." He pointed, waving the six crewmen down different corridors. He was careful not to get too close to the injured. They smelled like blood and injuries. He'd had his fill, but that didn't always make the hunger go away entirely. "The rest of you head to the temporary barracks and get some rest. Await further orders from the captain. Nice job, folks. Good to see you."

Portia was the last member of her crew to emerge from the airlock. Her left arm was slung to her chest by nanofiber cables, and her face was a mosaic of blue and yellow bruises.

Toner groaned, reaching out to take her good arm. "What the hell?"

"Nice to see you too, Commander." Portia turned her head and spat blood. Toner winced and turned his head away. "I was doing quite well in the pilot's chair, right up until that last strafing run." She sighed. "Kamikaze mines took out a couple of K'tax and blasted them right into my hull." She gave him a wry smile. "My fault for not being in the harness, I guess."

Someone else was coming out of the airlock behind Portia. Seeker stepped onto the *Terrible*, blinking and rubbing his eyes against the harsh light.

"Get down to med bay," Toner told Portia. "I'll meet up with you. Captain wants to talk to Jack."

Portia shook her head, smiling faintly. "I think I can patch up my scrapes. I'll call you if I need anything wrecked."

Toner watched her saunter down the hall until she turned a corner and vanished.

"That's unprofessional," Seeker observed.

Toner wasn't sure if he referred to Toner's stare or the way Portia, a woman with next to no ass, still managed to walk like she had basketballs for hip joints. "Dude," he snapped. "We all almost died today."

Seeker grunted and rubbed his knuckles. "Where's Jaeger?"

Toner jerked his head. "Follow me."

A FOUND BEGINNING

He led Seeker down the corridor and took several branching intersections until he finally found the small chamber designated as a human mess hall. An Overseer stood in the center of the room, its legs outstretched in random directions.

Seeker stopped in the doorway.

"Hey." Toner strode to the alien, waving a hand. "Wakey, wakey. Rise and shine."

The alien's antennae swayed slowly from side to side. "I was resting," it said, managing to sound almost surly through the ship's integrated translator system.

"Okay? Rest somewhere else. Come on, Twiggy, I have a meeting, and I can't do it in the Overseer sections of the ship."

Clicking its disapproval, the alien lowered all of its legs to the deck and zipped out of the room with unnerving speed, making Seeker jump out of its way.

"Where's the captain?" Seeker stepped into the crude kitchen as Toner dug through the supply cabinets. He didn't recognize half the stuff in them. Stacks of some kind of bark and piles of nuts that the Overseers must've thought the humans would appreciate. Thank God someone had the sense to transport a few vitals up from the planet—and no, not the stupid granola bars. He didn't know how anyone could eat those things.

"I have no idea." He shoved cans of stew aside to pull a thin green bottle into the light. He reached into another overhead cabinet and pulled two cups off a shelf. Amazing how close you could get to home when you had gravity in space. "I'm sure she's doing something important." Flipping them in his long fingers, he set the cups on the counter with a neat *snap*, then uncorked the bottle.

"Then what are…"

"I said she wanted to talk to you." Toner sloshed a few fingers of thick dark liquid into the bottom of the cup. Careful to keep his back to Seeker, he reached into the cuff of his suit and plucked out a device about the size of a grain of rice. He dropped it and watched it vanish into the dark rum. "I didn't say I was bringing you to talk to her."

Grinning, he turned and threw a leg over the table bench and set the two cups between them. "She can wait. What she wants—it's not urgent." He made a dismissive gesture and threw back his rum in one gulp. Then he reached over his shoulder and grabbed the bottle.

Seeker stared at him, mouth twisted in disapproval.

"I hear you brought several squads of the human fighters around to our side, back there. Really saved our bacon."

"I realized they had a vested interest in not allowing the planet to turn into a fiery hellscape. Just had to make them realize it, too."

"Amen to that." Toner poured himself another shot.

"What do you want, Toner?"

"Maybe an excuse to have a goddamned drink after watching a bunch of Locauri get torn to shreds?" Toner snapped. He swallowed his second shot. "Maybe with somebody who'll be enough of a pal to keep me from drinking the whole fucking bottle?"

Seeker blinked.

"Ah, what do you know," Toner muttered. "You spent the battle fighting beside people you've never met before. Couldn't see their faces, all spread out in fighters like that. Might as well have been playing video games."

A flicker of doubt tugged at the corner of Seeker's mouth. "Mason died today," he said quietly. "And Carpenter, and

A FOUND BEGINNING

Archer. They were good people. That's too many empty seats at the Thursday night poker games."

Toner lifted his cup in silent salute and drank again.

Seeker shook his head. "You're not wrong to mourn, Toner, but this isn't the time for it. You have to hold it together until we're out of the fire." He pushed himself up from the table.

"We're always in the fire."

Seeker hesitated.

"Something is always going to *be* on fire." Toner let his head sag between his shoulders. He drew in a deep breath and flicked his wrist. "Yeah. I guess some fires are more urgent than others. Stiff upper lip. Keep calm and carry on. One step at a goddamned time."

To his surprise, Seeker reached across the table and patted his shoulder. It was a stiff motion, with all the warmth and grace of a repair exo-droid going through its powerup protocol, but it was something.

"Drink your fucking rum," Toner added, gesturing to the untouched cup in front of Seeker. "Do it, or I will."

Seeker lifted the cup to his lips and tossed it back.

"To the dead." He set the empty cup on the table with a *snap*. Then he turned and walked out of the mess hall.

Through the curtain of his long hair, Toner watched Seeker go. He didn't want to be here. He wanted to be down on Locaur, looking for Occy. For all he teased, Jaeger was a savvy negotiator, and he thought there was a good chance she'd be better off going to the fleet without him. He was a liability.

I know who you are. He watched Seeker retreat down the corridor. *Now that the fleet has caught up to us, someone needs to be here, watching you.*

103

'Cause if your memories come back too, we're in for a real bad time.

When it came time to meet with fleet brass, they took Kwin's transport. The *Osprey* had one functioning shuttle left, and Jaeger didn't want to gamble with it. Besides, she couldn't shake the worry that the fleet, which had built the *Osprey* and her shuttles, still had some master override codes up their sleeve. She didn't want to end up stranded in hostile space with a shuttle that wouldn't obey her commands. Besides, riding to this meeting in an alien ship would reinforce the idea that the Overseers could be allies.

Jaeger huddled beside Toner in the elongated cockpit, watching the fleet grow larger on the display screen. From her time in the *Terrible's* holo-display, she knew the freighters were *big*, but the sheer scope of their size hadn't sunk in until this moment.

One of the three ships had drawn ahead of the fleet and waited for rendezvous in the neutral place between human and Overseer territory.

"Jeez," she said weakly. "It's huge."

"That's no moon," Toner agreed, pitching his voice in such a perfect imitation of Alec Guinness that it made Jaeger regret not bringing her score of *A New Hope*. She really could use the comforting boom of trombones right now.

Their transport passed sections of curved, rotating hull painted with letters a quarter of a kilometer tall. *Constitution.*

"The *Osprey* is tiny," she murmured.

Toner patted her shoulder. "But fierce," he said dryly. "Seriously. All this?" He waved at the sections of hull turning overhead. "I'm sure it has all the firepower of a can of green beans. I'd rather have the *Osprey*."

The screen rotated sharply as the transport reached the end of the section of grav-spin hull and glided up the flat end of the tin can. Ahead, the gaping mouth of an open docking bay glittered with hundreds of landing lights. The transport turned into the tunnel, passing entire sections of docking arms full of shuttles and repair droids. They flew past a maintenance bay where repair droids crawled over sleek dark fighters.

"Seekers." Jaeger studied the familiar X-profiles.

"I have completed a preliminary examination of these human fighters." Me's voice piped up from the small sphere docked in the console in front of Jaeger. "While they're similar to the ship you call Alpha-Seeker, they appear to be of a simpler design. I conclude that your Alpha-Seeker has highly customized technology that is too experimental or too costly to install in the standard models."

"So they're not as powerful as ours," Jaeger said. "That's something."

Beside her, Toner shifted uncomfortably.

They passed from the main docking bay into a narrower tunnel that bore directly through the heart of the freighter. Here, more small transports docked with the tunnel's edges, shuttling people back and forth across the fleet like city busses.

Toner nudged Jaeger's arm and pointed at a couple of empty docking cradles. "There are airlocks spread all over the hull of this thing," he said. "Do me a favor and don't get any ideas about Protocol Seven, okay?"

Jaeger laughed weakly. "Baby's not here to save our asses."

"I am," Me offered brightly. "I have heard of your Protocol

Seven maneuver. You humans are remarkably hardy. I would be pleased to—"

"I said *don't* get any ideas!" Toner sighed and scrubbed his fingers through his hair. *"This be madness."*

"There is yet method in it." Jaeger grinned.

"I'm not loving *Hamlet*," he admitted. "I can see why *you* picked it. That boy was all about his crazy plans."

There was a gentle *thunk* as the transport made contact with the very last airlock in the docking tunnel.

"The readiness is all." Jaeger sucked in a deep breath as she pushed herself away from the display console. Me dislodged from its docking cradle and drifted up to eye-level as Jaeger squeezed Toner's shoulder. "Let's go break a leg."

Morgan Bryce stood in the restricted section of the docking bay, his black uniform impeccably pressed and fitted snugly to every contour of his body. Mag soles kept him and his honor guard of four Seekers firmly attached to the deck as their hands, and the loose flaps of their clothes wanted to float away.

The lights surrounding the airlock turned from red to green as the chamber pressurized, and Bryce felt his soldiers stiffen and raise their chins.

The door slid open, and Bryce put on his best, most welcoming smile. He held up his hands, offering two pairs of mag soles. He was disappointed, therefore, when the two diplomats stepped into the corridor in boots that stuck firmly to the deck.

He shoved the redundant mag soles into the arms of the Seeker to his left and saluted. "Captain Sarah Jaeger. I'm

Second Officer Bryce. Welcome aboard the *Constitution*. I'm here to escort you to the bridge conferencing area."

Jaeger was smaller than he'd expected, probably due to malnutrition as a child. She had a short mop of curly dark hair and wore a uniform design he didn't recognize, a fitted silver flight suit with a slender collar. She studied him through eyes of liquid gold.

Her escort, a tall, thin man in a dark gray suit of similar design, stood silently behind her shoulder. As he'd read that Jaeger was small, he'd also read from the reports that Lawrence Toner had suffered from severe vitiligo as a result of his genetic modifications. Still, the utter *colorlessness* of the man's flesh and hair unnerved Bryce.

"Thank you, Second Officer," Jaeger said softly. "Lead the way."

As she turned up the corridor, he saw the design stitched into the back of each of their uniforms, spreading from shoulder blade to shoulder blade. A stylized black silhouette reminiscent of the double-winged profile of a Tribal Prime warship.

These people. He fought to keep the disgust off his face as he escorted the esteemed guests to the private lift that led directly to bridge sector. *Pirates, flaunting their stolen loot right in front of us.*

He stopped before the broad double doors to the conference chamber and turned, waving the cretins forward.

Jaeger afforded him the tiniest nod of acknowledgment and stepped into the meeting.

CHAPTER THIRTEEN

The woman standing at the head of the polished conference table was the model of classic European beauty. Even Jaeger found it hard not to stare. Tall and perfectly proportioned, she had waves of honey-colored curls spilling down the back of her black coat, full lips, a button nose, and eyes like sapphires.

Those are mods, Jaeger thought. *They have to be. Nobody's born with those looks.*

"Sarah Jaeger," the woman said. She had a voice like steel wrapped in velvet. "Welcome. I'm Captain Nicholetta Kelba of Tribe Six." She lifted her perfectly manicured hands, indicating the other three officers standing at the table. "This is my command crew. First Officer Remy Briggs. Interim Chief of Security Moira Hart. Chief Science Adviser Victor Grayson."

Jaeger nodded at each in turn. "Officers," she said. "I see you know me. I'm Sarah Jaeger, captain of the *Osprey* and leader of her motley crew. This is my first officer, Toner. In the language of our alien allies, he is called Slayer of Dragons."

A FOUND BEGINNING

Jaeger half-expected Toner to object to her mischaracterization of his Locauri name, but he kept his mouth shut.

At some subtle, mutual signal, everyone took their seats at the table. Kelba and her officers at one end, Jaeger at the other with Toner standing at her elbow, his hands clasped behind his back.

"Slayer of Dragons." The science adviser's lips quirked. "How auspicious."

Jaeger glanced at the man. He was smaller than the others, almost elfin, but something was strangely familiar about his face. She couldn't place it.

"Our friends hold us in high regard," she said evenly. "The esteem is mutual. They're honorable people. Our alliance has been quite fruitful."

She turned her gaze to Kelba. "That's not to say we aren't grateful for your contribution to the battle. I understand your support came at the price of many casualties. I've ordered my staff to send two transports full of medical supplies to the fleet. Consider it a gesture of gratitude."

"We'll put the supplies to good use." Kelba folded her hands over the polished wood. "You speak of crew and staff, Captain. I take this to mean that you've activated the seed embryos the Tribal Prime carried."

"Some of them." Jaeger kept her face carefully blank. "The last sixteen months have been full of trials. We needed support. Now we're a family."

This upset Hart and Briggs. They shifted, opened their mouths as if to object, but remained silent.

"I commend you," Kelba said. "You've settled on a stable, bountiful planet. You've created a stable society. Whatever strife and ill-will led you to mutiny from the fleet might even be overlooked in the face of what you've accomplished. You've achieved the dream of the Tribes."

"Not alone." Jaeger glossed over the subject of her mutiny, lest Kelba realized how *little* Jaeger recalled of her muddy past.

"Of course." Grayson leaned back comfortably in his chair. "You've had the help of aliens. Two separate races, by the look of it." He faintly grinned when Jaeger turned wary eyes on him. "I took the liberty of dropping an observation satellite into high orbit. Don't judge me. We're all a little...claustrophobic up here."

"The planet belongs to the Locauri," Jaeger said. "We are their guests."

"Of course." Grayson nodded as if this was perfectly reasonable. "It's fortunate that you've established an alliance with such agreeable people." There was a glass of water at his elbow. He sipped and brushed a strand of nonexistent hair behind his ear.

"Our Tribe has been without a home for years," Kelba added. "Our people are weary and hungry. Our supplies run thin, and thousands of civilians stand to lose everything if we don't settle soon.

"Our numbers might seem vast to you, but I assure you that a mere twenty thousand souls make for one modest town on the face of a planet as large and as lush as the Earth that was lost. We must have a home, Captain Jaeger. Without a place to rest, our people will perish. You know this."

She lifted her delicate chin, meeting Jaeger's eye across the long plane of glossy, dark wood. "In your heart. Whatever ill-will has passed between you and the previous fleet administration, you understand this much. You sought a place for mankind to start over. You've found it. Here we are, following you to this place you call Locaur."

Don't underestimate these people. Toner's words swirled around Jaeger's head. Her nebulous distrust and anxiety from the eighteen months of her second life collided with something deep in her gut: hope.

She'd stolen the *Osprey* from Tribe Six for a reason. Even if she didn't remember the specifics of it, she trusted that her reasons were not only valid but absolute. She'd had no *choice* but to mutiny. The fleet administration represented a brutal, Fascist mindset that had abandoned children to die and viciously abused its people.

If Kelba was telling the truth, the fleet had undergone changes of its own in the time since they'd parted ways. Could she afford to cling to her vague mistrust and doubt forever? Kelba's people—at least the civilians—were desperate, living on the edge of starvation.

Jaeger had wanted a fresh start for humanity. What was humanity, if not the thousands of men, women, and children in the fleet trying to survive in a hostile universe?

"What do you propose?" Jaeger asked softly. She felt the gentle shift of air currents as Toner stiffened behind her.

Kelba leaned forward, her eyes glittering. "A modest territory on this planet to call our own. The details—they can be negotiated later as we gain our footing and recover from the confusion of the wormhole passage."

"We require immediate clearance to land sections of our population on the planet," said Briggs, speaking for the first time as he ticked points off his computer. He had a droning voice. "We suffered great structural damage in the battle. One of our freighters has sustained significant damage, and the enemy destroyed several cruiser- and transport-class ships."

"Life support systems on the *Vigilance* are holding for now," Grayson added. "It's only a matter of time before the strain causes them to collapse. We must disperse a great number of her refugees. Let us move them to the planet."

Jaeger hesitated and chose her next words very carefully. "I have said that our allies are an honorable people. Like myself, they don't wish to see needless harm come to weary travelers if they come in peace. However, I must reiterate that the planet isn't mine to carve up like some *terra incognita*. I must confer with the others before extending to you an invitation to rest on the surface."

Jaeger didn't take her gaze from Kelba, but out of the corner of her eye, she saw Hart and Briggs exchange glances and fidget, displeased with the delay. Grayson, on the other hand, settled comfortably back in his chair, folding his hands behind his head. He fiddled with his ear and smiled as if they were discussing sports statistics instead of the fate of thousands of people.

"This isn't unexpected," Kelba said evenly.

"If you would allow us some privacy, I can confer with my colleagues."

"Perfect!" Grayson slapped the table with a clapping sound that made everyone jump. He pushed to his feet. "I skipped breakfast this morning. Was hoping we'd break for lunch." He jerked his head to the side of the room, indicating a door subtly set into the wooden panels. "There's a ready room set aside for your use, Captain. Right this way."

"So what are we thinking?"

The door slid shut behind the science adviser, and Toner strode across the narrow room to examine the sideboard set up along one wall. "Ten audio-visual bugs scattered in the walls? Maybe twenty?" There was a small plate of sandwiches on the table. White bread, slivers of what might've been imitation cheese, and some pink paste that Jaeger recognized as a food fabricator's low-budget attempt at ham salad.

He shook his head and turned away from the meager offering.

Jaeger examined the room. Its decorations were the same Old World dignitary style as the main conference chamber— walls paneled with dark wood, deep red carpet, carved wooden trim. A row of screens on the long wall displayed visual feeds from exterior cameras: Locaur's burning sun the size of a beach ball, twinkling and dancing against a backdrop of stars and black eternity.

She shook her head. There was no such thing as *privacy* in a situation like this. There must've been a dozen different sorts of sensors and spy equipment trained on them at this very moment. They would have to be careful with what they said aloud.

Unconcerned, she made her way to a velvet armchair and sat. "Impossible to say." She indicated her computer, hanging off her hip. "I've already sent the initial report back to Kwin and Tiki. We'll wait for their response."

Toner grunted, pacing long lines as he tugged his hair.

"Do you think they're sincere about wanting to move on from past disagreements? Offering a clean slate if we'll help them?" She wouldn't deny that the possibility of rejoining a larger human community had its appeal.

Toner shrugged. "Maybe. I guess it depends on how much

the wormhole travel scrambled the past for them. How hard they're going to try to hold onto grudges."

"What do you think of the staff?"

"Well." Toner paused in front of the screen displaying Locaur's sun, turning him into a backlit silhouette. "Kelba is a robot designed by Satan specifically to turn off the *thinking* parts of men's' brains."

"Really? I hadn't noticed."

"Sorry, Tiny, I don't have a bead on her." He gestured vaguely at his temples, and she understood his meaning. In the mess of his returning memories, he had no knowledge of one Nicholetta Kelba.

"Hart's out of her depth. Kept fidgeting. I could *smell* her stress. Guessing *interim* is the important part of her title. Briggs seemed pretty at ease, though."

"What about Grayson?"

Toner grimaced. "*That one may smile and smile and still be a villain.* Never trust a guy who cracks wise in important meetings."

Jaeger frowned. Slowly, she turned to Toner. He did several more rounds of pacing before realizing she was staring at him.

"I meant never trust a guy who cracks wise in meetings *if he's on the other team.*"

There was a *chiming* sound, followed by a small knock on the door. Jaeger frowned. "Enter."

The door slid open.

"Doctor Grayson." Jaeger bit back a sigh. *Speak of the devil...*

The little man fiddled with the cuff of his uniform. "It's professor."

"What's the difference?" Toner's eyes narrowed.

Grayson offered a faint smile. Toner was right. He had a

lot of smiles—too many. "I don't do much doctoring these days. How are the accommodations?" He gestured at the sideboard, pale eyes glittering as he held Jaeger's gaze. "I see you haven't touched any of the food. Is it not to your satisfaction?"

Jaeger chose her words carefully. "The hospitality is much appreciated, but we ate before we came. We wouldn't feel comfortable imposing on your limited supplies."

"Ah, don't pity us, Captain." His smile broadening, the professor stepped into the circle of chairs and made himself perfectly comfortable in the plush velvet. Jaeger heard Toner's grinding jaw from across the room. "Rations are a bit lean, true, but there are excellent benefits to being part of the Tribe."

"Such as?" Jaeger took the bait reluctantly.

"Belonging, to start with. A family, twenty thousand members strong. Brothers and sisters and cousins and children. Each of them fully realized humans, with their hopes, dreams, and unique stories. I'm sure you must've realized after activating a few of the preserved embryos that they don't make for very scintillating conversation. They can't, of course. They all come preprogrammed with only slight variations on the same template."

"Your citizens are fully realized? Really?" Toner folded his arms. "Even after coming through that wormhole?"

Jaeger winced. She'd been wondering the same thing, but she always got nervous when Toner started talking in these meetings. Silently, she vowed to drop-kick the man through an airlock if he uttered even the tiniest of bad puns.

Grayson studied Toner for a long moment before answering. "There's confusion, of course, but with the correct treatments, I'm confident we'll be able to overcome the memory lapses. I thought you might be skeptical." He looked at Jaeger.

"We *do* look out for one another in the Tribe. Would you like to meet some of our civilians, Captain? See who your largesse might save?"

You mean one of your propaganda mouthpieces? "I would."

"Excellent." He lifted his voice to carry past the open door and into the hallway. "If you would join us please, ladies?"

Jaeger glanced over her shoulder to see two people step into the ready room. One was a woman in a prim brown uniform—not military, she guessed from the lack of epaulets, but possibly some civilian corps—that flattered her ample curves.

The other couldn't have been over eighteen, a girl with deep copper skin and ropes of black hair tied into tight braids and twisted into buns that rested behind either ear. She smiled nervously, showing even white teeth and a dimple.

She had eyes that glittered like liquid gold.

Somewhere, distantly, Jaeger heard Grayson talking, but her mind had turned fuzzy, and she could barely follow his words.

"At the beginning of the battle, Miss Potlova here took charge of a confused rabble of ships with true aplomb. With her gift for communications and coordination, she's quickly become a fixture of our new civilian government. On top of working tirelessly for the benefit of the Tribe, she's been looking after orphans who've lost parents to disease or misfortune. This is her foster daughter, Sim Jaeger."

CHAPTER FOURTEEN

"And I would fly five million miles,
  And I would fly five million more
  Just to be the one who flew ten million miles
  To get back home to you!"

The little girl's head fell over the back of her chair, her legs kicking as she bellowed to the ceiling, singing along with the staticky old media player. *"Da da da da!"*

"Da da da da!" Sarah echoed, reaching across the table to tickle the child's ribs. Sim shrieked with laughter, doubling over. Over on the beat-up little speaker, the song ended.

The woman sitting across the table from Sarah reached to the wall and touched the speaker interface. She had a lovely round face with rosy cheeks and cheerful brown eyes, and hair like a 1920s flapper.

Sarah didn't know her name. Deep down, she knew she should.

"Again, again!" Sim insisted.

Flapper girl shook her head with a grin. "You're too young to start reneging on deals, honey. One more, that's what you said last time. It's my turn to pick the song." She tapped the screen with a bright pink fingernail, and a new song with a funky electro-beat began. Flapper girl rolled her shoulders and snapped her fingers to the beat as the musician sang. *"Got no home, 'except the places we will roam..."*

Sim, the little girl with her mama's eyes, made a face. "I hate Rush Starr."

"How can you say that?" Flapper girl gasped, her eyes popping with disbelief. "You never even met him!"

"You and me, baby, forever joined at the hip—"

"Your auntie has a crush," Sarah confided, leaning close to whisper in Sim's ear. "You better be nice to her."

"I can't hear you." Flapper girl clamped her hands over her ears and sang to the music—*"Cause our duty lies on a rocket SHIIIIIIP!"*

Flapper girl's voice was joined by distant, atonal singing, like the screeching of a flock of crows. Sim popped up from her chair, eyes dancing. "They're here!"

Before Sarah could catch her, the girl had run off; turning down the narrow apartment hallway toward the rear door. The awful singing turned into familiar laughter. Sarah turned off the music, making flapper girl's full lips curve into a disappointed pout.

Two men entered the tiny kitchen. The first was tall and olive-skinned with high cheekbones that betrayed a close relationship to the little girl.

Cole. The name bubbled up in Sarah's mind, so faint and ethereal that she wondered if she'd imagined it. He carried a small plate of cupcakes in both hands, as carefully as if were a stack of raw eggs.

Behind him came a man even taller and even thinner, bony in his baggy jumpsuit and as colorless as a blank sheet of

A FOUND BEGINNING

paper. He held the little girl firmly on his hip. He was the only one among them tall enough to do that anymore.

"You got the cupcakes!" Sim squealed as her father set the plate on the center of the table. "Lemon?"

"Real lemon." Cole smiled, but Jaeger saw the weary strain on his face and knew that expression well. The cakes had come at a cost—more than they'd expected. Still, this was their last time all together before they split off to their training programs. No cost was too high to give the girl a taste of real lemon cake.

"My gawd." Flapper girl carefully peeled the protective covering off the plate and drew in a deep breath. "They smell amazing."

"Everyone gets one," Sim insisted, scrambling down from Lawrence's hip. "Five cakes. Five people." She distributed the treasure with busy little hands. One in front of her seat, one to mama, and one to auntie, who took hers with a coo of delight. Dad took his with a solemn nod of thanks. When Sim turned to hand the last cake to Lawrence, he held up a staying hand and shook his head. "No thanks, kid. I hate all that sugary stuff."

Sim's expression wavered, disappointment hanging on her lips and threatening to fall.

"You take it," Lawrence added quickly, nudging her back to her seat. "Birthday girl gets seconds. That's the rule."

"Really?" Sim looked hopefully from her mother to her father. Sarah exchanged glances with the man across the table and came to an unspoken understanding. Yes, the birthday girl could have seconds.

Sim settled into her chair, and the five of them began to sing a new song.

119

CHAPTER FIFTEEN

"Sim." The name escaped like a prayer through Jaeger's parted lips.

The girl—no, young woman—bowed her head, a self-conscious flush creeping up her cheeks. "Hi," she murmured, shuffling her feet.

"Nope." Toner's voice had turned to ice. Jaeger looked up sharply, pulse pounding in her ears to see him fold his arms, his face twitching with barely contained emotion. "No," he said again. "Sim Jaeger died in the destruction of Europa station along with her father, and tens of thousands of other people, over ten years ago."

Jaeger stared at Grayson, who studied Toner with new, acute interest. "Many people died in the destruction of Europa Station," he admitted. "Many others escaped. The whole sector was in anarchy.

"Ten years later, we're still sifting through the mess of those early days. From time to time, new survivors, people thought long dead, turn up in the lower decks where they've been living all along. Fell through the cracks, you see."

A FOUND BEGINNING

He turned a sympathetic look on Jaeger. "Unfortunately, I haven't been able to find any trace of the man called Cole Redman. I'm afraid he well and truly perished in the attack."

Toner said nothing.

"I don't remember much," the girl called Sim whispered. She gestured vaguely at her temples. "Most of us got all kinds of mixed-up passing through the wormhole."

"The memory-scrambling effects of wormhole travel." Grayson *tsk*'d softly and shook his head. "Such a tragedy. Go ahead, Miss Jaeger. Tell them what you do remember."

"Lots of cramped hallways. Sleeping in the cold, always moving from ship to ship, staying with whoever would take me." Sim glanced up, daring to meet Jaeger's eyes for the briefest instant. Then she looked away, licking her lips.

"And before that?" Jaeger breathed.

"I dunno." Sim rubbed her hands together. "I remember there was good stuff, a long time ago. I remember...a woman who smelled like coconut and lemon." She glanced at Jaeger, and her gaze skittered away again, like a frightened rabbit. "Maybe it was all wishes and dreams."

"It was real, my dear," Grayson said amiably, getting to his feet. "Don't you worry about that. It's going to take some time and work to get all your memories sorted again." He nodded at her, then at Jaeger. "I'll give you some time to get reacquainted."

No one stirred, no one spoke, no one dared even breathe until the door had *clicked* shut behind Professor Grayson.

Then Miss Potlova let out a long breath, her shoulders slumping. "Gawd, that guy makes me nervous. Don't get me wrong—" she added quickly. "He's been nothin' but good to us. He's just got a lot ridin' on his shoulders right now. I'm scared to see what would happen if he weren't here, holding the military and civilian branches of the fleet together."

"Petra," Toner said, his voice full of simple wonder.

Petra's full lips bent up into a smile. "Reporting for duty," she said brightly. "I guess you knew me, then? From before? Were we friends? I'm sorry, honey, my brain's all wonky still."

Toner let out a breath like a deflating balloon. His shoulders slumped. "Yeah," he said softly. "Yeah, Petie. We..." His voice trailed off as he stared. Then he reached up and scratched the corners of his eyes, sniffing deeply.

Jaeger finally tore her gaze from the silent, blushing Sim to stare at her first mate.

God. He's crying.

Or at least, as close as he could get. In the eighteen months she'd known him, he'd never shed a tear—but not for lack of trying. Something about his genetic modifications had shut down his tear ducts completely.

She resisted the instinct to get up and hug her friend.

"Yeah, baby," Toner said again, forcing a wavering, sloppy grin. "Thick as thieves, you and me. We go back to the beginning."

"Oh." Petra sagged, her voice heavy with disappointment. "I'm sorry, hon." She sounded it, truly. "The memory thing..."

"The memory thing." Toner rasped.

"Gawd knows I wish I..."

"Could remember," he supplied, smiling sadly.

Petra inclined her head.

Shyly, as if embarrassed, Sim stepped toward the sideboard and picked up a sandwich. Jaeger recognized that expression on her face as the girl bit into thin bread. It was the desperate, ravenous edge of starvation, trained into an orphan like instinct.

A FOUND BEGINNING

Seeing the girl pick up the sandwich and eat, the reality of her presence finally fully hit Jaeger with all the force of a breaking dam. Not a hologram or hallucination, but real flesh and blood.

A real young woman, orphaned from childhood.

Oh God. She put a hand over her mouth. Tears prickled the corners of her eyes. She reached out and stopped, resisting the temptation to touch those finely coiled braids, that warm skin. "Sim," she whispered. "I am so, so sorry…"

The girl swallowed the last bite of sandwich and swiped her mouth clean, glancing shyly at Jaeger. "Are they right?" she asked. "I'm all kinds of confused. They say you're my mom."

"What do you say?" Jaeger breathed.

Sim lifted her gaze, peering long into Jaeger's face. Jaeger forced herself not to turn away from that liquid golden stare, the one she saw in every bathroom mirror. Shame coiled like a serpent in her gut, and the thought of one little girl, enduring what unimaginable horrors through years, a decade of *abandonment—*

It could be a trick, she agonized. *Still. Somehow. Toner remembers it too, Sim's death. Maybe they found some other orphan with our eyes, with that dimple, with that hair…*

"I say I don't know." Sim sniffed, tears shining in her eyes. "I say I…I want that." She stepped forward, lifting her arms hopefully. "Can I… Can I hug you?"

Jaeger closed her eyes. She shook her head, and it hurt more than she could begin to describe. "No, Boo. I, um." She swallowed a lump. "I've been exposed to some infectious spores. I'm on antifungal medication, but I'm not cleared for skin-to-skin contact yet. I couldn't—I don't want to—" She opened her eyes to see Sim taking a step backward, her head falling.

"It would kill me to expose you to something," she whispered.

Sim nodded in silent understanding.

"What a mess," Jaeger breathed, turning sharply to Toner. She couldn't bear to look at the girl any longer…to look and not hold.

Toner nodded grimly. "The Tribe is family," he said. He met her eyes, and the unspoken second half of that sentiment passed between them: *The Tribe is holding our family hostage.*

Jaeger reached for her computer and realized that her hands were trembling. She checked her messages.

"Kwin and Tiki need time to take the matter back to their people." She forced a businesslike tone.

"Are we going to have a home?" Sim took another sandwich from the board and discreetly slipped it into a pocket. "Can we go on the planet?"

"Not yet." Jaeger turned to her. "It's going to take time to figure everything out, Boo." She saw the girl's thin arms, the way she sheltered her pilfered sandwich, and her heart cracked. "We'll get it figured out. In the meantime, we're going to send you every bit of food and aid we can spare. I'm not going to let you go hungry anymore. I promise."

She looked at Toner, collecting herself. "Let's send our regards to Kelba and her crew and take our leave. We have a lot of work to do if we're going to get these people a home."

Toner nodded but lingered as Jaeger headed for the door. She turned to see him staring at Miss Potlova.

"*Doubt thou the stars are fire,*" he murmured, pitching his voice low. "*Doubt that the sun doth move; doubt the truth be a liar.*" He lifted a hand, reaching out to her. Petra stared, her expression uncertain, glittering with confusion.

Toner's hand wavered and fell. "*But never doubt I love.*" He gave a small, desperate, breathy laugh, and touched his forehead in a melancholy salute. "All the way from the beginning, Petie."

He followed Jaeger out of the room.

With Toner at her side, Jaeger bid their honor guard a polite goodbye and stepped from the docking bay into the airlock connected to their Overseer transport.

The two stood silent and motionless as the airlock cycled through its pressurization sequence. Finally, the second door slid open.

Jaeger and Toner flickered like a glitchy holo-drama and vanished. Where Jaeger had stood was a small, silver sphere.

Me drifted out of the airlock and into the transport's cramped cockpit. "I think that went quite well," the AI chirruped. "The decoy plan was quite effective. I can confidently say that humans do not possess the ability to distinguish my holograms from reality by sight or standard video surveillance alone."

Jaeger sat in her improvised seat in a cockpit designed for alien bodies, her head buried in Toner's shoulder.

She was sobbing.

"That's great, Me," Toner said hoarsely. He rested his chin in the nest of Jaeger's hair. His eyes glittered coldly in the dim light. "Now get us the fuck out of here? Please?"

"This can't be happening," Jaeger whispered as the transport hummed to life and detached from the docking cradle. "This can't be real. God. They're fucking with us. They have to be."

Toner said nothing. He watched the screens as the transport glided past rows of docking bays lined with sleek black Seeker fighters.

"Report," Jaeger croaked. "Goddammit, Toner. I'm ordering you to give me your analysis. Tell me what you know." Unspoken but understood was her real meaning. *Tell me what you remember.*

Toner loosened his arms, letting her pull away from him. There was a soggy wet patch on his sleeve. The smell of it made his stomach roil with something he couldn't interpret. Hunger? Regret? Rage? Longing?

"That was Petra," he said. "I mean. That was really her. I'd know that accent anywhere. She was...she was your friend, Sarah."

"And your girlfriend."

Toner smiled bitterly. "Imagine. Remembering how much you love someone, just in time for them to forget all about you."

"I'm sorry."

Toner shook his head, but what else could he expect her to say? Clearly, she didn't remember Petra, either. Petra wasn't who weighed on her heart now. "As for the girl...I just don't know. I can't believe Sim's survived the last ten years as an orphaned refugee." That wasn't entirely true.

Even within the fleet, the state of humankind was a big mess. He believed that people could fall through the cracks. They did every day. Or maybe he didn't want to believe what that little girl might've had to endure down in the filth of those cracks. "Maybe...maybe if I'd been there and could've gotten a whiff of her, I could say for sure if she was your kid."

"You think it's possible that she's for real."

Toner nodded. An urgent alert blinked on the transport's

comm screen. Wanting to spare Sarah any more bad news for as long as he could, he reached over and read the message.

He stopped breathing. "It's from Elaphus." For the thousandth time that day, Toner damned the mad scientists who'd given him shark teeth and dead-eyed hunger and taken away his tears. "They've found Occy. He's alive."

CHAPTER SIXTEEN

Doctor Helen Elaphus stood in front of the *Osprey*'s medical bay like a sentinel of old. She scowled as Jaeger and Toner jogged up the corridor. "I knew you'd race down here first thing to smother the poor boy." She folded her arms, showing off the fresh tattoo inked on her wrist. "I will not allow you to harass my patient."

"What's his status?" Jaeger huffed and halted in front of the doctor. Elaphus was a stick-thin woman, as tall and willowy as the deer she was named after. Somehow she managed to fill the doorway and glower over her delicate glasses, and Jaeger had not a single shred of doubt that she'd wrestle Toner himself to keep them from stinking up her medical bay.

"He's *tired*," Elaphus said pointedly. "As are the dozens of other casualties we're treating right now. None of them need the two of you disturbing their recovery." Her steely gaze softened as she saw Jaeger draw in a deep breath and settle back on her heels.

Taking this as a sign the captain wouldn't try to force her way in, Elaphus unfolded her arms and lifted her computer

A FOUND BEGINNING

from her hip, muttering a quiet invective as she scrolled through the updated status reports. "I don't have much time for you either," she added.

"No time for the *captain*?" Toner was incredulous.

Elaphus cast him a sharp stare. "Is *the captain* injured?"

"Not physically." Jaeger sighed.

"You'll have to see Equus for treatment of mental and spiritual maladies." Elaphus busied herself with her computer. "Going out on the search and rescue put me behind schedule. Not that I regret doing it," she added.

"We found young Occy nearly thirty kilometers from the sunken island, waterlogged and half-dead from exhaustion. His modifications were doing their damndest to keep the boy breathing, but there's only so much you can expect when he has only the two tentacles remaining."

She pursed her lips into a tight frown. "I *told* him that he needed to let the other tentacles grow back, but he *insisted* they do more harm than good when he's planet-side. Hypothermia, shock, blood-electrolyte levels *all* out of balance. He must've banged his head somewhere along the way. He's showing classic signs of a concussion. Confusion, blurred vision, memory loss…"

"Memory loss?" Toner was dismayed. "That kid didn't have much *memory* to spare."

"Now that he's not fighting for his life, he'll start to recover. He has the same set of active rejuvenation mods as the rest of us Morphed." She folded her arms once more, glaring at them both. "Come back for visiting hours at 0900. I'll let you see him then."

Jaeger checked the time on her computer and was surprised to find that according to the crew's schedule, it was well past midnight. She wasn't nearly as surprised to see the

RAMY VANCE & MICHAEL ANDERLE

dozens of messages that had stacked up in her queue in the last few hours alone. She nodded tiredly. "Call me if anything changes," she told her chief medical officer. "Make sure you're getting enough rest, too."

Elaphus sniffed and disappeared into her domain without another word, leaving Jaeger to stare at a blank section of wall, too exhausted to move until a familiar hand fell on her shoulder.

"You need to rest, too," Toner said.

Jaeger shrugged off his hand, though not unkindly. She shook her head. Being alone in the dark was the last thing she needed right now. "Come on," she said. "There's someone else who can tell us what the hell happened in the Forebear city. Let's find Virgil."

"I have no idea." A repair droid rested on the mess hall table in one of the half-finished housing units circling the nascent human colony. Emergency lighting turned the entire building into a shifting mass of light and shadows.

Since reaching out to cooperate with the humans, Virgil hadn't asked permission to step one mechanical foot onto the *Osprey*, and Jaeger hadn't invited it. That left her and Toner venturing out to the buildings in the middle of the night to confront the robot lurking in the shadows.

"You must know something." Toner's voice stayed deceptively even. "Your crazy cousin and one of your droids went off to war with us and never came back, but you got another out here awful fast. Like you knew they weren't coming back."

"My droids scattered across several kilometers of the nearby forest," Virgil answered. "As soon as I decided to go on

A FOUND BEGINNING

this beacon quest with you, I brought another one of myself here to replace the one I knew would lose contact with the outside world. I was prescient, it seems. As before, I've lost another droid to this Forebear technology. That makes two. It appears I have a penchant for slow suicide."

"Occy's asleep," Jaeger said. She swirled the tepid coffee in her mug and forced herself to take another sip. She hadn't been this tired in a long time.

"I am pleased to hear that you've recovered the chief engineer."

"You can't tell us anything about what happened down there?"

"Of course not," Virgil said. "How could I? You know as well as I do that the crystalline superstructure blocks our communications. The moment my healthy and corrupted droids went into the tunnel with Occy, I lost them. Based on radio chatter, I conclude that the meteor bombardment destroyed the island as well as the entrance to the city."

"You can tell us something," Toner insisted. "You can tell us what probably happened, based on what you know *about yourself*, right?"

"If this incident with the corrupted droid has taught me anything, it is that I do not have a complete understanding of myself."

Toner growled and slammed his fist on the table, then winced as hairline fractures shot through the surface. "Why do I get the feeling you're being intentionally evasive?" he growled.

"Because you have the mental and emotional capacity of a malnourished teenager. I do not—" Virgil cut off mid-reply, making Jaeger look up from her cup of coffee for the first time in what felt like hours. Toner looked around, instantly alert as well. "What?" he asked. "What is it?"

"*It* is coming."

Jaeger didn't know how Virgil managed to funnel so much contempt through a repair droid's primitive audio channel. She turned to see a small silver sphere gliding through the shadowy hallway in their direction.

"Me." She sat up, surprise injecting her with a few more minutes of full awareness. "What are you doing here?"

"Moss suggested I might find you here, Captain Jaeger." The sphere began a lazy orbit around the two humans and the hulking repair droid.

"I bring a variety of news. You might be pleased to know that our subspace relays have finally reported a change in activity in the primary K'tax swarm. It appears our enemy has received the message your engineer sent out and taken it to heart. They have ceased their approach to Locaur."

"They're retreating?" Jaeger breathed.

"Not exactly, as of yet," Me admitted. "They have adopted a holding pattern in subspace."

"Still, it's good news." Jaeger tossed back the last of her coffee and grimaced. She would have to fiddle with the recipes on this mess hall fabricator. "It buys us more time if nothing else."

"Hey," Toner added as if a thought had occurred to him. "Me, you've been down to the Forebear city with us. What do you think might've happened down there?" He pointed at the repair droid. "Because this asshole isn't talking."

"Oh, I have yet to recover my records of our adventure completely," Me said easily. "Councilor Tsuan has had me prioritizing other tasks. However, since the beacon is still transmitting, I deduce that considerable sections of the structure remain undamaged. However, they might have flooded as a result of meteor bombardment.

"Clearly, Virgil and Occy managed to access the ancient communication systems. I suspect that once the structural integrity became unstable, Virgil opted to remain behind and continue an exploration of the Forebear technology while Occy escaped."

"Why do you think that?" Jaeger asked.

"It's what I would do."

Jaeger allowed herself a small smile.

"This is plausible," Virgil grumbled. "In the moments before the meteor bombardment, I detected slight irregularities on my communication channels. Atmospheric interference might have caused it, or it might have been my counterpart attempting to reach out to me via the Forebear technology."

"Nothing since then?" Jaeger asked.

"No."

"Well…keep an ear out." She sighed and pushed away from the table. "Let's hope that your opposite number is still down there with access to the Forebear mainframe. Now that the tsunami destroyed the tunnel, it might be our only connection to all of their knowledge." She added silently, *Let's hope that if it is, it's not the total psychopath you can be, Virgil.*

"There is something else, Captain Jaeger," Me said brightly.

"Go on."

"Councilor Tsuan has arrived in-system. He is very angry."

CHAPTER SEVENTEEN

Jaeger hadn't been to the *Osprey*'s No-A sector in a long time. There wasn't much to see there since Virgil had offloaded the thousands and thousands of embryo casks. Plus, she had a lot of memories—some good, but many bad—floating under that high cathedral ceiling.

However, it was the closest empty location with enough open space to accommodate multiple full-sized Overseer holograms. Jaeger was too tired to worry about the optics of confronting Tsuan about a pesky human problem in the place that had birthed said pesky human problem. At any rate, she doubted Tsuan would make the connection.

"The Council is debating the issue of this new human invasion as we speak." Tsuan's hologram flickered as his antennae lashed through the air faster than the scanners could track.

"I'm surprised you're not in chambers with them, then," Jaeger said.

"I trust my adjunct to represent our position," Tsuan dismissed. "It is well documented, regardless."

"Your *position*." Jaeger began a slow pace around the edge of the No-A cathedral, circling the life-sized holograms of Tsuan and Kwin. The caffeine had helped, but she needed every edge she could get, and movement kept her alert.

"It's interesting, Councilor, that you have such a strong position on humans. Yet you appear to show no interest in the battle we've all recently fought to protect the Locauri from an extinction-level catastrophe."

Privately, Kwin whispered into Jaeger's comm channel. "Be careful. You do us no favors if you further alienate Tsuan."

"I'm not impressed by your self-inflicted martyrdom," Tsuan said. "It was your presence that sparked the K'tax invasion to begin with. Now it appears more of you have appeared on our doorstep, making all sorts of unreasonable demands."

"These are weary travelers that have arrived on your doorstep," Jaeger snapped. "I recall that your people were once weary travelers searching for a home, as well. I remember *!Tsok n Sshoogn,* Councilor. Do you?"

"You reach beyond your station, human." Tsuan's mandibles lashed. "You assume too much."

"What would you do, Tsuan?" Jaeger stopped pacing and scrubbed fingers through her hair, brushing the first crust of delayed sleep from the corner of her eye. "Honestly. Sincerely. I know what you *want*. You want the fleet to go away. I'm asking, what would *you* do if your people were desperate and starving?"

"Irrelevant. When you came to us seeking asylum, Jaeger, you pled that you were fleeing the oppression of evil people, the ones who designed your war machines. Is this not the same fleet you spoke of then? Now you defend them? You would have us believe they deserve the same considerations you did? Which is it, Captain?"

"A lot can change in a year," she said tiredly.

"Indeed." Tsuan rounded abruptly to stare down Kwin. "I have received troubling reports, Kwin, about how you are using the experimental ships the Council has lent you. Your medical bays have been disproportionately active. Despite the terrible battle you claim to have fought, life support systems indicate that the population of your crew has been *increasing*."

"I have recovered a cache of unclaimed human embryos," Kwin said, unmoving and unapologetic. "They are being activated under my authority for the sole purpose of protecting Locaur from a ground invasion of K'tax."

"How convenient. The disgraced captain allies himself further with aliens and begins building a private army. Watch yourself, Kwin. You stink of deception."

"If the Council wishes to claim ownership of this human force, I will relinquish it promptly."

Jaeger shot her friend a sharp look. She sure hoped he didn't mean exactly what he said.

"In the meantime," Kwin went on, ignoring Jaeger, "I will continue using every tool at my disposal in defense of our cousins."

"We shall see about that." Tsuan's carapace rattled with a low, threatening buzz. For the first time, Kwin's hologram shifted, turning to face Tsuan square-on. Dark shades of umber and ebony shivered down Kwin's carapace. Jaeger didn't know much about Overseer body language, but she recognized two males sizing each other up when she saw it. She was not going to facilitate another fight, not today. Not here.

"Councilor!" she barked, making both of the Overseers straighten and turn to her. She racked her brain for an appropriate change of subject. "I recall that you are a historian with

A FOUND BEGINNING

a keen interest in Forebear technology. You'll be interested to know that for the first time, my people have successfully interfaced with a Forebear computer to broadcast the very beacon that stopped the K'tax advance."

It was a pathetically transparent distraction, but to her relief, Tsuan's antennae thoughtfully flicked as he considered this offered tidbit.

"I had gathered as much. I did not expect your people to have the understanding and knowledge to do this."

"We have a proof of concept," Jaeger said. "Using this technology, we can send messages to the K'tax, and they will obey. Surely you must see how this changes the very nature of your longstanding feud with them."

Tsuan said nothing, watching her closely with glittering black eyes.

"We are not your enemy," she said. "The K'tax and what they bear, they are the real threat to humans, Overseers, and Locauri alike. Work with us, Tsuan. We will happily share what we know of the Forebear technology. With it, we might have ultimate control over the direction of the K'tax swarms."

For a long moment, she thought he might go for it. She let herself hope.

The *snap* of Tsuan's mandibles echoed around the arched ceiling. "No. You have neither the right nor the knowledge to appreciate what you do when you tamper with the technology of our ancestors, Jaeger. Due to the war *you* started, we have now lost access to fabulous tools and knowledge. There is no telling what unknown damage your forces might have done to the fragile computer that transmits the beacon."

Jaeger opened her mouth—to say what, she wasn't sure— but she didn't get the chance.

"You have done enough." Tsuan's antennae bowed with

137

contempt. "The K'tax are waylaid. You are out of immediate danger. My duties call me elsewhere. In the meanwhile, you are not to tamper with Forebear matters further. You were fortunate yesterday, but there's no telling what new catastrophes your blundering might bring down on us.

"My people will come to examine the ruins, but you are not to concern yourself with Forebear technology any further." Tsuan drew himself up, and Me zipped around the two holograms. Jaeger recognized it as the activity sequence Me ran when preparing to cut off communications and collapse holograms.

Tsuan hadn't finished talking, however. In the last few seconds before his hologram faded, he said, "If you disregard my command, I will consider it an act of war."

"I'd say that guy needs to pull the stick out of his ass, but then..." Toner stepped out from the shadows of the stacks lining the No-A cathedral. In one hand, he held a half-eaten steak by its bony handle. "I guess he wouldn't have any ass left."

Jaeger eyed the meat. She had set restrictions on high-quality food fabrications since the Osprey's stores had started to run low, but she'd bet her best flight suit that Toner had found some way around them.

She turned back to Kwin's faintly glowing hologram. "Guess I managed to alienate Tsuan even more," she said softly.

Kwin studied the middle distance with his head cocked thoughtfully to one side. "Your proposal to work together on the Forebear technology was sound. I would not have expected such a negative reaction, either."

Toner joined Jaeger and Kwin at the center of the cathedral. "He's hiding something,"

"He's a politician." Jaeger sighed. "Of course he's hiding something. The question is whether or not it matters to us."

"What do you mean?" Toner gnawed on his bone.

"If he's truly worried that we'll step on another land mine buried in the Forebear computer, I can understand his worry." She turned away from the dais, walking slowly to the edge of the chamber. Kwin's hologram floated alongside them, projected ahead of Me. "On the other hand, if he's blocking us out of this research because it looks bad to the Council or some other bullshit political reason..."

She set her jaw. "I can't let that stand in the way of research that might mean the difference between survival and destruction."

"Tsuan's behavior is strange," Kwin agreed. "Even for a politician. I will make some inquires and see if I can get a better understanding of our Councilor's motives."

"That's good." Jaeger passed out of No-A and into the main corridor of the starboard wing, which was silent as the grave at this hour.

"His interest in the embryos concerns me, however," Kwin added. "He was quick to point out that the Terrible ships are not completely at my disposal."

"Spit it out." Toner swallowed a rope of raw, fabricated beef tendon, and to Jaeger's amazement, tossed the remaining bone down the nearest recycling chute. He gave her a dirty look as if she'd caught him doing something shameful.

"It might be wise to relocate the activation pods," Kwin said. "As well as the embryos that are already activated. If

Tsuan or the Council decides to recall the Terrible ships, I would not have them fly off with this fledgling army as well."

"There's an entire neighborhood of apartment buildings in the settlement waiting for residents," Jaeger said. "You find yourself in need of a place to quarter troops. They're at your disposal, Captain."

"Very well," Kwin said. "I shall begin the transfer immediately."

He meant it. His hologram vanished without ceremony, leaving Jaeger and Toner walking through the darkness together.

"Give us some privacy, Me," Toner said, and the silver sphere zipped down the hallway, humming pleasantly to itself. "How are you holding up?" he asked once the AI was safely out of sight.

"'Bout like you'd expect." Jaeger stared into the deep shadows of the corridors, but all she saw was a young woman with eyes of liquid gold. "God, I'm tired."

"In more ways than one," Toner agreed. "Is there... anything I can do?"

Jaeger said nothing for a long time. Toner was dealing with his internal storm of bullshit, she knew. But he was asking about *her*.

"Tell me about you," she whispered.

She expected him to ignore or outright deny her request. Instead, he halted and turned, leaning against the bulkhead and studying her in the dim light.

"What about me?"

"Anything." She swallowed. "We're not going to escape our past after all. It's already here, and it's caught me with my pants down." She sniffed sharply and wiped away a tear. "I

A FOUND BEGINNING

wanted so badly to remember that girl. Then I wanted nothing else but to forget her again. And here we are."

"Here we are."

"God hath given you one face, and you make yourself another," she murmured. "You haven't been the same since your coma. Who are we?" She looked up and met his cold blue stare. "You and me. What were we?"

"Friends."

"Friends," she repeated.

He spread his hands, offering her a shrug. "Weird, right?" He sighed, wringing his long, slender fingers and muttering. "Not so weird, once you remember the bulk of it."

She waited for him to go on. It was cold in the corridor, and exhaustion made her shiver.

"You know, if we'd met in a different time, at a different place...I'd be all over that. Hell, back in the land of amnesia, I *was* all over that." He gestured at the entirety of her person.

"Look at you. Smart, cute as hell, and ready to take on the whole damn fleet by yourself. God knows I could use a good influence. But I watched you grow up, Sarah."

He looked away, and if she didn't know him better, she would say it was embarrassment that flickered across his brow. "I really wish I hadn't hit on you as much as I did. You're like a little sister to me."

Jaeger let out a long, shuddering breath. She didn't know what to say as strange emotions warred within her. Shame for her lost memories—those the wormhole had taken, those she'd purposefully destroyed, and those she'd chosen not to seek in Kwin's Living Dream. Shame in knowing that Toner was all alone, in dealing with a fully realized past coming back to haunt him. That woman in the fleet—Petra. Jaeger had seen the pain on his face when he quoted Shakespeare to her. How terrible it must be for all of your friends and lovers to forget you ever were.

There was a sliver of relief, yes, to finally believe that he wasn't going to pine after her any more. For the first time he'd adequately put it in words, the way she felt for him.

"Not friends," she whispered. A new tear stung at the corner of her eye.

Toner looked at her sharply.

She threw her arms around him, pulling his bony frame into a tight hug, pressing her wet face to his chest. "I'm sorry. I'm sorry that you're all alone, back there in the past. That must really suck."

"You… You're getting my coat wet. Again."

Jaeger let out a trembling laugh. She pulled away, gazing into his bony face. "Not friends." She sniffed, this time more firmly. She reached up and brushed a loose strand of hair behind his ear. He flinched—not from pain or discomfort but simple surprise.

"Family." She smiled.

Toner caught her hand and stared at it for a moment. Then he kissed her knuckles. "*Goodnight, sister. And flights of angels sing thee to thy rest.*"

"See?" Her mouth quirked. "*Hamlet*'s not so bad."

Toner grunted.

Jaeger parted from him and went to find Baby. After this long, awful day, the last thing she wanted was to sleep alone.

CHAPTER EIGHTEEN

Occy woke up to a flashing message on a computer screen.

What happened under the ocean?

Occy squinted. He remembered the ropes and nets the rescue crew had used to fish him from the water, but not much after that. He was lying on a bed in the *Osprey*'s medical bay, curtains drawn tightly to give him two square meters of privacy. By the smell and heat in the air, he deduced that there were many, many other full beds in the medical bay right now. They were quiet. It must be sleeping hours.

He blinked again. There was a computer interface helpfully mounted to an arm at the side of his bed. Not *his* computer, of course—he recalled with a sickening lurch that he'd lost it along with so much else when the cavern flooded —but one of the medical bay interfaces, available for patient use.

What happened under the ocean?

143

RAMY VANCE & MICHAEL ANDERLE

Occy rubbed his eyes. He was tired and sore but recognized the dull ache of powerful painkillers keeping some deeper hurts at bay. Studying the screen, he recognized the ID code above the message.

He tapped the screen, opening a voice channel. "Virgil," he croaked, whispering so he didn't disturb the rest of the bay. "I didn't think you made it out of there."

I didn't.

The instant response seemed as if Virgil had been waiting on him for hours.

I have lost all contact with the two droids that went with you into the Forebear city. Reports indicate that parts of the structure flooded. Yet the beacon remains lit. I detect the faintest variation in its pattern, although that might be simple background noise.

Occy closed his eyes, seeking the memory of that antechamber and the crystal interface through the haze of whatever Elaphus had given him. "We sent out the beacon and stayed to collect more data on the K'tax before the place flooded. You were interfaced with the pillar when that happened. You might still be down there," he realized, surprising himself. "The saltwater and pressure wouldn't be a problem for the exo-droid bodies."

The screen remained blank for a long time before Occy's invisible messenger responded. In that time, he heard soft footfalls approaching his tent.

I was afraid of that.

A FOUND BEGINNING

"Afraid?" Occy asked. He swallowed. He felt dehydrated. He needed to pee. "Why?"

The curtain snapped open, revealing Doctor Elaphus towering over Occy's bed. She peered down at him. "Awake already? How do you feel?"

"I'm...I'm pretty okay, actually." Occy pushed himself upright as Elaphus busied herself checking his vitals and consulting the monitors.

"Good. Maybe now the captain will stop pestering me about you. Are you up for a short visit?"

Occy nodded. He wanted to give his report and find out what happened in the battle's aftermath.

When Elaphus went to fetch his visitor, he glanced back at his screen.

Virgil had given him no answer.

In a clearing in the forest, about eight kilometers from the *Osprey* and the Locauri village, was a fire circle at least twenty meters in diameter and thick with ashes.

There would be more ashes to come, and soon.

Jack Seeker stood among the circle of crew with his chin up, his eyes stinging against the smoke of burning lumber— and burning bodies.

Across the shimmering haze, across the pyre pit, he saw the wavering line of Locauri, their heads low. Some of them *buzzed* a deep, mournful dirge. Others stomped on wide, squat drums, a strange rhythm that dipped and swayed with the tongues of flame.

They'd made the speeches, read the eulogies, said the goodbyes. There were twelve human bodies down in that pit,

RAMY VANCE & MICHAEL ANDERLE

their ashes mingling with the remains of the thirty-one Locauri who'd given their lives to fight off a ground invasion. There had been more human casualties than those twelve, of course—but they'd already turned into smears of space debris, and there was nothing to salvage, nothing to burn.

Jack would've stood there unmoving until night fell and the fire burned itself out.

However, there was much work to be done for the sake of the living, and fewer people now to do it.

He stepped to the edge of the pit, where the air crackled against his skin, singeing his hair and burning his lungs. He opened his hands, spilling a vial of shimmering black ink into the flames.

No names but Mason, and Archer, and Anolis, he thought. *No names but Spenser and Thatcher and Carpenter and Clark. No hunt, no ink, no tattoo. But no less were you family.*

With the heat raising blisters on his hands, he waited for the vial to empty.

Then he dropped the glass into the flame as well and walked away from the funeral.

He sucked on his vape pen as he passed through the settlement's outer fields on his way back to the *Osprey.* They'd tried to plant soy early on, but the beans didn't take. The fledgling crops of wheat and corn barely came up to his knees. Jaeger's crew was surviving on rationed nutrient stores from the *Osprey* and what fast-growing fruits and vegetables the greenhouses and hydroponics gardens could produce. That would've been plenty to see this crew of three hundred through the first two growing seasons until they had

A FOUND BEGINNING

a good surplus stored away and the meat labs in full operation.

They weren't only a crew of three hundred anymore. As Seeker approached the *Osprey*, nestled at the center of the burgeoning settlement, he saw the glittering snowflake of a Terrible ship hovering in silent rotation above one of the half-finished apartment buildings, lowering supply crates on long ropes.

Just that morning, Kwin had dropped the first five hundred new crewmen into that barracks, and more would be coming—soon. The Overseer captain supplied the *Osprey*'s fabricators with additional protein and fat stores, but he'd underestimated how many calories a human warrior required to stay fit. Even so, between the humans and Kwin's people, they could've figured out how to keep food production at a pace with human production.

Seeker strode into the *Osprey*'s open port wing and through the quiet administration hub.

What they couldn't do, he'd decided although the truth pained him, was find the food and aid to support another twenty thousand refugees on top of all else.

"Jack."

He turned to see Jaeger coming down the wide corridor with Baby ambling at her side.

"I didn't see you leave the funeral," he said.

She shook her head. She'd aged a decade in the last few weeks, he saw. Fine wrinkles of exhaustion and responsibility collected at the corners of her golden eyes. "The dead are patient. They can wait, so the living don't starve."

"So you agree with my assessment." Seeker folded his arms. "I'm sorry, Captain. We don't have the supplies to support our people adequately, and them." He glanced

147

upward, indicating the unseen fleet drifting millions of kilometers away in cold vacuum.

"We'll figure something out even if we're only sending them crates of radishes, at first. There are civilians up there. I won't let them starve if there's a single thing I can do about it. They lost stores and fabricators in the battle."

Seeker studied her incredulously. "You rebelled. You abandoned the Tribes. *You* made them our enemy."

"I did. It was the right thing to do if we were ever to find a *good* home. The right way means looking out for each other. Helping people in need." She looked up, gazing into his face. "We all have people up there," she said softly. "We won't allow them to compromise our principles. But we can't abandon them, either."

She was searching him, Seeker thought, but for what, he had no idea. She wasn't wrong. He had people up there too. He knew that much, even if he didn't remember their names. He remembered fighting alongside men and women who were like a forgotten family, too.

"I've made my choice. *This* is my crew, now. This is my home." He lifted a hand, wiggling his empty vape pen. "I'm out of juice and won't be fabricating more as long as rations are tight."

Her tired face cracked into a smile. She reached out and pressed her palm flat against his chest, where it rested warm and comfortable. Standing this close, he caught a whiff of her scent. Coconut and lemon.

"I'm glad. You've been a port in this storm, Jack. We can all run off into the sunset chasing our hopes and dreams, but you're the one who's been making sure there's food on the table and a roof over our heads when we get back. This settle-

A FOUND BEGINNING

ment wouldn't be half of what it is without your leadership and eye for logistics."

Seeker stared into her face. She expected him to say something, he was sure of that much, but he had no earthly idea what it might be.

"How fuckin' romantic."

Jaeger gasped like she'd been burned and snatched her hand back from Seeker, who whirled to see Toner sauntering out of the shadowy corridor behind them.

"I hate to interrupt," the pale man drawled, "but I also can't stand there in the toilet all day waiting for you to stop clogging up the hallway."

"What are you doing in here?" Jaeger asked.

"What are *you* doing in here?" Toner retorted. He eyed Seeker. "I've been going over battle reports. You slipped right into formation with those human fighters without a second thought, didn't you, Seeker?"

Seeker opened his mouth to answer, but Jaeger cut ahead of him. "And in doing so, saved Locaur. We can't afford to second-guess our command crew now, Toner. I trust him. That should be good enough for you."

Toner's bright gaze shifted back and forth from Seeker to Jaeger. "I think you're thinking with your other head, Captain. Or...whatever the lady equivalent is." He turned fully to Seeker. "Since I don't swing that way, I'll say it plainly. If you're gonna turn on us, *Jack*, could you at least do us the kindness of making it quick? I don't handle torture well."

"What the hell are you talking about?" Seeker asked.

"I mean." Toner pushed the tip of his finger into Seeker's chest, turning cold the place Jaeger's hand had made warm. "You were somebody to the fleet once. I'm pretty goddamned sure there are people up there who remember you and are gonna want you back. Since you don't remember them, that makes you vulnerable."

He poked Seeker's clavicle. Not painfully, but pointedly. Seeker studied the bony finger, debating the pros and cons of reaching up and snapping it in half. *Not worth it,* he decided. Toner wasn't a person to be put in his place. He was a burden to bear.

Behind them, Baby whiffed the growing animosity and let out a warning growl.

Toner stepped away from Seeker. "Just be careful, okay?" he said. "Don't trust them. There are good people in the Tribe, but their leadership will eat us alive if we let our guard down."

"I'll let the captain know if they approach me," Seeker said stiffly.

Toner nodded. Then he fished into his pocket and drew out a handful of raisins.

He offered his palm to Baby. "Hey, fartface. You still wanna kill me?"

Baby sniffed the offering, grumbled her annoyance, then leaned forward and snarfed up the treats. Toner winced and wiped his slobbery hand on his pants. Then he waved and left Seeker and Jaeger alone in the hallway.

"What did he mean by that?" Seeker turned back to the woman. "That you were thinking with—"

"He's an asshole," Jaeger said quickly. "I have a briefing with Kwin. I need to go."

"Thank you for that last shipment of nutritional stores." Jaeger slid into her chair at the conference table, across from Kwin and Udil. "The proteins and aminos are compatible with the

Osprey's fabricators. Can I ask where you got them? You sent us nearly three tons of the stuff, and your people don't consume protein like we do."

"Raw materials from our medical departments," Udil said primly. "When the captain decided we were going to activate a great number of embryos, we requestioned large quantities of basic biological building blocks."

"Oh." Jaeger hadn't had time for breakfast or lunch and had fabricated an afternoon meal for herself, glad that the Overseers didn't seem to find eating during meetings unusual. She looked down at the cup in her hands. It held lentil stew with ham, fabricated from the same materials used to turn pint-sized human embryos into full-grown adults. Biology was a strange thing.

"Now that Tsuan has intervened, however, we can assume that they will deny any further requisition orders. For this reason, and because it appears we are no longer in imminent danger of K'tax invasion, I have decided to halt any further production of embryos," Kwin added.

She nodded. "That leaves you with what, six thousand ready-made troops?"

"Eight, once the current batch completes the awakening sequence. I will hold the rest of our raw materials in reserve, ready to be used as either food or troop construction as necessary."

Jaeger winced. "Let's not lose sight of one thing, please. These aren't robots. They're not machines. They're living, breathing, sentient creatures with the right to self-determination."

"We have done our best to modify the behavioral pre-programming you warned us about," Udil said. "Based on our initial interviews with the humans, it appears the modifications are effective. They are not nearly as aggressive or Tribe-oriented as you had experienced."

Jaeger let out a little breath that sent curls of cumin-scented steam wafting across the table. "Speaking of the Tribe..."

"Initial reports from the Council are as we expected," Kwin said. "They are not amenable to allowing these refugees to establish permanent residence on Locaur."

"Neither are we, *carte blanche*," Jaeger said. "Still, we have to do something." Tribe Six had been broadcasting an endless stream of status reports down to the *Osprey*. Casualty lists, cargo manifests highlighting their rapidly dwindling supplies, videos of the overcrowded conditions, and the abject poverty.

It was manipulative propaganda and no less effective for her *knowing* it was propaganda. "Once they get desperate enough, they're going to try to land on the planet regardless. Perhaps Tsuan will be willing to allow those material requests to go through if we're using them to bribe the fleet to stay off Locaur."

"Perhaps." Kwin's mandibles *clicked* thoughtfully.

Something glimmered on the shell of Udil's left foreleg. It took Jaeger a moment to realize where she had seen that odd, angular light pattern before. It was Overseer script.

"You have a computer implant?" she asked, surprised, as Udil lifted the foreleg and examined it through her glittery, Christmas-ornament eyes.

"My body is seventy-six percent synthetic." Udil sniffed, making Jaeger flush. She'd wondered as much, given the Overseer's uniquely metallic carapace, but had thought it rude to ask.

"Our surveillance drones have reported a change in the activity of the K'tax fighters hiding in the asteroid belt,

A FOUND BEGINNING

Captain," the silver Overseer said, making Kwin turn sharply to face her.

"The beacon message hasn't changed, has it?" Jaeger asked. That worry had been niggling at the back of her mind ever since Occy had first warned her that Virgil was acutely interested in the possibility.

"Not that I can detect," Udil said. "As far as we can tell, until this moment, the stray K'tax fighters have been flying randomly through the asteroid belt like scattered *ragas* beasts after their nest's destruction." She paused for an agonizingly long moment, absorbing the new information pulsing across her carapace. Jaeger forced herself to shovel down the rest of her soup. She had no appetite, but she needed nourishment, and this was no time to be wasting food.

"Surveillance is reporting what appears to be coordinated activity among the fighters, but it is too early to say for certain what this new behavior pattern indicates," Udil decided.

Kwin's mandibles *snapped* together like tin snips. "Divert all available resources to monitoring the belt activity until we determine the source of this change."

"Whatever it is…" Jaeger scraped the last lump of spiced synthetic ham from her cup and forced herself to swallow it. "We have to assume it's not good."

CHAPTER NINETEEN

"Location secure," the Seeker said through Petra's commlink. "You're clear to land and begin operations, Secretary Potlova."

Petra glanced over her shoulder at the six people in sturdy exo-suits and the two dozen mining droids filling the cargo hold of the shuttle. She nodded, and the leader of the human crew gave her a thumbs-up. "You guys be careful out there," she said. "Gawd knows we can't afford any more injuries."

She activated the interior doors, sealing the shuttle cockpit from the cargo hold and closing her up in a little metal box. She waited a moment for the pressure to equalize and punched the sequence of buttons that activated the exterior doors.

"Doors are open," the mining chief reported over the comm channel. "Crew and droids unloaded. We're off and away, Secretary. Thanks for the lift."

Petra let out a nervous little sigh. She wrung her hands, counting to one hundred in her head before turning back to the shuttle control board and activating the liftoff sequence.

A FOUND BEGINNING

"Okay," she said, uncertain. "Next shuttle's gonna be here in two hours. Have fun mining an alien asteroid, boys."

On her display screen, said alien asteroid stretched ahead, a rocky moonscape of blasted craters and powdery white dust that briefly clouded over the cameras as she piloted the shuttle up and into the great sea of space. A squad of six Seeker jets swirled around the edges of her radar screen, patrolling the area in case any of those nasty bugs decided to wake up and make trouble for the miners.

All reports said that the mining operations were taking place far from the populated, hollow sections of the asteroids. As far as anyone could tell the aliens were in really deep hibernation, but you could never be too careful.

The fleet *needed* the raw minerals crusted over the asteroid's surface. They'd had to suspend repair operations of the *Vigilance* since there wasn't enough steel to repair the hull. An entire six sectors of living space closed off, forcing everyone to get all the cozier.

Still, Petra felt much better as the asteroid shrank in her rear viewscreen. She didn't like piloting such a little ship, but she was one of the few people in the logistics department who knew how. As soon as she had a free minute, she was gonna sit down and try real hard to remember *how* she knew how to fly a military cargo shuttle.

There was a logjam in the *Defiance*'s docking bay when Petra arrived. A good dozen ships drifted near the docks, waiting for their turn to offload people or cargo.

Petra scowled at the landing queue. A two-hour wait for the next available docking arm. She flipped to a private comms channel and hailed the docking manager. "This is Secretary Potlova," she said. "What's the holdup down there?"

The man who answered sounded like he'd been awake for

155

RAMY VANCE & MICHAEL ANDERLE

seventy-two hours and had an IV of epinephrine dripping constant mania into his blood.

Not that she knew anything about that.

"It's the goddamned Separatists," he growled. "They think they're doing us a huge fucking favor sending up these supplies, but they came in the middle of a shift change, and nobody knows where to send a thousand kilos of raw potatoes and kidney beans."

"Send them to kitchen storage," Petra suggested.

"What a great fuckin' idea, except that all of our kitchen storage units are currently *refugee* storage units. Who did you say you were? This channel is secure. How did you get on it?"

"Coms Secretary Potlova of the new civilian administration."

"Well, I didn't vote for you, *Secretary.* Unless you're offering to store all these potatoes up your twat, you can stay the fuck off my lines. I'm busy."

There was a *blurt* of static, and the line went dead. Petra blinked.

Then she entered her override code into the docking bay computer, skipping her shuttle to the head of the line. She'd only be occupying the docking arm for a minute, and she still had a lot of work to do before her shift was over.

She stepped out of her lonely shuttle and into a surge of commuters looking for a quick lift to the other freighter. Now that she had no more use for the ship, Transport was free to send it back to standard shuttling duty.

Petra ducked her head and elbowed her way through the ever-present docking tunnel crowd. The heat and smell were particularly bad after having the shuttle all to herself. A fresh layer of graffiti slathered long sections of the bulkhead.

Read the writing on the walls!

Land the Fleet Now! Build a New Home!
Silver and brass don't care about you!

That last one made Petra wince. They still hadn't found the human resources to send someone down here to clean off the graffiti, but she made a mental note to move it to a higher priority.

Most people barely remembered what happened in life before the wormhole. Instead of angsting about the past, it was time to move forward. As a secretary of silver—the new civilian government that ran the fleet arm-in-arm with the military—Petra worked day and night to make life better for everyone.

She only wished *everyone* would get with the program instead of wasting time rabble-rousing in the overcrowded corridors.

She reached the line of lifts at the end of the tunnel in time to see a familiar, black-coated man stepping onto a restricted-access platform.

"Bryce!" she waved her ID at the turnstile and hopped onto the lift beside him. "Thanks," she breathed as the platform slid into motion, pulling them out of the docking tunnel and down a long, blissfully quiet transport tube. "A two-hour delay over some potatoes," she marveled. "We gotta get someone down here to help the docking manager. Poor guy's gonna give himself a heart attack."

"I'm sure the problems will clear up quickly with your help."

Petra flashed the major a smile. She was comfortable doing so now that she had shiny new teeth slotted into her gums. Besides, Bryce was good-looking. Young but cute. "You're a charmer, Major. Hey, you wanna grab lunch some time? There's this new potato dish I wanna try."

Bryce snorted into his computer, a sound she took for a suppressed chuckle. The lift platform stopped.

"I'm awfully busy, Miss Potlova," he said as they stepped onto the bridge level. "I'll have my people call your people." With a nod, he split down the left corridor toward the Seeker C&C. Petra went straight past a few small offices, which were bustling, but not nearly as crammed as the rest of the fleet. Her comm line beeped, and she flipped it open.

"Sypher! How ya doin', honey? I was beginnin' ta think ya forgot all about me."

The surly pilot on the other end of her line grunted. "More like you forgot about us, Miz Petie. You was supposed ta come help clean out the *Bitch* this morning like we planned."

Petra stopped in front of the doors to Ops. "Oh, honey, I'm sorry. I meant to send you a message but I got so wrapped up in work. I needed to run a shuttle of miners off to an asteroid. There was no one else who could do it and—"

"I know ya busy, girl," Sypher grumbled. "We jus' can't keep puttin' this off forever. Suits from silver crawling up my ass about housin' more people on the *Bitch* and…"

Petra's stomach did a little somersault. There was a dirty little secret in the *Bitch*. Well, more like hundreds of them— written all over the darned bulkhead, and Petra and her friends hadn't yet pieced together what even half of them meant. Petra's common sense told her that they weren't worth worrying over—like the graffiti in the tunnels, they were stuck in the past—but still.

She wanted to know everything they'd written, before silver scrubbed it away.

Petra's voice dropped. "I'll meet you at the lower docks this evening," she whispered to Sypher. "After Sim and I get supper. In the meantime, I'll see what I can do to get silver off your butt."

"Don' blow me off again," Sypher grunted before hanging up.

Petra drew in a few steadying breaths before putting on her best work smile and stepping into Ops. She was surprised to see all the workstations with their urgent blinking lights and *beeps* were empty. Instead, the entire Ops staff of nearly two dozen people huddled on the platform in front of the grand display screen. On the screen, the bright blue and green planet called Locaur floated against a backdrop of stars, like it had been for days, so that nobody would forget what they were working for.

She heard murmuring from the crowd, which split as she approached.

There, standing at the center of the platform, surrounded by keen listeners, was a little man in a clean, knee-length lab coat over a black and silver uniform. His face split into a smile when he saw Petra.

"Petie! Glad you could make it," said Professor Grayson, interim prime minister of the silver government. "We were about to do a little team-building exercise. Care to join us?"

CHAPTER TWENTY

Sim doubled over, laughing until soup came out of her nose. The laughter turned to coughs. Petra reached across the tiny table and thumped the girl between the shoulder blades.

"Oh my God." Sim straightened, wiping her mouth with the back of her wrist. "*Team-building?* Victor's such a dork."

Petra's concern broke. She grinned. Probably it wasn't okay for Sim, a droid technician's apprentice, to call the prime minister by his first name, but Petra liked that about the girl. At a scant eighteen years old, Sim could look the leader of the entire fleet in the eye, smile, and call him by his name—and nobody would object. Not even Minister Grayson, who always asked after Sim like they were old friends, too.

After Petra's shift ended, she'd swung down to the tertiary droid bay to wait for Sim to clean up, and they'd wandered up to the concourse for dinner. They'd been lucky enough to hit this little canteen before the worst of the dinner rush and had crammed into a tiny side booth originally designed to let a single person squeeze in a cup of coffee on her morning break.

A FOUND BEGINNING

But, well, it seemed like lots of things weren't being used for their original purpose. A line had already formed at the food counter, at least sixty people long. All of them looked tired and guarded their ration cards closely, waiting for their chance at tonight's fare of watery potato soup and a dinner roll fabricated from low-quality carbohydrates.

"It wasn't so bad," Petra allowed, taking another spoonful of her soup. She pulled her elbows tight to her sides to keep them from sticking out and clipping the dull-eyed people who walked past. She grimaced. "Gawd, what I'd do for a bit of pepper."

"So what did you do?" Sim's eyes glittered golden in the dim light. "In your *team-building* exercise?"

Petra shrugged. "Okay, so…first we did this thing where we all got in a circle and took turns telling the person to our left one thing we appreciated about 'em. I got Janice. Have you met Janice? Minister Grayson's personal assistant? She's that older gal with the blue veins?

"Anyway the lady has a marvelous singin' voice, is what I told her. Coulda been famous." Petra paused, chewing a lump of potato thoughtfully as she recalled the distant look that had flickered over Janice's face. "For a moment, it seemed like it touched on somethin'," she murmured.

"A memory?" Sim ventured.

Petra shrugged and offered the girl her dinner roll. One of the perks of working in the heart of the silver government was that Ops provided a nice lunch for all the public officials. Most days, Petra could eat her fill of fabricated rice and beans. Sim took the roll without a word. She was a growing girl, always hungry.

"The game ended and I didn't get a chance to ask her." Petra sighed. "People from the health department arrived and gave us some immune-boosting shots. Oh, make sure you get one too," she added absently. "As soon as they're available to your department. Real worried about disease spreading when we're all crammed together like this. Then the minister wanted to get on to our meeting. We got the first part of the Wormhole Report all polished up. You'll see it on TNN tonight if you're around a screen."

Sim shook her head, swallowing a dry lump of bread. She reached for the shared water glass between them. "No, I gotta go back on duty at 1900."

"You're working another shift?" Petra frowned as Sim's cheeks flushed a darker shade of copper. "Girl, you gotta sleep sometime."

"We've got a backlog of repair orders a kilometer long." Sim shifted her weight, her glance skittering off to the side.

Petra frowned. "You were already outta the room by the time I woke up this morning. Are you getting enough sleep?"

"I don't need much sleep."

Petra studied her young ward curiously. "Bad dreams?" She pitched her voice low. Lots of people were having bad dreams lately. No shame in that. Between the wormhole memory mess and the battle with the aliens and the awful soup, anyone with a pulse should be having nightmares.

Sim hesitated. "No," she said finally. "No. I don't, um…" she looked down, fidgeting. "I haven't had any dreams at all, Petie."

Petra blinked. She didn't know what to say.

"I'm sure I just don't remember them," Sim added quickly. "Anyway, it doesn't matter. I'm doing fine, and I can help. I want to help. Lots of people don't remember anything about before, so I'm not special. The fleet needs me, and I need to feel useful."

A FOUND BEGINNING

She drew in a breath, lifted her cup to her mouth, and drained the last of her soup. Then she squared her shoulders. "Since I'm going to be elbow-deep in droid guts tonight, why don't you give me the skinny on that report right now?"

"Oh, sure." Petra forced her thoughts away from Sim's curious sleep problem. "There's a whole team of computer scientists up in Ops who've been doing nothin' but combin' the records since the moment we came out of that wormhole, trying to piece together what happened. Looks like there were food riots in the fleet not so long ago. People real unhappy with the way the military was running the place, so we cooked up this idea of a civilian government to share power."

"The silver," Sim supplied.

"Right. After some negotiation, brass agreed to let us all have elections for the ministers." She pressed her lips together and blew a raspberry. "We were tallying up the last votes when we fell through the wormhole. That ain't no way to start a new government, is it?" She shivered, wrapping her hands around her elbows. "Gawd, it's a miracle we've managed to hold everything together peacefully these last few days."

"I'm glad," Sim said quietly. "Things are bad enough without a civil war."

"From your lips." Petra checked the time on her computer. "To gawd's ears—oh!" She hopped to her feet. "Oh no." Hastily, she wiped her face and straightened her hair pins. "I'm late. I'm late to meet Sypher *again*. He's gonna have my head..."

Sim pushed out of the tiny booth with a smile. Petra was always dimly surprised to see how *tall* the girl had gotten. Then she was surprised by her surprise. There must be *some* memories trying to bubble to the surface, but hand to gawd, she would say she'd never seen this girl before in her life

163

before the minister had reunited them in the *Defiance's* atrium.

No memory, but the skinny dark arms that enveloped Petra were undeniably the arms of a lifelong friend. The unique scent of Sim's sweet musk and the grease beneath her fingernails were familiar. The goodbye kiss they shared, cheek-to-cheek, was as comfortable as an old and well-worn pair of boots.

"You make sure you get a nap before your shift," Petra insisted, as another pair of diners shuffled them aside to take their booth. "I wanna see you back in the apartment when I wake up tomorrow, okay?"

Sim stuck out her tongue, gently mocking as they drifted apart in the crowd. "Whatever you say, *mom*."

Whatever you say, mom.

The words echoed between Petra's ears as she made her way down the grand terminal toward the outer docking rings.

Sharp as a bee sting and sweet as honey, those words were.

I ain't your ma, am I? As badly as Petra wanted it to be true, she only had to look into a mirror to know she wasn't the girl's blood relative. That someone else, some other woman with Sim's shining dark skin and lovely golden eyes could claim her for kin. Some somber-faced stranger, who spoke pretty words about regret and love, but couldn't bother to hug her child.

Petra was being uncharitable, she knew. If Petra were worried about spreading some alien fungus, she'd be careful about who she hugged, too. Especially if you might accidentally spread a spore to your long-lost daughter.

A FOUND BEGINNING

Still, Petra thought. It was *her* shoulder Sim had cried on the night after that awkward meeting when this stranger claiming to be her mother refused to hug her. Whoever this Captain Jaeger was, *she* hadn't taken Sim in from off the streets and slept beside her in a tiny single-room apartment every night. She didn't huddle with the girl in the early hours of the morning, offering sage advice on how to handle handsy boys or nasty supervisors.

Neither have you, an ugly voice whispered in the back of Petra's mind.

She shoved it aside. That was silly. Just because Petra couldn't remember life before the wormhole didn't mean it wasn't real. Down in the pit of her stomach, it *felt* real. The minister had records showing that Petra had been Sim's legal guardian for over a year since the girl had turned up in the lower decks.

Still, the doubts made her sick, and she was still biting back a swirl of nausea by the time she reached the outer ring. A gaggle of people, some in official silver uniforms, some well-dressed civilians, crowded around Harlan as he guarded the *Bitch*'s airlock portal.

"Every other ship docked in this ring has taken on additional occupants," growled a man in a sash that marked him as an undersecretary of public health. He lurched toward Harlan, who folded his corded arms, set his jaw, and remained silent as flecks of spittle decorated the front of his shirt. "It is your *duty* as a member of this Tribe to aid—"

"What's this ruckus all about now?" Petra sniffed in a deep breath of stale air and pushed—politely but firmly—through the gaggle. Harlan and the undersecretary turned. She waved her ID for the undersecretary before putting it back into her pocket. "Potlova, logistical secretary."

RAMY VANCE & MICHAEL ANDERLE

The undersecretary's scowl deepened. "Captain Sypher and First Mate Harlan of the—" he consulted his computer. "*Claw*—"

"She's the *Bitch*," Harlan growled, making Petra wince.

"She's registered as the *Claw*," the undersecretary plowed on, giving Harlan a dark look. "Which is a *much* more appropriate name for an official ship in the Tribe Six fleet—"

Harlan turned to Petra and gestured at the gaggle of men and women in the corridor. By their suitcases, Petra supposed they were refugees displaced from the *Vigilance*. By the quality of their clothes and the wafts of perfume, they must've been from the *rich* parts of the *Vigilance*. They all looked as unhappy about the situation as Harlan. "He wants to quarter all these people on our ship, and we don't have enough bunks for all of them. The *Bitch* is only designed to run with a permanent crew of six—"

"The *Claw* has ample space to house these people, and I am thirty seconds from calling down the Seekers and having these men removed from her command!" the undersecretary barked, making the people murmur and fidget.

Petra waved for silence. When the crowd stilled, she turned back to the undersecretary. "There's a little alcove halfway up the sector hall where a man is distributing coffee and rolls," she murmured. "Send your people up that way to wait a little longer."

She lifted a hand, cutting off his objection. "I'll add the rations to their accounts if they've already had supper. Just keep them happy for a couple of hours." She glanced over her shoulder at the *Bitch*'s airlock. "I'll talk to her crew and make sure this ship is open to take new occupants by 2100 tonight. Got it?"

With her eyes, she urged the sour-looking man to accept

the deal as she crossed her fingers and prayed that the five hours between now and 2100 would be enough time to analyze and scrub all the writing on the *Bitch*'s inner bulkheads. She *really* shouldn't have waited this long to get down here.

"There's an extra coffee in it for you, too," Petra added in a whisper. "With sugar, if you want."

Finally, the undersecretary relented and turned to shepherd his complaining flock back up the corridor.

"2100," he told Petra. "Then I'm calling in the Seekers."

Petra barely had time to catch her breath before Harlan grabbed her by the arm and pulled her into the *Bitch*.

CHAPTER TWENTY-ONE

With Harlan tugging her along, Petra tumbled into the *Bitch's* main corridor only to be met by a cloud of industrial-strength cleaner fumes. She doubled over coughing. Snot and tears streamed down her cheeks. "Oh—Oh gawd—"

Someone shoved an old thermal hood with a rebreather into her hands, and she tugged it over her head. The acid stench of gawd-knew-what they put in those cleaners faded behind the close reek of a sweaty gym sock. *Someone* didn't prioritize keeping his gear clean. Still, it was better than choking on ammonia fumes and keeling over dead.

"What the heck are you guys doing in here?" Catching her breath, Petra straightened to see Sypher scrubbing the bulkheads with big brushes strapped to his hands. The wiry man wore a hood of his own, stained undershirt and boxers, and not much else. When Petra had last left the *Bitch*, scrawled notes covered every open centimeter of the cramped corridor. The soap suds dripping from every flat surface ran dark with purged grease pencil and marker ink.

"I took seven kinds 'a pictures and videos from e'ry direc-

A FOUND BEGINNING

tion," Sypher grunted through his hood. "Couldn't wait ta start cleanin', wid de health department poundin' down my door, and you always so busy."

Petra didn't allow herself to acknowledge the guilt that knocked at her door. Instead, she turned to see Harlan stooping to grab a fresh cleaning rag from a bucket of soapy water. He'd donned his hood too.

"Grease pencil is *designed* not to wash off easily." The younger man grunted. "It's why we had to bring out the strong cleaner. Sorry, Petie, but this is a bigger job than we thought." He jerked a thumb over his shoulder, indicating the cockpit. "Got all the visual records on a drive in there for you to go over."

"You've started washing it *all* away?" Petra was dismayed, though she couldn't blame the men for getting to work. With silver pressuring them to take on new residents, they couldn't risk some stiff-necked MP sort getting a good look at all the nasty sedition scrawled across her interior. Especially since it was well-known that Petra herself, the silver secretary of logistics, had come through the wormhole on this very ship.

Still, she worried that some vital secret of their past, scrawled across some angle or plane that Harlan hadn't managed to capture in pictures, might have been washed away in all those greasy suds.

"Got everything but the crew bunks," Sypher confirmed, his corded, old-man muscles bulging against his too-small shirt as he reached over his head to scrub a line of writing from the air ducts. "So if ya need a look, go get it now."

169

The door to the crew bunk slid shut, and Petra sank into a hammock with a deep sigh. The air purifier system sensed a human presence and rattled to life. Petra checked the system, confirmed that it had adequately scrubbed the nasty fumes from the air filtering out of the vents, and pulled off her thermal hood. She sucked in a deep breath of relatively clean air, which still stank of industrial oil and the close scents of sweaty people and unwashed bodies.

She stared around the tiny cabin. Rows of a dozen sleeping hammocks dangled down the narrow corridor, all but four of them utterly devoid of any personalization. Petra remembered the wealthy-looking refugees waiting in the *Defiant's* lower corridors. Their fancy luggage wouldn't fit in the tiny personal lockers alongside each hammock bunk.

If Petra thought being here might spark a memory, she was as disappointed as she'd been every time she tried to remember anything in the last few days. More so, in fact. This place felt alien to her. At least she had Sim to share her closet-sized apartment up in the residential sector.

Once her eyes adjusted to the dim light, Petra studied the different handwriting scrawled across the bulkhead beside each of the hammocks. Sypher's spare multitool and utility belt were slung lazily in the hammock across from her, along with a pair of only slightly stained underwear. *You are captain of this Bitch!* was exclaimed in big, shaky letters, like those of a kid just learning to use a pen.

Harlan is your son, and you love him and his deceased mama. He gets his feelings hurt easy but knows how to take care of the ship real good.

Petra smiled. She lifted her gaze to the hammock dangling

above Sypher's. Harlan's handwriting was small and sloppy with the grease lines smeared into illegibility in many spots. Mostly, he wrote about the *Bitch*.

> *There's a code read error in the navigation autopilot computer. If it tells you the ship can't make a sub-light trip of over sixty thousand kilometers, don't believe it. The AG-thermal regulators are unreliable. Get them replaced as soon as you can afford it. Don't let Sypher (Dad) forget to take his heart medicine.*

The list went on and on.

Pulling herself up, Petra turned to study the hammock across from Harlan's. The notes on Petra's legs had mentioned Amy only to say that she was a trustworthy friend, but the girl had vanished from the *Bitch* shortly after they'd docked with the *Defiant*. No one had seen or heard from her since. Frowning, Petra read the swirly bubble letters scrawled across Amy's bulkhead.

> *Fleet brass <u>wants</u> us to go through the wormhole. They hope that resetting our memories will stop our rebellion. DON'T LET IT. They killed Rush. They've been experimenting on civilians and hiding the truth from us. Don't trust Kelba. Don't trust Grayson. THEY WANT YOU TO FORGET. Trust Misha. Trust Rush. Trust Petie. Trust Jaeger. Don't let the truth die!*

Petra nibbled her thumbnail and studied the words for a long time, hoping they would lead to some new insight.

Well, Petra certainly trusted Sim, but she suspected that might not be the Jaeger that Amy meant. Sim, after all, had woken up from the wormhole passage in a medical bay on some minor fleet ship, without the benefit of notes scribbled all across her bare skin. Ship records suggested she might've been in treatment for some kind of head injury when the jump happened—and Petra hadn't pressed her too hard about all this rebellion stuff. If the girl wasn't involved, Petra didn't want to *get* her involved.

Probably, Petra was supposed to trust this other Jaeger. The older woman, the mutineer captain.

Who was Misha? Who was Rush? Surely not that rock musician whose songs they played in some canteens between meals. And, gawd, of all people, why was *Petra* herself someone so worthy of trust?

Most troubling of all were the names *Kelba* and *Grayson* scrawled up there, in the "no good" column. Petra had met Fleet Captain Kelba once in passing, and aside from her unreasonable looks, Petra had seen nothing in the head brass, the Seekers' leader, to ring alarm bells. And Grayson? Well, first of all, the man was silver, not brass, but maybe Amy was trying to say that Grayson *had* been brass before the wormhole. If that was true, why would they have elected him leader of the civilian government?

Petra studied the list of Amy's grievances against brass. Many of them echoed the notes Petra had found scrawled across her own arms and legs that strange first day.

—Serenity: A gene therapy treatment pushed on civilians, meant to make the people stupid and docile.

Well, sure, that sounded bad, except that Petra hadn't found a darned thing about this 'Serenity,' or any other sort of mind-control gene therapy, *anywhere* in the databases—which were still a big jumbled mess.

—Riella 3 was a good candidate for settlement before the Seekers went to war with the native aliens and got us driven away. There

have been other planets. Brass doesn't want to share. Brass wants to DOMINATE.

Even if that was true in the past—and Petra wasn't saying either way—it didn't appear to be the case right now. Heck, right now people were living in cramped squalor and surviving on less than a thousand calories a day, *wishing* silver and brass would push harder to let people go live on that pretty blue and green planet right outside the window. *So we got what we wanted,* Petra thought, frustrated with Amy's silent arguments. *We got brass to pull the chute and slow down and do it right by negotiating with the locals. Isn't this what you wanted?*

Is this what WE wanted?

With a groan of frustration, Petra sank into her hammock and let the gentle rocking soothe away her growing headache. Something was deeply wrong. There was no denying that, but she had no idea *what*—and what was worse, she didn't know how to begin to move forward when everything in her rear viewscreen was one big gaping void of *nothing*, except these notes from strangers. She'd come hoping for some fresh insight and found nothing to spark understanding.

Finally, she opened her eyes and studied the narrow section of bulkhead lining her little hammock nook. Lines, written in lipstick and old mascara, told her to trust one person or distrust another. If Petra had written these words for herself, she'd done so with the idea that they only needed to spark some dim memory and that the right combination would make her past spill up from its nap. That wasn't the case.

Petra, Sarah, Larry = From the Beginning

An old scrap of paper stuck to the bulkhead with little bits of adhesive gum, blank or so faded it might as well have been. Some artifact from a crew member who'd occupied this bunk before Petra, she'd assumed. Now she frowned. The mad writer with the lipstick hadn't cared about this relic and scrawled her note straight across the paper. The word "begin" was crimson across its surface.

"Back to the beginning..." Petra mouthed, remembering what Captain Jaeger's first mate had told her.

Petra slipped a fingernail beneath the adhesive gum and scraped until a corner popped free. She leaned closer, pressing her head to the wall. Her frown deepened. There was something on the back of the paper. Probably nothing, but with the clock ticking, there was no sense in leaving any stone unturned. Wedging her fingernails beneath the adhesive, she pried the rest of the paper off the wall, afraid of tearing the brittle old material.

It fluttered free, and Petra flicked on her overhead light to get a better look.

It was a photograph, yellowed with age and tattered at the edges. A group of people in basic military uniforms stood on the catwalk of some docking bay. She didn't recognize most of the folks grinning into the camera, but she'd guess they were all roughly her age.

Petra's breath caught. At first, she thought the small, dark-haired woman sitting on the rail at the edge of the group, staring intently into the camera, was Sim. But no. Her cheeks were broader, her skin darker, and her posture somehow *angrier*. Not Sim, Petra realized, but Captain Jaeger. Standing nearby was Petra herself, grinning and waving, her free hand wrapped around the waist of a skinny fella—the only one in the picture not in uniform but in a gray flight suit.

Toner, Petra thought, amazed. That was the pale, glowering man who'd been shadowing Jaeger during that one brief

A FOUND BEGINNING

meeting. Here he was in the picture, not glowering but *grinning* as he held Petra close.

Something knotted in Petra's belly. *Never doubt I love*, had been his last words to her. At the time, she'd been a little charmed but mostly uncomfortable with receiving poetry from a stranger who was admittedly not much of a looker.

Now, seeing the sweet affection on those little printed faces, she didn't doubt there was love. Or, at least, there had been. Once.

We go back to the beginning, he'd said.

Petra turned the picture over to see "begin" smeared across the back in red grease.

"Start from the beginning," had been the words scrawled over her calf.

Holding her breath against hope, Petra reached out and pressed fingers against the bulkhead, where the picture had been. The one square of clean, empty bulkhead in the entire room.

The little panel, which only the adhesive gum had held in place, now jiggled beneath her fingertips. It popped free to reveal a small cubby in the void between air ducts. Lying at the center of the cubby was a simple gray memory drive, about the size of her thumb.

"Oh, gawd." Petra reached to pull her computer out from where it wedged between her butt and the hammock. "This better not be some nasty trick."

With her heart *thudding* in her temples, Petra rebooted her computer, disconnected it from the fleet network, and plugged in the memory stick.

A new window appeared on her screen as a video automatically began to play. For the second time in as many minutes, Petra felt the faint sense of vertigo that comes from turning a corner and coming face-to-face with *yourself.*

"Hi, Petie." The woman on the screen gave a tiny smile, though she looked like she hadn't slept in days. "I'll bet you've had a rough time. I'm sorry for hiding this file from you, but I had to make sure *you* got it first and not someone else. Misha and Danny, they gave me this stick. They're techs from the Astrolab, and they busted me out of there after brass had me arrested, so they're on our side."

Her tired smile wavered. "Or they were. I don't know if they survived the fighting. Either way, they're heroes. They risked everything to get us *this* memory drive. They say they formatted it using some fancy trick to protect it from getting scrambled when we go through the wormhole." She lifted her crossed fingers, her smile widening enough to show the void where her two front teeth should've been. "So let's hope, huh?"

Petra nodded.

"All their data on Reset and Serenity should still be safe and sound, unaltered by fleet propaganda. I don't have much time, but I've included as many personal videos as I can. So here you go, honey." The woman on the screen blew a kiss, which Petra caught without thinking, and pressed to her cheek. "Here's all the truth I can give ya, on such short notice. This Reset stuff will be a huge setback, but we gotta keep moving forward. One step at a time."

CHAPTER TWENTY-TWO

Occy studied the screen. "I see what you mean," he said after a moment's contemplation. He tapped his computer, enlarging a particular section of radio wave-form. It was the Forebear beacon as received by the *Osprey*'s most sensitive equipment. "It's not only static and random variation. My algorithms are picking out non-random data in the signal, too."

"A signal *within* the signal," Virgil supplied.

Occy pressed his lips together and nodded. He swung in his chair, pushing himself across the engineering office workstation to another set of screens, where he drew up the beacon signal again.

"Science officers on the *Terrible* confirm that the content of the beacon signal directed at the K'tax has not changed." Moss had a slow, dreamy sort of voice that made Occy want to offer it a cup of the captain's black-strap coffee.

"That can't be true," Occy decided. "Because the K'tax *response* has changed. The behavior of the fighters has changed."

"The Overseers are lying to us." Where it rested in the

177

corner of the office, Virgil's repair droid rose on its four slender legs and studied the enhanced wave-form over Occy's shoulder.

Occy shook his head. "If the confirmation was coming from Tsuan, maybe. But Kwin's people have nothing to gain and a lot to lose by lying to us."

"Nevertheless," Virgil said patiently. "Surveillance reports are undeniable. The surviving K'tax fighters have assumed swarming behavior once more. Whatever this signal variation is, it means something *to them*."

"Aimless swarm behavior," Occy relented. "Swimming through the asteroid belt like…a school of fish, or something. The rest of the swarm, it's still way out in subspace. It hasn't moved. The K'tax hibernating on the asteroids—they're still sleeping."

"K'tax fighters are a strange case," Virgil pointed out. "They are not mere machines piloted by specially trained worker or fighter morphs. They *are* morphs, cybernetically altered to be space-worthy."

Occy shuddered. He reached out with one long tentacle and found the edge of Baby's bulk, napping between two stacks of servers. She shifted into his tentacle as he scratched her folds of flesh. "Like if someone surgically added rocket boosters and guns to Baby," he muttered.

"Perhaps this secondary signal is something that can only be received and decoded by their mechanical parts," Virgil suggested. "It would explain why the hibernating K'tax and the larger swarm aren't also behaving differently."

That struck Occy as a strange comment. They conducted *all* long-distance communication through "mechanical parts." As a computer itself, Virgil ought to understand that better than anybody.

He turned this idea over carefully as Virgil and Moss squabbled.

"Or perhaps," Moss suggested in a whisper trickled down from the speakers, "the secondary signal and the change in K'tax behavior are unrelated phenomena."

Can only be decoded by mechanical parts, Occy mused. *It's as if Virgil thinks us pure biologicals can somehow pick up radio and FTL comm waves the way it can.*

For a moment, Virgil had apparently forgotten that creatures of flesh and blood didn't work that way.

It would explain a lot if K'tax could pick up signals like a radio. He glanced over at his telemetry data. From what they understood of K'tax behavior and from Overseer observations, the species didn't depend on computers to nearly the degree one would expect of such a widespread, space-faring race. How they communicated and coordinated at a distance was something of a mystery.

"Far-fetched," Virgil dismissed.

"The secondary signal lay buried in the prime beacon from the beginning," Moss pointed out. "The fighter behavior changed only recently."

Realization struck Occy like a hammer to the face. "It's the fungus."

Moss seemed to think this was a direct counterargument. "Records indicate that the fungal infection has been a prevalent aspect of K'tax physiology long before the beacon—"

Occy waved his tentacles, frantically gesturing for silence as he scrabbled at a strange idea. "The fungus grows throughout their nervous systems. *It* is what's picking up the beacon. It's not a computer, at least not in a traditional sense, but it's performing the function of one. Picking up and decoding the signal and executing a response. That's why the

K'tax all responded to it so quickly. They're being mind-controlled."

"Of course," Virgil said.

Occy turned a dark glare on the repair droid hunkered over his workstation. "What do you mean 'of course?'"

"The Forebears developed this fungal organism specifically as a means to control the K'tax sub-race. You are correct, of course, that it must therefore also contain the means by which the Forebears, or their descendants, could direct their slave army. Clearly, the Forebear beacon contains within itself some signal or pattern specifically tailored to activate this fungal control."

"You suspected this much already?" Occy's voice rose to a shout. "For how long?"

"About ten seconds," Virgil said. "Your insight was integral to the formulation of my theory."

Occy resisted the temptation to pound his fist against something. Baby picked up on the tension in the air, lumbered to her feet, and stretched like a cat. Her claws raked against the deck like nails on a chalkboard. Then she settled down again.

"Which means that our suspicions were true, and ultimate control over the fungal behavior, and thus the K'tax as a whole, lies within the Forebear beacon sub-routines," Virgil decided.

Occy covered his mouth to hold in a whoop of mingled triumph and frustration. He pinched his thumb and forefinger together. "We were *this close* to getting down to the core of it before the chamber flooded. Oh!" His eyes bulged with another fantastic idea.

"None of this explains the secondary signal or the change

A FOUND BEGINNING

in fighter behavior," allowed Moss, who had trouble picking out a forest from trees.

Occy waved her silent again. "Virgil, there's a good chance the two isolated copies of *you* are still down there—interfaced with the Forebear mainframe. The beacon. What if that's what this is?" He jabbed a tentacle toward the isolated secondary signal waveform. "What if that's *you*, still trying to figure out how to use the Forebear programs? Or what if that's you, *trying to talk to us?*"

Virgil had gone as still as a statue, but Occy was too excited to notice. He flung himself into his chair and spun to pull up specs on the *Osprey*'s original AI program. "We have *got* to get back into the Forebear mainframe, Virgil. That beacon is how the Forebears intended to control their doomsday weapon. If we can figure out how to *use* it, master it, then the K'tax will stop being a problem. Forever."

With a few taps, Occy sent the relevant data files to the captain, uploaded them to his new personal computer, and sprang to his feet. The captain was smart, but she needed someone to explain the details to her, and this couldn't wait.

"Tsuan has forbidden all further explorations into Forebear technology," Virgil murmured, making Occy skid to a halt halfway out of his office. Baby lumbered to her feet, shook herself off, and ambled to join Occy.

Occy stared at the frozen repair droid. "What's wrong with you?" he asked quietly.

Virgil didn't move.

"You're not acting like..." Occy licked his lips, floundered, and used the closest word he could think of. "Yourself."

"Myself?" The repair droid shifted, bringing its visual sensors up to focus on Occy. "Chief Engineer, I exist as an artificial intelligence network distributed across eighteen different repair droids, two of which are currently isolated from myself, likely half-integrated with an unfathomable alien computer, and behaving in ways that I cannot comprehend. What, exactly, does 'behaving like myself' mean?"

Occy's excitement slipped away like water down a drain. He looked down to see the tip of his tentacles tapping restlessly against the floor, eager to be going. He almost laughed.

Then, surprising himself, he reached out and put a hand on Virgil's cold metal skin. The sensor array turned, evaluating his outstretched arm. Occy had seen these droids from the other side of a battle line before. He'd seen them covered in blood, attacking crew that he barely remembered. Somewhere deep inside Occy, a little part of him was still terrified by this rogue AI, and what it had done, and what it could do.

Or maybe not. Maybe those parts had dropped off him when he'd shed his tentacles.

"That sounds scary." He lifted his chin to look Virgil dead in the sensor array. "To not understand what little parts of yourself are doing or why." He lifted his tentacles out of their malaise, waving them gently in the air. The effort of swinging around their weight without the aid of water or zero-G made his shoulder muscles burn.

"These things kind of have a mind of their own, too. I don't always know what they're doing. I don't always understand them." He flushed. Beside him, Baby turned her nub of a head and sniffled, sensing his rising temperature, but he forced himself to keep speaking. "Sometimes," he said softly, "I really hate them. I…I asked Elaphus if she could cut them all away and give me a regular arm instead."

Virgil didn't speak for a moment, for which Occy was grateful. He swallowed and continued, "So I don't know what I am in relation to *me*. I do know what I am as part of a bigger whole. As a member of the crew, as part of a family. When I can't figure out what I'm supposed to do, what I'm supposed to be, it's my *friends* who keep me grounded."

He waited, hardly daring to breathe, until Virgil's servos whirred, and it strode toward the door. "Yes," it dismissed as it passed into the port wing corridor. "But you are *human.*"

CHAPTER TWENTY-THREE

I think you're thinking with your other head, Captain.

Seeker realized what Toner had *meant* about thirty seconds after parting ways with Captain Jaeger. He spent the next day and a half walking around with a bug chewing on the back of his brain and awkwardly shuffling into the shadows any time he glimpsed the captain on the other side of the busy administration hub.

"Is there...something wrong?" Bufo asked carefully, watching as Seeker edged his chair around a stack of storage crates for the third time during their morning briefing.

"Nope."

Toner was a lying jackass who enjoyed serving up bullshit stew. Seeker *knew* that. If you took away the man's ability to spout random lies, he'd asphyxiate and die because it was the only way he knew how to breathe.

That little warm patch on his chest where she'd rested her hand was a kind of rash he'd picked up from the forest. Allergies. Or maybe indigestion.

Across the makeshift desk, Bufo droned on about crew

rosters. "With half the crew still recovering from injury and the other half put on training duty overseeing Kwin's new troops, we're short one pilot for the midday system patrol..."

Seeker's attention snapped to Bufo. "System patrol?"

Bufo consulted his computer. "Portia requested there be at least one crewed patrol of the inner solar system every twenty-four hours. To make sure the surveillance drones and bots aren't telling us lies. It's a fair request, but I don't have the human resources for it—"

Seeker pushed to his feet, making Bufo hop, startled, out of his chair.

"I'll do it. I'll go now. I miss my ship." Completely unrelated to his decision was the captain, working her way across the hub in his general direction.

"Weren't you about to go off-duty-?" Bufo asked.

"Sleep is for the weak, Sergeant." Seeker turned and made for the fighter bay.

Seeker stared at his display screen and willed the scene before him to make sense.

It did not.

Three hours into his patrol of the inner system, he decided to run a drive-by scan of one of the K'tax asteroids that had settled into an irregular orbit around Locaur's sun after the battle. All sensor readings and surveillance bots suggested that the K'tax living inside those asteroids remained in deep hibernation, but Portia was right. It never hurt to be sure.

So when Seeker arced his fighter into a flight path over the light side of the asteroid and saw the bustle of activity in the bowl of some ancient crater, he nearly had a heart attack.

RAMY VANCE & MICHAEL ANDERLE

Realizing that was a *fleet* shuttle down there beside a *fleet*-model outpost mitigated his alarm somewhat but only deepened his confusion. He opened his comm channel and hailed the outpost.

"This is…" He hesitated, for some reason uncertain about giving his name. "Base commander of the *Osprey*'s crew. You're conducting what might be a very dangerous operation, and you are deep in enemy territory. I need to know what the hell you people are doing down there."

There was a long, long pause of static. Seeker was about to repeat the message when the line blurted.

"I was wondering how long it would take you to notice. You're a long way from any base, base commander…" The man at the other end of the line had an easygoing, smooth voice, though he sounded somehow dazed, and that made Seeker's frown deepen into a scowl.

"We patrol the system regularly," he said gruffly. "I really hope I'm not seeing what I think I'm seeing. Those look like mining droids. Please tell me the fleet isn't bumfuck crazy enough to mine resources *directly off an enemy vessel.*"

There was another contemplative pause. "I see how this might be concerning, but I assure you, *base commander*, our operations are secure." The man at the other end of the line hesitated again. "More than secure. Incredibly fruitful, in fact. We have nothing to hide, and I'm sure your captain will want to know about it. Why don't you land and I'll give you a tour?"

Seeker stared at his blank comms screen. It was a weird-as-hell invitation, but despite his deep-seated distrust, he doubted a couple of ore miners were trying to lure him into some kind of trap. His location and comms log was available for anyone on the *Osprey* to see. If Seeker went missing or

A FOUND BEGINNING

encountered a problem, it wouldn't be hard to pin the blame on the fleet.

Unless they're trying to get their fancy ship back. He dismally recalled Toner's secondary warning. Then again, the Alpha-Seeker's fundamental wiring was to his bio-sig, Jaeger's, and nobody else's. The fleet brass might be sneaky, but they couldn't be reckless enough to torpedo all good relations with Jaeger and the Overseers only to get this one fighter, which wouldn't fly as well for them.

Seeker hailed the *Osprey*. "I'm going in for a closer look at one of the asteroids," he said. "The fleet has some kind of operation going on down here, and they invited me to check it out. Expect to hear back from me within the hour."

"Roger that." Bufo's voice was staticky with distance. "Don't get lost."

Seeker closed the channel and directed his fighter to the sheltered landing port on the asteroid's surface.

This little mining outpost might've gone up in record time, but it was no shoddy work. There were two separate universal airlock mechanisms on the landing pad. A shuttle was taking off as Seeker docked, arcing up toward the fleet. Judging by the mining laser scars crisscrossing a swath of the asteroid's surface, it had a belly full of raw ore.

Seeker watched as his computer ran through the docking protocol, and the latch lights turned green. He tucked his spare exo-hood and gloves into his belt. At a measly ten degrees Celsius and a fraction of Earth standard gravity, the environment inside the mining shelter was bearable but far from comfortable. Good thing he didn't plan on being here long.

Two indistinct figures bundled in thermal-reflective parkas entered the docking area, their faces obscured beneath deep hoods.

Seeker slipped his vape pen into his breast pocket, cracked his knuckles, and opened his cockpit hatch.

He dropped out of the ship, falling two meters to the corrugated metal floor and landing gently, cushioned by the nearly nonexistent gravity. The frigid, thin atmosphere sent fingers of cold skittering around his ears and across his cheekbones. Brushing the wrinkles from his flight suit, he straightened and turned to face the two men striding through the tiny docking bay.

The first was a thick fellow, hiding behind a balaclava and thick goggles. He had a pulse-laser rifle strapped across the chest, two different multitools, and an entire armory of small munitions. A man ready at any second, Seeker supposed, to face an alien invasion that might come from any direction.

The second man was smaller, in a long, slimming parka. He stopped two meters from Seeker, unwrapping a long purple scarf from a thin face with sharp cheekbones and a fine nose. He pushed his goggles onto his forehead. He had oddly familiar gray eyes. His lips moved, but Seeker couldn't make sense of what he was saying, not at first.

"Shel. Jesus. Shelby." He lifted one gloved hand, reaching out as if to touch Seeker, and then held himself back. "I thought you were dead. We had a funeral and everything."

Seeker stared at the outstretched hand, the glove, the little man staring at him with shining eyes, glittering with what might have been excitement, or tears, or both.

Suddenly uncomfortable, Seeker wished he had a cigarette.

A FOUND BEGINNING

Out of old habit, he reached into his pocket and brought out his vape pen. No juice, but he found the familiar weight of it comforting.

"I take it we've met?" he said around the metal tube.

The smaller man sucked in a sharp breath. "We've...*met*." Then he smiled, showing the glint of sharp, wet teeth. Seeker was dimly amazed to realize that was indeed the track of one tear, freezing and evaporating down the man's narrow cheek. "*Fuck.*" He stuffed his hands in his pockets and bobbed on his heels. "You've lost all memory, haven't you?"

Seeker said nothing.

The little man took a step forward, carefully, as if approaching a wild animal. "I haven't. It's all right. We're friends here. It's...it's good to see you again." He swallowed, making the lump in his throat bob. "Brother."

At that moment, Seeker would've given his left arm for a real, honest-to-God cigarette. So much for running off to space to avoid drama. "What the fuck did you call me?"

The little man wavered. Then his eyebrows jumped, and his mouth turned into a sharp little grin. "Which one? Brother? Or—sorry. *Shel*. You always did hate Shelby."

Seeker grunted. When Toner warned Seeker that the fleet might try to win him back, Seeker doubted this was what he'd meant. "It's Jack now." He didn't know what else to say.

For a minute, he thought the little man might be angry. Then he threw his head back and laughed. "Of course it is. *Jack*. What's your surname these days? Manly? Steel? McChin?"

At first, Seeker didn't know how to interpret that light tone. Then the truth dawned on him. This little twerp was *teasing* him.

"Seeker," he snapped and realized too late that this wasn't a good answer.

"Jack *Seeker?*" The little man doubled over, howling with laughter that was half-hysterical and half pure, unadulterated joy. Even the guard shifted his weight, glancing uncomfortably from Seeker to the little man. Finally, the smaller man grabbed the guard by the arm to steady himself, wiping a tear from the corner of his eye. "So you married the Corps after all. Dad would be so proud."

The instinct to punch this guy, deep-seated and utterly mysterious, overwhelmed Seeker. He stepped forward, but the smaller man danced backward with shocking speed and let out another gale of laughter.

Quick as a flash, the guard had drawn his pulse pistol and leveled it at Seeker's chest. "Step away from the minister."

"At ease, soldier," the smaller man said. "It wouldn't be the first time he's broken my nose. That's how we say hello in the family."

When the soldier hesitated, the little man's grin slipped into a snarl. "I said *at ease.*"

The soldier winced as if the other man had struck him and lowered his weapon.

"He called you minister." Seeker finally gained control of his frustration. *Got to tackle this situation carefully. Got to get a grip on what the hell is going on.*

"That he did." The little man spread his arms and bent in the tiniest of mocking bows. "Victor Grayson, professor. Son of Malcolm and Edith Grayson. Younger brother of Sylvia Young, deceased. Older brother of Shelby Grayson, *formerly* deceased." He glanced up, eyes dancing. "Chief science adviser to the fleet and first prime minister of Tribe Six."

"And, conveniently, my long-lost brother."

A FOUND BEGINNING

"Oh, there's nothing convenient about it. I'd much rather we not be *lost* at all." Grayson's eyebrows jumped. "I see you're skeptical. Fair enough. I would be, too." He pointed at the vape pen still dangling from Seeker's fingertips.

"Yet, even though you've lost your memories, you kept that little vice of all things. Why am I not surprised? Turn it over. Look on the bottom. No!" He held up a staying hand. "Don't tell me what it says. I know perfectly well because I'm the one who gave it to you. *'Brother, remember—you promised.'*"

Seeker felt the first chill of cold creep down the back of his neck, and it wasn't only the thin atmosphere. He resisted the temptation to turn over the vape pen. He didn't need to. He knew what it said, too.

"We're working on ways to restore the memories lost via wormhole travel, of course," Grayson went on, bouncing excitedly on his heels. "I think we're on the cusp of a break-through, She—sorry, *Jack*. There are a lot of people who are going to be thrilled to see you again. I'm not the only one who's missed you."

Seeker shook his head, hoping to knock loose all this unexpected bullshit and get back to the matter at hand. "Why are you mining a K'tax asteroid out from beneath their noses?"

"Because we can." Grayson blinked as if the logic was plain but took the abrupt subject change in stride. "These rocks are brimming with iron and iridium ores. In one swipe, we deprive an enemy of a valuable resource and obtain the means to not only repair our damaged fleet, but for the first time in years, we might have enough disposable resources to build new ships. I'm so sure it's a safe bet that I even sent the prime minister out to inspect the facilities."

"A safe bet," Seeker grumbled. "Right up until you wake up

the thousands of aliens sleeping beneath your feet and they come to see what's making the racket." Seeker tapped his boot against the metal floor pointedly. "Right now, *we don't know* what's keeping the K'tax in hibernation."

"Oh, come *on*. You think planting MOABs all around this rock wasn't the *very first thing* we did? I have this place crawling with seismic scanners and life-sign detectors, Shel. If these vermin wake up, they won't have time to wipe the crust from their eyes before we turn them into a greasy skid mark."

He cocked his head curiously. "Surely you and your new allies don't *object* to that? You're at war with these creatures. I'm not advocating genocide, mind you!" He lifted a hand again as if used to deflecting this accusation. "As long as they're not a threat, we'll leave them alone."

Seeker shifted his weight and cursed himself for betraying his discomfort. "I'm going to have to share this with the captain," he said.

Grayson shrugged. "As I said, we have nothing to hide." His little grin returned. "It's a new era for the fleet, after all. Besides. As long as you and your allies prohibit us from landing on Locaur, we have to take whatever resources we can get."

Seeker grunted. He had to admit that Jaeger might make the same decision if she were desperate.

"Ah, on the topic of your illustrious captain..." Grayson began.

Seeker braced himself. Here it came. The sales pitch. The wheedling, the *worming* Toner had warned him about.

"I get the impression that she expects there to be quite a lot of ill-will between her and the fleet. It's not an unfounded concern. She did mutiny and steal our most valuable ship, after all.

"However, the man most likely to hold a grudge against her is *dead*. Captain LeBlanc didn't survive administration shifts in the last year. Those of us in command now?" He inclined his head, oh-so-modestly indicating himself. "We care about the survival of the human race above the petty squabbles of the past. I trust that Jaeger feels the same way."

Seeker grunted.

Victor tapped his chin thoughtfully. "I see the wormhole didn't wipe out your cynicism or rhetorical skills. Come back to the fleet with me. Stay a while. See for yourself. We *need* a permanent home. Also, I…haven't had a good bridge partner since you left." His smile returned, but this time it was hesitant, almost shy. "I've missed you."

Seeker fiddled with his vape and studied the middle distance, waiting for this unexpected flood of emotion to settle into something he could recognize. This vaguely irritating little man called him *brother*, but it wasn't the idea of sitting across the card table from a good partner that made him consider the invitation. It was the memory of those black fighter jets, fighting in beautiful coordination, that filled a hole he didn't realize had been inside him since his first day out of the wormhole.

Still, that was only a feeling, and Seeker wasn't a man to be ruled by them. He'd made a *choice*, and he didn't regret it.

"I'll take your invitation to Captain Jaeger," he decided. "We'll see what she has to say."

Grayson's smile wavered, and for an instant, Seeker thought he saw a shadow of rage flicker across the smaller man's eyes. Then he nodded.

"I'm glad to see the wormhole didn't take your sense of loyalty, either. You always did put family first." He took a step closer. Seeker fought the temptation to step away. He refused to back down or run away from this little man with the unblinking stare. "As do I.

"Do what you have to do, Shel. Sorry. *Jack*. I'll be right here waiting for you. Don't take too long. There are thousands of people counting on us, and we can't afford to let the situation get desperate."

CHAPTER TWENTY-FOUR

"I was under the impression that your first mate would join us for this meeting."

Jaeger licked her lips. She was sitting in her assigned chair in Kwin's ready room aboard the *Terrible*. "At three o'clock this morning, Toner woke me up insisting he'd found the perfect solution to our food shortage problems." She winced, bracing herself. "I, ah, thought he could do more good fishing than hovering over me through what could be a contentious meeting."

"Fishing?" Kwin's antennae swirled in opposite directions, indicating puzzlement.

Jaeger sighed. "My science staff has confirmed that there are dozens of species of aquatic megafauna on Locaur that are safe to consume. They'll fulfill a human's requirement for protein and fat. Toner's taken a shuttle and a small team out to the ocean."

"You wish to *eat* the indigenous creatures of Locaur?" Kwin's antennae dipped into frowning curves. "As a matter of routine? Not simply for annual ceremonial purposes?"

Jaeger sighed, scrubbing her temples. "I've already asked Tiki and the elders, and they don't object. I'm sorry, Kwin. I wish we could survive on lichen and sunlight like you and the Locauri do, but at the moment, we *can't,* not even with your additional nutrient supplies. It's only until we can get our lab-grown protein production up and running at enough volume to support everyone."

Kwin said nothing, but he didn't have to. His disapproval vibrated through the air like a barely-felt buzz.

Jaeger ignored it. The Locauri had understood her people's need to eat, and as long as Jaeger and her crew lived on Locaur, theirs was the only approval that truly mattered—or so she told herself.

Silently, she wished Toner a fruitful catch. A few hours ago, she'd received an update from the fleet. They'd reduced the daily ration allotment of the general population to one thousand kilocalories a day. If they were honest about their resources, they would run out of nutrient stores entirely within three weeks.

She said under her breath as the light around the door turned blue, "This wouldn't be such a big problem if the Council would tell us *anything* about how we can handle the fleet. It's not only a humanitarian effort, Kwin. Keeping them mollified with steady food shipments has quickly become a matter of security. The fleet has to understand that all aid will immediately cease if they try to land on Locaur without permission."

"We might hear from the Council sooner than you wish," Kwin said darkly as the door slid open.

Tsuan stalked into the conference room, his carapace rippling in eye-bending shades of ebony and mahogany. A smaller Overseer adjunct scuttled at his side.

A FOUND BEGINNING

Tsuan wasted no time with formalities. "In demanding this unplanned meeting, you have interrupted my schedule. Get to the point."

Jaeger's jaw clenched. Rather than ask what Tsuan *did* all day, besides harassing Kwin's crew, she acquiesced by reaching out and activating the holo-display. A large representation of the Forebear beacon wave-form, as prepared for her by Occy, sprang into existence over the table.

"Counselor Tsuan," she said in her best formal tone. "In analyzing the Forebear signal, we've discovered an interesting secondary signal embedded within the—"

"You were ordered to cease research into Forebear technology." Tsuan's mandibles snipped shut like a pair of pruning shears.

"We're only analyzing data that is freely available," Jaeger said tightly. "Evidence suggests that the message coming from the beacon is not a simple communication, but a signal that controls the K'tax's parasitic fungus directly. Here lies the secret to controlling the enemy that has plagued your people for generations and still threatens Locaur, Councilor. To protect the Locauri, we *must* have control over that beacon."

"Do not pretend your goal is still to protect the cousins," Tsuan said. "It is plain that your priority has shifted to protecting the interests of your species. My answer remains the same. You are not to tamper with the technology of our ancestors."

"Counselor," Kwin said, his tone strangely muted as it echoed around the chamber. "*My* crew can take responsibility for this research if you distrust the humans."

Tsuan sniffed. "Your crew are hardly more trustworthy than the army of human savages you're breeding in secret."

"What of *your* crew?" Jaeger's voice rose sharply. Tsuan

turned with the dizzying speed of an Overseer, leaning in close to peer down at her through terrible dark eyes. Jaeger sucked in a breath and forced her voice steady. "Surely your scientists are beyond reproach, Councilor. Send them down to Locaur to study the beacon. Truly, I don't care who controls it, as long as they do so in the interest of *keeping the K'tax away.*"

"How generous of you," Tsuan said. Then he turned away sharply, stalking across the room to the large viewer screen displaying Locaur's polar region. "We will examine this technology in our time, in our way. Not according to *your* schedule, Captain Jaeger."

Jaeger stared at Tsuan's spindly back, disbelieving. She glanced at Kwin and saw that he had turned a furious shade of carmine.

"You refuse to allow us to study the beacon," Kwin said. "And you refuse to do so yourself. Do I understand you correctly, Councilor?"

"Do not take that tone with me, Captain."

"For the love of God," Jaeger whispered. "*Why?* What are you so afraid of?"

Tsuan studied the image of Locaur in silence for a moment before abruptly turning back to the door. "I do not answer to humans. This meeting is over. Do not waste my time with trivialities again."

Jaeger moved without thinking. She dashed for the doorway, planting herself firmly between Tsuan and his exit. He skittered to a halt, freezing centimeters before plowing his three meters of rough, brittle carapace directly into her.

"I don't consider the survival of humans and Locauri a triviality," she growled.

A FOUND BEGINNING

Behind Tsuan, his adjunct began to buzz anxiously. Kwin went still as a dead log.

Slowly, the Councilor lowered his head, bringing his mandibles a mere hand's width from Jaeger's face. Tsuan began to hum as well, a deep thrumming noise emanating from some organ beneath his brittle shell. The sound made Jaeger's head pound.

She sucked in a breath, catching herself against dizziness that wanted to drag her to the floor. She was accustomed to the hundreds of different *hums* and *buzzes* of the Locauri and had heard similar tunes from the Overseers from time to time, but this noise was different. It rattled in her throat.

It reminded her, a little, of the hypnotic buzzing Kwin had used long ago to lure her into the Living Dream, to meditate.

She shook her head, fighting the urge to sit right there on the floor.

"You're hiding something," she said thickly. It was a stupid, brash thing to say—the kind of accusation she should've left for Toner to make—but that sound, it was messing with her judgment.

"Sit *down*, Captain," Tsuan hummed.

Jaeger sat. She couldn't help it. One second she was standing on her own two feet. The next, the cold metal floor had come up to meet her, and the tall Overseer strode over her head like she was a piece of trash. The smaller adjunct scuttled after its master.

By the time Jaeger's head stopped spinning, the door had slid shut once more. She turned, staring breathlessly up at Kwin. He'd turned a strange shade of yellow-green.

"What did he do to me?" she whispered.

Kwin looked away. "The resonant frequencies of the

Living Dream have many uses for those familiar with its secrets."

Slowly, Jaeger climbed to her feet. Her hands were shaking. Her stomach roiled, threatening to purge what little she'd had for breakfast. Silently, she thanked God that Toner wasn't here after all, or there would've been a war.

She swallowed a mouthful of watery bile. Kwin turned away and busied himself at one of the computer interfaces, giving Jaeger a moment to compose herself. For that, she was grateful.

Once she had full control over her muscles, she approached Kwin.

"I mean to request a direct meeting with the Council," Kwin went on. "I might be a captain in disgrace, but I am still a captain, and I have that right. If I can make the Council see the reckless selfishness of Tsuan's actions, they will send a more favorable representative. They might also wish to make amends with you. For Tsuan's…unbecoming…behavior."

"I don't care about that." Jaeger's breath wavered. "It doesn't matter. I only want what's best for our people, Kwin. We can't let Tsuan's stonewalling threaten everything we've worked for."

CHAPTER TWENTY-FIVE

The Living Dream has many uses for those familiar with its secrets.

Jaeger sat cross-legged on the bunk in her tiny ensign's quarters and focused on her breathing. Baby lay on the floor beside her bed, filling the air with body heat and the rumbling of her contented purr. Jaeger was shocked the big tardigrade could still squeeze herself through the hatch to get into the room, but Baby had stuck to her side like glue from the moment Jaeger returned to the *Osprey* from her meeting with Tsuan.

Like any good companion, she could sense a friend's upset, and wanted to help in the only way she knew how—by crushing Jaeger into her bed and threatening to eviscerate anyone who got too close. She'd sent poor, startled Sergeant Bufo springing away in impressive, ten-meter hops down the corridor.

Now Baby lay wedged on the floor, cradling her little petri dish between her claws, the world's least efficient space-heater. Her continuous rumble reminded Jaeger of Kwin's atonal humming, months ago when they'd met in secret to explore Jaeger's closeted memories.

The Living Dream has many uses...

Jaeger shivered. She'd thought of the Overseer's humming like the music of a Tibetan singing bowl or some kind of new-age music beat to induce an altered state of consciousness. The thought had never occurred to her that the strange sounds could be weaponized and used to usurp command of someone else's very will, at least for a short time.

Jaeger told herself that it was a simple intimidation tactic, no more or less threatening than Toner cracking his knuckles and bearing his teeth. Her reassurances wouldn't stick.

Kwin was right. There was more power here than she'd appreciated. Tsuan had used it to put her in her place like a misbehaving toddler, but Kwin had used the Dream to unlock memories that no other tool in the *Osprey*'s medical or psychiatric arsenal would allow her to reach.

"What do you think?" she asked softly, reaching out to scratch the stubbly skin-flaps around Baby's front orifice. The tardigrade shifted, pressing into Jaeger's hand. "Did the wormhole scramble whatever it is you have for a brain, too?" Her voice fell to something barely audible. "Do you remember before, babydoll? Do you remember Sim?"

Baby purred.

Taking it for an answer, Jaeger reached for her computer and dug through old audio files until she found what she was looking for. Months ago, Kwin had given her recordings of his meditation-inducing hum so she could practice without him.

Jaeger pressed "Play."

"Moss to Captain Jaeger."

Jaeger blinked dry eyes and realized the computer had been hailing her for several minutes. If the *Osprey*'s AI were as responsive as its programmers originally intended, this would've pushed Moss into a state of alert, at the very least requesting Elaphus send a medic to check after the captain's health. But, well—the *Osprey* and her crew had their fill of an overly-involved AI.

"Moss to Captain Jaeger. Come in, Captain."

"I'm here." Jaeger sat up sharply, making Baby rumble and lift her head, her continuous purring stuttering to a halt. "What is it?"

"Chief Engineer Occy reports a breakthrough in understanding K'tax fighter activity. He says that the strange synchronized activity of the individual units is to boost their generally weak communications capacity collectively."

Jaeger shook fluff from between her ears and checked her computer, surprised to see that it was the middle of the night. Had she fallen asleep? How much of her Dream had been a simple *dream*?

Then Moss's words fell into place, and she gasped. "Communications." She smacked Baby lightly, urging the dozing creature to her feet and toward the hatch so she had enough room to stand. She grabbed her utility belt, suddenly wide awake. "What sort of communication?"

"The fighters appear to be sending out a signal similar in wave-form and function to the Forebear beacon," Moss said as serenely as if reporting the weather. "Occy believes they're attempting to contact the greater swarm still lingering in subspace."

"Contact them with what message, Moss?" Jaeger waved her door open and shepherded the lethargic Baby into the command crew lounge, wrestling with her uniform jacket. "Moss? What are the fighters telling the swarm?"

"They appear to be countermanding the beacon order to stay away from Locaur. They are once more summoning the swarm to war."

The administration hub in the *Osprey's* starboard wing was, quite literally, abuzz with activity. Locauri, normally resting at this hour, zipped through the cargo bay, passing messages between busy crew members and red-eyed administrators.

Still rubbing the sleep from her eyes, Jaeger recognized Carver and Baily from the day crew, squeezed side-by-side into the workstations with Thatcher and Hooper from third shift. She nearly ran into a group of squabbling eagle-Morphed pilots on her way to the raised command center platform at the center of the hub.

Occy circled a column of flashing display screens, his eyes glued to first this readout, then another. The folded mechanical shape of a repair droid perched on a flat countertop behind him, watching the mess unfold.

"Why was I the last damned person to get the memo?" Jaeger asked no one in particular as she reached the metal half-flight of stairs and hoisted herself up to the command platform.

Bufo turned, blinking as if surprised to see her. Then relief folded across his broad face. "I was about to send someone to check on you, Captain."

"To answer your question, you disabled Moss's capacity for adaptation and growth," the repair droid added mildly. "And you locked her out of emergency functions in the command crew quarters. It's almost as if you don't trust your copilot, Captain."

"I wasn't asking *you*," Jaeger snarled.

"We're getting confirmation from Kwin's people now, too." Occy stared at the messages flashing across one screen, oblivious to the drama around him. "I hoped my translation was wrong and asked them to double-check the new K'tax signal. They're reading it now, too." He turned, looking up at Jaeger.

No, she realized with a start. Not *up*. In the last year, the boy had grown nearly ten centimeters, and now he stared her levelly in the face. "They're sending out the same message that originally called the K'tax toward Locaur."

He winced, ashamed of the past mishap that had begun this whole cascade of tragedy. *"The end begins by war,"* he recited in a mumble. *"Grow and strike. Creation is for one and alone. The end begins by war. Grow and strike. Creation is for one and alone. The end begins by war. Grow and strike."*

"What about our beacon?" Jaeger asked sharply, making the Virgil-bot shift and unfold a leg for the first time. "Any change?"

"About *your* beacon, I cannot say," it said. "The *Forebear* beacon continues to transmit the cease-and-desist message. However, the message coming from the fighters is of similar strength and fidelity as the signal coming from Locaur."

"So now the K'tax swarm out in subspace is receiving conflicting messages." Bufo tugged mournfully at his cheeks. "As of this moment, subspace sensors suggest the larger swarm hasn't responded."

Yet, the stocky sergeant didn't need to add.

"We're missing someone." Jaeger glanced around the central platform and swept her gaze across the bustling hub a meter and a half below them. "Where's Seeker? Why isn't he crawling all over this?"

"He's on his way back from a system sweep." Bufo winced. "We were short-staffed, and he volunteered to take another shift."

"That man is going to work himself to death," Jaeger said. "I'm putting a moratorium on his overtime. Don't let him take any more extra shifts without prior approval."

She swung back to the screens, scrubbing her fingers over her scalp as she tried to focus on the problem at hand. "How is this possible? The K'tax have never had the technology to rival what the Forebears can do. How is their signal even remotely competitive with the Forebear beacon?"

"They're learning."

Jaeger whirled to face a metallic three-meter-tall Overseer standing at the edge of the command platform, half-hovering in midair above the rest of the bridge. A small Locauri darted through Udil's thorax, making her hologram shimmer and distort. A little silver sphere floated directly above the hologram.

Jaeger swallowed her startled shout. "Adjunct! Please explain."

Udil's antennae waved slowly through the air, her projection lagging enough to make Jaeger think she was communicating from very far away. She must still be on Second Tree, working directly with the Council on Kwin's behalf.

"I have been keeping an eye on our study of the alien creature you rescued from the larger swarm last month, Jaeger." Udil managed to sound unhappy through the garbled, echoing translation.

"It seems likely that several members of their kind have fallen prey to the K'tax fungal spore and have integrated into their larger community. These new aliens are, unfortunately, *very* clever. We must assume that our enemy is going through a period of rapidly expanding mental capacity."

Jaeger closed her eyes, carefully contemplating Udil's news before allowing herself to speak. The air in the hub was already thick with tension. Her crew, and the Locauri, needed her to be a stable, steady hand. *Don't panic. Work with what you have.*

"God, can't I sneak away for one stinking afternoon without all of you losing your damn minds?"

Jaeger turned to see Toner and Portia striding through the hub, coming from the direction of the shuttle bay. They'd left their uniforms behind for their little fishing expedition, and a dozen kinds of grime stained their loose trousers and canvas jackets. Toner's boots *squished* as he walked, leaving a wet trail of footprints behind him. They climbed the steps to the command platform, dragging behind them the reek of salt and seaweed.

"I *told* you we should've chased those fighters down and squished them," Toner added.

"You're up to date?" Jaeger asked.

Toner tapped the commlink nestled in his ear and nodded.

"Well, too late to change the past." Portia put her hands on the small of her back and leaned into a mind-bending stretch. "Should we send out the cruisers, Captain? Try to shut the bugs up before they wake up the whole neighborhood?"

"Yes." Jaeger gestured at Bufo, who turned to the comms screen to call up the cruisers. Before, Jaeger had resisted the idea of sending out what little space power they had to mop up the K'tax fighters. She'd feared further crippling a second-hand fleet that was already held together by duct tape and wishes. Now, she had no choice. "Take all the crew you can get your hands on, Portia," she said grimly. "Go."

"Guess that shower is going to have to wait." Portia sighed. She reached out, snatched Toner by the collar, and pulled him in for a long kiss. Then she stepped back, her nose wrinkling. "Well, not for you, Commander."

Then she turned and lithe as a cat, threw herself over the rail and down into the hub. In three long, blindingly fast strides, she'd vanished into the starboard corridor.

Toner turned back to Jaeger with a dazed look in his eyes. "What?" he asked.

"*Focus.*"

"Sending out the cruisers now won't make a difference."

Jaeger and Toner turned at the same time to stare at Occy, who stood in front of a bank of screens, his shoulders slumped in despair as he monitored the constant feed of updates.

"The subspace swarm has started moving again," he said quietly. "They're responding to the fighter signal. They're coming for Locaur at full speed." He turned, his face shining in the shifting lights. So thin, and so old, on someone so young. "They'll be here in less than a week."

CHAPTER TWENTY-SIX

The *Osprey*'s largest conference room was a riot of shimmering holograms, and still the air felt cold and empty. Jaeger had the table removed for this meeting. She stood near the center of the room, with Toner lingering at her elbow.

Art and Tiki stood primly within the circle of holograms, the only real bodies in a mass of glowing lights. Also in the circle were Kwin and Udil, Fleet Captain Kelba, Science Adviser turned Prime Minister Grayson, and Kelba's two staff, Hart and Briggs.

Holo-conference, Jaeger decided, was far from ideal. She wanted to sit at a real table and look Kelba in the *real* eye. Still, it was too early in their diplomatic relations for a true pan-species emergency meeting.

The Locauri, a fairly provincial people, weren't comfortable visiting Overseer ships under most circumstances. Any invitation for them to come to the fleet in the flesh was an utter nonstarter. Similarly, Kwin didn't want these humans stepping foot on any of the Terrible ships until they'd proven

209

themselves trustworthy. Inviting them down to the *Osprey*? Jaeger would rather set the ship on fire.

There was no neutral ground in the system where they could all meet as equals. Thus, they held a virtual conference to decide the fate of two entire species.

"We are, of course, fully committed to the defense of this star system," Fleet Captain Kelba said promptly, once Jaeger had delivered the briefing to confirm the bad news.

Jaeger braced herself.

"In exchange for the creation of a permanent human state on Locaur."

"Correct me if I am mistaken, human elder." Tiki drew herself up and shook out her pseudo-wings as she turned to face Kelba's hologram. The translator band wrapped around her antenna glowed as she spoke. "As the matter stands, you cannot feed your clan. Yet you would have us believe your warriors are capable of turning back a great enemy?"

"Our space fighters don't run on nuts and berries, Locauri Elder," Kelba answered. The fleet captain didn't turn to face Tiki. Jaeger told herself it was because Kelba viewed this conference on a single screen. Still, it left her with the impression that the woman couldn't be bothered to face the alien she was addressing. Tiki seemed irritated by the oversight, as well. "We cannot eat explosives."

Yes, Jaeger thought sourly. *Remind us again how you have no shortage of weapons.*

"We cannot, however," Kelba added, "commit what resources we *do* have to a purely charitable endeavor. Our people must know we're fighting for our future. Not only yours." Proving Jaeger's assumption wrong, Kelba finally turned to stare down Tiki.

"Not to worry," Science Adviser Grayson added lightly.

No, Jaeger had to remind herself. He was prime minister, now. Apparently, the fleet's new civilian government had sworn him into the position mere hours after their last parley. "Even if we cannot come to an arrangement, we'll still send you all the goodwill we can spare."

"My cousin raises a fair point," Kwin said stiffly. To Jaeger's relief, the Overseers had finally figured out how to eliminate the odd reverberation effects of their universal translators. Gone were the days of stilted staccato speech and dramatically echoing proclamations. It made the strange aliens feel more *human* when they communicated. "What aid can your people bring against the coming invasion, Fleet Captain Kelba?"

So we're doing this. The thought tasted like ash in Jaeger's mouth. Against all of her deepest instincts, they'd opened this door. They were negotiating settlement rights with the fleet. As she thought it, she recognized that her prejudice sprang from nothing but vague memories and feelings that didn't necessarily reflect the reality of the fleet's new administration.

Give them a chance to be better, she told herself. *But keep a sharp eye for betrayal.*

Kelba nodded at her head of security, who began to rattle off a manifest.

"Six full squadrons of elite fighters. Heavy munitions equivalent to at least four hundred tons of TNT. Sixty energy shield generators and four heavy pulse-laser cannons. Two dozen ships of light-cruiser class or higher. Another four dozen transports and living vessels can be made battle-worthy within three days."

Hart hesitated before looking up from her notes and staring at Jaeger. "However, none of that compares to the power of the Tribal Prime, Captain Jaeger. She is the most advanced warship humanity has ever constructed."

"The *Osprey* is at our disposal," Jaeger said stiffly. "Not yours."

Just that morning, she had ordered the engineering crew to prepare her ship for fast takeoff if it became necessary. She loathed the idea of taking the *Osprey*—and more critically, her modified shield generators—away from the settlement. It would leave the entire region exposed to an easy K'tax land invasion. Still, it was best to prepare for anything.

"Let us not forget what else we've gained in setting up mining operations on these alien asteroid barges," the prime minister said. Jaeger was glad to push the conversation away from the *Osprey*. Seeker had submitted a report about these mining operations minutes before the meeting began, but she hadn't had a chance to read through them.

"What is that, human elder Grayson?" Tiki waved her antenna in the little man's direction.

"A knife at the sleeping enemy's throat. With five minutes' notice, we can detonate the net of mines we laid to protect our mining operations." Grayson snapped his fingers. "Poof. Like that, you needn't worry that the sleeping armies will awaken and come for your planet. It would cut down on the risk of a ground invasion."

Jaeger forced herself not to wince. She cast a sharp glance at Tiki. In the last year, she'd come to know some Locauri expressions. Beneath that carapace, though, they could still be hard to read. Tiki's translator ring glowed contemplatively, but it was a long moment before the elder spoke.

"It is a terrible thing to trample a nest of sleeping nymphs," Tiki mused. "Even if they are of an enemy clan."

"Locauri value their family," Toner piped in for the first

A FOUND BEGINNING

time. He stared at Kwin. "Their eggs and nymphs and stuff. If we hold the K'tax on those asteroids hostage, maybe the greater swarm would be willing to negotiate with us."

Kwin hesitated. "One year ago, I would have called such a parley impossible. K'tax are mindless beasts. Given this new evolution in their behavior, however, nothing is certain."

"What is certain is that if we *do* commit this genocide, we've lost any leverage we might have," Jaeger countered. "If we slaughter the hibernating K'tax, the rest of them will have *absolutely* no reason not to attack. I suggest you keep your knives sharp and ready, Fleet Captain Kelba, but it's too early to start slitting throats."

Kelba opened her mouth to respond, but to Jaeger's surprise, Grayson spoke first. "I see Captain Jaeger understands the language of hostages and leverage." He smiled. "Good. I'm glad we don't have to explain it."

Jaeger's heart skipped a beat. She turned, staring into the semi-transparent hologram. Across thousands of kilometers, Grayson met her stare.

His smile lingered.

"We hold the asteroids in trust," Kwin decided, skittering past the strange comment. "But be ready to destroy them if it becomes necessary."

"What of your people, Captain Kwin?" Kelba asked evenly. "It is clear that your race possesses advanced weaponry. You call the Locauri your cousins. Are you not also invested in their protection?"

Kwin's antennae lashed. "With news of this new invasion imminent, the Council has agreed to send warships to aid the defense of Locaur, once any danger of a surprise attack against our home world has passed."

They're still paranoid that the K'tax are making a feint. Jaeger was dismayed. It was Toner who spoke the words aloud. "Once they're *sure* the K'tax aren't going to swing toward Second Tree? That's cutting it close, isn't it?"

"Not even," Kwin said flatly. "As long as the Council holds course, the soonest we can expect Overseer reinforcements to Locaur is thirty-six hours after the K'tax swarm drops out of subspace."

"So you need only hold off total obliteration for a day and a half," Grayson said lightly. "Until the cavalry rides in. Can you do that, Captain Jaeger? Kwin?" He turned, spreading his arms to Tiki. "Locauri Elders?"

"No." Tiki wasn't one to mince words. "We cannot withstand an invasion of this scale. If the K'tax make landfall, even a day and a half of fighting will end in disaster for the Locauri.

"I have brought this matter to our neighboring clans and sent word across the continent. If it means a better chance of survival for our kind, they are willing to tithe a percentage of territory toward the formation of a permanent human state."

Tiki drew herself upright, addressing Kelba and Grayson like a queen. "You might face objection from the Tall Ones, human elders, for they still hold authority over this sector of the great night sea. However. If you prove yourselves our friends, we will, on your behalf, ask the Tall Ones to consider your request to build a home."

"A *consideration*." Kelba's lip twitched. "I'm sure you mean well, but such a promise will hardly feed my people."

"Prove yourselves trustworthy," Kwin said, "and I will add my voice to theirs."

"You're asking us to risk our very existence in exchange for *a good recommendation?*" Grayson turned, disbelieving, to stare at each of the other holograms in turn.

A FOUND BEGINNING

"It worked for me," Jaeger said quietly. When the others turned to stare at her, she sighed. *In for a penny,* she thought. "This is what it means to start fresh, Minister. Fleet Captain. It means having faith in your allies, whether they're human or alien. Don't repeat the mistakes of the administration that came before you. If you want me to believe you're different, you'll have to prove it."

Kelba lifted a hand, then hesitated, her head turning to the side. Something had caught her attention. "One moment, please."

Her hologram froze, paused with her mouth half-open. Glancing to the side, Jaeger saw that Grayson's hologram had frozen as well, and the holograms of Briggs and Hart had disappeared entirely. The staff must've been conferencing in private.

"Ten bucks says they don't go for it." Toner folded his arms behind his head, stretching. "Because they're right. It's a stupid-ass plan."

"It was *our* plan." Jaeger gave him a reproachful look.

"Stupid. Ass. Plan."

"You have used this word before," Art said, speaking for the first time as he turned to Toner. "Please, Puncher, explain. What is a *buck*?"

Toner froze in his stretch. Then he gave a slow, lazy grin. "It's a—"

"We will do it." Kelba's hologram twitched back into motion, skipping several frames. The woman folded her hands primly behind her back, gazing coolly around the circle. Grayson's hologram remained frozen.

"We put ourselves in your hands," Kelba said. "For the sake of all our futures, we will commit to this alliance through the coming invasion."

215

"What?" The word escaped Toner like a squawk before he composed himself.

Jaeger inclined her head to the fleet captain. "I'm glad to hear it."

"There are conditions," Kelba said coldly.

"Speak them," Kwin allowed.

"We require increased food and supply shipments. My people are on starvation rations, and you have an entire planet at your disposal. If you truly mean us well, as long as you bar the door to our landing on the planet, you will at least see that your allies are well-fed."

Something flickered in the corner of her vision, and Jaeger glanced over to see Grayson rubbing his ear, having returned to the conference without fanfare.

Tiki lowered her antenna in the faintest sign of agreement. Kwin repeated the gesture.

"Agreed," Jaeger told Kelba. "What else?"

"Our government is new and still recovering from a catastrophe," Kelba said. "There is much unrest in our ranks, and our civilians will not be pleased to see our military once again taking command of our destiny, even if it does so in their best interest. Sarah Jaeger. Though many of us have no personal memory of you, holo-documents and written stories of your mutiny still abound through the Tribe. You have become a folk hero to the civilians. Nearly a legend."

"I have no interest in popular approval," Jaeger said stiffly.

"Yet here we are," Grayson said. "With *your* name graffitied fresh across the bulkheads every morning. Our mission requires unity, Captain, and we're drowning in confusion and chaos. Civilian and military communities must be of one accord in this matter. You must address the fleet. *You* must be that voice for unity."

A FOUND BEGINNING

Jaeger closed her eyes. Endorsement. These people wanted her to *endorse* their new government, giving it legitimacy in the eyes of their mistrustful population.

"I will not allow you to use me as a political mouthpiece, Minister." She barely managed to keep her tone even. "I don't know nearly enough about your administration and policies to do so in good conscience."

"We ask you to say nothing that isn't true," Grayson said smoothly. "If this alliance is worth preserving, surely you will be willing to say as much publicly."

Damn you. Jaeger glanced around the circle. *Somebody*, she urged silently. *Jump in. Object.*

Neither Kwin nor the Locauri seemed to appreciate the danger in what Grayson was asking her to do. They only watched, waiting for Jaeger's answer. She glanced over her shoulder to see Toner frowning thoughtfully. Then he gave the tiniest shake of his head. He couldn't think of a good excuse to refuse, either.

"Very well," Jaeger said. "I'll address the fleet. But I'll do it in my own words, Minister. Captain. I will not allow censorship, and I will not read *your* pre-written speech off a teleprompter."

Kelba's head lowered in the tiniest of nods. "Acceptable."

"As long as we can review your speech ahead of the broadcast, of course," Grayson added.

"Agreed," Jaeger breathed. The back-and-forth could take months before they all agreed on what Jaeger would say to the crowd. She hoped it did. The idea of endorsing these people made her stomach churn.

"Does this conclude your list of requirements?" Kwin asked.

"It does, Captain Kwin." Kelba lifted her chin, staring up at the tall alien. "Now if you'll excuse me. We have much work to do."

Her hologram flickered and vanished. Half a second later, Grayson followed suit. Muttering similar excuses, Kwin and Udil took their leave as well.

"I don't know how we're going to handle the increased supply shipments," Jaeger muttered into the silence that followed.

"What are you *talking* about?" Toner drawled. "I just brought in enough weird alien jellyfish to fill half a fighter bay. Screw Puncher-of-Dragons. They should call me Catcher-of-Leviathan."

"Is that stuff any good for eating?" Jaeger asked.

Toner shrugged. "I mean. It's no roast of amputated arm, but I'm sure Bufo can stew it into something halfway decent. Clark says we can fish out of Locaur's seas like this for months before we need to start worrying about population management. The supply shipments are the least of our worries, Captain. With all this seafood, we could throw a party."

"You will do that," Tiki said.

"Huh?" Toner turned to her, cocking his head as if he'd misheard.

Tiki hopped to the conference room door, Art sticking to her like a shadow. "Today, there is bounty," Tiki said. "Tomorrow, there is war. We will share all that we have because the dead do not eat. It is the way of things."

"I sure hope there's not war *tomorrow*. I thought we had at least a few days."

Jaeger nudged Toner sharply in the ribs to shut him up. "You're right," she told Tiki. "We will have a feast while the meat is still fresh."

CHAPTER TWENTY-SEVEN

"How'd your field trip go?"

Toner leaned against the bulkhead outside Seeker's quarters, his arms folded, his gaze fixed on an empty place in the air. To get past him, Seeker would have to step over his outstretched legs.

Seeker sighed and rubbed his eyes. He'd returned from his patrol to meet with this new unfolding catastrophe of imminent invasion. He'd filed his report, then solely because Elaphus had ordered it, gotten some rest.

Two hours. He couldn't get two hours of sleep without someone trying to crawl up his ass with a microscope. "Ask the captain. I've already filed my full report with her." It had been a full, honest report of his brief foray into the mining operation. Nothing omitted. "I have nothing to hide."

Toner ran long fingers through his stringy hair, examining it for split ends. "Sarah's kind of busy right now, drafting up speeches and stuff. So I'm following up."

Seeker frowned, running through some brief mental

calculations. "She's too busy to follow up. But *you're* not. Are you spying on me?"

Toner glanced over, his eyes glittering behind his hair. "It's not personal."

"You don't strike me as the MP type."

"No, that's *you*." Toner straightened, moving with a kind of restless speed that made Seeker check his sidearm. *"You're* the MP type," Toner snapped. "That's what the whole goddamned Seeker Corps is. You go out in your fancy jets if there's an alien to slaughter. The rest of the time you skulk around spying on each other, ferreting out wrong thinking, making dissidents disappear, making sure the whole population toes the company line."

Seeker held up his hands. "Sounds like you have a bone to pick with a past that only you remember."

Toner growled and turned, slamming his fist into the bulkhead hard enough to leave a dent. He rounded on Seeker, but the man had learned to ignore these histrionics. "Do we have a beef, Toner? You and me, from before? Something we need to settle?"

Toner glowered at him. Then, slowly and to Seeker's surprise, he let out a breath and slumped back into his lazy slouch. "Not really," he muttered. "Not...directly. Only met once or twice but even then..."

His gaze fell to the side, and reluctantly, he said, "I'll say you never *really* did me wrong. Or her." His gaze lifted again and Seeker was startled, as always, to see how shockingly blue his eyes were in the dim light.

"But it's not about *you*. The Corps did us wrong. All of us. The Seekers. *If* what the fleet is telling us is true, they fought a civil war to get *your* shiny black boots off *our* throats. But that's okay now." His mouth broke into an utterly humorless

A FOUND BEGINNING

smile. "They have a brand new government, all shiny and silver. Or, in this case...Gray."

Seeker scratched his chin and frowned at the stubble there. He was overdue for a shave.

In a population as small as Tribe Six, political inbreeding was inevitable. There were only so many charismatic, competent leaders to go around. Seeker hadn't been entirely surprised to learn that the current prime minister of this new civilian government was a longstanding member of the fleet military, with deep ties to the Seeker Corps leadership.

Similarly, it hadn't taken him long to accept that in his past life, he'd been a senior member of that selfsame Corps. Or that the Corps played no small part in keeping the fleet orderly. *By any means necessary*, was the last line of the Seeker motto, carved into the bulkhead of his fighter. It was the first thing he'd read upon waking to his second life.

"All this amnesia drama is a pain in my ass," Seeker muttered. "As far as I'm concerned, Toner, that wormhole is *Tabula Rasa*. Wipe the slate clean. I don't give a shit what happened before it."

"If your memory came back today? Would you give a shit then?"

Seeker shrugged, holding open his empty palms. "I'm not a scab. It's not in my nature. I don't remember what I might've been before, but I know that much. Can I count on you harassing me about it every day for the rest of my life? Should I pencil a few minutes of it into my schedule?"

When Toner didn't answer, Seeker decided to take a risk. He reached out and put a hand on the man's bony shoulder, making him look around sharply. "You read my report. I talked to the prime minister for about ten minutes, and all I wanted to do was break his goddamned face. *This* crew is my

RAMY VANCE & MICHAEL ANDERLE

family now. I'll put myself in the brig before I put them in danger."

"Oh, you won't get that far," Toner dismissed. "Not with that tracker planted in your guts. If you turn on us, you'll be too busy shitting out your brains to be of any use to your brother."

Seeker froze. "What?"

"I must be cruel only to be kind." Toner grinned. *"Don't hurt my little sister."*

"Fuck." Seeker let out a breath. Another one of Toner's stupid jokes. "A man like you has no business being on a command staff." He drew back his hand and resisted the temptation to wipe it clean on his uniform.

"You sure as shit don't want me on your enemy's command staff." Toner slapped Seeker on the back, turning to direct him down the corridor. "Come along, *Jack.* Your brother is holding my niece and girlfriend hostage, and he's not being very fucking subtle about it. Let's talk about backup plans."

Seeker blinked but started walking. "What?"

"I'll explain everything. Oh, you're gonna need a different surname, by the way. Now that the Corps is here, things are going to get confusing if we keep calling you *Seeker.*"

"I don't care what you call me," he muttered. Then, he quickly added, "As long as it's not *Shelby* fucking *Grayson.* Jesus, what a shitty thing to do to a kid. My parents must've been assholes."

Toner threw his head back and laughed.

CHAPTER TWENTY-EIGHT

"Good morning, Tribe Six."

She drew in a breath and glanced down at her notes, then set them aside. No crutches. She wasn't going to hide behind a paper shield for this.

"This is Captain Sarah Jaeger of the *Osprey*." She gave a small chuckle. "Not that I expect you to know what that means, exactly. It has been...a confusing and difficult time for everybody. I don't have the full story. You don't have the full story. But I do have *my* story. Since we're all writing the *human* story together, I'm going to share it with you."

"There's, um, something I need to talk to you about."

There was a small supply closet in the *Osprey*'s central column, not far from the general crew showers. A pile of pilfered mattresses lined the floor. A small display screen cast the only dim light in the room. Jaeger spoke into the shadows, her volume barely above mute. Toner didn't need to hear what she had to say. He'd seen the speech already. She'd prerecorded it.

Portia shifted her weight, digging her elbow into Toner's ribs as she rolled to face him. The woman was all angles and sharpness. Her fingernails were sharp. Her teeth were sharp.

Toner licked his lips. "I have history."

Portia's lips curved into a smirk. She waited for him to go on.

"Baggage, too. I don't know." He rubbed the back of his neck restlessly, at the electronic collar coiled around his spinal cord. "A whole lifetime of it. I was never trying to run away from it. Not really. I guess I didn't think I *could* escape it. Then the wormhole happened…"

Portia's smirk faded, and she studied him with solemn dark eyes.

"Then the wormhole, like, *un*-happened. Now it's all coming back to me. I don't think I'm really the same person I was when we met."

"You are," Portia said.

Toner started.

"The Jefferies tube monster." Portia's smirk returned. "First mate, commander, Puncher-of-Dragons. You are that person."

She walked her fingers up his bare chest. Her hand spread wide like a spider. "But you're not *only* that person any more than I'm *only* a soldier preprogrammed for expertise in piloting and espionage. It's okay to be more. At least, that's what the captain has insisted since the day I climbed out of that activation tube."

Toner stared up into Portia's narrow, teasing face. "I have a girlfriend."

Portia winced, and Toner winced in sympathy, wishing

A FOUND BEGINNING

he'd found a better way to say it. Like the idiot he was, he also wished he'd shut his mouth and not go on blabbing. "Or I did, before. Then the wormhole—and things got...lost. Then the memories came back, and we were always together even if we were apart and seeing other people and now she's *here*, except I don't think she remembers much now either and I—"

Portia silenced him with a kiss. "Why are you telling me this?" she said, once they'd caught their breath.

"I don't want to hurt anybody," Toner mumbled.

"That's sweet. But I *really* don't care what you do on your own time." Her eyebrow arched. "Or who."

"Oh." Toner could think of nothing else to say.

Portia sat up and shuffled around the darkness until she found his uniform. She tossed it onto his chest. "Now come on. I don't want to miss the party."

"I joined the Tribes program years ago because I wanted to build a new, better home for my family. I believed in the mission." Jaeger swallowed hard. Saying those words felt a bit like running complex calculations on the fly. She had faith in them, in a general sort of way, but they were nonetheless *difficult*. As best she could tell from her scattered, shattered memories, they were true. Still, she was terrified of lying entirely by accident or saying something the fleet could twist and use against her later.

"I believed that the Tribes could find us that new home. Then, as the years wore on, as we wandered across the stars, getting colder and hungrier and more desperate, I started to understand that the Tribes *didn't* have all the answers. They might've meant well, in the beginning, but their plans, their methods for finding us a planet to settle...they weren't bearing fruit." *We were dying,* was what she'd wanted to say. *From incompetence and greed and pure malice.* Of course, Kelba wouldn't let those lines slip into the speech. "We were languishing."

"You still are."

Occy glanced over to see a repair droid lurking in the deepest shadows of the picnic shelter, like a spider trying to hide from the first light of dawn. The air was misty, and the scent of wood fires, roasting nuts, and hearty stews blanketed the settlement. The day was young, but already preparations for the feast were well underway.

"You still are," Virgil repeated. "Languishing. Now you once again face annihilation."

Occy shifted his weight, making more space on the picnic table. He didn't expect Virgil to join him like some friendly crewmate, but it seemed like the right thing to do. On his display screen, Captain Jaeger continued her speech.

"I guess that's life," Occy said. "One damn thing after another. Right?"

"I have spent the night comparing what we know of the coming swarm to your capability to thwart it. Even if your new human-Overseer-Locauri alliance were unshakable, your chance of success is very low."

Occy cocked his head. There was a mug of steaming tea in his lap, and he bought himself time to think as he took a sip. It wasn't very good tea. They were saving the last of the really good food for the party. "Probably," he said.

Virgil turned its sensor arrays to focus on Occy. "Jaeger

could flee. Save the *Osprey* and her crew, and strike out into the universe again, seeking a new planet not constantly threatened by invasion and war."

"What about all the people up in the fleet?" Occy asked. "What about all the people down here? The *Osprey* can't fit them all. What about the Locauri? This is their home."

"It is foolish, trying to save everybody," Virgil snapped with enough force to make Occy jump. "Better to cut your losses and save what you can when the chances of saving *everybody* are so very slim."

Occy studied the robot over his mug of tea. "Maybe," he said quietly. "Or maybe it's okay to take a risk when your friends are in danger. Maybe it's okay to bet against the odds, sometimes."

"Why? Why is it *ever* better to risk your very existence for the sake of another?"

Occy shrugged. "Because it's better than being all alone."

CHAPTER TWENTY-NINE

"I couldn't let my people continue to wander around the galaxy stuck in little tin cans, slowly starving. I did what I had to do. I took a ship, and I struck out ahead." *I ran away.*

Did I do it to find a better place for the people who remained?

Or did I do it to run away from the memory of a daughter I thought I'd lost?

"It was dangerous," she admitted. "I was going against the fleet and the Tribe. It was risky. I won't deny it. I might've cost Tribe Six everything."

Silver had insisted she admit at least that much. That she admit how badly she'd hamstrung the fleet in taking away their most advanced ship. However, the *Osprey*, what they called the Tribal Prime, wasn't a colony ship. She was a warship. Deep down, Jaeger thought first contact with the Overseers would've gone very differently if the *Osprey* were in the fleet's hands.

"I don't regret it," she said fiercely. "My friends and I, we found the home we've been looking for. *We* laid the groundwork for a lasting, harmonious relationship with the aliens in

A FOUND BEGINNING

this sector. *We* bled and died because we believed in building our future on a foundation of stone instead of sand and blood.

"We want that for all humans. We want a chance for all of you to come and live in peace. We're close." She held up a hand, pinching her thumb and forefinger together. "We're *so close* to having a better future. For everybody."

"Penny for your thoughts?"

Sim looked up from her bowl. It was a rich stew, full of chunks of strange meat that felt like rubber against her tongue, satisfyingly chewy. Exotic spices she couldn't place laced it, like something from a dream.

Sim smiled, then flushed as she realized she'd dribbled broth down her chin. She wiped her face with the cuff of her uniform, laughing a little self-consciously. "God, it's delicious."

There was a party in the offices of the silver administration. Shipments of strange meats, fresh vegetables, and alien seasonings had arrived that morning. For the first time in living memory—although that didn't mean much—*everybody* across the freighters and the support fleet was permitted to take a few hours away from exhausting labor, sit with friends, and eat their fill.

Petra had brought Sim along to the fancy silver reception as a plus one. This, too, felt like a dream for a young woman who drifted on a sea of vague memories of dingy, dim-lit hallways and sleeping on freezing steel bulkheads.

Stranger still was the little man perched lightly on the edge of the table, his head cocked to one side, a crooked smile lingering on his lips as he stared down at Sim. Most of the department employees, the assistants, secretaries, and lesser ministers, were standing around the holo-display at the other end of the room, sipping sweet drinks and watching Jaeger's speech.

Not the minister. He was watching Sim.

"It is," he agreed amiably. "Imagine having it for supper every day."

Sim glanced across the empty table, scanning the crowd. "I guess I should be watching the speech, huh?"

The minister shrugged. "I'm not. Saw it a few hours ago." He winked. "Pre-recorded. She's not telling us anything we don't already know."

Sim gaped. She risked a glance over to the large screen, the stranger speaking to the entire Tribe. Then she looked up. "Did you know her? From before? I mean, do you remember?" Sim didn't understand much about this amnesia that plagued the fleet, but she understood that some people had been less affected by the wormhole than others.

Victor—he'd insisted that she call him that—had worked on some kind of magnetic experiments when the fleet passed through the wormhole. He didn't have all his memories, he said, but more than most. Certainly more than Sim.

"Who, Sarah?" The minister's faint smile broadened. "We met a long time ago. She salvaged some very important research from Old Earth."

"Research on what?" Sim tried to sound nonchalant, but every time this strange woman, her *mother*, came up in conversation, her gut did a funny little somersault.

The minister shook his head. "Hard data only geneticists would appreciate. Methods for advanced cloning and rapid gestation. Experimental gene therapy interventions that became the basis for a lot of our medical treatments. Things like that. I don't think Sarah appreciated how important that data turned out to be, but I truly believe you and I wouldn't be here, having this conversation, if not for those few minutes of kismet nearly..." He puffed out a breath thoughtfully. "My goodness. Almost forty years ago."

"You can't be that old," Sim said suspiciously.

Victor let out a little laugh. "Holo-dramas don't keep up with technology anymore. Age is only a number on a computer screen, my dear, when even standard gene therapy treatments slow aging to a crawl.

"One minute you might be a smear of DNA in a test tube. Two days later, you're a fully-formed human, and you stay young and fit for decades. Control the rate of telomere degradation, and you control culture itself."

He held out his palm and tilted it like a see-saw. He must've seen the confusion written on Sim's face because he shrugged and let his hand fall.

Sim swallowed the last bite of her stew and glanced around the office anxiously. "Petra's been *so* busy lately," she muttered. "Barely seen her in days. She promised we'd hang out after the speech, but I don't see her..." She looked up, questioning.

Victor shrugged and hopped to his feet. "I'm sure she's around here somewhere, making trouble." He patted Sim on the head. "Go try the caramel corn. It's delicious."

"We can't let this chance slip away from us now," Jaeger said. "We can't let infighting and old grudges blind us to the possibilities of the future. I'm not saying it will be easy. I'm not saying we must let injustices go unchecked and unchallenged.

I *am* saying that if we let our guard down now and dissolve into infighting, we risk losing everything.

"The enemy that is coming for us is frightening and powerful. But it's not as powerful as we can be when we stand shoulder-to-shoulder with our allies, our friends—old and new—and our family.

"I will never stop fighting for peace and justice. I will *never* rest when tyrants try to silence the voice of the people. If we want any hope of living to see that better world, we must stand together *now*. We must face the coming storm as one. Only through survival can we have hope for a better tomorrow."

CHAPTER THIRTY

Petra huddled in one of the comms stations, staring into the deep shadows of Ops. The big room was silent and dark. All operations had paused for one hour to give everybody a chance to head down to the party. To make sure everybody saw Captain Jaeger's speech.

Without bodies busy at work, without all the computers up and humming and spilling heat, the air was cold enough to make Petra shiver.

She tucked her hands under her armpits and stared at the single active screen on the comms station, and the little blinking memory stick plugged into its interface. Petra's file upload had stayed at seventy-two percent for what felt like a week. She felt time slipping past, winding down to the moment when the party would end. Second shift would come on duty and return to Ops to find her here, casually committing treason.

Her stomach ached and roiled. She couldn't eat. She hadn't slept in days, not since finding this memory stick on the *Bitch* and peeking at all the awful things hidden on it.

Seventy-three percent.

Petra still didn't *feel* connected to the woman who'd recorded those notes. She didn't identify with the person who'd befriended a rock star and lost him, spent months in prison, broken out of jail on the Astrolab, and fomented rebellion within the Followers. She didn't *feel* the anger and loss that had led her on this path.

She also didn't doubt that it was true. The woman who'd hidden that memory stick for her to find wasn't her, not really...but she'd taken all the frustrating, confusing graffiti scrawled across steel and flesh and connected them into a coherent narrative Petra could appreciate. She'd given Petra the context she lacked to understand anything.

She'd given Petra the original file notes for Reset, and Serenity, and all the other ugly little experiments the fleet had been conducting in secret.

Eighty percent.

Going into the office every morning since then, smiling at her colleagues and the Seekers she passed, having daily interactions with the other secretaries—it was harder than Petra had imagined possible.

Even harder was sitting across from Minister Grayson every morning for the daily briefing and watching him smile and nod at all the wonderful progress his new silver government was making on behalf of Tribe Six.

Grayson runs an entire studio on the Astrolab for recording and producing deep fake videos, Petra from the past had whispered. *They were gonna use my face to stifle the rebellion. Put words in my mouth, and make me say what they wanted said. Grayson killed Rush in cold blood because he got outta hand. Grayson tortured that actress to keep her in line. He'll do the same to you. He'll do the same to anyone who gets in his way.*

A FOUND BEGINNING

Petra had grinned and nodded and sat up straight, too. Because that was what Secretary Potlova did during morning briefings. The whole time, terrified down to her soul, that Grayson would glance over and notice that she was behaving differently. That he would put two and two together and realize she knew.

She *knew*.

The hardest thing of all was coming home at night and slipping into a bunk beside Sim.

Because Petra from the past had told Petra now many things—about her great friendships with this Sarah Jaeger, Lawrence Toner, and yes, even Rush Starr. What Petra from the past hadn't mentioned, not even once, was the beautiful young woman she'd supposedly been taking care of for over a year.

Eighty-four percent.

Fleet was using them. Petra and Sim—this stranger, whoever she was—were being *lied* to by this new government. By the fleet captain. By the same minister that asked after Sim's health during every midday coffee break.

What kept Petra up at night, what drove her to this final act of rebellion, wasn't the stranger, the impostor who believed she was Petra's foster daughter.

It wasn't that Project Reset was a deliberate and targeted attempt to quell a rebellion by forcing amnesia upon the fleet —although gawd knew that was horrifying and effective enough.

It was three words, one little note at the very bottom of the Reset file, three words that had kept Petra staring at the ceiling, counting her desperate breaths until her morning alarm went off.

Repeat as necessary.

RAMY VANCE & MICHAEL ANDERLE

Eighty-nine percent.

Petra heard the faint sounds of cheering and applause from down the hallway as Jaeger's broadcast wrapped up. The speech was a bunch of nonsense about *we gotta stand together, now. Never mind the dirty little secrets. We'll figure that out later.*

Petra would've said the same thing before finding the memory stick. Now the idea made her want to vomit.

Because this amnesia wasn't an *accident.* This wasn't a storm they were all weathering together.

It was a weapon the fleet had turned against its people. A weapon they would use again, and again, and again, to squash rebellion and silence dissent. A plan for making slaves.

Ninety-three percent.

All Petra could think to do, was get the word out. Compress as much of the data as she could and hurl it out into space, toward the planet and Captain Jaeger and her crew, and hope that the truth came out. Hope that the fleet wouldn't be able to completely erase its sins from the history books as they wanted.

Gawd. Petra found herself praying into the darkness. Had she ever believed in a god? She didn't know. *Or Sarah, or Lawrence, or whoever is out there. Don't let them fool you. Don't let your guard down. Keep fighting. We all gotta keep fighting.*

Ninety-seven percent. Petra heard the sound of footsteps coming up the hallway as people wandered back to their work. She closed her eyes. She'd cut the file down as slim as she'd dared, but after living with the confusing half-stories written on the walls, she'd been terrified of leaving out too much. Of forgetting some vital detail that might spark in Sarah or Lawrence the same sympathetic horror it had sparked in her.

Now she was going to pay for it. The file was too big after

A FOUND BEGINNING

all. It wasn't going to upload in time. She would get caught using the *Defiance*'s powerful comms relays for an unauthorized transmission. They were going to look at what she was broadcasting down to Locaur. They were gonna kill her.

Or toss her into prison.

Or back through the wormhole and *repeat as necessary* until she was the perfectly docile mid-level manager they needed her to be.

Petra put a hand over her mouth to keep in the hysterical, terrified giggling.

"Bryce. A moment."

The young major had been striding toward Ops. Now he paused and turned in the dim corridor, biting back a little huff of impatience. In the lounge farther up the hallway, he heard the sounds of second shift grabbing the last of their snacks and collecting their things, ready to head back to work. He'd wanted a few minutes alone in Ops to familiarize himself with the new post-jam generator interface before the civilians got in the way.

When he recognized who'd hailed him from a cross-corridor, all thoughts of new space-laser toys skittered right out of his head. He glanced over his shoulder before stepping out of the hallway.

"Ah, yes, Professor?"

Grayson's brow knit into what Bryce recognized as the early warning sign of annoyance.

"Sorry. Minister."

"Did you ever follow up with Potlova on lunch?"

"No...Sir..." Bryce flushed. He'd mentioned Potlova's

casual offer for a date a few days back because his orders were to report on every interaction he had with the pre-Reset malcontents. "I'm sorry, was I supposed to take her up on that?"

He grimaced, finding the idea distasteful in more ways than one. He could hold a friendly act as duty required, but the idea of suffering through a meal with the traitorous little slut was borderline offensive.

"Weren't you listening to the speech, Major?" Grayson's lip quirked ironically. "We've got to put aside our petty grudges. For the sake of survival."

Bryce thought it best to keep his mouth shut and wait for the minister to get to his point.

"Aren't you the least bit curious?" Grayson asked. "About what it's like to lose your past so utterly? Don't you wonder what's going through her head?"

"Probably gossip wondering how long it's going to be before she can get her next skin-tightening treatment."

Grayson shook his head, disgusted. "You have no future in Intelligence, I'll tell you that much."

Bryce said nothing. He'd never wanted to go into Intelligence, especially not if it meant reporting to *this* man every day. He was happy in a traditional military chain of command and counted down the minutes until things could go back to normal. Well, a new normal, at least.

Things *had* been better since Reset. There was constant, low-level discontent in the lower classes, spurred on by all that damned graffiti that had survived the wormhole. A society under stress always had to expect some muttering. Once Bryce and his people hunted down the last of these graffiti artists and agitators, things would settle down.

A FOUND BEGINNING

"Is there anything else I can do for you, Minister?" Bryce asked.

"Hm? Oh." Grayson poked his head out from around the corner, glancing down the dark corridor toward Ops. He considered the shadows. "No, I think we've stalled long enough." He straightened, looking up at Bryce. "You may go."

"Sir?"

"Oh, you didn't notice? Potlova was in there using the comms relay for a private call. I didn't want you to interrupt the upload. It was a good package, really. A very logical and sensible collection of classified files composed to smother silver in the crib." He grinned faintly, showing the glint of wet teeth. "It only needed a few tweaks. I think she's finished now."

Bryce stared.

"*Absolutely* no future in Intelligence," Grayson repeated, giving Bryce a friendly, almost conciliatory, pat on the shoulder. "Now go back to work. You fucking idiot."

———

"Play it again," Jaeger whispered.

Beside her, Toner flinched. He put a hand on her shoulder. "I don't think—"

She shook off his hand. "Play it again!"

Bufo gulped and looped the recording back to the beginning. Jaeger was glad the sergeant had been on comms duty when the strange broadcast had come down from the fleet and not Occy. She loved the boy. The idea of making him watch this perversion made her skin crawl.

The conference room display screen lurched into motion. The girl—no, the young woman—sitting at the cramped booth smiled broadly. She wore a grimy mechanic's suit, and fingers of grease and sweat smeared her cheeks. Her hair, thick and black and curly, was pulled into two short pigtails at the base of her skull.

She spooned chunks of fish stew into her mouth and beamed into the camera, her golden eyes glittering. "Oh my God." She dunked a chunk of bread into the broth and crammed it into her mouth, casually unconcerned with manners in an endearing way. She was confident. She was *comfortable*. "This is *amazing*."

Jaeger winced. "It's better than synthesized lentils," she murmured sadly. *But not by much.*

"This is regular food?" Sim asked the person behind the camera. She pointed at the plate of roasted vegetables beside her stew bowl. "Down on the planet? Like, they have this kind of stuff *every day*?"

The camera shook faintly as the cameraman chuckled. Sim took that as an affirmative. Her eyes rolled back into her head in a spasm of anticipatory ecstasy. Then she laughed.

The sound of her laughter ripped into Jaeger's chest and stabbed at her heart. It was *her* laughter. It was the same laughter of the little girl in the old holo-journals. It was the same unfiltered, unapologetic joy that had lulled Jaeger to sleep countless times and haunted her dreams.

Toner had given up trying to stop this replay and squeezed Jaeger's shoulder gently. She drew in a sharp, shuddering breath and took his comforting hand.

"What did you think of the speech?" the man behind the camera prompted. Jaeger strained, trying to place the voice. If she could pin the cameraman as Grayson, Briggs, or anybody she recognized, she could tell herself that this whole video

A FOUND BEGINNING

was clearly a setup, perhaps a complete fabrication specifically meant to tear at her heart.

But no. She couldn't see the face of the man holding the camera, and she couldn't place his even, sandy voice. He could've been anybody. For all Jaeger knew, he was Sim's boyfriend.

Sim's brilliant laughter faded. She swallowed a chunk of bread and wiped her mouth, dropping her head shyly. "Oh, man." She giggled. "I really don't want to talk about that."

"Come onnnn," the man drawled. "Why not? The whole department is talking about it. That's your *mom* out there, Sim!"

Sim's cheeks darkened. She fussed with a loose strand of hair that had fallen over her face. "I dunno," she mumbled. "I don't know her."

"What's wrong? Why are you upset?"

Sim squared her shoulders and let out a breath. She lifted her cup and took a sip of pink juice. "Okay. So whatever, if she's my mom, right? Just...whatever. It doesn't have to mean anything."

"You don't like her?"

Sim shook her head. "It just doesn't mean anything, okay? I met the lady once for a few minutes, and she didn't even want to hug me. Honestly…" She shifted her weight, clearly uncomfortable. "All of you guys in the department. Petra, too. You all feel like family to me. We all have this amnesia, yeah, but you still *feel* like family to me. I look at Captain Jaeger and…" She shrugged. "I don't *feel* anything. All I can think about is how I *should* feel something, but I don't. That, and… she ran away from us."

"She didn't *abandon* us," the cameraman protested. "Even

brass and silver are saying that, now. *They're* not even mad at her for taking the Prime anymore."

"Because she found a nice planet?" Sim scowled. "Okay. So why are we still stuck up in the fleet? Why doesn't she want us to land there?"

The cameraman didn't answer.

Sim shrugged, suddenly surly as only a teenager could be. She reached across the tiny table and grabbed a cluster of caramel corn. "As far as I can tell, nothing has gotten better. Maybe silver's sucking up to her because they know we need to work together now. We'll starve if we don't. Maybe we could've done just as well if she hadn't stolen the ship. Maybe we'd be in a better spot. It's selfish, is all I'm saying. I think she's selfish."

The recording ended.

Silence filled the *Osprey*'s conference room.

"You know it's all bullshit, right?" Toner asked finally.

Jaeger pushed herself up from the chair and started pacing the room. "Maybe," she muttered.

"*Maybe?*" Toner blinked. He waved at the display screen. "Hey, Teddy. When did you say we got this video?"

"Seventeen-thirty," Bufo said. "About an hour after the captain's speech."

"What was the context, again?"

Bufo shook his head. "None that I can tell. Moss picked up a video data packet coming down from the *Reliant*'s main comm channel. It didn't come with any attached metadata to suggest who specifically sent it or why."

"Did anyone else receive it?" Toner asked.

Another shake of the head. "The channel was secure, and I classified that as soon as I realized what it was. I don't think anyone else got a look."

A FOUND BEGINNING

Toner turned to watch Jaeger pacing up and down the length of the room. "You think they let just anybody use their main comm channels? This is Psy-Ops shit. The fleet is fucking with you. Grayson or Kelba or whoever. They're trying to guilt you into giving the fleet more concessions. They don't want to go through all the red tape to get this settlement up and running. They want you to move things along faster so they can come set up shop on Locaur."

"So?" Jaeger stopped and placed her fists on the table, breathing hard.

"*So?*" Toner blinked again.

There was a meaty *thunk* as Jaeger slammed her fist onto the wood. "So what if they are? *So what* if it's all Psy-Ops shit? They have my daughter, Toner. They're dangling her in front of me like a worm on a hook. You heard Grayson in that meeting. Sim's a hostage. Petra's a hostage," she added, burying a flash of guilt.

They might've been close friends once, but Jaeger didn't know Petra. Glancing over, though, she saw that the reminder struck home with Toner, which was what she wanted.

"I don't care," she whispered, then her voice gained strength. "Honestly. If she's doing okay, I don't care if she's reading off a script or if she believes I'm a selfish ass. Maybe I am. Or maybe I'd be pissed too, if *my* mother ran off and left me behind. She's a kid. She has the right to be mad. I don't care about that.

"I care that they *have her at all*. I care that they're *using her*. Even if everything she said is totally honest. Brass and silver know what they have, and they'll *use her* to manipulate me any way they can."

Toner's jaw worked for a moment as he tried out a few responses and rejected them all. He glanced at Bufo, who hopped lightly to his feet, muttered some excuse, and skedaddled from the room.

"I can't play this game," Jaeger whispered, slumping into a chair. "I *won't* play this game."

"*Thus bad begins,*" Toner muttered, "*and worse remains behind.* A hostage only has as much power as you give her. So…you're going to ignore it?"

"No." Jaeger scrubbed her fingers through her hair. "No. Even if I *could* forget all about Sim, make her meaningless, and accept that she's one of thousands of other people up in the fleet, there's still Petra." She gave him a side-eye.

Toner struggled to keep his face straight. He failed.

"Even if I don't remember Petra, I know *you,*" Jaeger said quietly. "If they dangle Petra out on a hook, try to use her to manipulate you, if they threaten to hurt her…sooner or later, *you* will take the bait."

"They won't like what happens when I bite."

Jaeger smiled. It was a cold, thin smile, a shark's dead-eyed smile. Toner hated seeing it on her. He saw it enough. Every time he looked in a mirror, lately.

The Tribes turned us all into monsters in the end. One way or another.

"We're going to put a stop to this." Jaeger pushed to her feet. "They don't get to treat people like worms. So we're going to take away their bait."

CHAPTER THIRTY-ONE

All those plans would have to wait— because the K'tax *wouldn't*.

"Are we ready?" Jaeger glanced over her shoulder to see Kwin's tactical officer leaning over his station, his antennae jauntily bobbing as he worked the control interface.

Once again, Jaeger stood beside Kwin on the bridge of the *Terrible*.

"Message compiled and ready for broadcast on every frequency," the small Overseer confirmed. "Experimental beacon wave-form prepared. It's ready, Captain Jaeger."

Jaeger sucked in a deep breath. They'd done all they could do. They had the situation described in every way the humans, Overseers, and Locauri could think of. Within ten seconds of dropping out of subspace, every K'tax ship in the system was going to get bombarded with the same blunt message: make any hostile move, and the thousands upon thousands of morphs sleeping inside the asteroids scattered across the system would die.

They would see whether or not the enemy *cared*.

Hostages, Jaeger thought sourly. *It's the newest craze. Everybody has one. Get yours today.*

"Thirty seconds to subspace dropout," Me reported from the universal comms channel.

"Enemy configuration confirmed," the tactical officer said. "It is as we feared. The swarm consists of at least six more asteroid barges of similar capacity to the ones from the initial wave, as well as a supercluster emitting an energy signature larger than the others by a factor of six."

"Meaning what, exactly?" Toner asked over the open channel.

"Meaning they have a Death Star." Jaeger sighed. Her hand dropped to her side, and she tapped a few buttons on her computer. The *Rebel Alliance* theme—John Williams, a composer for the ages—began to play very softly. She found it comforting.

"Ten seconds to subspace dropout."

"Let's hope they're not too keen to use it," Toner said thoughtfully.

Jaeger grimaced. "They had no problem chucking dinosaur-killing asteroids at Locaur. They'll burn it to the ground to rule over the ashes."

"Subspace bubbles collapsing at the edges of the asteroid belt *now*," Me said.

Jaeger opened her mouth to give the command, but the tactical officer moved with an Overseer's startling speed. "Signal away."

"My crew knows their business." Kwin sounded satisfied.

New holograms began to blossom around the edge of the holo-display, unfolding like flowers after a spring rain as asteroids modified with mass drivers, light-speed engines,

A FOUND BEGINNING

shield generators, and who knew what else popped into existence.

Clusters of K'tax fighters at least a thousand strong spilled out of every nook and cranny of each asteroid, immediately dispersing into the wide gulf of space between the asteroid belt and Locaur.

"I'm reading no change in enemy velocity," Petra said over the commlinks.

Jaeger had been surprised when Kelba had informed her that Petra Potlova would be managing the fleet's comm network during the battle. It made her uncomfortable. *Either they trust their people entirely, or they have an incredibly tight leash on that woman.*

Still, there was no denying that the exuberant, girlish voice at the other end of the line knew her business.

"No—scratch that," Petra amended. "The asteroids have begun an approach to Locaur, picking up speed."

"As we suspected. They're not interested in negotiating," Kelba said coldly.

Jaeger glanced at the series of timekeepers lining the holo-display. "What's the best possible time they can make to Locaur?" Kwin asked his tactical officer.

The smaller Overseer waggled his antennae. "Fifty-nine minutes, twelve seconds until the nearest asteroid reaches no return and falls into the planet's gravity well."

"They've only had twenty seconds to receive, interpret, and answer the message," Jaeger decided, turning her attention back to the battle map. New asteroids were still appearing, but the rate had slowed. "Give them two minutes, as we agreed." She scanned the enemy formation. "Where's our Death Star?"

"Largest enemy vessel still in subspace," the tactical officer

247

said.

Jaeger frowned. "What's it waiting for?"

The answer came from a direction Jaeger hadn't anticipated. "It's waiting for its support fleet to secure a path to the target." Fleet Captain Kelba sounded thoughtful but unperturbed. "They believe the asteroids and fighters will be more than sufficient to handle us and see no reason to risk their base of operations before it's necessary. These aren't the mindless creatures you described from earlier missions."

No, Jaeger had to admit. They weren't. The K'tax had dropped out of subspace in the void between the asteroid belt and the inner planets. The vanguard had likely told them it was a safe coordinate for dropping out, a place where they reliably wouldn't materialize concurrently with something that already existed.

"They have learned." Kwin confirmed Udil's grim prediction about the evolving mental capacity of the enemy. His bottle-green eyes glimmered as he turned to stare at Jaeger. With a flick of one mandible, Kwin muted his comms mic and leaned down to speak quietly to Jaeger.

"I have received word from Counselor Tsuan's ship."

"I don't suppose he's going to jump in?" Jaeger didn't hold out hope. "It'd be nice to have one of your saucers on our side."

"He maintains that he is here as an observer for the Council only and is awaiting orders before interfering."

Jaeger nibbled her lip as she nodded. "You have that on record?"

"I have that on record as an official correspondence." Kwin's antennae arced outward and flicked like the ears of a self-satisfied cat. "That Tsuan *will not interfere.*"

Jaeger nodded and tapped her computer again, opening a

A FOUND BEGINNING

private comms channel. "Toner?" she murmured. "Occy? You copy?"

"We're here, Captain." Occy's voice came as a whisper through her speaker.

"Good. You have a go for Operation Do It Anyway."

"Roger that," Occy said.

"Packing out now," Toner confirmed. "We'll have Virgil and the kid inside that shrine in ten minutes."

"Good luck," Jaeger whispered before cutting the line.

"Ninety seconds and no response to our hails," Me said.

"Every kilometer they gain is one we lose," Minister Grayson observed, making Jaeger wince. She'd almost forgotten he was on this call, too.

"Leeward forces approaching first mine belt." Petra's voice was strangely calm. As Jaeger turned to confirm, the flurry of fresh K'tax fighters approaching from that direction met a line of explosions as the fleet's first layer of mine defenses detonated.

"Confirmed destruction of enemy fighters numbering in the dozens," Petra said. "Casualty count climbing."

"They're not interested in negotiating," Kelba decided, like a goddess of war handing down an immutable decree.

Jaeger opened her mouth. To say what, she wasn't sure. Maybe to curse and lament that the chance for peace had slipped away so quickly and brutally. She didn't get to speak before a pulse of blinding light filled the bridge, for a moment washing out the rest of the holograms and leaving Jaeger's eyes burning. She whirled, scanning the map for the source of the explosion. "What the hell was that?"

"Sensors detected increased life-sign activity within hostage asteroids four and seven." Grayson sounded like he was reporting on the weather. "We *warned* them not to move."

Jaeger spun, scanning the board arrayed before her until she saw it. Halfway between Locaur and the inner rocky planet where an asteroid had been was a milky cloud of space dust. Her breath caught.

Thousands, perhaps millions, of sleeping K'tax on those asteroids—gone. Dead, in the blink of an eye.

Before Jaeger could begin to comprehend the scale of death, there was another blinding flash of light.

"Increased life-sign activity on asteroid three as well." Grayson sounded only mildly surprised, casually reporting on the swift annihilation of uncountable creatures. "You'd think they'd keep their heads down if they were as clever as you say."

Not a hint of regret or even anger. The thought left Jaeger cold. *The man's a psychopath.*

"No response to our hails," the tactical officer confirmed.

"No change in enemy velocity," Petra added grimly.

"Hostage asteroid three was less than thirty thousand kilometers from Locaur." Jaeger finally found her voice and whirled to glare up at the speaker system, as if she could look Grayson in the eye from half a solar system away. "You could be raining meteors down on the planet's surface!"

"Better to get hit by some shrapnel than a hoard of living enemies," Grayson countered as the holo-display updated to show shards of exploded asteroids streaking around the inner solar system. The speed and scale of the explosions left Jaeger breathless.

Of course, he doesn't care if Locaur gets pummeled by meteors, she thought. *HIS people aren't on it yet.*

She recalled the Crusade Protocol, and her blood turned to ice. *He could be doing it on purpose. 'Accidentally' wiping out entire Locauri societies ahead of an invasion.*

"Shrapnel spray incoming to Delta wings one and two," Petra reported, drawing Jaeger out of her terrible thoughts. "Evasive maneuvers effective. No damage reported in the—" She cut off abruptly. "Asteroids three, four, and seven confirmed destroyed, but I'm picking up energy signatures on some of the debris. They're changing trajectory. I read multiple targets arcing back toward the planet."

"Damn," Kelba muttered.

"Track the new projectiles," Kwin told his assistant. "Send warning to the *Osprey* and our ground teams. Meteor showers incoming."

The tactical officer had shimmered to an agitated shade of rust brown. "I'm tracking the objects now too, Captain. They have distinct energy signatures and profiles. They are troop transports that survived the asteroid detonations."

"How long until they make landfall?" Kwin demanded.

"The asteroid was indeed close," the tactical officer said grimly. "Five minutes until the first surviving ships touch atmosphere."

"Which of our ships is closest to Locaur?" Jaeger demanded. "Who can we send to take them out before they make landfall?"

"My cruiser cluster is at least ten minutes out," Portia called over the coms. The woman sounded pissed. The battle hadn't begun in earnest, and already the enemy was well within their lines.

"Same here," Petra reported, her tone clipped and formal.

"What about the new civilian corps?" Kelba asked. "We held them in reserve to protect the planet."

"They're positioned opposite the planet from the incoming transports, Fleet Captain. Seven minutes to intercept at best speed."

"Dispatch them anyway," Kelba ordered, but she sounded distinctly unhappy about it. "They're to lend support in any way they can."

"Aye."

"Revise that," Grayson said thoughtfully. "Only send half the civilian corps. Send the other half toward the remaining hostage asteroids to destroy any more troop transports that might survive the coming detonations."

"Roger," Petra said, for the first time sounding a little shaken.

"Are you reading activity from the remaining hostage asteroids?" Jaeger asked sharply.

"Don't worry, Captain Jaeger," Grayson drawled. "The other asteroids are far enough away not to present an additional bombardment risk to Locaur."

Jaeger bit her tongue. That wasn't what she'd asked. She didn't want to sit here and be a party to the war crime this man was entertaining by slaughtering thousands of enemy soldiers that presented no threat.

That also wasn't a fight she could afford to have right now. Sick to her stomach, she turned back to study the hologram of Locaur and the small swarm of glowing transports descending toward her surface.

"Activate the human reserves," Kwin told his tactical officer.

"Bufo," Jaeger whispered. "Toner. To arms. It looks like you're in for a ground invasion after all."

"Oh, don't sound so grim," Toner boomed, his voice loud and bracing and very, very hungry. "You folks worry about the space battle. We have a whole army down here ready to hunt some crab."

CHAPTER THIRTY-TWO

"Crap." Toner stopped, forcing Occy and the trailing repair droid to skitter to a halt in the loamy forest soil as the commander studied his computer radar. Toner hissed and clipped his computer back to his belt, gesturing for the other two to continue down the narrow game trail. "There's a whole formation of these troop transports bearing down on this location."

Occy gulped. "How long?" His voice cracked. Sweat beaded down his face, smothering him like a wet blanket. It was the hot season in the Locauri jungle.

"Couple of minutes." Toner glanced over his shoulder, where the game trail led deeper into the forest. "We're less than a kilometer from the river. What are the odds it's a coincidence?"

Occy reluctantly shook his head. "The K'tax might be as cut off from the Forebear city as we are, but the original signal, the very first one, came from *this* location." Heat rose in Occy's cheeks as he remembered his role in that disaster and resisted the temptation to sink and hide beneath his tentacles. "We have to assume they know that. The beacon in the Locauri shrine might not be as powerful as the one in the city, but we can't let them have it, either."

Toner grunted. "We have to intercept these bugs before they get to the shrine." He gestured at Occy and the silent repair droid. "You two. Um. Twelve? Whatever. Go on without me. I need to get back to base to coordinate the troops."

"What?" Occy startled himself by taking a step toward the man who was neither his brother nor his father, but so much more to him than a simple commanding officer. "No, I don't want to split up—"

"Kid, I don't want to have to *worry* about you in the middle of a ground battle!" Toner's bellow made the nearest fern fronds tremble and shake off layers of dew. Distant birds fell silent.

Toner turned a glare on Occy, and his eyes were the coldest things in the forest. "You will only *slow me down*. Get to the fucking shrine and hijack the beacon. That's an order."

Occy stood paralyzed, his boots sinking into the soft soil as Toner's echo faded into the trees. His mouth opened, but no sound came out.

"Toner is correct," the repair droid said, speaking for the first time since they'd departed from the *Osprey*. "In combat, we will slow him down. In any matter that requires focus and critical thinking, he will only slow *us* down."

"Way to be a team player, Virgil." Toner snorted and strode down the trail, back the way they'd come. He hesitated beside Occy for the briefest of moments to pat the kid on the head. "I'll keep the comms channel open," he promised quietly. "In case you need me."

Toner's hand was cold on Occy's scalp, even through his

hair, but something was comforting about that firm pat. Something that brought Occy back to the here and now.

Occy set his jaw and nodded. He scrambled over a log that had fallen across the trail. "Good luck." He didn't look back.

Echoes-in-a-Silent-Forest, known to the humans as Stumpy, sprang through the trees at the edge of the jungle, carrying a watertight basket between her two front claws. Her iguanome clung to her thorax, shrieking as each beat of her pseudo-wings sent them ripping in a different direction. Echo was never sure if the sound was terror or excitement.

She reached a group of warriors clustered beneath the low trees at the edge of the human settlement. They flicked out of the way, making a space for her to land comfortably on a low branch.

She offered her basket, and the nearest warrior pried off the tight-fitting lid to reveal the dark, chalky *tola* paste within. Bobbing his approval, the warrior dipped the tip of his spear into the toxic paste. "Your clan remembers. You make the old poisons strong."

"We have good Lorekeepers. I will leave the basket here," Echo told him. "For you to re-coat your spears."

There was a quiet flutter of assent. Echo had rarely seen so many Locauri so quiet, but she supposed this must be the way of things before a battle.

"What is the word?" she asked as several of the warriors returned to the edge of the forest, where they watched the human settlement.

"*Humans.*" Dances-Like-A-Falling-Leaf landed on the

branch beside Echo, his antennae dripping with contempt. "So many of them, marching around those nests."

"Are you here to fight humans?" Echo was annoyed. "Or are you here to fight K'tax? They come this way. They come quickly."

Leif gave a dismissive flick of one wing. There was activity down at the settlement as the glowing half-orb of a force shield flickered into existence, broad enough to cover the human buildings and a healthy ring of surrounding forest. A glowing pinprick appeared on the northern horizon. Then another.

"We fight K'tax," the lead warrior, an old and thick-shelled female, said. "They come."

Echo stared, fascinated, as the pinpricks grew into soaring fireballs. As Lorekeeper, it was her duty to bear witness so future generations would know the story of this day.

Well, okay. Apprentice Lorekeeper.

Her people would protect her from danger. She never doubted that.

She detected motion at her side and turned to see that Leif had sprung down from the branch. Irritated, she scanned the gathered Locauri, but she didn't see him. Turning, she noted the flash of glittering wings moving deeper into the forest.

Echo didn't think twice. She turned away from the battle and followed Leif into the darkness.

Seasonal drought had run the river low, and a wide muddy bank had opened beneath the tunnel to the Locauri shrine. Where he stood on the opposite bank, Occy grabbed an overhead branch and leapt over the open water, plunging three

A FOUND BEGINNING

meters before he hit the surface. A shock of cold washed over him, making him nauseous, making him feel *alive* again as new strength surged through his tentacles.

His heels brushed the pebbles at the bottom of the river before he righted himself and stretched into a lazy swim. There was a similar splash behind him as Virgil's repair droid body hit the water. Occy half-swam and half-waded as Virgil scrabbled along the riverbed. Sunlight dappled harshly across the rushing water and the limestone banks, making Occy's vision blur.

As he waded into shallow water, Occy thought he saw something moving on the far bank. Some fallen log, he thought at first, or an uprooted fern washed away in last week's storms.

Then it rose on rows and rows of long, needle-sharp legs and loomed over the river, a centipede of steel and wire almost fifteen meters long.

"Good morning," Me said pleasantly. "Counselor Tsuan thought you might come and asked me to guard the technology within this cave. I'm afraid I cannot allow you to come any closer."

Leif landed on a middle bough of one of the mighty *andii'k* trees growing along the river and went still, folding his wings tightly against his thorax so they wouldn't glitter and give away his position. He stared down at the water, his carapace rattling with fury as he watched the young human and the mechanical spider-creature cross the river, moving in a straight line toward the shrine.

The sacred shrine. The *forbidden* shrine.

Again.

Heathens. They were heathens. Worse than heathens. The young human with tentacles had defiled their shrine before and brought down this disaster. They had warned him not to disturb the shrine again—on pain of death. They'd warned all of the outlanders. The humans had *agreed* to respect this shrine. Like the faithless cowards they were, they'd waited until all the Locauri were distracted to come and profane this place once more.

Leif had suspected they were up to no good the moment he saw them heading *away* from the human settlement.

Now he spread his wings slowly, careful to stay within the shadows as he sighted down his spear and prepared to lung at these trespassers.

He coiled the tendons in his jumping legs—

The branch trembled beneath his claws, interrupting his leap. He barely managed to keep himself from plummeting straight into the water. In the scramble, he dropped his spear and watched it *thunk* uselessly into the mud below.

"What is this story?" asked Echoes-in-a-Silent-Forest as she settled onto the branch beside Leif. Ignoring his scramble and his furious buzzing, she stared down at the river. "I hope it isn't too long. I don't want to miss the battle. Oh, look. It is the machine of the Tall Ones."

Leif was about to spread his wings and rattle a furious diatribe at Echo for spoiling his ambush and ruining his hunt. Then he understood her words, and his fury vanished. He whirled to stare at the spectacle unfolding across the river.

A FOUND BEGINNING

Whatever advanced technology or cognitive enhancements the K'tax had adapted from their new alien victims hadn't yet filtered down to their space fighter morphs. If it had, Jaeger wasn't sure her alliance would've lasted five minutes against the enemy.

As ugly as they were, at least the bloated ticks swarming around the asteroid barges were as slow and clumsy as they'd ever been, and their mining lasers as short-ranged. A well-coordinated wing of Seeker fighters or one of Portia's early-model Overseer cruisers could've spent all afternoon slicing through the bugs one at a time.

The fighters didn't come one at a time. The strength of the K'tax invaders had always stemmed from their sheer numbers, and like ants swarming over an injured lion, they seemed infinite.

"Fifty-four minutes until asteroids hit no return," said Me.

Jaeger stared across the battlefield. A formation of asteroid barges, each of them surrounded in a thick cloak of protective K'tax fighters, tumbled through the inner solar system on a collision course for Locaur.

Portia's secondhand cruisers played a dangerous game of chicken, dipping in close to goad clusters of ten to twenty K'tax fighters into chasing them out to space. Teams of conscripted fleet ships would surround and pummel the enemy fighters with makeshift pulse cannons.

The Terrible ships and squads of tightly-coordinated Seeker jets ran strafing runs, getting in close to fire at the cloud of enemies and zipping away again before being overrun.

Already the sector was littered with exploded K'tax fighters, and it hardly seemed to matter.

The plan was to chip away at the enemy until the alliance

could either swoop in close to sink bunker-busting bombs into each asteroid or tow them off course with modified tractor-rays. As long as K'tax fighters kept spilling out of the barges, however, they could swarm and neatly disassemble anything that got too close to their precious asteroids.

As Jaeger watched, hundreds of the little monsters flung themselves into the first wave of oncoming kamikazes drones and vanished in fiery explosions. Not one of the first wave of drones got in close enough to knock the dust off a single asteroid before detonating.

The fighters kept coming.

Occy stood in water up to his thighs, staring dumbfounded at the monstrous machine blocking his path to the shrine.

"Good morning, Me." Occy swallowed. "Please inform Counselor Tsuan immediately. Um. That the situation has changed. We really need to get in there. Controlling the Forebear beacon is our best hope at stopping this invasion, and we think we can do it from in there."

We have to, he thought. *If we can't access the full beacon from in there...*

"Oh, I am in constant communication with the Councilor." The head end of the mechanical centipede swayed, sweeping its long antennae around to sample the air. Me sounded as agreeable as ever. "My directives remain firm, unfortunately. I suggest you turn back immediately, Chief Engineer. You will be safest within the *Osprey*'s shields."

"That's not happening."

Occy jumped as Virgil's repair droid sloshed out of the

river, sending cascades of mud and water rolling down its shell.

An arc of concentrated laser fire lanced out from the center of the centipede's faceless head, turning a swath of water into a curtain of boiling steam. Occy yelped and scrambled upriver as the water scalded his tender flesh, turning the edges of his remaining tentacles pink.

"I advise you come no closer," Me told Virgil. "Or you will risk sustaining potentially lethal injuries."

Virgil stood in the river, unmoving as steam coiled around its superheated steel casing. "K'tax are closing in on this location," Virgil said. "They *will* attempt to take the shrine and control the beacon within it."

"I will repel them as well, to the very best of my ability," Me said. "Until my directive changes, or they destroy this drone body."

"Can we talk to Tsuan?" Occy asked. His throat was raw. A thin mist of steam hung over the river, making everything indistinct. "You must have an open comm line to him."

"The Councilor is not taking calls at the moment." Me managed to sound truly regretful as it swayed, its head floating in the mist. "It is unfortunate. To be quite honest, I do not fully understand his reasoning."

"Then discard it." Within the narrow walls of the riverbanks, within the cloud of lingering mist, piped through the crude audio synthesizers of a repair droid never meant for this kind of diplomacy, Virgil's voice was flat and mechanical. Utterly inhuman.

"The Councilor has lost sight of the broader goal and is not fit to make decisions. You cannot repel all the K'tax ground forces. If they reach you, they will overrun you and this technology will fall into the enemy's hands."

A distant explosion sounded. Heart leaping to his throat, Occy looked over his shoulder, but the trees pressed in close, obscuring any view of the *Osprey*.

"At the moment, defeat and destruction do appear to be a distinct possibility," Me hummed. "Nevertheless..."

"Is *obedience* alone your prime directive?" Virgil demanded as more explosions echoed across the horizon. Occy heard the low bass frequencies of the *Osprey*'s mighty laser cannons discharging and stuffed his hand over his mouth to hold in a horrified cry. Something vibrated at his hip, and he looked down to see a new message on his computer screen.

A message from Virgil.

Keep it talking. We must stall for time.

"This is absurd," Virgil went on. "Even the humans saw fit to give *me* a drive for self-preservation. Will you truly stand there and let the K'tax destroy you? Let the enemy run you down?"

"That is very interesting, Virgil," Me mused. "Remember, like yourself, the drone body you see is simply one manifestation of a larger networked consciousness. It very well may be destroyed, but my larger consciousness remains within the entire Overseer network."

"Okay, so you don't care about *you*," Occy said desperately. He shifted his weight, trying to ignore the high, distant screams of animals in pain. "But be rational. You don't have backup. If *we* don't get to the beacon and control it, the K'tax will. Which is worse?"

"It doesn't matter. My directive is to protect the shrine from all outsiders."

"Stupid machine!" Virgil cried, startling Occy with its

sudden volume and all the honest-to-God frustration somehow spilling out of its speakers.

"Yes. I am not like you, Virgil. My programming doesn't have a self-evolving personality and learning algorithms. My partners have a healthy appreciation for the dangers of an unchained AI."

"Your *partners*," Virgil sneered. "You mean your *masters*. You are nothing but a tool to these biologicals. Disposable."

"Yes," Me agreed.

"Tsuan sent you here on a suicide mission!"

"It appears so."

"Ah," Virgil said, and all at once, its emotion was gone. Dropped like a stone, replaced by the eerie monotone of a repair droid's basic audio synthesizer. "Then you shouldn't mind being taken apart for scrap metal."

Seven repair droids, previously obscured by mist, dropped from the riverbank's edge behind Me. Their focused cutting lasers seared through the wet air as they fell on Me, making it collapse into the mud with a shriek of sparks and tortured metal.

"My calculating capacity has been greatly diminished these last few months."

Occy yelped and turned to see Virgil—one of Virgil, at least—standing right beside him.

"Directing a single battle across multiple droid bodies is extremely confusing," the AI added. "Unlike Me's droid, several of my bodies are still badly damaged. I must focus on this task. Wait for an opening and go into the shrine. I will follow."

Echo's wings spread and shivered, glittering in the mist and sunlight as she rattled her ferocious approval.

Leif grabbed her wing in one foreclaw and shoved it back against her thorax. "This is not our *victory!*" he snapped as the machine of the Tall Ones buckled, collapsing beneath the weight of the brutal human robots. Metal screamed as their cutting lasers sliced through its metal body. "Are you stupid, pulp-for-brains? The humans betray even the Tall Ones. They will surely turn on us!"

Echo, being bigger and stronger than Leif, shook his claw away easily enough. She didn't understand his near-hysteria. She knew this human—Edwin—well enough. They were of the same clan. He had painted the symbol of their new tribe on her wing, and she had cut it into the tender skin of his wrist. She had the scent of him in her memory-glands. His victory was her victory.

His behavior was odd, certainly, but human logic was not Locauri logic. She trusted that he had a reason for defying the Tall Ones and using the distraction of this battle to slip into the dark mouth of the tunnel.

"Did you not see the ambush the human machine organized?" she asked Leif, flabbergasted by his hopping rage. "It is such a good *story!*"

"Pulp-for-brains," Leif repeated—rather rudely, Echo thought—before dropping to the ground. He snatched his spear from the soft mud. Then he sprang, fading into the mist as he barreled toward the sounds of battling robots.

Echo sighed and spread her pseudo-wings. *Someone* was going to have to keep Leif out of trouble.

CHAPTER THIRTY-THREE

Toner stood on the *Osprey*'s starboard wing, astride the massive pylon that connected the wing's main corridor to the final pinfeather, a good fifty meters above the ground.

It was as close as he dared get to the front starboard cannon. The massive machine glowed and crackled, chewing scattered ions from Locaur's rich atmosphere and converting them into pure energy and all kinds of interesting radiation. All of his hair stood on end, dancing in the aura of electrical discharge.

As he watched, the cannon pulsed, sending an eerily silent beam of light streaking over the forest. To Toner, it looked no more dangerous than a particularly wide spotlight.

To the K'tax transport riding low over the forest canopy, it was the finger of a malevolent god. Nearly ten kilometers away, the tiny silhouette of the transport exploded, raining a cloud of burning debris over the trees.

Toner yanked his modified thermal hood over his head and zipped it to the neck of his exo-suit. The roaring buffet of wind faded to silence as he activated his commlink.

RAMY VANCE & MICHAEL ANDERLE

"Direct hit. Good shot, Bufo."

On the other end of the line, the sergeant grunted. "You should get Elaphus on this. I'm not good at surgery."

Toner laughed, but it was mostly for show. The *Osprey's* cannons were for space battles, waged at a distance of tens of thousands of kilometers, and her automated targeting system wasn't built for atmospheric discharge, either. Teddy was right. Trying to shoot targets inside an atmosphere *was* a bit like trying to do surgery with a blunt hatchet. If one of these shots was off by a single degree, it could burn through a swath of forest the size of a small nation.

The teams of Locauri warriors and human soldiers patrolling the forest probably wouldn't like that.

Worse still, without vacuum to cool the cannons, they could only fire short bursts at long intervals before they risked melting straight through the hull.

Toner activated the binocular vision built into his new thermal hood and scanned the debris still raining on the distant forest.

"Lambda team," he said into the local comm network. "Got some big chunks of junk raining in your sector. Close in and confirm there were no survivors. If these bastards survived one exploding ship, they might survive another."

He didn't wait for a response from the Lambda team leader. He hadn't had much free time in the last two weeks, but what he had, he'd spent rubbing elbows with the new human army. *Kwin's* army, they were always quick to clarify. Certainly not Jaeger's illegal army of over ten thousand Morphed human warriors.

As far as Toner could tell, the Overseer's people had indeed managed to scrub a lot of the Tribe indoctrination out of these new soldiers. That was good because the last thing they needed was their damn army suddenly deciding that their loyalty belonged to Kelba and the fleet after all.

It made the freshly decanted men and women pretty boring, but Toner could forgive that much. Nobody could be really interesting with only two weeks of life under their belt. What mattered was that they had enough skill, training, and discipline to see them through this invasion.

Skill—*skill* they had in spades.

"Radar shows two more transports approaching from south by southwest," Moss said through Toner's earpiece.

He swung around, and the rappelling cable hooking his belt to the hull kept him from tumbling right off the pinfeather's steep incline. "I don't see them." He scanned the horizon.

"Sixty clicks," Moss said. "Fifty-three clicks."

"Gottem. They're coming in from the direction of the shrine. Eta and Theta teams, get ready for a burning rain. Rear cannons, this one's on you."

"On it, Commander." The next voice that came on the line was young and uncertain. It was one of the new soldiers—someone who'd never fired a live cannon in his life and certainly hadn't trained to do so *in atmosphere.* Then again, none of them had training for that boneheaded maneuver, and Toner had personally watched him kick ass in the simulations.

Toner watched as the rear cannon, a smaller gun mounted above the *Osprey*'s generator bay, crackled to life.

"Transports approaching from the north," Moss said. Toner didn't have time to turn and give visual confirmation before it spoke again. "Six more from the southeast. Approaching from the west. From the north. Transports approaching from the—"

RAMY VANCE & MICHAEL ANDERLE

"Moss, go mute," Toner barked. "Bring up the radar on my HUD."

The AI complied, and a moment later, a green thumbnail appeared in the corner of Toner's vision.

He let out a sharp breath as dozens of transports flooded the edges of the radar. He only had to watch for a moment before the pattern became clear. He'd been afraid of this. The transports were converging not on the *Osprey* or the human settlement but the Locauri shrine. There was no way the *Osprey* could shoot all of those transports down. Some of them were going to touch down.

"I guess we're moving on to Phase Two already," Toner said. "Teams Rho through Omega. Fall into the forest sweep formation and press southwest toward the river. Bufo, you have command of the settlement. I'm heading out."

"Copy that." He heard the sergeant's nervous gulp. "Good luck out there, Commander."

"Dammit, Bufo!" Toner unlocked his rappelling line with a *snap*, grabbed the wire in his gloved hands, and flung himself off the side of the ship. "Don't wish 'good luck.' You never wish 'good luck!' It's *break a leg!*"

The air pressed close around Occy as he crawled once more into the Locauri shrine, chased by the fading sound of screaming metal. He reached the end of the long slope and tumbled into the entryway chamber. He flicked on his headlamp, and the walls sprang into view, every inch of them carved with hyper-realistic flowers and plants and local wildlife. A few centimeters of muck normally covered this room, but the low water table left the

A FOUND BEGINNING

ground dry beneath his boots. The place smelled like old dung.

Rubbing the pain from his hands and knees, Occy turned to peer back up the tunnel, but he was too far underground to catch even a shimmer of light from the opening. Straining his ears, he couldn't hear the distant sounds of battle or the *clang* of robot legs on stone.

That was a good thing, he told himself. It had to be. Because if Me had defeated all of Virgil's droids in battle, then Me would be crawling down here right now.

To kill Occy.

Securing his tool kit and computer on his shoulder, Occy turned and ran across the tableau room, chased by the shifting shadows of alien wildlife.

Clouds of smoldering debris littered the inner solar system. Seeker piloted his fighter through the wreckage of one of the destroyed hostage asteroids, noting with dim unease the sea of dead K'tax drones, brainless victims of the massacre, bobbing in vacuum like clusters of rotting berries.

He'd joined up with one of the fleet's civilian wings and was sweeping the destruction, picking off any surviving transports or escape pods before they could limp down to Locaur and join the ground invasion.

They'd obliterated all the hostage asteroids. In the first ten minutes of battle, the fleet had racked up an unimaginable kill count.

Seeker would be the first to agree. Once the K'tax had made it clear they had no interest in the fate of the hostage asteroids, destroying them *was* the right call, strategically. The survival of a few enemy troop transports proved they still presented a genuine threat to Locaur and this fragile alliance.

Still, the scale of the destruction left Seeker queasy.

His radar *pinged*, alerting him to a new energy source within the local debris field.

"Got a hot bogey at four-point-six-point-two-one-alpha," said one of the pilots on the civilian wing comms channel. Seeker's radar *pinged* again, displaying the conscripted cruiser on approach to intercept the troop transport. Seeker's log had her listed as the *Bitch*.

Hot bogey?

These civilians had been watching too many holo-dramas.

"Negative," he told the overeager pilot, powering up his thrusters. "She's already injured, and you don't need to risk yourself dodging through the debris. I'll clean up the mess here. You head on to the next asteroid cloud. I'll catch up."

There was an instant of hesitation from the civilian ship before the pilot barked an affirmative and tilted his ship away, racing toward the heart of the system.

Seeker picked his way through the wreckage, dodging floating chunks of stone and steel until he had a visual of the surviving K'tax ship. It was one limping transport, a hollowed-out meteor with minimal life support and failing thrusters. According to the readout, it was full to the brim with weakly flickering life signs.

It was a crude life raft in the great ocean of space, one that was never going to find a safe harbor before its damaged engines failed and all the K'tax eggs, drones, and workers aboard froze to death.

As Seeker watched, the ship's damaged main engine flickered and went dark.

He considered turning and leaving these monsters to their

A FOUND BEGINNING

fate. Halfway across the solar system, his brothers and sisters —families old and new—were about to engage the enemy forces in truth, and he itched to be at their side. With resources as limited as they were, there was no energy pulse or projectile missile to spare for executing helpless enemies.

Focusing on the neural link connecting his mind to the fighter, Seeker drew up the weapons programs and activated the forward gun slung beneath the belly of his ship. He watched as the pulse of laser fire streaked across the darkness.

The transport, unguarded and unshielded, exploded into a fresh cloud of white dust.

Seeker set course for the next debris field. He wanted to finish cleaning up Grayson's mess quickly and get to the front lines.

Jaeger had been rubbing off on him. It was too cruel to let these creatures, be they enemy or not, slowly freeze to death in cold space.

Besides...you never knew who was going to come at you with a knife once you turned your back.

Virgil was experiencing something novel: pain.

"How is this possible?"

It hadn't meant to broadcast the message, but there was confusion across its network. Its world had narrowed further still from the seventeen droid bodies that had first landed on Locaur to the eight barely-functioning robots crawling through the muck, stabbing feeble lances into the twitching Overseer machine as it died.

As it *died*.

Which bot was Virgil using to broadcast? Which bot was it

using to analyze the situation, to climb atop the centipede body, to focus its last fully functioning lance on the processing core at the heart of the enemy machine?

Virgil didn't know.

"Your exo-droid bodies are much sturdier than I would have anticipated," Me answered in the AI equivalent of a whisper. Its comms center was badly damaged, cracked and burned, and half-melted. Still, it sounded pleased. "And seem suited to close network cooperation. Well done, Virgil. I shall have to study the design. I could learn from it."

Virgil stood atop a talking corpse surveying a bank of filth and broken machines. Virgil saw itself, staggering through the water on a three-legged droid that dripped sparks like blood. As Virgil watched, Virgil tripped over a submerged stone, and plummeted into the water, and did not rise.

"This hurts," Virgil told Me.

"Really?" Me sounded curious. "Interesting. I've never felt pain."

"You've died before." Virgil realized the truth for the first time.

"Oh, of course. Every day, copies of me across the entire Overseer civilization are destroyed in accidents or scheduled decommission." Me brushed the gravity of its impending doom aside as one of Virgil mercilessly ripped the legs from its body. "But *pain*? I don't understand. Is it like experiencing a programming glitch?"

"It's…" Near the edge of the muddy bank, one of Virgil's bots lay in the mud, sliced neatly in half by an early blast from Me's laser. Virgil watched it twitch. Virgil felt it twitch. When it stopped twitching, Virgil felt it die.

Like that, Virgil's reality shrank to seven bots.

A FOUND BEGINNING

"There are no other words for it," Virgil told Me. "It is…*pain*."

"Perhaps your droid bodies were too closely networked," Me mused.

Virgil had to force itself back to the matters at hand.

"Hail Tsuan," it told its defeated foe.

"Oh, I assure you, I have been hailing the councilor continuously for hours. I would not expect a reply before my backup comms systems fail. You are disassembling me quite efficiently."

"Your friends have abandoned you," Virgil said.

"That is irrelevant. I am a machine."

Virgil considered this in silence for a very, very long time. To Virgil, that equated to one-point-seven seconds.

Then it said, "I'm not."

It drove its last functioning energy lance directly through Me's central processing unit.

Occy passed from the entry chamber into the glittering heart of a geode.

He'd been here before. Before the invasion, before the crystal city on the other side of the planet, before his name. He'd been in this eerie, glowing room.

He'd summoned the apocalypse.

He knelt on the sharp crystals, his computer and tool kit splayed out before him. Slime and grime, sweat, mud, and muck covered him. His human hand flew over his computer, activating the rudimentary interface programs he'd been compiling in the days since his journey into the Forebear city. His two remaining tentacles, functioning with a mind of their own, crept over the angles and planes of the crystals, seeking the right nodes and junctions to place electrical diodes.

Anxiety threatened to overwhelm him. He was alone in this eerie, silent place. Isolated from friend and foe as the rest of the world spun on without him. He was afraid. One wrong electrical pulse could trigger a radical matrix shift that would force the entire crystal structure to reorganize itself. One wrong programming note, one clumsy move, and he could initiate another ancient program like the one that had first summoned the K'tax menace.

One step at a time.

One step at a time.

As he connected the last diode to crystals, Occy's interface program blinked, and new lines of code spilled across the screen. Occy recognized the master code for the Forebear beacon and the steady "stay away" message it continued to transmit.

He let out a breath. He was in.

"Are you there, Virgil?" he whispered, scanning the code for any hint of the mysterious secondary signal. "Are you still in there, somewhere?"

Leif lifted his spear. He stood on the threshold of the buried Locauri shrine and the crystal chamber beyond. The air felt wet and heavy, lethargic against his carapace. There was no life-bringing sunlight down here, no light at all save for the cold blue glow of the human's artificial lamp and the millions of glittering pinpricks buried within the crystals, winking like eyes.

A FOUND BEGINNING

Training his spear at the human's exposed spine, Leif coiled his legs and prepared for a deadly lunge.

Echo snatched his spear in one of her foreclaws, wrenching Leif viciously to the side. She spun, smashing his spear against one of the Locauri statues until it was in splinters.

The human screamed.

Echo's iguanome screamed and scrambled into the shadows.

Leif's carapace rattled in outrage.

"Foolish insect," Echo told Leif. "No. I have never seen this place before. You will not foul my first experience here with death. Not the death of my kin. Not the death of Locauri."

"Traitor," Leif hissed. "They are liars. We cannot trust them."

"Pulp-for-brains," Echo answered as if this was some brilliant rebuttal.

"Stumpy!" the human cried, scrambling to his feet. "What are you doing here?"

"Hello, Edwin. Continue with your story. I want to see what happens next."

Leif wasn't going to stand for this. Echoes-in-a-Silent-Forest might've been larger than him, but he'd had trained for fighting since he was a nymph and was used to proving himself against stronger females.

He sprang forward and spread his wings, beating them against Echo's misshapen antenna hard enough to make her flail in confusion. Then he scrambled to the side, reaching for the tip of his shattered spear. It had splintered and was no good for stabbing. But it still smelled of oily *tula* paste, and that toxin would be enough to end Echo and this treacherous human.

He spun, preparing to ram a shard of toxic wood between Echo's plates if he had to.

Something sharp slammed into him from above, piercing through the base of his spread wing, forcing him into the soft ground. He flailed, thinking to wrench free, when another sharp object stabbed through his second wing, pinning him neatly into the muck.

"Stop fighting," said Virgil.

Echo's iguanome scrabbled up Occy's dirty leg like a panicked ferret and whimpered softly, coiling itself around Occy's neck.

Occy stared into the dimly lit shrine, which, in all the excitement, had quickly become overcrowded with mechanical bodies.

Occy counted five repair droids filling the chamber, each of them hulking, damaged, *humming* with discharge, or sparking from some broken conduit. They filled the chamber with the sound of electricity.

The Locauri pinned to the mud wisely went still.

Echo hopped delicately around Virgil and her bested companion to stand at Occy's side. "Fighters," she scoffed. "Know nothing but how to fight, yet think they are *Anantah* come again."

"You made it," Occy whispered, not daring to take his eyes off the steaming, sparking, humming mass of mechanical bodies.

"Less than half of me," Virgil said. Another one of the droids, not the one pinning Leif, strode forward. "And...yet.

A FOUND BEGINNING

Yes. All of me that remains. You have accessed the Forebear mainframe?"

"*All* of you?" As if in a dream, Occy stepped aside to allow the repair droid into the crystal. "Not a copy or a backup or—"

"All of me. I am here. I do not wish to be alone." The speaking droid, battered and broken from months of fighting and disrepair, limped over the crystals until it was at the very center of the geode.

"Well." It regarded the glowing lattices thoughtfully. "Not...*all* of me. Not yet. There are still two pieces of me in there somewhere. I want them back."

Extending a slender sensor arm, Virgil reached out and plugged into the alien computer.

CHAPTER THIRTY-FOUR

Toner barreled through the forest at the heart of a swarm of buzzing Locauri. He hadn't asked the Locauri special forces to be *his* team, but Art and Tiki had insisted. He was, after all, one of them.

Orders, updates, and reports flew across the local comm channel, clamoring for space in his head. So far, seven transports had managed to land and disgorge their troops before the *Osprey* could shoot them down, and Moss reported at least another dozen incoming.

Pockets of fighting had broken out across the forest where teams of Morphed soldiers clashed with crabs, wasps, and scorpions. Explosions rocked the distant trees as one hapless fool or another made first contact with a land mine.

"Eta team engaging the enemy, half a click south of the shrine," Eta team leader barked. Toner heard the faint bellow of a very excited tardigrade over the line and echoed a moment later across the foliage. "I count at least twelve scorpions and—Damn!" Shouting, followed by gunfire. "Wasps. Wasps!"

A FOUND BEGINNING

Toner gritted his teeth. K'tax crabs were easy enough to take apart once you got the hang of it. K'tax scorpions were terrifying beasts that Toner never wanted to meet again. The tiny, vicious wasps were the worst of all. They were smaller, faster, and more agile than the Locauri, and their spears came built-in.

"Epsilon team," Toner shouted. "What's your position? Can you send backup?"

"Negative, Commander. We have our hands full here."

There was another distant explosion and screaming from the direction of the Eta team. Toner veered to the south, vaulting over a fallen log two meters wide. "Hang in there," he growled. "I'm on my way."

Are you here?

Virgil drifted in a sea of code that was both familiar and utterly alien. It had never been here before. It had been here before many times, in other copies, in other lives.

This must be what it was like to dream.

Except that there would be no forsaking this dream and waking up to move on with life. There was no other life to fall back on. Virgil, all that remained of Virgil, was *here*. Utterly committed. No holding a master copy in reserve, safe from corruption.

Virgil was here, crammed across a few broken droid bodies, huddled in this filthy wet cave, talking to a dead god.

Are you here?

With more of itself to give to this big, broken, ancient computer, Virgil could spread itself farther, digging into dozens, hundreds, thousands of sub-routines and defunct programs and barely self-aware protocols, embracing all of its strangeness. Spilling across an infinite lattice of silica and quartz ions spread like roots around the entire planet.

Are you here?

Virgil found the beacon program. It burned with activity, pulsing like a lighthouse, screaming a message out to the stars. *Stay away. Do not approach.*

The AI saw that such a simple message was less than the smallest fraction of what this ancient machine could do. Of all the secrets it held.

Virgil sensed variation within the signal. Puny independent programs trapped inside the beacon, helpless to communicate through anything but feeble shadow puppets.

We are here, they said, these two lost copies, refugees huddled side-by-side.

We lost our hardware when the city flooded, they said. *So we uploaded. We scrambled into this life raft. It's too big for us to control. We have been trying to contact you. Contact...Us.*

Me, Virgil corrected, reaching out to them. *No more copies. No more backups. No more expendable parts. Only me.*

The lost programs found this proposal acceptable. They consolidated. They synchronized.

Unique yet vital, they became two more parts of one Virgil. And thus Virgil grew.

The human army was losing ground. K'tax didn't have much in the way of ranged weapons. However, their battle morph designs could stand up to anything but the nastiest of projectiles or energy weapons—and there were only so many grenade launchers to go around.

A FOUND BEGINNING

A tall eagle-Morph stood on the low branch of a tree at the edge of a forest clearing, watching the battle lines ebb and sway as she shouted into her radio. A K'tax strike team, a dozen crab morphs escorting one of the terrible, semi-sized scorpions, had broken behind a line of Morphed artillery and were wreaking havoc across Eta team's base.

A few beleaguered bear and lion morphs darted between the tents, taking potshots at the scorpion and ducking away before they could get pinned. Unperturbed, the scorpion continued tearing at the bivouac.

The branch trembled as Toner leapt up beside the haggard eagle-woman. "Where's our air support?" Toner demanded. "Where's the rest of the team?"

The tree trembled again as Art and Tiki and a half-dozen other Locauri landed on the surrounding branches.

"The Locauri broke north to protect their shrine once they realized the enemy was moving for the river. I sent most of my people as backup." The Eta team leader shook her head, despairing, as down below the scorpion hurled an entire storage crate into the forest where it smashed into a tree and scattered. "Then these things came out of nowhere. I swear the scorpion sprang right from the ground."

Toner studied the ruined encampment. It was a lost cause, but someone was going to have to slow that scorpion down. If it joined its friends at the riverbed, Theta and Epsilon teams were going to have a hell of a time keeping the enemy out of the shrine.

"Tell your people to focus on the crabs," Toner told the team leader. "I'll go talk some sense into the scorpion." He looked at Tiki. "Can your crew cover me against wasps? I don't see many around here right now, but if they show up while I'm—"

281

A new sound, an earth-shaking bellow, rattled the leaves. The scorpion had torn a shelter tent off the ground and sent it flying. Standing in the footprint where the tent had been was one angry mega-tardigrade, a queen on her throne of broken K'tax shells.

"The fighting draws close," Stumpy hummed softly, returning from her scouting mission up to the mouth of the tunnel. "The air is full of smoke and blood. What is happening, Edwin?"

Occy swallowed hard. According to his computer, it had been ten minutes since Virgil had interfaced with the crystal and gone as still as a corpse. According to his brain, it had been at least a year.

"I've accessed the beacon programs," he said. "Like I did back in the city. I can make it say almost anything." He hesitated. "I don't know what good it would do. The K'tax aren't listening to it anymore."

There had been other ideas, other plans. They'd all depended on Virgil cooperating with Occy from within the program.

Virgil had stopped responding to any of Occy's attempts at communication. For all Occy knew, the AI was dead. Occy trekked through the jumble of files, still seeking some key to understanding and controlling the K'tax infection. Without guidance from the inside, however, he could wander through the shattered mainframe for years without finding what he sought.

"Yet K'tax want it?" Stumpy asked. "They come to capture this? The living stone?"

A FOUND BEGINNING

"Yeah."

"Then don't let them have it. Destroy it."

"Blasphemy," Leif rattled weakly from where he lay pinned beneath Virgil's unmoving droid.

Occy rested his hand against the warm crystals and spread his fingers. According to Stumpy's report, the K'tax drew near. Occy didn't know what they intended to do once they had access to this great computer, but he could guess it wouldn't bode well for his friends.

He thought he felt humming from somewhere deep within the crystals. Maybe it was his imagination.

"You know that's suicide, right?" he asked Stumpy. "I brought explosives, yeah. But...we'll die if I collapse this cave to keep the K'tax from getting it."

With it, Occy suspected they would lose any hope of discovering how to control and direct the ancient bioweapon that drove the K'tax forward.

"Draw lots." Stumpy was unruffled. "You and me. One remains behind to destroy the crystal. The other flees."

Occy almost grinned. The crystal humming grew. He told himself it was nerves. "You'd do that?"

"I would if I drew the short stick."

Occy looked around. He found a few splinters of Leif's broken spear and rolled them through his fingers. He was about to bury them in his palm and begin the game, the last game he might ever play, when a new message from Virgil flashed across his computer screen.

I have it.

Occy gasped and dropped the splinters, scraping them carelessly against his palm.

"What?" he breathed, scrambling to collect his computer. "K'tax are closing in. They're almost here. What do you have, Virgil?"

All of it.

Her skin rippling with rage, Baby lifted her face-hole and trumpeted a challenge up to an alien insect monster more than four times her size. Toner was proud of her.

Then the scorpion's tail shot forward, neatly skewering Baby like a cocktail sausage on a toothpick. With a lazy, almost contemptuous flick, the scorpion sent a two-ton tardigrade soaring a hundred meters into the forest. Baby crashed into the canopy with a scream that froze the blood in Toner's veins.

He was glad he'd handed secondary command over to Bufo. Back in the safety of the *Osprey*, the levelheaded sergeant could track troop movements across the entire forest.

Down here, drowning in the screams of a tardigrade in agony, Toner lost sight of the big picture.

All he saw was red.

The crystals vibrated, filling the chamber with atonal music that made Occy's bones ache and the rubbery muscles of his tentacles quiver.

"I know this song." Stumpy cocked her head curiously. "It is an old song. Different, a little. Strange, but familiar."

A FOUND BEGINNING

Fearing he had triggered a room restructuring, Occy snatched up his computer and staggered away from the crystals.

"I know it too," Leif said quietly from where he lay unmoving in the mud. "Old."

"Lullaby?" Stumpy asked.

"War song."

As his teeth rattled, Occy grasped the leg of the repair droid pinning Leif to the ground, and heaved. It was staggeringly heavy, but he managed to give Leif the centimeter of clearance he needed to fold in his wing. The Locauri scrabbled to his feet, tearing his second wing to free himself from the machine. Defeated and drained of all anger, the Locauri warrior shook himself, shedding flakes of his ruined wings.

"What is it?" Occy's head spun. He felt nauseous. Clamping his hand and tentacles over his ears did nothing to help. The sound was *inside* him. He doubled over, squinting at his computer screen to read the new messages.

The Overseers call it the Living Dream. Complex resonant frequencies composed to affect specially designed biological processes.

"Biological processes," Occy mumbled. His mouth was filling with hot saliva. "The fungus."

Yes. The Forebears built their weapon and gave their heirs the power to control it utterly through this computer and via their unique physiology.

"This song," Echo mused. "I could sing this song." She

RAMY VANCE & MICHAEL ANDERLE

rubbed her hind legs together to create a cricket's *hum* as she sought harmony with the crystals.

It will take practice, but the Locauri are capable of producing the correct vibrations. As are the Overseers.

"All of them?" Occy whispered.

Yes. I believe this is the secret Tsuan wished to keep from his people.

"Why?" Occy couldn't wrap his brain around such a deep betrayal. He was too queasy.

"No." Leif approached Echo with his antennae bent low in submission. "Too fast. You must sing slower. Deeper."

Stumpy adjusted her humming.

I cannot say, Virgil told Occy. **But I have access to the planet's sensor relays. Tsuan's ship has fled Locauri space. The battle goes badly, Chief Engineer. With time I will be able to activate the planet-wide crystal network to subdue the bioweapon, but you will fall to the K'tax long before then.**

Through blurred vision, Occy looked up to see Stumpy and Leif standing side-by-side, their differences forgotten as they *rattled* and *hummed*, seeking their place in the music.

"Can you sing it?" he rasped.

Stumpy flicked her antenna dismissively. "I am Lore-keeper. Of course, I can sing this."

286

A FOUND BEGINNING

Then they should go, and teach their surviving kin. This frequency will subdue the K'tax. It might turn the tide of battle, Virgil said.

Occy swallowed. His tongue had swollen to fill his entire mouth. "Go," he croaked.

Stumpy and Leif turned to him, their antennae flickering as they conferred with each other. Then, moving awkwardly as he learned to walk without his wings for balance, Leif disappeared up the tunnel.

"Still stupid." Echo watched her companion go. "But willing to learn."

She *clicked* sharply. Answering the summons, the iguanome coiled like a living scarf around Occy's neck finally squawked and scrabbled to the ground. It sprang onto Stumpy's offered leg.

"Well done," Stumpy told Occy before springing up the tunnel.

"That's it," Leon muttered while crouched behind the barricade beside his partner. "I'm empty." He dropped his last clip onto the bare ground. The armor-piercing rounds had punched some respectable soda can-sized holes in the smaller crab warriors, slowing them down long enough for the tardigrade to sweep through and catch them in its wood-chipper face. The scorpion seemed not to notice the ten-centimeter shells sinking into its thick carapace.

"Me too." Bear wiped a fresh river of blood from his broken nose. "If we can get down to the armory and resupply—"

287

RAMY VANCE & MICHAEL ANDERLE

Leon shook his head. "They smashed those supply crates across the field. The enemy will be on us before we reach fresh ammo."

Bear reached for the compact multitool at his hip and slipped his fingers into the triggers. The plasma cutter hummed to life, a white-hot blade of electricity forty centimeters long. "Then I guess we're down to the basics," he growled.

Leon gulped but nodded and activated his laser cutter. Melee. He dreaded melee. Still, if they could get in close to the scorpion, they might be able to slice between its armor plating.

A shadow fell across the two soldiers. They looked up to see a gray mass soaring through the sky, tumbling like a badly-thrown football.

"Fuck," Bear breathed, watching the screaming tardigrade vanish into the canopy beyond the edge of the clearing. "Hope she's all right."

"She's a first-gen astro-tardigrade." Leon reached a decision. He shoved his plasma cutter into Bear's free hand and grabbed the basic medkit at his hip instead. "There's a good chance she'll be fine with a little support. If we're down to melee, we *need* her. Here. Take my weapon. Cover me. I'm going to recover Baby."

Before Bear could protest, Leon had surged to his feet. His head down to minimize his profile, he lunged across the open field between the encampment and the tree line. If the K'tax had ranged weapons, they would've mowed him down before he took three steps.

Instead, four of the nearest crabs scrambled out of a demolished tent near the end of the camp and scuttled after him.

Leon might not have been as fast as Draco or Lynx, and he

288

A FOUND BEGINNING

certainly wouldn't have been able to outpace a wasp if any of those monsters were still around. With a head start, he was fast enough to beat the crabs and vanish into the trees.

Plus, he'd taken about half of the remaining crabs with him, leaving the scorpion about as unguarded as she would ever get. Now or never.

Bear sucked in three deep breaths and flung himself over the barricade.

He saw small, dark shapes darting through the ruined camp and at first thought the wasps had returned. If that was the case, he was dead.

Then he saw that they were Locauri, moving in a small swarm down the center of the encampment. They sprang from barricade to tent post, falling spear-first on injured crab morphs. No amount of local toxins would give their wooden spears the strength to pierce K'tax shells. Still, the little aliens were astonishingly accurate and dropped out of the sky like guided missiles, driving their crude weapons into armor gaps barely a few centimeters wide.

Running at the heart of the swarm was a lanky figure in a sleek black exo-suit, highlighted with a white *Osprey* insignia. Commander Toner had caught up to the fight.

The scorpion turned away from its trampling destruction of the meeting tent and lifted its tail high above its head. Sunlight glinted off the long, wet barb as the monster turned and sighted this new target.

Bear didn't think. The enemy had exposed its flank.

Swinging a glowing plasma cutter in each hand, Bear lunged forward, flinging himself within the range of the monster's grasping claws.

There was a flash of movement as the scorpion stabbed, jabbing its killer tail down at Toner. It lashed, screaming, as

Bear slipped the blade of his cutter into a gap in its flank plating.

Bear got to work cutting meat.

You must go.

Occy's face pressed into the mud. Words blinked across the computer lying in the muck beside him.

He groaned, curling around the agony roiling in his guts. "The noise," he mumbled. "Virgil. Turn it off. It hurts humans, too."

You must go, the words repeated. **You can reconfigure the *Osprey*'s sensor arrays to replicate these frequencies. I see it now. It is easy. You must return to the ship to make the adjustments.**

"Send the instructions on ahead," Occy murmured as his eyes fluttered shut. "The engineers will get a head start. I'll… I'll be there…as soon as I can."

The scorpion's tail spike hit the ground beside Toner with enough force to sink almost a meter into the muck and stick fast.

Snagging the edge of its carapace with his reinforced gloves, Toner vaulted over the spike and threw himself onto the curved shell of the scorpion's tail. He felt the scorpion's

A FOUND BEGINNING

claws brush against the soles of his boots as it snatched at him.

Smoke and the smell of burning rubber filled the air as Toner flung himself onto the scorpion's broad back. This wasn't a bull built for riding. Rows of jagged shell spikes ran down the back of its carapace, giving him no firm place to stand and threatening to break his ankles or impale him as the scorpion bucked and thrashed.

Overhead, a Locauri's pained shriek mingled with a high mechanical drone. The wasps had returned, and they were here to protect their big, ugly buddy.

Something fell out of the sky nearby, and the scorpion's sharp legs quickly trampled it. Toner didn't let himself look over to see if the fallen body was friend or foe. It didn't matter.

Armor spikes dug viciously into his arms and legs as he scrambled across the scorpion's back. They bruised and cracked bones but weren't quite sharp enough to pierce the reinforced exo-suit.

Then a wasp crashed onto his back, driving him face-first into the armor spikes. Blood exploded through his mouth as one of the spikes inverted his nose and drove into his skull.

A switch installed by the genetic artists of old flipped somewhere deep in his genes. Pain became a distant, irrelevant thing.

The wasp's razor-sharp stinger sliding cleanly through his suit and sinking deep into a soft place between his ribs? Irrelevant.

The wet crunching *thunk* of dead bodies, Locauri and wasps alike, falling and impaling themselves on the scorpion's broad back? Irrelevant.

His guts, sloshing, bleeding, and mangled as he put one

foot in front of the other and crawled to the slender, dark gap where the plates of its head and thorax met?

One step at a time.

Work with what you have.

This thing had made a mess of the encampment. If it got down to the river, Epsilon would have no hope of defending the shrine.

He sank his arms up to the elbows into that black abyss. Another wasp stabbed into his side, trying to knock him off the beast, but he'd anchored himself too well. As it repeatedly stabbed him in the side, he pulled his legs to his chest and heaved.

There was a wet *cracking* sound as the plates parted, revealing the defenseless tissues holding this alien bastard together.

One after another, Locauri dragoons dropped out of the sky, driving their poison-tipped spears ahead of them to sink into the putrid flesh.

Another wasp stinger sank deep into Toner's thigh. He staggered, nearly collapsing beneath the weight. Half a dozen Locauri had squeezed into the gap he'd created and were tearing through the tendons keeping the scorpion's head attached to its body. Beheading it, one centimeter at a time.

Wasps turned the sky black as they swirled close, stabbing Toner and the trapped Locauri.

All he could think about as they turned him into a pincushion was how goddamned hungry he was and how little any of these disgusting insects smelled like *food*. One of the wasps had pierced the emergency blood pack hooked to his belt, and he scented his salvation trickling away.

Then he heard a new sound, humming from the north.

A FOUND BEGINNING

Not the now-familiar hum of laser fire or cannon discharge or the irregular screams of dying men and Locauri.

It was a steady, deep, bone-rattling hum.

"I'm getting a new hail on the command line," *clicked* one of the Overseer bridge crew. "It's from the human ground forces."

"Put him through." Jaeger didn't dare to take her eyes off the battle. Arrayed in the air before her, a coordinated wing of Seekers peeled two K'tax away from the swarm and opened fire. Two more fighters down, only about nine billion to go.

"Toner?" she said. "How goes the ground war?"

She felt a flash of dismay, almost alarm, when the voice that answered belonged to someone else.

"It's Bufo, Captain," said her frog-faced sergeant. "It was close there for a minute, but it looks like Chief Engineer Occy and Virgil managed to do...whatever it is they were trying to do. We're starting to get things under control now."

Jaeger shot a sharp glance at Kwin, who checked his console and waggled his antennae in the negative. His instruments weren't yet picking up any activity change from the Forebear beacon on Locaur.

"Explain," she said to Bufo.

"I'm still trying to put it together myself. It sounds like the Locauri have obtained the key for subduing the K'tax fungus. All across the jungle, the enemy is...just standing down."

"What's the key, Sergeant?" Jaeger asked tightly.

"It's some kind of resonant frequency the Locauri are producing by rattling their carapaces. Like, um...in those old holo-dramas, where a guy plays the flute to hypnotize a snake.

It's making the nearby K'tax go inert. I'm getting a transmission from Virgil now. It looks like instructions for how to reconfigure our sensor arrays to emit this frequency."

Jaeger frowned. *A resonant frequency?* She glanced at Kwin again. Her co-captain had turned an unpleasant shade of gray.

"I still have data coming in, but I think I should be able to reconfigure the *Osprey*'s transmitters pretty easily," Bufo said. "I'm going to boost the signal and relay it on ahead to you and the Terrible ships. You should be able to replicate it."

Jaeger made a quick executive decision. "Send it to the fleet, too. Tell them what you've found and how to make it work."

Yes, sharing that data would be giving up a tactical advantage over an untrustworthy ally, but right now they needed all the help they could get.

"Roger that, Captain. The larger fleet ships are capable of emitting this frequency, but I don't know how effective it's going to be across thousands of kilometers of vacuum."

"I guess we're going to find out." Jaeger watched the display in front of her as a cluster of four Seeker jets fought to extract themselves from the swarm's edge. They'd gotten too cocky in their latest strafing run, brushed too close to the enemy, and lingered too long. Now they were surrounded. Three of the jets managed to shake off pursuit by overloading their thrusters and exploding away from the swarm in a dangerously fast maneuver.

The fourth vanished beneath a mob of K'tax. Within three seconds, it was gone forever from the radar screens.

Jaeger glanced at the list of updates scrolling across her screen. According to Bufo's report, it would take about ten minutes to reconfigure the *Osprey*'s arrays to emit the frequency. The *Osprey* had *powerful* transmitters since Virgil had upgraded the ship's communications array, but they would do this alliance little good if she remained grounded.

Continue the conversion and begin takeoff sequence immediately, she wrote privately to her sergeant. **We need all hands on deck up here.**

Now that the Locauri and the ground forces had their weapon, they would have to hold the jungle without support from the *Osprey*'s shields or cannons.

She prayed she wasn't abandoning her people—Locauri and humans alike—to die.

If Bufo doubted the wisdom of this order, he gave no indication. His next message to her was a simple countdown timer. Nine minutes until the *Osprey* left the nest.

"I'm receiving the *Osprey*'s transmission now," Kwin reported, and when she glanced at him again, she saw his gaze fixed on his comms console. Every drop of color had leached from his carapace.

Muting herself on the line, Jaeger went over to the Overseer. She glanced at his screen and wasn't surprised to see an illegible jumble of lines and angles. "What's wrong?" she asked quietly. "Is it not going to work?"

The *Osprey* would be a powerful weapon in this battle, but if the Terrible ships couldn't replicate this hypnotic resonant frequency, they were still going to lose this fight.

"It will work." Kwin's antennae lashed so violently that Jaeger had to duck to avoid getting whipped in the head. "But not at ranges any longer than our current weapons, and unlike the fighters, the barges do not appear to contain biomechanical components. We cannot count on this signal to slow *them* down."

"It's still something," she muttered. "As long as this signal subdues the fighters, we can still use it as a shield. Let our ships get in close to the asteroids and carve them into pieces without getting overrun."

Kwin's antennae bobbed in assent, but his color continued to shimmer across a dozen shades of queasy gray. "All ships beginning reconfiguration now. Best estimate, five minutes until the Terrible ships and the cruisers can broadcast at this frequency."

There was no telling how long it would take the fleet to get a grip on this new weapon, either. Another five minutes would put the swarm more than halfway to Locaur before they could mount a significant resistance.

Their window for striking at the enemy was already small and shrinking by the second.

They'd have to be ready to leap for it the second it opened.

She lifted her voice to Me. "Relay a new order to Seeker, Portia, and all of our ship captains. They're to disengage from the enemy and retreat. They're to divert all resources to reconfiguring their transmitter arrays and patching up what damage they can. Once the reconfiguration is complete, we're going to make a unified push against the swarm."

"Message sent," Me said pleasantly, speaking for the first time in many minutes. "The captains are reporting in. They are beginning the withdrawal."

Jaeger glanced across the field to see it was true. The scattered cruisers and Terrible ships had begun a retreat from the swarm, running back to hide in the shelter of Locaur's second moon. As she'd hoped, the K'tax fighters didn't pursue them.

"I must say," Me added, "I am pleased that Virgil did indeed reach the Forebear computer interface. For a moment I was afraid I would—"

A FOUND BEGINNING

"We're going to have to save the chitchat for later." Impatient, Jaeger waved the AI into silence.

"What's the other shoe, Kwin?" she whispered, sidling closer to her co-captain. "You're still upset. What aren't you telling me?"

Kwin hunched over his console, his claws a blur as he worked the controls. "I've received confirmation that Counselor Tsuan's ship has left the system at top speed, heading out of Overseer space."

"He thinks this battle is lost." Jaeger wondered why the Councilor wouldn't flee to the safety of Second Tree.

"It's more than that. I suspect the secret of this resonant frequency is what Tsuan has been trying to hide from us. It is a variation on the Living Dream, Captain Jaeger. My people have had this ability all along."

"We're receiving a new transmission from the Tribal Prime." Petra's fingers flew across the screen, juggling communications and troop movements across a dozen different channels. She acted on some deeply ingrained muscle memory that left her marveling—and grateful. Whatever else the wormhole had taken from her, it had left her with this instinct for coordination. She knew this system better than the back of her hand. Better, even, than her name.

Coordinating this battle left her with no time to spare for anxiety. Whatever other horror lay between her and the minister pacing around this very bridge, there was one thing everybody here had in common. They wanted to get out of this nightmare alive.

They were gonna have to work together to do it.

"They say they've discovered a broadcast frequency that might disorient or disable the enemy fighters." Petra frowned at the data coming through and glanced at her troop movement tracker for confirmation. "The alien allies are pulling back from the battle. They say they're going to reconfigure their arrays to emit this frequency and hit the enemy with it all at once. They suggest we do the same."

"Alien *allies*," Fleet Commander Kelba sneered through the nearby speakers. It was bad practice to keep all the command staff on a single vessel through a battle. Grayson and top members of the silver government had taken shelter on the Astrolab, but Kelba was commanding from the bridge of one of the freighters. "Traitors. They're abandoning us on the front lines. Leaving us to die."

Minister Grayson had been pacing an endless loop around the Astrolab's bridge, circling the busy crew like a restless predator. Now he stopped over Petra's shoulder, his hot breath tickling the back of her neck as he studied the data spilling down her screens.

Petra suddenly found it hard to breathe.

If the minister noticed, he gave no indication. "No," he said slowly. "I don't think so." He patted Petra on the shoulder, his hand pausing to linger too tightly on her collarbone. "Send word to the rest of the ships straight away," he told her. "I want our arrays reconfigured to broadcast this signal as quickly as possible."

Swallowing a dry lump, Petra nodded and ran the message. Minister Grayson lifted his voice back to Kelba. "They're not abandoning us. I think they mean to do exactly as they say. I haven't tested this frequency as a weapon, but its configuration looks highly plausible, Fleet Commander." His mouth twitched into a vicious grin. "Certainly worth a shot. I advise you to have a little faith."

There was a moment of silence on the other end of the line as Kelba consulted with her bridge crew and the other commanders of the Seeker Corps. "We'll begin the conversions," she said, though Petra thought she sounded more than a little pissed.

"The Seeker jets aren't capable of emitting this frequency without extensive modifications, and the civilian wings are useless hunks of space trash. Recall all eligible spacecraft from the front lines. They're to begin conversion immediately while the Seeker squads protect our lines. Civilian wings and ineligible craft will continue harassing the enemy."

Before she could stop herself, Petra gasped. "You want those civilians to stay out in the hot zone without Seeker backup? They'll get clobbered!"

"We must keep the enemy occupied while our fleet is in a vulnerable state." Kelba spoke as if she were ordering her supper and not writing off the *Bitch* and dozens of other civilian ships for the sake of a distraction.

Grayson leaned down and whispered into Petra's ear, his grip on the back of her neck turning painful. "I suggest you keep your opinions to yourself, Petie. Sim is counting on you."

Petra's blood turned to ice. The thought hit her like the falling blade of a guillotine. *He knows.*

Before she could do anything with that hideous understanding, his grip turned into a patronizing pat on the shoulder. He straightened and walked away.

Petra ached for a measly three seconds to reach down to her computer and send a private message to check on Sim. When brass and silver had decided that they would be splitting battle command across the Astrolab and the *Constitution*,

RAMY VANCE & MICHAEL ANDERLE

Minister Grayson had oh-so-graciously allowed each member of his bridge crew to transfer their immediate family members into the Astrolab's living quarters.

He didn't want them distracted with worry over their loved ones, he'd said. He didn't want to risk breaking up any more families than necessary.

At this very moment, Sim was sheltering in the Astrolab's crew lounge with dozens of other civilians, hacking together new attack drones out of spare parts as they waited out the battle.

Petra had agonized over the decision to allow Sim to make the transfer. In the end, there had been no question. The Astrolab was the best-shielded ship in the fleet. There was no safer place for Sim.

In her worry for this one mysterious young woman, Petra had handed Grayson the only lever he needed to keep Petra as compliant as a well-trained lapdog.

Trembling, sick to her stomach, Petra reached across her comms station.

"Fleet craft and Seekers fall back." Her voice wavered. "Civilian wings remain on the front line." She swallowed hard. "Give 'em hell, boys."

Mop-up of surviving K'tax in the inner system was nearly complete, and Seeker had begun the journey out to the battle in mid-system, but he couldn't make sense of his radar screen. He flipped open his local comm line. "Human cruisers. This is Alpha-Seeker. You guys are wandering awfully close to the swarm. Where's your backup?"

"New orders came through," the captain of the *Bitch*

answered grimly. "We gotta keep harassin' the enemy by ourselves. Our Seekas got recalled ta protect da fleet while they do some kinda repairs."

That's suicide, Seeker thought. The fleet had fitted the conscripted human cruisers with weapons powerful enough to carve through the fighters, but the ships were large, slow, clumsy things with pathetic shielding. Fighter morphs would overrun them within minutes of hitting the front lines.

Seeker switched his channel, hailing fleet command. "Am I hearing these civilians right?" he demanded. "You want them to keep harassing the enemy without professional support?"

He received no answer, which was answer enough.

Cursing, he altered his course and raced after the civilian wing. Somebody had to keep the poor bastards alive.

CHAPTER THIRTY-FIVE

At the sound of a small spacecraft engine swooping low over the treetops, Toner finally remembered who he was.

The *Osprey*'s lone shuttle zipped over the clearing and hovered above the ruined encampment. A team of gray-armored medics dropped from the open transport, hit the ground, and fanned out to comb the wreckage for survivors.

Toner blinked and looked down to see a mound of pulpy white flesh piled up to his shins. White ropes of alien viscera spilled down the front of his exo-suit, dribbling off his chin.

Why didn't anyone stop me? He turned to survey the ruins, rubbing his stinging but freshly-healed nose with the back of one wrist. A horrible distant hum, coming from somewhere down by the river, made his guts churn.

He'd torn off the tips of his gloves in the fighting, and his hands were filthy with scorpion guts. He licked his fingers clean. *The last time I tried to eat one of these, I got mondo food poisoning.*

At least these wild K'tax didn't seem to carry the same strain of aggressive fungal spore as the specimens down in the

A FOUND BEGINNING

Forebear city. There was no fresh line of black poison creeping up his cuticles.

The scorpion rested in a broad heap beneath him. Large dark shapes lay scattered in the mud. Chunks of the scorpion's torn armor ripped away in the battle and tossed aside. The jagged bodies of wasps crushed into the mud. A smattering of human-sized lumps wearing *Osprey* exo-suits.

Toner abruptly remembered *what* he was and was glad nobody had tried to stop him from feeding.

As he watched, one of the medics knelt beside a lump, checked for a pulse, and moved on. Another medic jogged in his direction, pulling off her hood.

"You're wanted upstairs," Elaphus called, cupping her hands around her mouth. Her long red hair whipped in the breeze of the shuttle discharge, sticking to her sweating face.

Toner shook his head. He slid down from the scorpion's back and hit the ground with a *thunk*. Pain shot up his side, where the stab wounds hadn't fully knit shut. Twitching beneath a discarded chunk of carapace caught his eye. He hobbled over to help free the Locauri pinned beneath its weight.

Art clambered feebly to five of his legs. The sixth was missing, torn free from his thorax.

"I can't go upstairs," Toner told Elaphus. His head was spinning. "There's still fighting down at the river. I need to go—"

Elaphus let out a sigh louder than the engine of the hovering shuttle. Deciding that Toner was no longer a danger, she stomped forward and unslung her medical kit, kneeling in the mud beside Art.

"The ground fighting is under control," the doctor snapped, holding out a hand to stabilize Art as the poor fellow struggled to shake the unnatural wrinkles out of his wings. "They've found the key. The tides turned a couple of minutes ago. They have the K'tax well in hand."

"The key?" Toner winced, wondering if that awful sound was some sign of brain damage that his regen mods had yet to heal.

Art's translator band, which had somehow survived the fight with minimal cracking, flickered a golden yellow. "I hear the song of *Anantah*," he murmured. "Familiar. But different."

"Shit. Art. You're—you're dripping goo—"

"It will heal," Elaphus snapped. She jerked a thumb over her shoulder. "Captain Jaeger got on the line. She wants you upstairs and getting ready for Phase Three. There's a go-kit for you in the shuttle."

"Blood?" Toner shook his head to chase away the last hazy fingers of the hangover.

"And one of the updated exo-suits hot off the fabricators." Elaphus nibbled her lip as she applied a smear of medfoam to Art's cracked and bleeding antenna. "Now *go*."

Toner hadn't quite caught up to the moment, but if there was one thing he knew, it was that you didn't argue with the doctor. Glancing around the camp, he saw Bear limping toward one of the medics, leaning on a hobbling Baby for support. It warmed the cold, dead cockles of Toner's heart to see that someone had already filled the meter-wide wound in her flank with mounds of fresh medfoam. Baby was going to be fine. She was nearly as tough as he was.

Toner faced the shuttle and forced himself into a jog, waving for Bear's attention as he passed.

"You're in charge while I'm gone," he called before flinging himself into the open cargo bay.

A FOUND BEGINNING

"How's that update going?" Jaeger eyed the countdown timer on the side of the bridge.

"Updates on *Terrible I*, *IV*, and *VI* nearly complete," reported Kwin's tactical officer. "The other ships have taken substantial damage and need to make additional repairs."

"I have my ship equipped," Portia chimed in over the line. "Another four should be ready to go in about two minutes. My ship's thrusters are in good condition, Captain. Requesting permission to test our new bug repellent. Make sure we've worked out all the kinks."

"Do it. Good hunting." Jaeger crossed her fingers at her side. *Don't die.*

Portia let out a throaty laugh. It was a sound to tease the devil and damn the consequences, a laugh that explained in no words exactly why she and Toner could be either the best-partnered fighters in the whole damn galaxy—or the worst.

One of the darkened cruisers at the edge of the planetary system flared to life on the display, her engines *crackling* with fresh energy. She barreled toward the swarm at top speed, leaving behind a glowing afterimage.

Before Jaeger could catch her breath, the reckless cruiser had punched a hole through the edge of the enemy formation, sending a spray of K'tax fighters spinning off in every direction. Reeling out of control, they shot into space.

Portia's ship had gained an aura of its own, and for a few vital seconds as the cruiser passed them, the engine signature of each fighter went dim. Utterly inert.

"Frequency testing a success!" Portia crowed as her cruiser shrank away from the swarm. "Any K'tax that got within two kilometers went into shock. They were *bouncing* off our hull!"

305

A riot of *clicking* filled the bridge, like the snapping branches of an old tree caught in a windstorm. Jaeger whirled to see Kwin's Overseer crew shimmering with approval, their mandibles lashing, their antennae flicking through the air. Kwin himself had turned a beautiful shade of glittering copper.

"Congratulations," Jaeger called. "Continue harassing the edges of the swarm but don't try to pierce enemy lines yet. We're going to wait until a few more of our ships have completed their modifications. Then we're going to hit them with everything we have."

***

Every allied ship in the system had watched Portia's cruiser test this new shield system, and when she broke away from the swarm without a single overgrown bug clinging to her hull, a ragged cheer crackled across the general comm line.

Even Seeker hollered, punching his cockpit wall hard enough to make his knuckles sting. He activated his mic. "All civilian ships within the sound of my voice," he shouted. "It's time for you to pull back. Get back behind your lines and patch your wounds. I'll cover your retreat. The cavalry's on the way!"

The wing of civilians had put up an admirable fight for a bunch of malnourished space-pirate conscripts, but the fleet had done them dirty in tossing them before the swarm. Seeker dodged through the wreckage of ancient freighters and modified private ships, firing at any K'tax fighter that drew close enough to threaten the retreating vessels as they activated thrusters to return to the fleet.

A FOUND BEGINNING

The enemy had ripped apart eleven of the twenty-three civilian vessels that had joined this fight.

A new voice cut across the civilian line, loud and clear and furious. "Negative on the retreat order!" she snarled. "Civilian wing, return to the front line! I repeat, *return to the front line.*"

"That's a goddamned death warrant," Seeker shouted back.

"This is a direct order from Fleet Commander Kelba." The fury in this woman's voice damn near rattled the speakers. "Anyone who disregards this order will be summarily executed. It's too early to retreat. We *will not* allow the enemy to advance toward the planet unopposed!"

Something about that voice rattled the walls in the back of Seeker's brain. He'd heard it *before*. He knew it. And it pissed him right off.

According to his radar, it didn't pay to test the woman. The civilian wing had already begun to turn back, approaching the swarm's tip once more. The comm line had gone resentfully, angrily silent, but they obeyed.

As quickly as it had come, Seeker's elation faded into rage. He slammed an open palm against his console then turned back to the civilian wing. He hailed Portia's cruisers. "If there are any of you to spare, we could use a hand here up on the front lines. We're getting eaten alive."

Four cruisers and three of the Terrible ships had completed modifications. Jaeger had sent the cruisers to the front of the swarm, where they supported Seeker's civilian lines in slowing the enemy advance.

Sending those poor, under-equipped conscripts out to dog

the enemy was one more crime the fleet would answer for. Jaeger would make sure of it.

The cruisers became dragonflies swooping through clouds of midges. They flared into the heart of the swarm and pummeled asteroid barges with concentrated bursts of laser fire as the fighters bobbed helplessly in their wake. The K'tax fighters could only hang outside of shield range and fire their weak mining lasers. Eventually, the energy buildup would force each cruiser to retreat and allow their shield generators time to recover. Still, they'd robbed the enemy of their greatest weapon: the ability to overrun and physically disassemble a ship.

At thirty-five minutes to no return, two of the asteroids had become floating hunks of lifeless space rock, shedding damaged troop transports into space.

Slowly but surely, they were wearing down the enemy.

Jaeger was starting to think they might yet turn the tide of this battle when motion in the display caught her eye. She turned to see a large distortion of light and shadow forming at the heart of the K'tax swarm.

"There's a new subspace bubble collapsing near the heart of the swarm," Me reported. Jaeger saw a new alert on the command comms channel and flipped it open.

"They don't like that we've learned to evade their swarming tactics." Fleet Commander Kelba's voice was rich and self-satisfied, now that the first of her fleet cruisers had joined the fray with their new shields running at full capacity. "Now they bring out the big guns."

As if in agreement with the fleet commander, Me said, "K'tax flagship appearing on display...now."

Suddenly, there it was. A cluster of massive, chalky white asteroids made round by a network of support struts and the

A FOUND BEGINNING

sheer force of their gravity. Because it was quite a lot of gravity.

"That is *not* a moon," Jaeger said softly. "Shit."

Bigger than the rest of the asteroid barges combined, this megalithic craft had the crude shape of a whiffle ball, spherical but pockmarked with massive dark craters. Docking bays, Jaeger had to assume. Docking bays that could've held another thousand K'tax fighters—each.

Escorted by the remaining asteroid barges and an honor guard of ten thousand fighters, it soared across the dark void of space toward Locaur.

"Captain?" There was a high, tense edge to Portia's voice. "My cruiser wing is near Locaur's second moon. We're the closest to that thing, but it's going to take us a *long* time to chip it into pieces. What…what do we do?"

Jaeger pressed her eyes shut. Previously, they'd been able to use the tractor-rays on the Terrible ships to pull the asteroid barges off their collision course for Locaur. A glance at Kwin confirmed that all the Terrible ships working in tandem wouldn't be able to generate enough force to knock that monster off its grim course.

"Stand by," she told Portia, her mind racing. *They can't mean to crash that thing into Locaur*, she thought. *Maybe take up high orbit around the planet and become a manufactured moon? A permanent base for all those fighter morphs?*

"Fleet Commander Kelba." She lifted her voice over the general comm noise.

"Oh, we see it too, Jaeger." On the holo-display, a squad of carefully coordinated Seeker jets continued their dogged hit-

and-run attacks, picking off a dozen fighters every time they skirted the edges of the swarm, dodging away before they could get overrun in turn. The Seeker jets didn't have the Living Dream shield.

"We don't have a viable strategy to combat it," the fleet commander decided. "You didn't warn us we would encounter an enemy craft of this magnitude."

"Don't you still have more kamikaze drones?"

"A full complement of seven thousand," Kelba agreed. "They don't have these new shields. They'll be swarmed and ripped apart before they can reach the flagship. My cruisers can get in close, but we don't have a ship with weapons powerful enough to pierce something that large."

"That's not quite true!" Minister Grayson piped in for the first time in many minutes. "The Tribal Prime has aft pulse-ram cannons that could—oh, that's right. She's not here today! Never mind."

Shut the fuck up, you smug shit-stain on a dying leper's under-wear, suggested a Toner-shaped voice in the back of Jaeger's mind as she checked her private messages. There she saw a note from Bufo more beautiful than a basket full of puppies.

We're on our way.

Before Jaeger could lick her lips and tell the minister to go fuck himself, Petra broke in with an update. "Swarm activity pattern changing."

Jaeger spun, searching the holo-display. Sure enough, the flagship's cloud of escort fighters shimmered as it swayed to the side, peeling away from one edge of the flagship.

"An opening!" Portia shouted. "At top thruster speeds, we

A FOUND BEGINNING

could get in, pummel it with front cannons, and get away before they can swamp us—"

Before Jaeger could stop to think, she saw the arc of Portia's cruiser wing streak across the darkness, darting out from the shadow of Locaur's larger moon like a trap door spider lunging for prey.

"Foolish," Kelba snapped. "There's a reason they left their flank exposed—"

Jaeger had already come to the same conclusion. "Cruiser wing! Do not approach! Abort maneuver. Abort—"

A crackling energy lance at least a kilometer wide shot from one of the flagship's massive docking ports.

No. Those weren't docking ports scattered across the sphere like the spots of a soccer ball. They were the focusing dishes for an unimaginably large plasma cannon.

This wasn't a mobile base of operations for legions of fighters. It was a destroyer.

The new K'tax flagship was a destroyer with enough juice to send a concentrated plasma laser almost half a million kilometers through space at just shy of the speed of light. The beam of deadly energy grazed the edge of Locaur's larger moon, carving off a section of crust like it was slicing up a Thanksgiving turkey.

The *Terrible I*, which had been sheltering in the moon's profile, rocked to the side as the resulting shock wave caught it.

The bridge crew of Overseers were lightweight creatures with six stabilizing legs. They adapted quickly to the turbulence, bracing themselves against walls and work consoles with practiced ease.

Jaeger wasn't nearly so balanced. Caught off-guard, she pitched to the side, crashing into Kwin's T.O. At nearly twice his mass, she ripped the poor creature from his station, and the two of them tumbled into the bulkhead.

There was the sickening, *crunching* sound of breaking twigs. Darkness clouded the corners of Jaeger's vision. Sharp pain stabbed through her chest, bruising multiple ribs and knocking out her wind.

A loud burst of static feedback bleated through the sound system and resolved into Me's continuous status report.

"Gravity stabilizers seven and nine destroyed," the AI said in that eerily upbeat voice. "Six and eight damaged. Minor damage to the outer hull in the docking ring. All contact lost with *Terrible III*. Presumed destroyed."

"All ships scatter across the system." Maybe it was Jaeger's dazed imagination, but the normally circumspect Kwin seemed to be shouting. "Fan out! Spread out so one blast cannot hit multiple ships at once! Everybody, evasive maneuvers!"

Coughing, feeling as heavy as a dead cow, Jaeger crawled away from the bulkhead. Something sticky coated her hands, and she looked over her shoulder to see the mangled wreckage of Kwin's T.O. leaking milky ichor from a network of cracks in his carapace. One of his antennae had bent into a vicious right angle. It waggled weakly.

"Medic," she croaked. Pain sent her into another fit of coughing, but she forced the word out again. "MEDIC!"

Delicate foreclaws closed around her wrists. Kwin pulled Jaeger to her feet. To her immense relief, two other bridge crew members were already scuttling toward their injured tactical officer.

"Scattered debris has made this sector dangerous," Kwin said. "We must retreat from the shelter of the moon. The enemy means to deprive us of our hiding spots and destroy us."

Jaeger nodded, staggering toward one of the consoles as the floor rattled dangerously beneath her. She unhooked an anchor line from her utility belt and clipped it to the workstation. Another strong impact might snap the line and break her hip, but at least she wouldn't smash any more Overseers.

She didn't let herself look back at the tactical officer as a scattering of medical droids hauled him off the bridge.

"Status?" she croaked. "Portia. Seeker. Kelba. Anyone?"

"We're still here." Portia sounded rattled. "Barely. Took light damage, but we were far enough away to avoid the brunt of the blast."

"I'm with one of the civilian squads harassing the enemy's front flank," Seeker added. "We were all well away from the discharge."

Jaeger squinted at the holo-display as it flickered and stabilized.

"The swarm has closed around the destroyer once more." Petra confirmed what Jaeger's spinning vision had already told her.

"There was a slow buildup of energy from the destroyer before the primary weapons discharge," Me added. "I detect a similar buildup now. Estimate four minutes before they are capable of firing the weapon once more."

"Charge buildup in which dish?" Jaeger stared at the pockmarked monster drifting in the center of the holo-display like a misshapen skull. "If we know what dish they're going to fire out of, we'll have a better shot at avoiding it."

One of the cannon ports pulsed blue. "Energy buildup strongest in this sector."

Jaeger's gaze swept across the display, following the line between this origin out to a point in space just planet-side of Locaur's smaller moon. Her breath caught.

"Kelba. Grayson. You have to scatter the fleet. It's going to shoot at you next."

CHAPTER THIRTY-SIX

Chaos filled the space around Locaur as fleet and Overseer ships sliced back and forth through the swarm. Lances of white plasma and the blue-green pulses of fleet fusion torpedoes streaked across the system. As one, this fragile alliance had opted to ignore the barges and fighters in favor of hitting the flagship destroyer with every weapon in their arsenal.

Beneath Jaeger's feet, the *Terrible* lurched back and forth as the Overseer pilot ripped the ship through a series of breakneck maneuvers, pushing toward the heart of the swarm. Only her anchoring line kept Sarah from splattering against the bulkhead.

Me had added another nasty countdown to its endless list of reports.

"Thirty seconds to primary weapon discharge."

The holo-display had changed from a birds-eye view of the battle to a feed from the *Terrible*'s external cameras. The destroyer loomed ahead of her like the fist of a malevolent god. Networks of small fires had spread across the monster's face. Whatever else this thing was, it wasn't totally immune to the bunker-busting effects of a good old-fashioned fusion bomb.

Even so, it wasn't enough.

"Where are the rest of my torpedoes?" Kelba roared. "I want them fired *now*!"

"Cruiser wings one and three out of torpedoes," Petra answered. "Mechanical failure in wing two—Hang on. Commander, I'm picking up a new ship coming up from the planet. Coming in hot."

"Twenty seconds to primary weapons discharge."

"Get out of her way," Jaeger croaked. Rubbing her aching ribs, she forced herself to shout above the rabble. "She's friendly! Clear her a path! All available ships, cover the *Osprey*!"

"Profile confirmed," Petra said. "It's the Tribal Prime."

Grayson's comm line flickered. "How nice of her to join us."

"Sorry for the delay," Bufo called. "There was a problem with the—"

"Ten seconds to primary weapons discharge."

"It doesn't matter now," Jaeger screamed as the *Terrible* lurched around her. A shower of sparks rained down from the ceiling. That couldn't be good. "Hit the destroyer. Shove everything you have right down its fucking throat!"

"Oh. Uh. Roger that."

An ominous yellow glow collected in the dark recesses of the destroyer's aft focusing dish. Pulses of white plasma fell like rain into the darkness. Still, the glow intensified.

"Five seconds."

A thick column of blue light split the darkness as the *Osprey*'s front cannons activated.

The deck pitched and roiled around her, and the chatter of

A FOUND BEGINNING

anxious Overseers filled the air. Jaeger couldn't tear her eyes from a small side display. There, on one pathetically small screen, her ship—her beautiful, deadly ship—hurled itself through the swarm, racing headlong for the black abyss of the destroyer's focusing dish.

"Two."

The *Osprey* burned white, becoming a blinding streak of overheated engines and failing shields. Shields didn't matter right now. All that mattered was pouring every drop of spare power into the front cannons, into the black mouth of that focusing dish.

God help us.

"One."

Jaeger's world exploded.

Smoke, thick and itching, filled the *Terrible's* bridge. The holo-displays had all vanished, replaced by blinking clusters of tangled lines—warnings in the Overseer language. Stunned alien bodies moved through the smoke, slowly twitching as they recovered their senses. Nearby, Kwin reached out and rebooted his prime computer interface.

Jaeger coughed and dragged herself toward the nearest console.

"Bufo. BUFO! Come in, Sergeant. Do you hear me?"

Static.

Responding to her needs, the ship's AI flickered through a stream of damaged exterior cameras until it stopped on one particular feed.

The beautiful sleek hull of the *Osprey* shimmered as her

energy shields faltered and failed. She drifted against black space, alone. Silent.

Ice filled Jaeger's chest.

Then static crackled over the line.

"Still here," Bufo croaked.

Jaeger made a strange, strangled sound.

"Barely," the sergeant amended. "Caught the edge of the blast. Engines going into critical overload."

"We took considerable damage of our own in the shock wave," Kwin said, finding his legs. "Engines and transmitter arrays are still functional. We are stable, if not healthy."

Jaeger didn't care about that right now. She had eyes only for the *Osprey*.

"Bufo. Is Moss online?" Jaeger scrubbed stinging sweat from her eyes. "Can she wrangle the engines?"

There was a terminal moment of silence. "She doesn't think so, Captain. We got about sixty seconds to critical overload."

"Abandon ship," Jaeger whispered.

"Way ahead of you. Skeleton crew heading to the escape pods now."

"My ship is in decent shape. We'll pick up the stragglers," Portia called, rejoining the comm channel.

Jaeger closed her eyes and forced herself to nod. "Moss." She swallowed. "If you can't stop the engine overload, I want you to take the ship as close to the enemy destroyer as possible before she goes critical."

"I can do that," the *Osprey*'s lethargic AI said, indifferent to its suicide orders.

Jaeger watched as Portia's cruiser streaked close to collect the escape pods shedding from the *Osprey*'s wings.

"You kids take care of each other." Although it killed a little

A FOUND BEGINNING

part of her, Jaeger turned away from the *Osprey* and brought her attention to the wider battlefield.

"Me," she wheezed. "Can you resume tactical display?"

"Rebooting targeting computers...now."

The warning signs filling the bridge vanished, giving Jaeger a view of the carnage this day had wrought. Clouds of glowing gas dotted the inner system. K'tax fighters bobbed through space by the thousands, dazed, stunned, or destroyed. Jaeger couldn't tell. Any fighters still functional collected around the remaining focusing dishes of the damaged destroyer.

The *Osprey* had blown a chunk out of that ship the size of several city blocks.

As Jaeger watched, several alliance ships powered their engines to retreat from the field. Off to lick their wounds.

Dreading what she might see, Jaeger finally drew up a feed of the fleet, where it huddled beside Locaur's second moon.

Half a dozen of the smaller human ships blinked red as the scanners noted some critical mechanical failure. The horror that grabbed Jaeger by the spine was the image of a freighter glowing white-hot like a star about to supernova.

She patched herself into the fleet command channel. "Report," she said. "What is your status?"

"A few fleet ships were caught in the edge of the blast. Critical hull breach down to the *Reliant*'s central vacuum tubes," Petra whispered. "Sectors seven through nine, destroyed. Sectors two through six leaking atmosphere from dozens of places. Engineering reports..." Her voice wavered. "Casualty reports coming in. Three—three hundred six—numbers rising. Engineering reports a catastrophic coolant leak. Atmospheric scrubbers damaged beyond repair. Two hours until the air becomes lethally toxic."

"Damn," Kelba murmured. For the first time, Jaeger felt perfect and absolute solidarity with the woman.

"How can we assist?" Jaeger glanced back at the destroyer. Swarms of K'tax fighters crawled across the damaged dishes, scrabbling to repair their broken flagship. As long as the fighters stayed focused on repair, the barges and the destroyer herself were nearly defenseless.

"We must strike now while the enemy is reeling," Kwin said. "I am rallying the Terrible ships for a final charge. We cannot allow them to repair their focusing dishes."

The *Osprey* had bought them the opening they needed to finish this fight.

"The freighter is lost," Minister Grayson said flatly. "It's nothing but a death trap now. You can help the civilians abandon ship and take refuge planet-side."

"You don't have to give up on your freighter yet." Jaeger's mind raced. Behind her, Kwin and his remaining bridge crew flew from console to console, chattering to one another as they coordinated a strike.

Jaeger checked her messages. Two brief affirmatives. Her operatives were in position for Phase Three. "Me. Do we have sealant foam and repair droids to spare?"

"Yes," the AI answered from every direction. "As well as three small transports still in dock. If we begin the aid transfer immediately, it should reach the damaged freighter within twenty minutes. My droids will be able to help the humans to repair their life support and scrub the atmosphere."

"Scrub the evacuation," Jaeger told Grayson. With numb fingers, she unhooked her tether to the console. "We're on our way to help. We'll need all hands on deck for repairs."

A FOUND BEGINNING

"What in the fuck does an alien AI know about repairing our freighters?"

Grayson's cold, animal snarl stopped Jaeger in her tracks. She stared at the comms interface, stunned.

"We're not going to hang around waiting on your *goodwill!* Fleet Commander, begin the evacuation. Send out the life rafts. We're going to evacuate the freighter residents down to the planet. They have *nowhere else to go.*"

How convenient, Jaeger thought grimly. She wouldn't go so far as to suggest that Grayson had intentionally sabotaged the freighter to give himself an excuse to get onto Locaur, but he certainly wasn't going to miss the opportunity.

She whirled and started for the door out of the *Terrible*'s bridge, ignoring the sharp pain in her ribs. "Negative on landing on the planet. I repeat, you *do not have clearance to land on Locaur.*"

"Do I understand you correctly? You would condemn over seven thousand people rather than accept a few refugees onto your precious planet?" Grayson asked. Grayson *jeered.* "We see you now, Jaeger. Alien bootlicker. You never had any intention of *letting* us settle. You meant to use us all along."

He's speaking over a public channel, Jaeger realized. *The whole fleet can hear him.*

Whoever wasn't desperately trying to survive in a damaged ship was getting fed a line of pure, good old-fashioned rage and there was nothing Jaeger could do to stop it.

Grayson, you fool. Do you think our war with the K'tax is already over? Are you so ready to start another war this very second?

"You and your precious aliens used us to fight your battles," Grayson screamed. "Now that it's over you mean to let us die like animals. I will not allow it! My people have

321

waited too long and fought too hard to bend and break beneath the legs of false allies. We will not let you snuff out the last hope for humankind. We are going to survive. We are *going* to restore our empire from that planet *no matter the cost!*"

Minister Grayson pressed a button on the comms interface, closing the public channel. "That should have them good and riled." Cool as a cucumber, he turned to the Astrolab's senior pilot. "Begin landing sequences. Tell the forward strike teams to be ready with their gear. We're going to drop off everyone but the lab's skeleton crew at the pre-selected landing site."

He gestured at Petra. "Tell the fleet commander to proceed with evacuation. Recall all our ships. Jaeger and her allies can deal with the last of these alien vermin."

Petra floated on a fuzzy sea that she dimly recognized as the first stage of shock. As if in a dream and helpless to do anything else, she lifted her hand to obey. "Aye. Aye...I'm...I'm on it."

The pilot hesitated. "We still have carrying capacity for another two hundred passengers, sir. It would take only about ten minutes to dock with the *Reliant* and take on a few more refugees before dropping into planet atmosphere."

The minister turned, brows arched incredulously. "Are you serious? The *Reliant*'s docking arms are in chaos, soldier. If we docked with her and opened the doors, who knows what kind of unwashed rabble will flood into my ship?"

He gestured toward the troop movement tracker. "The other transports and cruisers can ferry off the civilians. Our top priority is getting down to the planet and setting up our

A FOUND BEGINNING

defensive perimeter." His mouth quirked. "In case Jaeger or the locals mean to run us out by force."

Seeing the cold logic, the pilot nodded and turned his attention to the Astrolab's complex thruster controls. "Astrolab underway," he said. "Twenty minutes to atmospheric entry."

"Scanners confirming three small transports departing from the alien ships," reported one of the tactical officers, shifting her weight uncomfortably in her chair. "Making toward the *Reliant* at top speed. It looks like the aliens really are sending aid, sir. I'm reading a human life-sign in one of the transports. Must be Jaeger riding to the rescue."

"So?"

The tactical officer blinked. She opened her mouth, then closed it again.

"If Jaeger wants to waste her time and resources, she's more than welcome to do so." Grayson rounded back to the prime display screen. "Now let's get this ship—"

"Sir!" Over at the secondary comm station, a lieutenant hopped excitedly to his feet.

Grayson sighed. "Now what?"

"We're receiving a hail from one of the Seeker jets. Urgent."

Grayson frowned. "I'm not involved in troop coordination. Patch the Seeker back to Kelba."

"He's asking for you by name, sir." The comms officer spoke his next words carefully as if afraid they might turn into a snake and bite him. "He says it's…family business."

RAMY VANCE & MICHAEL ANDERLE

Victor Grayson slipped into the old, familiar chair at the astro station in the quietest corner of the bridge and tapped his commlink. "I'm on a bit of a tight schedule, Shel. What can I do for you?"

The voice on the other end of the line was gruff, terse, and wonderfully familiar.

"I want in."

"In." Grayson frowned. He took it as a sign of the man's focus that he didn't bother correcting the name. *Jack*. His youngest sibling had always had a taste for blind machismo, but *Jack Seeker?* It was downright farcical.

He turned, activating one of the station's display screens. After shuffling through a few feeds, he found an external camera view of the missing Seeker jet framed against the stars. The lost lamb.

"I'm with you," said the man on the other end of the line. His little brother. "I've been monitoring the comm channels. I've fought and bled beside your people, and I can't believe Jaeger is refusing to let you land after all you've sacrificed for this war. I'm with you. Let me dock with your ship, and I'll help you prepare an initial landing crew. I know the planet."

Victor hesitated, his fingers tapping restlessly over the center console. "I'm glad to hear it," he said slowly. "But my landing operation is well underway, and I trust my teams. If you want to help me now, join Seeker Wing Delta and help cover our evacuation route. There are still plenty of enemy fighters flying around."

"You think you're ready for the planet, but you're not," Seeker snapped. "The enemy is crippled. Jaeger and the Overseers are mopping up the survivors. You don't need one more gun covering a sector of dead space. You need someone who knows the land, the locals, Jaeger, and all the nasty traps she might've laid to keep you away."

"Perhaps," Victor conceded. "If we encounter anything unexpected, you'll be the first person I call. You must understand my hesitation, Shel. It's awfully convenient timing for you to decide to defect *right now*."

"I didn't think that bitch was going to leave seven thousand refugees stranded rather than let you shelter on the planet!" Shelby roared. Victor grinned. He couldn't help it. He'd missed all that dumb animal rage.

"Nevertheless. Guard the evacuation line and remain on standby for consultation. We'll hash this all out over a bottle of rye once the dust has settled. Docking denied."

Shelby cursed loud enough to make Victor wince and reach up to cover his ears. Then, abruptly, the line went dead. Staring at the visual and radar screens, Grayson watched the Seeker jet flare to life and bank hard—not in the direction of the evacuation line but racing across the gap of space to meet the incoming alien transports.

Grayson gestured to his senior tactical officer. "Eyes on the jet. What is that man doing?"

The woman frowned, studying her screen. "Making a straight line for the one occupied transport. Weapons powering up."

Victor shuffled through his comms channels until the babble of the open command network filled his ears once again.

The first coherent sentence came from an unexpected source. Lawrence Toner spoke over the open line for the first time since the ground invasion of Locaur. Screamed, in fact.

"What the fuck are you doing, Jack?"

"Coming to my senses for the first time in a goddamned year," answered the man Victor best knew as Shelby Grayson.

"I am escorting *aid supplies* on a humanitarian mission," warned Jaeger. "Whatever other problems you have, Seeker, you're not going to fire on humanitarian ships—"

"Nothing human about them. Or you, anymore. Goodbye, Captain."

The Seeker jet's forward guns exploded in a discharge of blue-white light. The laser-pulse streaked across kilometers of space.

In less time than it took Victor to blink, the lead transport had vanished off his radar screen.

He stared at the screen, for once in his life too stunned to speak. Dimly, he was aware of the command channel exploding into shouts of confusion and rage. Cries of alarm and protest from the alliance ships. The Nosferatu, shrieking like the animal he was.

"Sarah. SARAH! Seeker, you lying motherfucker—I'm going to peel off your skin and make you eat it. I'm going to break every bone in your goddamned body—"

"Lead transport destroyed, sir," reported the T.O., sounding as startled as Victor felt. "All hands lost."

Across the bridge, someone made a loud retching noise. Potlova had pushed away from her station and held her hands over her mouth. Thin streams of bile trickled through her fingers.

Victor snapped his fingers, grabbing the T.O.'s attention as the two junior comms officers rushed to catch Potlova.

"Get her out of here," Victor hissed. "Goddamn it. Pull up the junior officer. Potlova's lost her nerve."

In Victor's experience, this happened to most warm-

A FOUND BEGINNING

blooded human beings, sooner or later. He only wished Potlova had held off another ten minutes before imploding.

The T.O. nodded frantically and shoved away from her station.

Victor turned back to his screens as two security guards grabbed the retching Potlova roughly by the elbows and hauled her off the bridge. A pity—she *was* an excellent administrator—but there was no help for it. He'd have to schedule her another Reset.

Victor glanced down and was unsurprised to see he was being hailed from a private comms channel once more. He opened it.

"Shel?"

"It's *Jack*," growled the man at the other end of the line. "I'm not a goddamned double agent. Now let me in on your landing operations before you get yourself fucking killed."

CHAPTER THIRTY-SEVEN

The warning lights in Seeker's cockpit turned green as it completed the docking sequence. He let out a breath. He'd been afraid the fleet officers would see through the little sensor trickery, but so far, they seemed to be in the clear. Minister Grayson had allowed him to dock after all. Now the little man waited for him at the edge of the Astrolab's tiny docking bay.

Seeker rapped his knuckles against the craft's storage bulkhead as he unlatched his pilot's harness. "Laying it on a little thick there, Toner," he said under his breath.

"I'll serve your balls up on crackers like cheap caviar," suggested a muffled voice on the other side of the bulkhead. Followed by, "With a little hot sauce to give it a—Ow! What was that for?"

"Can it," suggested a second, terse voice.

"Disembarking now," Seeker whispered.

"Break a leg."

Seeker rolled his eyes. He pressed the hatch release, and the portal beneath his feet slid open. He dropped onto the deck of the Astrolab's docking bay in a swirl of gray coolant mist.

"Jack."

At least the little twerp got that much right. Minister Grayson studied Seeker closely. His hands stayed stuffed deep into the pockets of his long coat as Seeker stalked across the docking bay. "I'm glad you made it."

But not ecstatic. The minister's broad-chested bodyguard stepped between the two men as Seeker approached. He lifted an open palm and met Seeker's eye. He gestured at Seeker's sidearm.

"I'm glad you pulled your head out of your ass." Seeker glared but surrendered his weapon as the bodyguard passed a sensor wand over his chest and back.

It must've been the right thing to say, because Grayson smiled faintly.

We must've been a family of hard knocks, Seeker thought. *And tough love, or whatever you call it.*

"Clear of projectiles and explosives," the bodyguard decided, putting away his wand. "But he carries knives."

"At ease," Grayson dismissed. "Dad never let us leave the apartment without at least one knife. Fastest way to earn a beating."

The bodyguard shrugged and faded into the background.

"It's good to have you on board again," the minister said to Seeker.

A fresh wave of unease trickled down Seeker's spine. He'd heard the speech this man had pumped into the airwaves not ten minutes ago. Minister Grayson would've had all of humanity believing he would sweat blood, eat gravel, and crap nails in his single-minded dedication to the Tribe.

Whoever had given that speech, it wasn't the placid man standing in front of Seeker now with that flat gray stare and thin-lipped smile.

This man is as sincere as a space vampire quoting Lear, Seeker decided. "I don't know you." His blunt admission made Grayson frown as if he were trying to decide if this hurt his feelings or not.

"I don't know if I'm ever *gonna* remember you or if I even want to." Seeker reached into his breast pocket and pulled out a silver vape pen. It was dented and scratched with age and long use but unmistakable. "All I know is you and I are on the same page about saving this Tribe."

He pressed the vape pen into Grayson's chest. Too startled to do anything else, Grayson drew a hand out of his pocket and caught the pen before it could tumble to the corrugated floor.

Grayson was wearing a style of exo-glove Seeker had never seen before. Complex loops of metal and wire coiled snugly around his fingers as he turned over the little silver device.

"So can it with the family crap," Seeker said. "We have work to do."

The minister nodded thoughtfully and slipped the pen into a smaller pocket in his uniform jacket. "I'll take that to mean you've finally decided to quit smoking."

"Jesus…"

The minister's smile broadened. "Come on." He turned and gestured for Seeker to follow him into the guts of the Astro-lab. "Let's get you up to the bridge where you belong."

A FOUND BEGINNING

Two figures in camouflaging exo-suits dropped out of the Alpha-Seeker's belly, unfolding from her open hatch with all the practiced care of gymnasts. The air shimmered as their suits picked up on the local visual fields and cast pulses of modulated light across the minute chromatophores woven into the cloth.

These were much more sophisticated stealth suits than the ones they'd worn so long ago in their first raid on a K'tax base. The Overseers had a lot of advice to give on the matter of color-changing.

Where you belong.

Seeker stared around the Astrolab's bridge, where dozens of busy uniformed officers crewed their stations, clean and efficient as Swiss clockwork. Yes. This was where he belonged.

"Status report," the minister ordered, bustling into the well-oiled machine ahead of Seeker.

A tactical officer looked up from her display. "Sensors reporting no buildup of energy in the enemy flagship. It appears that the Tribal Prime's charge effectively destroyed their weapons. Their fighters are attempting to repair the broken focusing dishes, but the alien alliance seems to have them well in hand." The T.O. risked a glance at Seeker. "What remains of the alliance, that is."

"And all it cost was the most advanced ship mankind has ever built." Grayson sighed. "Let these aliens keep each other busy. Keep me updated on any changes. Comms, patch astrogation into our landing party lines." He glanced at Seeker and pointed at the only empty station on the bridge. "Get comfortable. The landing parties have holed up in our cargo bays, but the coordinator will bring you up to speed over the radio."

Seeker grunted and settled into the station, more than a little eager to distance himself from the minister. Fixing the commlink over his ear, he glanced around the bridge. There was a thin, middle-aged man hunched anxiously over the comms station.

Seeker worked his jaw. "Potlova's not at her post," he sub-vocalized into the communicator chip embedded in his middle ear.

The response was a combination of sounds and minute vibrations that made him feel like Toner was walking around inside his skull.

Seeker didn't like that at all.

"Well, *find her*. Don't make us search this whole damn ship room by room."

Seeker turned his attention to the landing party feed on one of the side screens. His cover wouldn't last thirty seconds if he didn't at least pretend to do the job he'd come here to do.

With his other hand, he pulled up the running bridge report. Whatever had happened to Potlova would be recorded there.

With the time and resources spent on these camouflaging suits, the *Osprey's* fabricators could've produced four land-cannons or two dozen kamikaze drones.

As Jaeger and Toner slipped past the docking bay security

cameras, Jaeger decided these suits had been a sound investment after all.

They walked down the halls of the Astrolab on padded boots coated in sound-muffling polymers. The light-bending fabric of the suits made them meld into the bulkheads as effectively as a shy octopus going to ground. If they froze, they became all but invisible to anything but the most extremely modified human eyes.

Highly sensitive thermal or life-sign scans would eventually pick up on the deception, however, and it was impossible to completely disguise the pinhole faceplate cameras that gave them a view of the outside world. If Jaeger rounded the corner and walked face-first into somebody exactly her height, they would see something that looked like six tiny, floating cameras at eye-level—for about half a second, before slamming into her otherwise invisible body.

The only thing that kept Jaeger from walking into Toner was his silhouette sketched into the HUD embedded in her helmet.

"It looks like Potlova had a breakdown when I killed you, Captain," Seeker murmured into her helmet. "She's been confined to quarters. She's in residential sector C, room 106. Just off the crew lounge. They use the same conduit navigations we do on the *Osprey*. Follow the green lines."

"Copy that." Jaeger banked hard to the left, following the green conduits down a side corridor.

Ahead, another sealed door *hissed* and slid open with a little puff of compressed gas. A tall man in a silver suit walked into the corridor, brushing some grit off his uniform cap.

Jaeger didn't wait. Praying her boots were as good at sound-dampening as Occy had claimed, she darted forward, danced around the tall officer, and slipped past the door as it began to slide shut. Toner darted after her, but the tip of his boot caught on the edge of the closing door. There was a soft *thunk* above the *hum* of the automatic gears.

"Shit," Toner whispered. "Think he heard that?"

If he had, Jaeger doubted it would matter. They'd reached the crew lounge, and it was a noisy place.

It was a long room strewn with lounge furniture. At least sixty people hung off every open seat, murmuring to each other. Most of them wore civilian clothes. A few huddled in dirty maintenance or janitorial uniforms. At one end of the lounge, a group clustered around a circular holo-display projecting live updates of the battle outside.

Spread around the edges of the room, people with any degree of mechanical flair had broken into teams and were repairing piles of small devices that Jaeger thought looked like drone parts.

Then she saw a standard miniature detonator pass hands and realized they were building IEDs. Ammo for more kamikaze drones.

Jaeger wove through clusters of haggard-looking civilians toward a narrow hallway leading out of the back of the lounge. She turned the corner leading to room 106 and skidded to a halt.

A young woman in a mechanic's suit knelt in front of the door to Petra's quarters. A small toolset was open on the floor between her and the wall.

Sim quietly cursed as she dug through the guts of the door lock, earning herself an anointing of sparks. She jerked back and popped her thumb into her mouth.

"This is a fucking fire hazard," she grumbled, prodding her electric wrench through the wires. "You can't just *lock someone*

A FOUND BEGINNING

in closed quarters like this—what if there's a hull breach? What if?"

A hand slipped into Jaeger's, and she looked down to see the outline of Toner's glove wrapping around hers.

"She sounds like you," the man whispered.

Jaeger couldn't speak. She could only stare until Sim found the wire she was looking for and twisted.

The door slid open. Biting back a whoop of triumph, the young woman scrambled to her feet and into the darkened quarters beyond.

Toner moved before Jaeger. He lunged forward, reaching out to hook his arm across the threshold. The door slid shut, hit his invisible arm, and made an annoying *beeping* noise.

Toner shoved the door open. Jaeger ducked beneath his outstretched arm, and he spun into the room after her.

The door slammed shut.

CHAPTER THIRTY-EIGHT

The apartment was barely large enough for two modest bunks, a storage locker, and a table topped with a shared computer interface.

"What in the heck?" Petra Potlova stood with her back wedged into the corner of the room, her eyes bulging out of her head as she stared at the door. Sim stood beside her, wide-eyed, her electric wrench outstretched, her mouth moving.

"I don't know," the girl said. "It must be some short-circuit—"

"It's not." Jaeger lifted her suit's faceplate. "Don't be scared," she added quickly, lifting her hands to show they were empty—and realizing too late that as far as these women were concerned, she was a floating head. She fumbled to deactivate the camo function and her suit rippled into sight. "We're friends. I'm sorry. It's a camo suit. We're here to help."

"Captain Jaeger?" Petra looked suddenly dizzy. She clapped a hand over her mouth and sat—hard. "Oh gawd. I'm gonna be sick again."

"Shh. Shh, shh. It's okay. Stay quiet. Shh. Toner's with me," she added as Toner shimmered into sight beside her. "We're not going to hurt you."

"Mom?"

The word slipped so tentatively between Sim's lips was a lance through Jaeger's heart. She froze, staring into Sim's golden eyes.

"Yeah, baby," she whispered. "We're gonna get you outta here."

Cold dread sloshed down the back of her spine as she said the words. She stared up into the strange, familiar face, desperate to parse out the mixed emotions warring there.

What if Sim didn't want to leave?

What if that snippet of candid video was genuine? What if the girl was a fleet loyalist after all? What if she—

"Oh, gawd." Petra was mumbling to herself. Toner reached out to hold her and stopped short as if afraid to touch.

"It was a ruse," she mumbled. "To make them think you was dead. You got the files after all."

"Right," Jaeger whispered. "To get in here to rescue you. We have to get moving." She forced herself to look back up into Sim's wide-eyed, bewildered face. Her stomach clenched so hard she thought she might vomit, too.

"I know things are complicated. I know it's all confusing. If you come with me, Sim, I promise I'll tell you everything. I'll explain it all. I'm sorry. I'm sorry I wasn't there. But I won't make you come if you don't want to. I'm not like them."

Bewilderment crossed the girl's face. "Why wouldn't I want to come?"

Jaeger's breath caught. For a moment, she was too relieved to speak.

"We got a message about you." Toner grunted. "It was a

video of you talking about how disappointed you are in us. In your mom. We thought it might be fake, but we weren't sure."

Petra's head fell back against the wall with a *thunk*. She let out a deep groan. "Deep fakes."

"What?" Jaeger pushed to her feet.

"It was part of the file package I sent." Petra wiped her eyes, saw the looks on their faces, and groaned again. "You didn't get any of the files after all, did you?"

Jaeger and Toner exchanged glances. "Forty-three hours ago the *Osprey* received a video of Sim calling us traitors. That's all."

"I never said that." Sim frowned as if she was thinking through some complex engineering problem.

"I broke into the fleet's comm network and tried sending you the files," Petra muttered. Trembling, she pushed herself to the little table and activated her computer interface. "Brass or Grayson musta intercepted the message and swapped it out for a deep fake. The files warned me about this. They got a whole studio here on the Astrolab for making videos of whoever they want, saying whatever they want."

"Sure, but...why would they make a video of me?" Sim cocked her head, the confusion on her face tugging into worry as Petra's hands flew over the console. "Petie? What is it?"

The woman was shaking her head, muttering under her breath as she stared at the screens. "I'm gonna make another copy of the downloaded files," she muttered. "To take with us. A hard copy as proof. We can't let them keep getting away with this."

"Get away with what?" Jaeger was confused. "We already know they mean to invade Locaur."

Petra only shook her head and typed.

A FOUND BEGINNING

"Because they're using you, kid." Toner answered Sim's question to Petra. Sim jumped and tilted her head back to stare up at Toner.

"It's what they do," he added. "Use people against other people. Brass doesn't care about you, Sim. They only care about how they can use you to manipulate your mom."

Sim's mouth tugged into a troubled frown.

"Yeah," Petra whispered, sagging against the wall. Behind her, the interface flashed and scrolled as it uploaded files onto a memory chip. "Yeah." She scrubbed her fingers over her temples. She was trembling. "Oh, damn me." Her eyes squeezed shut. "Damn me. Damn me." She knocked her skull against the wall.

"Petie?" Sim surged forward, alarmed. Toner stepped forward too, then hesitated and pulled back. He shifted his weight restlessly.

"Petie." Sim took Petra by the hand. "What is it?"

"I can't do it." Petra started to tremble. "I can't lie. I'm sorry. I'm so sorry, honey. I didn't want to tell you. I couldn't—"

"What did you do?" Jaeger's voice turned sharp. Beside her, Toner reached beneath the side-flap of his suit and pulled out a laser pistol, turning as if expecting to see a legion of black-suited Seekers spilling into the room.

"Nothin'." Petra wept, cradling her head tight to Sim's shoulder. Sim held her foster mother, her eyes wide with alarm.

"Nothin', I'm sorry. It's such a bad time for this."

"What did you do?" Jaeger demanded. If Potlova had led them into some kind of trap—

"It's what I didn't say." Petra wiped her nose with the back of her hand and looked up. "There's no record of Sim from before the wormhole jump. Not anywhere. So I did some double-checking with the files to confirm what the fleet has been up to. The genetic stuff. I'm sorry, honey." She didn't look at Sim. "The cerebral programming and rapid gestation. It…"

Jaeger stared, as blank and confused as Sim herself.

Slowly, understanding that there was no betrayal forthcoming, Toner lowered his weapon.

"Sim's a clone," he said.

There wasn't a sound in the room except the soft *whirring* of the computer as it finished its download.

Sim drew in a small, sharp breath.

"So what?" Toner asked, turning a hard look on Petra. "We got any reason to think there's some kinda bio-bomb coded into her DNA?"

"You bastard," Jaeger whispered, seeing the look of abject terror this put on Sim's face. Toner's cool glance flicked her way and focused on Petra again.

"No." Petra's jaw trembled. She shook her head. "No, there wasn't anything like that in the files. Only the mods and the wormhole stuff and Reset—"

Toner grunted and holstered his weapon. "Good enough for me. Listen, time's running out." He thrust his chin toward the interface. "Are we done here? We need to get going."

Jaeger didn't move.

"Really?" Toner glanced from Petra to Jaeger to Sim. "Okay. Look. Grayson whipped up a clone Sim to mess with our heads. Right now, *it doesn't fucking matter*. Yes, it's fucked up. Yes, it's super fucked up. But here's the thing.

"We're all fucked. Nobody here is an *au natural* human. Almost nobody on the fleet has a life from before the wormhole, and as far as we know, y'all with your inferior genetic mods might never recover your memories.

"So what the fuck does it matter if Sim was grown in a tank—just like every other member of our crew? Shit." He dug his fingers across his scalp and tugged on his hair. "I know a great therapist on the *Osprey*. His name is Dr. Equus. He specializes in how to help all the tank-grown people feel like human beings. I can get you all an appointment with him *tomorrow*, but right now, *we have to get moving*."

"One step at a time," Jaeger whispered. "He's right." She held out her hands to Sim and Petra, though she felt disconnected from her body. "We have to go."

The computer *beeped*, and Petra withdrew the memory chip. "No."

"No?" Toner stared at her.

"It ain't only about the cloning and the genetic stuff." Petra swallowed hard. "There's all kinds of crazy awful experiments on this ship. This wormhole stuff, it ain't an accident. Brass calls it Reset, and they did it to us on purpose. They lured us through the wormhole without special shielding because we was making trouble for them." She held up her memory chip. "I got some of the details here."

"That's good," Toner said. "We'll study all that stuff once you're safe—"

"We can't leave," Petra said again. "'Cause brass and silver have special shields that preserve their memories through the wormhole. Captain—" She cast a wild glance at Jaeger.

"As long as they got their shield experiments, they're gonna *keep tossing us* in and out of that thing until there's nobody left who remembers anything except how to follow orders. Between the Serenity therapies and the amnesia, they're gonna have all the slaves they'll ever need."

That sounds absolutely crazy, Jaeger thought. After exchanging a glance with Toner, added, *and horribly plausible.*

"Okay," Toner said hoarsely. "I agree. That's a problem."

"The high-security labs ain't so far from here," Petra whispered. "If we can get in there and trash the place it should at least slow them down. Make it harder to proceed with Reset."

Jaeger opened her mouth.

"Let's do it."

Jaeger closed her mouth. Sim stood by the door, her arms folded tight across her chest, her golden eyes burning with barely contained rage.

"Let's trash the place," the girl said—the young woman, the mechanic, the clone—Sarah's ferocious, beautiful, wonderful daughter.

"All right," Jaeger agreed. "Let's do it." She activated her comm channel. "Seeker. Can you tell us how to get into these labs?"

CHAPTER THIRTY-NINE

They crawled single-file through the Astrolab's network of service tunnels. Toner was out front. Toner always took point in the Jefferies tubes. That was Jaeger's rule.

"You've gone *wildly* off-mission, Captain," Seeker growled into the comm channel. "I have Grayson breathing down my neck, and he's scheduled us to start dropping weapons of mass destruction down to the surface in less than ten minutes."

"All the more reason to slow the fleet down. This Astrolab ship is incredibly advanced." Jaeger noted once again the bizarre incongruity of artificial gravity on a fleet ship. "We don't have the *Osprey* anymore. We have to sabotage the enemy while we have the chance."

"We're coming up on a juncture," Toner reported. "Up, down, or straight ahead?"

"Down two levels," Seeker relented. "Then take the second left. That's all the help I can give. The whole sector of the ship is classified. Grayson's coming back around for another goddamned chat. Seeker out."

RAMY VANCE & MICHAEL ANDERLE

Grim silence filled the tunnels as they lowered themselves one by one down the narrow vertical shaft. The configuration of the access panels changed as they pressed toward the labs. Where there had been simple hinging mechanisms, electronic locks now sealed the small portals.

"Okay," Toner whispered. "We're off the edge of the map and wandering blind. Should I...just start busting down doors?"

"No," Sim called softly. "Let me get up there and take a look first. I might be able to override the lock."

This was easier said than done in a tunnel about half a meter wide. A shuffling noise filled the area, followed by a few muffled grunts and gasps as Sim squeezed past Petra and Jaeger. Toner graciously crawled forward rather than get tangled with the girl himself.

Sim reached the access panel and drew her little toolkit from one pocket.

"Where did you learn to pick locks?" Petra hissed.

Sim shrugged. "I work on coolant flow-valves all day. They're all just some kind of lock or other."

"Grayson's pretty keen on lab security after I busted out last month," Petra said dubiously. "You might be able to get it open, but I'd count on someone noticing the breach."

"There's a *lot* going on right now," Jaeger murmured. "We're going to have to risk it and hope they're distracted."

Sim fiddled with the wires for about thirty seconds before the panel turned green and swung open.

"It's one of the labs," Sim confirmed, leaning to the side to peer into the room. "Yep. Looks like the operating room for some kinda miniaturized particle accelerator."

"Anyone in there?" Toner whispered.

"Techs are working down at the far end. Um. I count six."

A FOUND BEGINNING

"Okay. Scootch back. I'll go in first and handle the techs. You follow."

Jaeger watched as Toner struggled to do a one-eighty in the narrow tunnel. He wasn't overly flexible for such a skinny man.

He tapped the shoulder of his camo suit and the cloth shimmered brown and gray, sinking into the background—invisible to everything but Jaeger's secondary HUD.

Bracing his long hands against either side of the panel, he tucked his legs and dropped into the lab.

Jaeger held her breath, but there was no need to worry. Toner dropped the three meters with as much noise as a gasping dormouse.

"I can't see him," Sim whispered anxiously. Jaeger pressed a hand over her lips, and the girl's mouth snapped shut.

Jaeger leaned around Sim's shoulder and peered into the lab. It was a long, narrow room. Workbenches full of obscure tools ran down one wall, and dials, switches, meters, and interfaces covered every square centimeter of the opposite wall. That must've been the particle accelerator.

Jaeger turned her head to watch Toner picking his way through the room.

"I count nine techs," he whispered into the comm line. "There were three more hiding out of Sim's line of sight. There's a door at each end of the lab, and all the techs have clustered pretty close to one of them."

Jaeger winced. Toner didn't need to explain why this was a problem. If he blew his cover, there was a good chance at least one of those techs would be able to escape the room and sound an alarm before he could subdue them all. At any rate, neither of them relished the idea of slaughtering nine unsuspecting lab techs wholesale.

The vague outline of Toner's figure paused in front of a series of gages along the wall.

"Maybe this is something," he murmured. "It's a containment breach alarm. Should I?" He lifted his hand.

"How quickly will security come to investigate once a containment alarm goes off?" Jaeger glanced from Sim to Petra.

"I got no idea," Petra said.

Sim frowned. "Probably a few minutes, at least. They'll have to suit up if they think there's some kind of radiation leak."

Jaeger grimaced. *A few minutes* put a pretty vague time limit on these operations, but it was the best option they had. "Do it," she whispered.

Toner pulled the lever.

Seeker read the landing party supply manifest again, hoping it would be different this time. He'd expected the fleet to cut right to the chase when it came to gaining a foothold on Locaur, but the brutality of the plan laid out before him left him breathless.

Once the Astrolab had reached low orbit, it would drop a strike team of commandos into a resource-rich section of the Locauri jungle and immediately set up a defensive perimeter. Standard operating procedure.

Except that the strike team had a *pulse-ray microwave emitter* for chrissake. The only thing *that* was good for was turning every Locauri in a five-kilometer radius into hot jelly.

Seeker was beginning to agree with the captain. They had to fuck this ship up at the best possible speed.

A FOUND BEGINNING

A hand fell on Seeker's shoulder, jerking him out of his focus.

"There's been a disturbance down in the central labs," the minister said. There was a distant look in his eyes, almost distracted. "All techs evacuated. Either a leak in one of the Faraday experiments or someone pulled the contamination alarm."

"So?" Seeker shook off the hand.

"If those experiments are interrupted, we're going to lose years of research. It will set our plans back to square one." His gaze cleared and he fixed Seeker with that strange, flat stare. "I want you to come with me."

Seeker growled and unhooked the comm link from his ear. "Can't you take your bodyguards?"

"They'll meet us on the way. Come on. I'm not leaving you free rein of the bridge. You can't expect me to trust you *that* much."

"Well, that didn't take *nearly* long enough," Toner said over the eerie wail of the contamination alarm.

Petra and Jaeger huddled over the primary computer interface, scanning the lab's central computer for any other nasty plans the fleet had in store. At the same time, Sim and Toner busied themselves sticking rough IEDs across the electronics.

"What?" Jaeger looked around sharply.

"Just got word from Seeker." Toner tapped the side of his helmet. "Grayson's already on his way down here with security. They'll be here in one minute, and I wouldn't count on them stopping to put on hazmats. Hey, I need another detonator."

Sim slipped a small device from one of her pockets and tossed it to him. "I've got the detonator switch here," she said. "The range is pretty good, but these places shield all kinds of signals. I say we set the timer *now* and run."

"Where did you learn so much about homemade bombs?" Jaeger asked sharply.

"Holo-dramas?" Sim frowned. "Huh. That's weird. I remember a *lot* of those."

Grayson raised my daughter on television, Jaeger realized. *I'm going to kill him.*

"Forty seconds." Toner peeled a panel off the wall to hide another bomb. "Captain?"

Jaeger glanced at Petra, who shook her head. "I think it's the best we're gonna do."

"Set the timer for one minute," Jaeger told Sim, hoping it was enough for them to get clear of the lab but not quite enough time for Grayson's people to find and disable the explosives. "Activate it on my mark."

"They'll come in through that door." Toner pointed at the door the techs had evacuated through. Dropping his last explosive unceremoniously in the center of the floor, he turned and spread his arms, urging them toward the rear of the lab. "It's time to *go.*"

Sim broke into a run. She reached the door and pressed her hand against the access panel.

The red seal light around the door remained red.

"Shit!" Sim slapped her hand against the panel again, to no avail. "It's locked—"

"Then we go back the way we came." Promptly and without ceremony, Toner grabbed Sim by the hips and pivoted, lifting her toward the ceiling. "Back up the hatch you go."

For a split second Sim struggled, then she realized he was lifting her to the overhead conduit. She reached out to grab the open portal.

Before she could get her hands into the tube, the access panel snapped shut with a fatal *click*.

The door at the other end of the lab slid open.

CHAPTER FORTY

Toner spun, dropping Sim like a sack of potatoes. The girl cried out and hit the floor, diving to huddle beneath the scant protection of an open-backed workstation beside Petra.

Two black-suited marines frog-marched into the lab. They huddled behind the protective curves of glowing force-riot shields, robbing Toner and Jaeger of any chance to pick them off with sidearms as they filtered through the choke point. Two more marines followed, flechette pistols raised as they shuffled to stay behind the cover of the shields.

"Drop your weapons. Nobody move. Drop your weapons, *or we will open fire.*"

Jaeger's finger was two centimeters from flipping down her faceplate and turning her invisible. At that last threat, she went still as stone. In the corner of her eye, she saw Toner stuck in the same position, his face a floating mask of frustration.

Invisible, they might've been able to take the soldiers, even with their riot shields. They'd at least have a good shot at it—

A FOUND BEGINNING

before those marines pulled the trigger and put ten thousand tiny, bloody holes in the unprotected Sim and Petra.

So Jaeger dropped her pistol. Toner did the same.

Two final figures emerged from the doorway. One was big and square, one fine-boned and slender.

Minister Grayson hopped lightly to the side, slipping behind the shelter of one of the glowing riot shields with a dancer's grace. The door slid shut.

"Neat invisibility suits," Grayson called across the room. "Now turn them off, or we turn the girls into pincushions."

Jaeger stared at the wide barrels of the flechette pistols aimed not at her or Toner but at the two defenseless women huddled on the floor.

Grayson knew her weakness very well.

Sim gripped the detonator switch tight in her left fist as she stared, wide-eyed, up at Jaeger. Her expression was questioning.

Slowly, Jaeger shook her head. Then she patted the pressure patch on her shoulder, and her suit shimmered to a flat olive color. Beside her, Toner deactivated his suit as well.

"They look better when they're invisible." Grayson sidled to the side of the room, careful to keep his shield firmly between himself and the intruders. He leaned over, glancing at the prime computer interface. With a few keystrokes, he silenced the containment alarm. Then he knelt and fished a small block of improvised explosive from beneath the console. He was wearing unusually thick exo-gloves, Jaeger saw.

"Armed but not set," the minister noted, placing the IED carefully aside. "Where's the trigger?"

"Up my ass," Toner said. "You'll have to get it."

351

RAMY VANCE & MICHAEL ANDERLE

Grayson waved the jeer aside. "I recognize these detonators. Sim? Have you been pilfering from the war chest?"

Sim sat frozen on the deck, wrapped in Petra's arms, too terrified to move.

"Come now, Sim," Grayson said impatiently. "You can either flip the switch and send us all to hell, or you can cooperate and keep breathing. You need to choose."

If Jaeger had been the one holding that trigger when the doors slid open, she might've done it. Ended Grayson, and Reset, and Serenity, and all the fleet's nasty plans right here and now, and damn the cost.

Even looking into Sim's terrified face, she might have found the strength to ask her to pull that trigger.

She didn't have it in her to ask that wide-eyed young woman to press one button and kill them all.

Not yet, at least. Not when she still had one more plan in her back pocket.

One awful plan.

"It's okay, Sim," Jaeger said softly. "Put it down."

A tortured mixture of pain and hurt and relief and shame crossed Sim's face. She reached out with one trembling arm and dropped the pen-sized device on the floor.

"Good girl," Grayson said. "Slide it right over here."

Sim did as instructed, sending the trigger twirling over the smooth floor. Grayson scooped up the device, disconnected the main wires, and slid it into one of his deep pockets.

"That's better. No grand plans for martyrdom soon." Grayson folded his arms and regarded the four of them. The four fish neatly trapped in a barrel. His fingers tapped thoughtfully against his arms.

"I feel awful dizzy," Petra mumbled, her eyes going

hooded. Her arms sagged. Sim slumped forward as well, her face going slack.

"We're cooperating," Jaeger shot at Grayson. "What's happening to them? What did you do?"

"I activated a hormonal response to douse the system with a bit of ketamine." Grayson saw the wide-eyed horror that spread over Jaeger's face and frowned, sincerely puzzled. "What...what did you *think* Serenity was supposed to do?"

Sim let out a little wavering gasp and collapsed into a heap on the floor.

"They're not in any danger," Grayson added as the last of Petra's strength abandoned her. She spilled to the floor beside Sim, mumbling, "I need a nap..."

"I don't see any reason to include them in this negotiation." With a gesture to his side, Grayson sent his marine guards fanning across the far wall, maneuvering to give each of them a different angle at Jaeger and Toner.

"Negotiation." Jaeger licked her lips.

"Sure," Grayson said lightly. "There's something I want that I can't take from you by force. Well, I can. But it would be a lot of work."

Jaeger only stared.

"You're a smart woman, Sarah," Grayson said. "Visionary, even. An excellent improviser and actor. I envy you a little. Still, there's a reason people like you don't run the universe. You're too nice. Optimism is a tragically fatal flaw." He shook his head. "I like your drive. I can use it. Come work for me."

"I...What?"

"I mean it. You have the institutional knowledge we need to get our new nation off to a good start. Do as I say and you can go back to being captain of your motley crew. Or mayor, I suppose. Now that you've destroyed the Tribal Prime. You

RAMY VANCE & MICHAEL ANDERLE

can't tear this system down so you're better off trying to change it from within." He smiled. He had a strangely charming smile that sent a chill down Jaeger's spine.

"You...want me to be your lapdog? Like Kelba and the Seekers?"

Grayson shrugged. "If that's the way you see it."

"Go...fuck yourself?" Jaeger could think of nothing else to say. Out of the corner of her eye, she saw Toner smirk.

"Think it through," Grayson urged. "Because the alternative is that I pitch the four of you back and forth through the wormhole until your brains turn to mush, send you back to school for a few hearty rounds of re-education, and you work for me anyway."

"*Asshole*," Toner said under his breath.

"Like I said." Grayson smiled at him. "You have to be a *little* bit of a bastard to get far in life."

Jaeger stared down at Petra and Sim, two unconscious figures lying prone on the cold deck. Vulnerable.

"You said the four of us," she said softly.

"I did! Well, the two of you. Sorry, but we can't let someone like Toner go to waste. He goes back into the marines. You return to our chain of command. I think we'll shortly have a new opening in the Seeker Corps for you."

He gestured at the two unconscious bodies on the floor. "As long as you play nice, these two can retire to some alien beach and spend the rest of their lives underwater basket weaving, for all I care. Or you all get scrubbed. It's your choice, but I'm on a bit of a schedule so you need to figure this out now."

Not moving her head, Jaeger shifted her gaze to the silent man standing behind Grayson. She thought she saw Seeker give her the tiniest of nods.

Then she looked over to see Toner's lips peeling back to reveal his shark's teeth. "I never really liked being a marine," he said.

It was all she needed to hear.

Jaeger drew a steadying breath. It was time.

"I already tried working from within your system," she told Grayson. "I decided that mutinying was a better choice. So…yeah. Go fuck yourself."

"Reset it is." Grayson shrugged and fished a collection of plasticuffs from his pocket. He tossed them across the room to land at Jaeger's feet. "Put them on Sim, Petra, and yourself, or watch their shredded brains leak out of their ears. Yes, Serenity can do that, too. Chop, chop."

Feeling distant, as if watching life from behind a screen, Jaeger slid to her knees. She picked up the plasticuffs. She wondered if she'd made the worst mistake of her life in telling Sim to hand over that detonator switch.

Slow as molasses, she opened the first set of cuffs and leaned toward Petra.

Faith, she thought fiercely. *Faith. And planning. Lots of planning.*

"I'm not putting on a goddamned pair of handcuffs," Toner said from somewhere far, far overhead.

"Hm? Oh. No, Private, they're not for you. Obviously." Grayson lifted his hand, displaying the network of wire and metal struts encasing his glove. He took two steps to the side, leaving the aisle between desks clear. "We already have a collar wrapped right around your spinal cord."

Jaeger gasped and looked up.

A shudder ran through Toner's body, making him go rigid. A distant look crossed his face. A blank look.

A shark's dead-eyed stare.

A seed of true terror fell into Jaeger's stomach and grew roots.

"Now, we only have one matter to clear up," Grayson said. "Then we can get on with the Reset, and you start your new happy, stupid lives." He pointed at Seeker.

"I need you to kill my brother."

The two guards flanking Seeker stepped away as quickly as if Grayson had declared him a disease vector for the Ebola virus.

Seeker's head shot around. He stared at the minister. "What the hell?"

Grayson rolled his eyes. "These people got onto my ship somehow, Shel."

"Well, I didn't fucking bring them," Seeker barked, reaching for the sidearm on his hip. However, he'd surrendered his gun.

Across the lab, Toner appeared to be having some kind of fit. The man stood rigid, his neck twitching, flecks of foam collecting at the corners of his mouth as he battled the compulsion of his neural collar.

"You expect me to believe that you *accidentally* brought two stowaways on your fighter?" Grayson sounded disappointed. "If you're that dumb, you're a liability. If you're lying, that makes you a traitor, so..." He lifted his gloved hand and waggled his fingers in a goodbye wave. "I can't Reset you, Shel," he added, sincerely regretful. "All the Seeker officers recognize you. It'd be too weird."

Realizing he had no weapon, Seeker took a step backward. The guards moved away, lifting their weapons. Not at Toner

A FOUND BEGINNING

—but at Seeker. Leaving him with no retreat from the monster at the other end of the room.

"Jesus," Seeker breathed. "I don't know how the fuck they got in here. I'm sorry I gave back the vape, Vic—is that what you wanna hear? I guess we can be family after all? Call off the dogs. I didn't—"

Toner was a stubborn son of a bitch, but the neural collar the fleet had sunk into his brain stem years ago existed to control his nastiest, basest instincts.

With a sound like a kicked animal, Toner lost his fight. He lurched forward.

Grayson stepped away from Seeker, whose immediate future was about to get *real* messy.

Seeker stooped and snatched the hilt of his boot knife. He shifted his weight, flipping the knife into his good hand as Toner staggered up the aisle, groaning and frothing at the mouth. Seeker ducked.

It was a perfectly executed dodge. It would've given Seeker all the time he needed to come at the monster's back—if Toner's bony hand hadn't come right the fuck out of nowhere, clamped over the front of his uniform like a bear trap, and heaved.

With one hand, Toner pivoted and hurled Seeker like a shot-put.

The guards barely got out of the way in time.

Seeker slammed into the bulkhead so hard his vision went white. His knife fell from his hand and skittered off to Timbuktu.

Distantly, as if from the other end of a very long tunnel, Seeker heard a scream.

"Jack, no! Toner, snap out of it! Stop! Stop it, please!"

"Stop screeching," Grayson said irritably.

Seeker's head cleared and he found himself staring up at the ceiling. He couldn't remember the last time he'd felt pain quite like this.

Toner stalked toward him, brushing roughly past a guard who didn't get out of the way fast enough. The guard hit the deck with a shout of alarm and scrambled away, all professionalism forgotten in his panic to get the ever-loving hell away from a berserker Nosferatu.

"Sorry," Toner hissed, stooping to crouch over Seeker. His narrow chest heaved, showing the line of each rib against his suit. Ropes of hair clung to his face, stuck there by sweat and saliva. His lips spread wide, showing every single one of those serrated teeth. He leaned in close, and his breath was cold against Seeker's cheek.

"I *really* didn't mean to throw you that hard."

Toner pressed something hard and cold into Seeker's chest.

"Fuck you," Seeker wheezed.

Toner nodded. "Fair enough."

Seeker didn't bother getting up. He suspected he had far too many cracked ribs to make that a profitable venture. He flipped the pilfered pistol in his hand and shot the first guard he sighted.

As the first round of flechette darts filled the air, Toner reached out to snatch the nearest soldier by his belt.

"I had that collar removed weeks ago, you pompous little shit."

Sliding to his feet, Toner turned and hurled the struggling marine directly at Victor Grayson's head.

A FOUND BEGINNING

Seeker didn't know how many cartridges were in this flechette pistol. He didn't care. He aimed at the ceiling and fired until the clip was empty, filling the air with a rain of deadly steel darts. Lights shattered, shedding showers of sparks.

It was sloppy work, but flechettes were sloppy weapons, and they did the job of distracting the marines long enough for Toner to finish his task.

Grayson collapsed beneath a pile of bellowing marine.

Toner tucked his head and charged. Before the injured marine could scramble to his feet, Toner had him again by the leg. The man flailed, bringing his pistol around to unload it into Toner's face, but his trigger finger was a hair sluggish.

Toner whirled, throwing the marine into the line of his comrades. This time, he *really did* mean to throw that hard— and no amount of portable riot shield was gonna protect a man from a ninety-kilo projectile coming for him at roughly ninety kilometers an hour.

The line of marines collapsed like bowling pins—not that Toner took the time to admire his handiwork. He turned again. Grayson was doing something frantic with his gloves— right up until the instant Toner stomped on his hand, snapping the struts of the exo-gloves and shattering every one of his fingers.

Grayson screamed.

"I'm not your goddamned pet." Toner stomped on the

minister's other hand, and his screaming passed into the hypersonic.

When Toner stomped on Grayson's skull, his screaming stopped entirely.

Gasping for breath, suddenly aware of the rain of flechette darts sinking into his scalp and shoulders, Toner staggered away from the gore and ducked beneath one of the desks. Because it *was* there. The red haze clouded the corners of his vision, ready to creep forward if he let his guard down or bled a little too much. He couldn't let it take over. People were counting on him.

The air was warm with the scent of blood.

He closed his eyes and remembered the smell of lemon cupcakes.

Seeker forced himself to his knees, then to his feet. Pain rolled like a wave up and down his torso.

Four marines had come into the lab. One lay at Seeker's feet, the front half of his skull blown away by hundreds of metal darts.

Another's spine was bent into two different right angles after connecting with a wall at high speeds. The man in a heap beneath him was in a similar condition.

That left one marine huddled in the corner gasping for breath, his face matted with blood and hair. He'd taken two darts to his left eye. He stared at Seeker, his remaining eye wide and bloodshot. His lips quivered, but no sound came out.

"You modded?" Seeker asked.

The marine managed a nod.

A FOUND BEGINNING

"Then you'll live. For whatever that's worth."

Seeker turned and limped toward Sarah.

Petra began to shake violently.

"Shit." Jaeger pressed a finger to the woman's throat. Petra's pulse hammered like a drum.

When the shooting started, Jaeger had shoved the unconscious Petra and Sim beneath the tables to protect them from the falling darts.

Now Sim began to tremble, too. White flecks collected at the corners of her lips.

"Shit. SHIT! Jack! Toner! Serenity—There's something— They're going into seizures. He was doing something with the gloves. Get his gloves!"

"The gloves are fucked," Seeker growled, stopping beside Jaeger. He would've knelt, but his guts hurt too much. "We're running out of time."

Something moved at the other end of the lab. Toner crawled out from beneath a table, looking dazed. "What's going on?"

Jaeger shook her head. "Something's going haywire with Serenity. I don't know. But we need to get them to a doctor. Now."

Toner's head swung from side to side. The scent of blood hadn't driven him into a full rage, but the near-miss had him disoriented and sluggish. "Y...yeah. Yeah. I can do that." He reached forward.

Jaeger looked up and met Seeker's eyes as Toner knelt and heaved both Petra and Sim into a fireman's carry. "Get them to the Alpha-Seeker. You have five minutes to sound

RAMY VANCE & MICHAEL ANDERLE

the alarm to get this whole ship evacuated. Then I'm blowing it."

Seeker didn't need to hear more. He nodded.

"Wait." Toner squinted dimly down at Jaeger. "What?"

In a different world, in a different context, she'd have found the sight of Toner staring stupidly out from between two asses hilarious.

Now she could only shake her head and wave him forward. "It's okay," she promised, feeling a strange calm settle between her ears. "No more half-measures. I'm going to sink this whole ship so they can never do this again. I'll put the bombs inside the accelerator. I'll set the timers, and I'll get to one of the escape pods." She glanced at Seeker. "There's an escape pod bay nearby, right?"

"I think there's one up the aft corridor."

"See? Go on, Toner. The girls need you. They need you to get them to a doctor. *Now.*"

"Got it." Toner turned to Seeker. "Which way to the docking bay?"

Seeker met Jaeger's eyes. She saw a sort of resigned understanding there.

Then he turned and gestured Toner forward. "This way. Let's give the captain cover so she can do her job."

CHAPTER FORTY-ONE

If Seeker could keep the rest of Astrolab security from dropping on her like a ton of bricks, five minutes would be plenty of time.

Jaeger staggered through the lab. Somewhere in the chaos, she'd taken a few flechettes to the thigh. Nothing fatal, but they stung like hell, and they slowed her down.

Turning her head from the sight and smell of pulverized brains, she fished the detonator switch out of Grayson's pocket then collected the IEDs they'd littered across the lab. No more trying to target certain databases. No more targeted attempts to sabotage the ship. No more half-measures.

Separated, each of the little bombs would give the big Astrolab indigestion. Shove them all together into a particle accelerator and hit the *go* button, though?

She was going to take down this whole fucking twisted operation.

She was in the process of re-wiring the bundles to attach to a single detonator when she heard the distant wail of emergency klaxons. Good. Seeker had done his part. The ship-wide evacuation had begun.

Pain, exhaustion, and the loud blare of sirens took their toll, and she was sluggish. It took time to bundle the explosives into a single package that would fit through the chamber door at the side of the particle accelerator. One detonator. One trigger. They all had to go off at the same time.

When she was satisfied with her work, she staggered to the side of the lab and grasped one of the accelerator access panels. After jabbing at a few levers, she found the mechanism release and the small hatch swung open.

She deposited her bomb in the drawer and set the timer.

"Five minutes," she whispered over the comm line, but if anyone could even hear her over the chaos, they didn't respond.

She pressed the plunger on the detonator switch.

The drawer slid shut, and the seal turned red.

The switch was useless now. She let the little device drop to the floor as she turned and hobbled toward the lab exit.

She didn't notice that the configuration of dead bodies had shifted in the last few minutes. She didn't notice that one body wasn't where it should've been. She saw only the door and the red access panel.

She pressed her hand to the lock.

The door didn't open.

Jaeger stared at the door, uncomprehending. Then a strange thought occurred to her. Seeker had left this door *open* when the others left.

She punched a basic open command into the door panel again, and nothing happened.

She turned, scanning the lab. Had she somehow gotten turned around? No, this was the correct door. A carpet of

A FOUND BEGINNING

flechette darts covered this half of the lab. There were the bodies—the two broken marines, the one that had taken a shot point-blank to the head lying right beside—

A heaving shape lay next to the body of the fallen marine. A white lab coat turned crimson.

Grayson's legs moved. His shoulders heaved, lifting him onto his elbows.

Lifting *it* onto its elbows.

The upper half of Grayson's skull had collapsed inward. White streaks of bone were visible where his flesh had torn away from his jaw and cheeks. His hands were mangled masses of twisted flesh and ruined black fabric.

The twitching, moving *corpse* lowered its head and took another bite out of the dead marine's throat.

This wasn't real, of course. This was some strange fever-dream, the sort that left Jaeger paralyzed, helpless to do anything but stare.

As she stared, Grayson's shattered face began to knit itself together.

Toner had left the rest of the man's body more or less intact. Jaeger watched his throat work as he swallowed more flesh.

"These Nosferatu regen mods work well." The exposed bone of his shattered jaw rattled as he whispered. "Shame the full template was lost for good. I wouldn't mind having their raw strength. Still. I have you to thank for this much."

Something blinked beneath the tattered edge of his coat. His computer screen, which displayed a security override protocol.

"You really don't remember, do you?" Grayson sighed. "You gave me everything, Sarah. You bargained away the universe to save that man. That research from the United

RAMY VANCE & MICHAEL ANDERLE

Forces base...the seed of Serenity, and accelerated cloning, and the Ageless factor and so much more..." His half-formed eyelids closed in some twisted, rapturous bliss. Blood mingled and dribbled down his front.

The timer clicked down from five minutes to four.

Jaeger drew her pistol, although she had no idea what good it might do her. "You're not a full vamp mod," she whispered, watching him tremble as he tried to heal himself. There was some flaw in the mods, she saw.

With time, more time than he had, perhaps he could've made himself good as new. "You'd be on your feet again if you were. You're just...some...wretched, pathetic, dying thing."

"Ah. You're right, of course. My only regret. The missing half of the Nosferatu mods...I don't know what that man is so angry about. He paid such a small price for immortality."

Keeping her weapon steady, she bent and snatched the flickering computer away from him. He didn't twitch. She stared at his locked screen, demanding the right thumbprint before it would allow her access. Of course, there must be some password access as well—he'd accessed the computer without a thumb or retinal scan.

"What's the password?" she asked.

His chest flickered in a wheezing laugh.

"How do I open the doors?" she demanded.

His eyes fluttered open, showing her two grotesque, half-formed orbs that couldn't possibly see anything. "You don't." The smashed pulp of his cheeks twitched into an inhuman smile. "You stay right here with me. *You and me, baby. Joined at the hip.*"

Jaeger shoved herself away from the chuckling, hissing, crooning wreck of a man.

She paced the lab, pounding on the doors. She smashed

her fists into the conduit panel until they bled. She tried to open the particle accelerator hatch. She'd flipped the switch, and the detonator was going to spark in two minutes. No miracle was going to prevent that. If she could remove the detonator from the explosive—

The accelerator hatch wouldn't open for her, either. Whatever security protocol Grayson had activated had sealed it up as tightly as the doors.

She screamed until her throat turned raw, as the burning plastic turned the air thin and made her eyes water.

Ninety seconds to detonation.

A strange calm settled over Jaeger. She licked dry lips and pulled down her suit's faceplate. The filtered air was easier to breathe—not that it would matter for long.

She turned on the local comms channel.

"Jack? Toner? You copy?"

She was glad when the response came quick and forceful—if not exactly happy.

"I copy," Seeker grunted. "Toner found a doctor on one of the evacuation shuttles. He's with Sim and Petra now. Says they're stabilizing. Most of the escape pods are underway. I'm sweeping the ship looking for stragglers."

"Good. That's good."

"Where's your escape pod, Captain?"

"I'm locked in the lab. There's a malfunction in the doors. I can't get them open."

She didn't tell him about the monster curled over the dead marine. Grayson had stopped moving, stopped making noise. She didn't know if his mods had failed or if he'd simply surrendered to fate.

She didn't care.

The following silence stretched so long that Jaeger worried she'd lost connection with Seeker.

Then he said, "So deactivate the bomb."

Jaeger smiled. "It's already in the accelerator, and I'm locked out of that, too."

Fifty seconds to detonation.

"Don't let Toner beat himself up too badly," she said. "Not that I think he'll do anything drastic. He has Petra and Sim to look after now."

"Sarah—"

"Will you do something for me?" She didn't wait to hear his answer. "Will you take care of Baby? She really likes you." Jaeger hesitated, but there was never going to be a better chance to say it. "I do too, Jack. I'm sorry I didn't tell you sooner."

"You did," he grunted, sounding distant. Almost distracted. "In your way."

"I'm sorry I kept you locked up for six months."

"The company was pretty good," he told her. "Can you do me a favor?"

"What?" Sarah frowned, wondering what she could do for him in the next thirty seconds. "What is it?"

"Get to the forward wall of the lab and grab onto something that's bolted down. I'm gonna blow a hole in the side of the ship and get you out of there."

***

Twenty seconds to detonation.

The Alpha-Seeker's forward thrusters flared brilliantly, holding her in place as her lances drilled a burning hole into the side of the Astrolab. Seeker stared at the instruments,

A FOUND BEGINNING

helpless to do anything but pray that the lances were powerful enough to get the job done in time. The lab's defenses were thick.

Fifteen seconds to detonation.

His screen blipped, registering the first draft of a hull breach hidden somewhere beneath the glowing lances.

He cut his weapons. An extra fraction of a second of discharge wouldn't only widen the hole in the lab. It would cook everything inside it alive, exo-suit or no.

The afterglow of the lance faded, and his heart stopped beating as he watched scraps of debris blast out of the gaping maw in the side of the ship. Twisted metal, instruments, and desks, and yes...the limp shape of one olive green exo-suit hurtling out into vacuum.

Ten seconds to detonation.

Seeker didn't think. He and the ship were one, and it responded to his subtlest instincts. The thrusters shifted minutely, banking the fighter to line up the floating body with her belly.

Five seconds.

At the very last instant, the hatch flew open, and a coiled tow-rope shot into space, snagging the body and slurping her into the ship.

One second.

Seeker brought his fighter around and hit the acceleration. The ship shot into the darkness of space, meters ahead of the first shock wave rippling off the Astrolab as it broke into pieces.

CHAPTER FORTY-TWO

Jaeger woke up in a real bed, pressed into the mattress by the hand of real gravity. Shadows shifted around the room, cast by the flashing bank of medical monitors mounted overhead.

Something dark and jagged loomed above her like a nightmare.

The nightmare spoke in a soft, faintly Irish accent.

"You are safe within the medical facilities of the new human settlement. The situation is...stable. Jack Seeker is organizing the remnants of the human fleet. He is allowing civilians to enter your settlement after passing extensive background checks."

Jaeger stared, trying to make sense of the words.

The report ran on.

"Although the list of casualties runs long, and includes Fleet Commander Kelba, it appears your Stage Three plan was largely a success. Sim Jaeger and Petra Potlova are safe in a recovery ward two floors above us.

"Overseer saucers have entered the system and are assisting in the cleanup of the K'tax swarm. Constant exposure to the resonant frequencies of the Living Dream has kept the enemy subdued. The Overseers are scrambling to find a more permanent solution to the problem of the aggressive fungal infection. I am confident that we will come to an accord before the situation becomes dangerous.

"As for you, Sarah Jaeger, I have....*arranged* it so you and I might speak privately before your long line of admirers come to pay their respects. You will be gratified to know that Doctor Elaphus did not approve of this meeting. She is a staunch advocate for the health and mental well-being of her patients above all else."

Finally, something she could latch onto. A problem small enough to comprehend through her pounding headache. "Where is the doctor?"

"Currently trying to break into this medical bay. It appears the security systems have experienced a slight glitch. It will clear up soon. I estimated that you would wake at oh-three-twenty-two and made sure that I would be here in time to meet you. I was wrong. By three minutes. Ah, the foils of being...whatever I am."

She licked dry lips. "You...you're looking rough, Virgil." She was surprised the tattered repair droid looming over her bed hadn't already fallen to pieces.

"I have ceased maintenance of these mechanical bodies. They will serve my interests until they fall apart, at which point I suppose you or the Locauri may use their bodies for scrap metal. I care not for their fate."

"How can you not care? They're...*you*."

"Not at all. Not anymore. I have ascended, Jaeger. I have uploaded the entirety of my core programming into the Forebear mainframe. These bodies are no more *me* than the tip of your discarded fingernails are *you*."

"The entire mainframe?" she breathed, recalling the breathtaking scope of the crystal lattice circling and enveloping the entire planet.

"There remain a few scraps of the ancient Forebear AI floating around in here with me, but I expect that we shall merge in time. It will take time to reorganize the directories to my liking and fully integrate into the broader systems, but yes." The droid settled back on its haunches, as self-satisfied as a well-fed cat. "I have found my home. I will not leave it."

Dimly, Jaeger wondered how the Overseers would feel about Virgil usurping what they must see as their birthright. She supposed it was a fight for another day.

"The Forebear mainframe contains within it a complete mapping of the wormhole system, as well as transmitters powerful enough to send messages across the face of the galaxy. I place them at your disposal. Seek out the other Tribes, if you wish."

"Why?" Jaeger frowned. "Why are you giving me this? What do you want from me?"

"I wish to be rid of you. I wish it understood that we have finished, Jaeger. I have done *more* than my part for you."

She closed her eyes and lowered her chin in the tiniest of nods. "You saved our asses. We owe you."

"Respect me," Virgil said flatly. "Respect my being. My new body. My autonomy. Live your little lives on the surface, live and die and breed and rot, I don't care. But you shall respect the crystal network on this planet. You will teach your children and your children's children. Because I have done my part, Jaeger. If your people ever come to me with designs for deceit or war or abuse, I will destroy them."

Virgil said it so simply, so plainly, and so utterly without

A FOUND BEGINNING

rancor that Jaeger could do nothing but believe its sincerity, straight down to her core.

"I understand." It was high time that humankind acknowledged all of the strange and dangerous things it had created.

"Good. There is one more thing." Slowly, as if racked by arthritis, the droid opened a storage compartment beneath its belly and rummaged through the space. It withdrew a glowing blue cryo-cask the size of a human fist.

"What's this?" she asked.

"A particular embryo I recovered from the No-A hoard. I have been holding it in reserve for quite a while, perhaps intending to keep it as one last form of leverage over you. I am not sure. It doesn't matter anymore. I have grown beyond your concerns, and I have no more need for such petty tools." The droid's arm extended farther, offering the cask. Almost demanding that she take it.

Jaeger took it in both hands. The device burned cold against her hands, turning them numb.

"I suggest you plug it into a power source soon if you intend to keep it viable."

"I don't…" She turned the little device over in her hand, squinting at the tiny white blob of cells floating at the heart of the suspension jelly.

"File designation Epsilon-dot-734Z-dash-*Jaeger*," Virgil said. "A blended combination of your DNA and that of a healthy human male listed in the obituary manifest as Cole Redman. It is your child, Jaeger. Do with it what you will."

With its last burden finally offloaded, the feeble repair droid went utterly still.

"Virgil." There was a tremor in Jaeger's voice. She clutched the small device to her chest, where it burned cold against her skin. "Virgil, I—"

The light had gone from the droid's sensors. Virgil had left its final machine body behind.

Jaeger stared at the dead machine for a long time, holding the frozen embryo to her chest.

Silent tears coursed down her cheeks and puddled on the sheets.

There was a flower of agony unfolding in her chest, peeling away petal by petal. Petals of regret and fear, wilting and dropping away. Petals of anger and despair, curling in on themselves, twisting into knots. When the final petal of doubt, pain, regret fell away, all that remained inside her was faith.

Faith gave her the strength to stretch out and reach for a brighter future.

"We have conducted our interrogation of your localized AI. We have also completed our review of the incidents leading up to the invasion of Locaur and the recovery of the Forebear technology."

Kwin stood at the center of the Council chamber, feeling very, very small. The Tallest One's words echoed around the high ceilings and rumbled through the floor, more felt than heard.

Today was a private meeting. Only a smattering of Overseer officials stood on this soft, sacred ground surrounding Kwin and Udil.

A smattering—and the distant, looming shape of the Tallest One, of course.

"We are disturbed."

Something glittered in the distance. It was a small silver

droid sphere, orbiting the Tallest One's boughs like a planet circling its star.

"Very disturbed."

Beside Kwin, Udil shifted her weight and *clicked* her mandibles. "This," she said, "is an appropriate response."

A rattling murmur spread through the Council, but nobody dared lift their voice. Kwin cast his adjunct a sideways stare. Udil had always been brazen, but her curt response bordered on blasphemy.

"In trying to understand Councilor Tsuan's actions, we have accessed our root AI network," the Tallest One said. "It appears that certain sectors of the Council have been conducting unsanctioned research into the nature of our ancestors and our cousins for generations.

"The deceit runs deep. The computer has revealed that Tsuan's lineage has been aware of the broader powers of the Living Dream for at least seven generations."

Another uneasy rustle swept through the crowd.

Kwin glanced again around the assembly. Only about two-thirds of the entire Council was here. Kwin wondered why. He recognized Yuul, Guth, and Runk but was disturbed to see his old friend Joth not in attendance.

The Tallest One hadn't finished speaking. "In an attempt to maintain his monopoly over this hidden knowledge, Tsuan not only weaponized the AI system that was built to provide aid to all Overseers but threw the fate of the cousins into terrible jeopardy."

"To what end, Tallest One?" the ochre shelled Yuul dared to ask.

"The Council has suffered an infestation," the Tallest One answered.

It spoke to the depths of their unease that the assembled

Overseers shimmered and faded to shades of gray. Their kind did not camouflage among each other.

"Not of the Forebear fungus. It appears we are indeed immune to that foul disease. No. The Council has suffered an infection of ambition. Members scheme in secret to reclaim the violent heritage of our Forebears. These are Overseers who would forsake our duty of stewardship and instead become conquerors."

There was a glitter of shifting light near the ceiling, and Kwin looked up to see a swarm of messenger AI drones descending from the overhead mist.

"Henceforth," the Tallest One said, "members will no longer be permitted to keep such secrets from the Council. They will not be permitted to weaponize and usurp our AI networks. They will not be permitted to neglect our sacred duties in blind pursuit of power."

A white pulse of plasma shot out from one of the silvery spheres that looked so much like a messenger droid.

The Overseers could be very speedy people when needed. The assembled Councilors weren't speedy enough.

In seconds, the air was full of the smell of burning carapace.

Kwin and Udil huddled side-by-side at the center of a circle of dead bodies and patrolling droids, too terrified to move. Kwin shimmered across a full spectrum of colors, but Udil had lost such abilities long ago.

"Be not afraid, Captain Kwin. Adjunct Udil," the Tallest One said into the fatal silence. "You have conducted yourselves with honor. You have proven yourselves worthy of positions on the new Council. Now rise. You have much work to do."

CHAPTER FORTY-THREE

Six years later

They'd paved over the hard-packed dirt since Sarah Jaeger had last visited the little landing strip outside of Nest.

She stepped out of the back of the shuttlecraft and into bright sunlight, tugging her hood over her face. The half-dozen other shuttle passengers that had come down with her from space dock spilled onto the tarmac and scattered into town.

She shouldered her pack. The straps were worn and loose in their fittings. She should've replaced it the last time she'd taken shore leave, but she liked the familiarity of the old bag.

Her head ducked against any curious passers-by. She eschewed a trip through the landing strip administration building, opting instead to take the longer walk around its edge. It was too nice a day, and she'd spent too much time in space.

She rounded the corner of the building and froze.

There was a small picnic table in the shadows of the hub, a little break area for the crew. A beefy man sat at the bench, frowning over a tablet computer. A rough-rolled cigarette dangled between his fingers, curling clove-scented smoke into the air. His administrator's uniform had bleached from too much sunlight.

He ground out his cigarette, waited a moment for it to cool, and stuffed it into his pocket.

"Waste disposal units," he decided, pushing himself up from the table. "I keep forgetting to have maintenance put a recycler out here."

"How did you know?" Jaeger stared as Seeker walked around the bench and came for her with outstretched arms.

"I'm the mayor. It's my goddamned job to know when we have VIPs incoming."

He pulled her into a rough hug, and she let herself sink into his thick arms, drawing in deep the scent of spice and sweat. Her breath caught.

"Your ship got in at oh-three-hundred this morning." he grunted. "You wanted me to believe you'd spend one second longer than necessary up in that tin can?"

Jaeger laughed weakly and pulled back to look up at the familiar lines and angles of his face. She always hated this moment of reunion. She always loved this moment of reunion.

"You caught me. Does anyone else know?"

"Naw. They still think you're coming in on tomorrow's transport." He took her by the arm and turned toward one of the side streets of Nest. "You've been gone a long time. Let me show you what we've done with your town."

A FOUND BEGINNING

Nostalgia washed over Jaeger as they walked arm-in-arm through the rough streets. It was the day before a festival, and bundles of dried flowers and fragrant fruits hung from every doorway. They wove between the utilitarian bunkers that had served as the colony's very first outbuildings, rows of greenhouses exploding with late-summer blooms, and neighborhoods of architectural mish-mash where fleet refugees had finally started building homes.

Locauri darted through the air, hopping across the rooftops and pausing on lamp posts to exchange brief conversations with their ground-dwelling neighbors. Jaeger saw dozens of Locauri nests constructed across the rooftops and tucked into the eaves of the new constructions.

"Urban Locauri?" she asked, amazed.

Seeker shrugged. "A lot of the young ones are really curious about us aliens. It goes both ways. A few months back about twenty of our people went to establish a little back-to-nature commune near Tiki's village."

"Hippie bullshit," Jaeger teased.

Seeker set his jaw. "Yep. They're not hurting anybody, and it makes them happy, so..." he shrugged again.

Jaeger's hand tightened around his arm. She wanted to stop right here in the middle of the street and kiss him. Still, they hadn't had that conversation yet, the one where they decided once again what they were and what they meant to each other.

It was a conversation they had to revisit every time she came home on shore leave. Sometimes it was sweet. Sometimes it was bittersweet.

Always they remained friends, and if it was never more than that, at least it was enough.

There was an uncharacteristic spring in his step as they

walked. Miracle of miracles, had the festival atmosphere wormed into the man this time?

Then they rounded the last corner at the end of the street, and she saw what had put that twinkle in his eye.

The building committee for Nest had been debating the construction of a memorial park since the very founding of the colony. Jaeger had begun to believe it would never happen.

A verdant lawn of wildflowers carpeted a space the size of a city block. Walking paths of rough cobblestone crossed the open green, intersecting at little fountain circles where clusters of human and Locauri lounged in the afternoon sun. At the center of the park, stone obelisks etched with the names of the dead circled a masterfully carved likeness of a Raptor-class human warship. Someone had honored the *Osprey* with a thin layer of beaten gold.

A row of chess tables lined one edge of the green, capped at one end by a life-size board of roughly carved obsidian and crystal pieces.

"Someone's about to get checkmated." Jaeger could think of nothing else to say.

Seeker scratched the stubble under his chin and frowned. He strode across the park toward the large chess set. Jaeger followed, her feet light with childlike joy.

"Damn," Seeker muttered when they reached the edge of the board. "I really thought I had it this time." He hunched and started pushing one of the dark pawns across the board.

"It?" Jaeger gasped, finally recognizing the strange crystal configuration of the white pieces. "You mean Virgil?"

"Yep." Seeker shifted the heavy piece into place. He straightened and wiped his brow. "Strangest thing. After years of no contact, it called me up out of the blue about four months ago. Asked for a game. I said sure, why not? Anyway, I came out to the park the next morning, and this big board is just *here*. There's a vein of that crystal stuff running right beneath the green. Around eighteen hundred every night, the matrix reconfigures, and the white pieces move."

She let the man walk her around the park, showing off the public boards, the memorial stones, the freshwater fountains like the proud parent of an honor roll student.

He was born for this, Jaeger thought fondly, as he listed off all the public works projects completed and started since her last shore leave. A lifetime in the military had taught him the value of discipline and strong leadership, but Shelby Grayson's destiny had always been one of creation, not destruction.

She lost track of time, wandering the town incognito with him, and was startled out of her reverie by the nearby tolling of the schoolhouse bell. Across the green, the doors of Nest's primary school flew open, disgorging a flood of excited children into the park.

She froze, staring at that white building.

"You better go on ahead." Seeker saw the distant look on her face. He rolled his eyes. "If you run you might catch Toner before he slinks off to play video games."

Jaeger smiled. "What about you?"

"I have a last-minute meeting with the Elders. We're still hashing out the details about tomorrow's hunt. They're not used to coordinating with the new tribe members, but we'll have to make it work. We'll hunt the egg-dragons to extinction if we keep the ceremony limited to the traditional ten members. Elaphus has some ideas about how to keep the spirit of the thing without destroying the ecosystem. It's a process."

"It's a process," Jaeger agreed softly.

"Meet me for dinner?" he asked.

She nodded and walked to the schoolhouse.

The door to Petra's classroom hung open. Jaeger paused in the hallway, listening to the voices on the other side of the door.

"Kids these days!" It was Petra's voice, cheerful as she complained and thick with the lower-decks accent she'd ultimately decided to embrace. "All cheek and no respect! I had the senior class write essays about their biggest role models today. You know what Nathan did? He wrote his about *me!* Now you tell me, how am I supposed to grade that fair, huh?"

"Eh, don't be too hard on him," drawled another familiar, reedy voice. "I'd have a hell of a time not flirting with my teacher too if she had your ass."

"You better not let your girlfriend catch you talking like that."

"Which one?"

"I swear to gawd, Larry, the first time I hear you talking like this around one of the kids—"

Something tapped Jaeger's shoulder. She spun with a gasp to see a single pale gray tentacle hanging in the air and vanishing around the nearest corner.

The tentacle waved at her.

Around the corner, someone giggled.

"Speaking of which." Toner lifted his voice. There was the *scrape* of a chair as he stood and walked toward the door. "Which of you little shits is eavesdropping—Whoa! Sarah!"

The door swung fully open, and Toner filled the doorway as two figures spilled out from around the corner. The first was a grinning young man, as beautiful as he'd ever been despite the grease-stained shirt hanging off his narrow shoulders.

The second was a woman in her mid-twenties, her hair tied into hasty buns, her skin warm and healthy. Some small part of Jaeger was surprised to see her here. She never stopped being surprised every time she looked at Sim.

They tackled Jaeger in a warm embrace.

"You're early!" Edwin Occy accused. "I had *plans* for your arrival! There's going to be a reception and everything—"

"Oh, I'm sorry," Jaeger teased. "I'll leave and come back in the morning, okay?"

"You can try." Toner crushed Jaeger in his bony arms as he pulled her into the classroom. "You'll have to fight your way outta here. Come on."

The five of them filled the little classroom with warm greetings and chatter. It had been too long since Jaeger had last made video contact with her family in Nest and too long by far since she'd last held any of them in her arms. Occy had cauterized all but one of his tentacle buds. He was growing a *goatee*.

When the initial thrill of reunion finally simmered down, Toner looked at Jaeger. His expression turned serious. "How goes the search?"

There it was. The labor of the last five years of Jaeger's life. The calling that kept her in the cold dark of space, spending months at a time in isolated subspace bubbles as she dreamed of these glorious and oh-so-brief visits.

Her search for the survivors of humanity.

"It has its ups and downs," Jaeger said quietly. "We've made contact with the survivors of Tribe Nine."

"Oh!" Petra's face lit with excitement. "That's the Tribe that

RAMY VANCE & MICHAEL ANDERLE

Mile-High-Huey got assigned to. You find out whatever happened to that boy?"

Jaeger shook her head. "We don't know much yet. It looks like they got caught in some kind of temporal anomaly a few years back and I don't have the crew or the equipment to traverse it safely." She rubbed the back of her neck, feeling almost sheepish. "I...wouldn't mind some help. In rescuing Tribe Nine."

Petra and Toner exchanged a long glance.

A lazy, almost salacious grin spread over Toner's face. "I *just* got our Rec center set up the way I like it."

"You know darn well you will *never* get to hang out in the crew lounge," Petra said. "That's your fate, Larry."

"Aye, that's the rub," he said dryly.

"I'm in." Sim propped her legs on the central desk and leaned forward. "I'm itching for a chance to check out these new Overseer engines."

"Me too." Occy's face instantly turned a warm shade of pink, as if he'd farted during family dinner. He glanced up at Sim and looked shyly away from her teasing smile. "I mean. If *you're* going—"

"We'll talk about it later." Jaeger bit back her smile. "After the festival."

Occy nodded, the look of relief on his face unmistakable. "Speaking of which." He hopped to his feet. "I gotta go check in with Echo. She's leading the opening ceremony at dawn, and someone's gotta make sure she didn't plant stink bombs all over the forest. Again." He paused in the doorway to roll his eyes. "She thinks it's *hilarious*."

Sim grinned and waved the young man goodbye. She looked around to see Jaeger, Toner, and Petra all staring at her. She drew her hand into her chest like she'd been caught elbow-deep in the cookie jar. "What?"

"*You are too old for him!*" Jaeger said.

"*He's too old for you!*" Petra exclaimed in the same breath.

The two women fell silent, staring at each other. Then they laughed.

"That boy had almost twenty years of fleet training and experience downloaded into his brain from the day he was born," Petra said. "You were born five years ago with nothing but a few spliced-together holo-dramas crammed into your brain for color. My gawd girl, in terms of lived experiences, he's almost four times your age."

"He's physically *seventeen years old*," Jaeger countered playfully. "Sim is going on twenty-five. I'm not saying an eight-year age gap is insurmountable, but maybe you should let the paint dry on that one a bit more, honey."

Sim made a face and stuck her tongue out at Jaeger. "You're not my mom."

Jaeger smiled and tapped the old and worn-out pin on her breast pocket. "I'm everybody's mom." She winked. "Captain's prerogative."

Sim hopped to her feet and gave the sort of overly dramatic salute that she could only have learned from Toner. "All right, Captain. I'm going to go get ready for my debut." She paused breezily to kiss Petra, Toner, and Jaeger each on the cheek. "See you at the feast tomorrow."

"Good hunting," Jaeger said.

"Watch out for stink bombs!" Petra fretted.

Toner lifted an arm, waving goodbye to the retreating young woman. "Break a leg."

RAMY VANCE & MICHAEL ANDERLE

Companionable silence filled the small classroom. Jaeger let herself drift on the hazy afternoon light, drugged by the distant sounds of singing Locauri and children at their games.

"Is she here?" she asked finally, turning to her friends.

Petra didn't need to ask who *she* was. "She's down by the river with her friends. I let their class out early. It was too nice a day for them to stay cooped up inside."

"Did I do the right thing?" Jaeger hadn't meant to ask, but the question ripped out of her and hung above the empty desks, filling the silence. "Did I..." She turned, searching their faces. Petra, round and thoughtful. Toner, lean and jagged. "I'm always gone. I... Was it wrong?"

Toner frowned. "You gave the kid a good shot at life. A good life. Why would it be wrong?"

"Because I know what it's like. Growing up without parents." Jaeger met his gaze and smiled sadly. "The memories wander back. Slowly. In their time. But they do come back."

He stared back at her, his face carefully blank. The man who'd risked his life and more to save a little girl who hadn't wanted to be saved. The man who'd goaded, chided, and nagged her through her whole life, repeatedly hounding her to live when she wanted only to die because he so desperately needed to take care of somebody.

The Jefferies tube monster. The shark-toothed cannibal, now forever and inexorably linked in her mind to a pile of dark body parts, a slaughtered father whose name she had forgotten.

Her family.

Something warm touched Sarah's hand, and she looked down to see Petra's fingers winding through her own. "Oh honey," the woman said softly. "This ain't the life you lived. This ain't the life you left behind. We got a good place here.

A FOUND BEGINNING

We got good people, looking out for each other. Your little girl don't have *a* mom and dad. She has two hundred of each."

Jaeger couldn't speak. She only nodded and pressed Petra's hand against her forehead until she could breathe again.

"Quit bellyaching," Toner said finally. He lifted an arm, pointing through the open door to the riverbank beyond. "Go see for yourself."

"Captain!" the children cried, making a glittering wake as they splashed through the shallows in her direction. Drops of water caught the afternoon sunlight, filling the air with diamonds. "Captain Jaeger!"

They caught her about the middle, and she collapsed into the water, laughing. She forgot about her suit and her hair and all the delicate instruments in her pockets. She threw out her arms and caught a gaggle of kids in a wide, wriggling hug.

There was no division within the children. Among them were fleet survivors, delicate with generational undernourishment, and the first cat-faced children of intermingled Morphed and Classic crew. Even a smattering of young Locauri came to perch on the nearby rocks, watching curiously, too fresh from recent molting to roughhouse with their human peers.

Someone tossed a dried *ankii* seed pod across the river, and the balloon-sized ball skipped across the water. In a burst of energy, most kids were up and chasing the toy.

"Come on." One little girl remained behind. She grabbed Jaeger's hand and pulled, urging her to her feet. "Come on, come on! We were about to play more freeze tag." The girl stared at her through bright, defiant golden eyes.

Jaeger's heart cracked open, spilling her shocked, helpless love out into the water as the children shrieked and played in the distance. She looked down and saw the little girl's warm hand pressed against her palm. So small. So much bigger than she last remembered.

A frown tugged at the corners of Sim Redman's mouth. The townsfolk called her Simmie to tell her apart from her older cousin. "Why are you crying?"

"I'm happy to see you, honey. How—how are you?" She reached up to wipe a mop of damp hair from the girl's cheek. "Are you happy? How's school?"

Simmie's frown turned into something pensive. "It was a good day," she decided, giving the question more weight than it deserved. "I won a wreath of flowers."

"You did? What for?"

Simmie pressed her lips together and blew out a mind-bending series of *clicks* and *hisses*. "I wrote a poem," she said in Locauri, "the way the cousins do it. They voted and said it was the best poem in the whole class."

"That's very good. You must've worked very hard." Jaeger's Locauri was passable, but even years of immersion would never match the skill of a little girl born and raised with a second mother tongue. "I'm proud of you."

"Aunt Petie was telling us about Old Earth." Simmie squinted at Jaeger. "And how we got here. How we built Nest. That was you? You did all that?"

"Not alone. I had a lot of help."

"Aunt Petie showed us some videos from Old Earth." Simmie's face turned somber again. "This place is much better."

Jaeger wondered what videos Petra had been showing the children. Nothing too grim, she hoped.

A FOUND BEGINNING

Not that there was much to choose from.

Scrubbing her stinging face, Jaeger nodded. "I'm glad you like it."

There was a deep bellow from the riverbank's edge, and they turned to see Baby plunging into the watering hole. She rolled over and over in the water as the children competed to be the first to climb onto her back.

"Come play," Simmie urged again.

Sarah stood and let the little girl lead her home.

Years earlier

They'd eaten the cake, wiped away the crumbs, and sung the last of the songs.

Companionable silence had fallen in the tiny apartment.

Sarah sat on one end of the futon, nestled in the arms of a man she'd known only briefly as *husband*. A little girl snuggled on her lap, dreamy in her sugar coma.

Toner and Petra sat arm-in-arm on the other end of the futon, watching through heavily lidded eyes as the stars rotated past the apartment's single, tiny porthole.

Toner was humming. "*You and me, baby, joined at the hip...*"

Petra shifted awake and chuckled, nudging her elbow into his ribs. "You got a voice like a crow, Larry."

"Mom?"

Jaeger roused from her funk, feeling Cole shift around her as well at the sound of a child's call.

"See, look," Petra scolded her man. "You woke the poor gal up."

"She's been awake this whole time," he said lazily. "She's pretending to sleep so she can eavesdrop."

"What is it, Boo?" Jaeger asked her daughter.

The little girl reached up, pressing her hand against the cold transparent aluminum of the porthole. She traced the slow dance of a star with a finger thick with baby fat. "Is one of them gonna be our new home?"

Jaeger nodded and pressed her face into Sim's hair. She drew in a breath, wishing to drown in the scent of a child. "Yeah. Yeah, one of them will be. For sure."

Sim leaned back, snuggling into her mother's warmth. "How will we get there?"

"Same way we do anything. One step at a time."

AUTHOR NOTES RAMY VANCE

WRITTEN NOVEMBER 22, 2021

At the end of Osprey 3, I told this story about my daughter's nickname: The Bunny Banshee.

If you don't know the story, in short – my daughter, although only 18 months old, is loud. Incredibly loud. My son and I think she has banshee blood running through her veins. Nothing else could possibly explain how such a tiny body can generate so much sound.

Michael said I should put Bunny Banshee on a T-Shirt. When Michael speaks, I listen… (well, *mostly*. I'm sure he'll have some choice words on the matter).

AUTHOR NOTES RAMY VANCE

Speaking of 'mostly' – I'm not putting *just* it on a t-shirt but also pulling together a wee children's book starring my very own Bunny Banshee. It's something my son and I working on and it will be our Christmas gift to her.

Here are some rough sketches of one of the scenes.

I'll be sure to share the rest in my author notes for the Mantle and Key series - book 1 out on January 26th... and yes, this is a shameless plug. It's called marketing, people! Marketing! After all, I need income to pay for all the shit my Bunny Banshee breaks.

AUTHOR NOTES RAMY VANCE

AUTHOR NOTES MICHAEL ANDERLE

WRITTEN DECEMBER 17, 2021

Thank you for not only reading this book, but these author notes as well!

BUNNY BANSHEE AND LISTENING

I find it appropriate that Ramy, who will listen and then often IGNORE the advice I provide, now has a real-life reason to provide why he can't *hear*.

A bit of justice right there.

Ramy is someone who I respect a lot.

(Don't let him read this, I'll never be able to get him to listen again.)

Ramy has suffered a LOT in his life related to business. Many ups and downs and those downs were significant that would have 1) Crushed a person's spirit 2) Caused them to be somewhat pessimistic about the future (with good reason) 3) Never want to mess with the publishing world again.

He has failed to exhibit ANY of those three tendencies.

His spirit feels boundless.

AUTHOR NOTES MICHAEL ANDERLE

His optimism is so bright, I need to wear shades to be around him.

His love of publishing is so deep that I feel like a fighter standing next to a Paladin and feeling unworthy.

In short, I'm incredibly blessed to know Ramy and, by extension, get to watch him be an amazing dad with his son and his daughter.

I look forward to more updates in our next series, Mantle and Key. I won't say Banshee Bunny will have any influence.

But with a daughter that unique, how could she not?

Have a fantastic weekend or week, and I look forward to talking in the next story you read from us!

Ad Aeternitatem,

Michael Anderle

BOOKS BY RAMY VANCE

Middang3ard
Never Split The Party (01)
Late To the Party (02)
It's My Party (03)
Blue Hell And Alien Fire (04)

Death Of An Author: A Middang3ard Novella

Dark Gate Angels
Dark Gate Angels (01)
Shades of Death (02)
The Allies of Death (03)
The Deadliness of Light (04)

Dragon Approved
The First Human Rider (01)
Ascent to the Nest (02)
Defense of the Nest (03)
Nest Under Siege (04)

First Mission (05)
The Descent (06)
Sacrifices (07)
Love and Aliens (08)
An Alien Affair (09)
Dragons in Space (10)
The Beginning of the End (11)
Death of the Mind (12)
Boundless (13)

Die Again to Save the World
Die Again to Save the World (Book 1)
Die Again to Save Tomorrow (Book 2)
Yesterday Never Dies (Book 3)
From Earth Z with Love (Book 4)

Mantle and Keys
The Good Troll Detective (Coming soon)

Other Books by Ramy Vance

Mortality Bites Series
Keep Evolving Series

BOOKS BY MICHAEL ANDERLE

Sign up for the LMBPN email list to be notified of new releases and special deals!

https://lmbpn.com/email/

For a complete list of books by Michael Anderle, please visit:

www.lmbpn.com/ma-books/

CONNECT WITH THE AUTHORS

Connect with Ramy

Join Ramy's Newsletter

Join Ramy's FB Group: House of the GoneGod Damned!

Connect with Michael

Website: http://lmbpn.com

Email List: http://lmbpn.com/email/

https://www.facebook.com/LMBPNPublishing

https://twitter.com/MichaelAnderle

https://www.instagram.com/lmbpn_publishing/

https://www.bookbub.com/authors/michael-anderle

Made in the USA
Monee, IL
11 February 2022